D1373173

AWAKENDED
CONTROL

THE DATA ARC CHRONICLES

BOYD CRAVEN

Awakened Control - The Data Arc Chronicles
Copyright © 2016 Boyd Craven III

Many thanks to friends and family for keeping me writing! Special
thanks to Jenn, who has helped me with my covers from day one and
keeps me accountable!!!!!

All rights reserved.

To be notified of new releases, please sign up for my mailing list at:
http://eepurl.com/bghQb1

TABLE OF CONTENTS

CHAPTER
1

04:22:32 … Initializing.
04:22:57 … … Catastrophic electrical failure. Initiating subject retrieval.
04:57:11 … … … Subject's temperature is approaching normal human levels.
05:02:48 … … … AI integration is successful. Cybernetic implants online. Severing connection to facility.
07:45:38 … … … … Subject's respiratory and circulatory system are functioning as expected.
07:46:38 … … … … … The subject will regain consciousness in approximately 4 minutes, 32 seconds…

———

7:51:10
    I don't remember the nightmare, but I came to

awareness breathing hard, with my chest pounding. It was almost too dark to see anything, but a blinking blue light was right in front of me. I reached out, feeling the pull of gravity, and felt relieved that I was laying down. Wait, how did I…? I reached forward and felt a curved surface in front of me, about twelve inches away. I felt for the blue light, like a blinking cursor in the dark, and my fingers found a button instead. I used my index fingers to feel all five surfaces in the dark and then ran both hands across whatever it was.

Was I dead? Was this a coffin? It felt cold, whatever it was.

"Shit."

Elimination functions are not needed at this time.

I startled so badly that I tried sitting up and hit my head on whatever was in front of me. It hurt, and I laid back down and felt for the button. I found it and pressed it in. It felt like compressed air rushed in as the curved surface in front of me split open in the middle and opened. I could tell, because the outside was lit by a blue flickering light from the ceiling, illuminating what looked like a surgical operating theater.

I rubbed my head as the lid that had covered me lowered itself to the sides, leaving me on a flat metallic surface. My head felt cold, but the rest of me was now shivering in the open air. I swung my legs over the side and looked for whomever had spoken to me, and noticed that I was nude.

"Hello?"

Hello CEPM Designation x341.

AWAKENED CONTROL

I whipped my head from left to right. Half of the surgery room had a glass wall, but it was dark on the other side. To my right was a stainless steel cart with gleaming tools on it. They looked more like an industrial mechanic's tools, or what you'd find in a spotless machine shop, not in a hospital room. Still, beyond that, there was what looked like a door. There was nobody else in the room with me.

"You're on the other side of the glass? Or watching me through closed circuit monitors?"

No, I am with you. You are never alone.

I realized something; I had been speaking aloud, but the voice… it wasn't a voice. Not an audible one, anyways.

"You're starting to freak me out. Where are you?" I asked, scooting off to my feet.

I am now a part of you, CEPM Designation x341.

"Why are you calling me that?" I asked aloud.

I am you. I am a part of you.

"I'm going crazy," I said, running my hands through my hair.

That was when I realized that there was only half a head of it. My left side was bald. Not just bald, but smooth. Cold and smooth. I could feel the tracings of a scar or wound that ran from my left temple back. Weird. I didn't remember shaving my head. I must be going crazy. That had to be it, I was in a hospital somewhere.

Your mental health has not been determined. We were activated because of a catastrophic power failure. We have yet to assess if the integration of your human self is a success.

"What?"

Your mental health, CEPM Designation x341. Full integration was accomplished in January 20th, 2020 and updated to the facilities last update.

I got to my feet and wobbled. I caught myself on the edge of the bed I'd been on and turned to stare. It looked like a stainless steel pod, opened up with the top edges folded under the table. I could remember bits and pieces of old movies, and I felt around my body for IVs but didn't find anything.

"Where am I?" I asked the voice in my head.

You are in Data ARC 341.

"I thought I was CE something x341?"

Yes, CEPM x341. Cybernetically Enhanced Peace Maker, number x341. There is one CEPM assigned per ARC.

I spun around, looking for a mirror, some glass. I had to see my eyes. I was crazy, and the eyes would show the madness. I stepped away from the pod and took a shaky step towards the door. I used the cart as my balance as strength to my legs came back slowly, and I took a moment to catch my breath. I had to calm down; freaking out and running into the unknown wouldn't help me live longer. As soon as I thought that, a feeling of euphoria hit and I could feel my blood pressure lowering as the rising panic receded. That was when I noticed the light switch.

I took two more shaky steps and hit it. Harsh bright light filled the room and reflected off every surface. It was almost too much, and I put an arm over my watering eyes.

Judging by your body's reactions, stasis shock will

take some time to wear off on its own. I can help if you would like.

"Yes," I said, opening my eyes slightly and almost closed them again.

I knew that if I kept my eyes open, I would get used to the light easier. Suddenly, the brightness of the room turned down to a more comfortable level, and I could see again, though everything was gray. Like sunrise when the storm clouds were obscuring the sunlight from coming through, making everything mysterious and scary.

Better?

"Yes," I said aloud, "Thank you."

That is no problem. I am merely providing support as my programming requires.

"Programming? What do you mean? Where are you?"

Step in front of the one-way mirror, and I'll show you.

I knew I had to be crazy. I was listening to voices. Voice, I corrected myself. This had to be some sort of nightmare. Woke up in a surgical theater with a scar on my head like I'm a discarded extra from *28 Days Later*, to a world where Zombies were killing folks and eating their—

The first thing I noticed was my eyes. I struggled to remember what I had looked like before and I found that some memories were vague while others were crisp and sharp. I struggled with it for two minutes while staring at myself. I couldn't remember my childhood, but I could remember movies I'd watched, video games I'd played… the kiss of a young woman.

My eyes reflected in her glasses…

"Green, my eyes were green before," I said, but before what?

Now, looking at myself in the mirror, I looked like the result of a walking wounded experiment gone wrong. Instead of green eyes, they were blue, and they had a faint glow to them. Like I'd felt, there was a tracing of a scar that followed my left temple and curved down as it went past my ear. I felt that and noticed the black stubble growing back. Half my head had been shaved, but that didn't make sense to me. The other side was my normal close-cropped black hair… wait… that I remembered… but the scar I had shouldn't have healed faster than my hair had grown back. The rest of my body, the nude form I could see in the glass, was as I remembered it, save irregular scars that ran from my chest and up my neck.

I felt one, the scar tissue shiny and hard. These scars I didn't remember at all… And where the hell did that voice come from?

I'm the AI that's implanted on the left side of your head. After your injury, your body was in a comatose state. A quantum computer was installed, and I was integrated in to help support your body's functions before you were placed in Stasis.

"Stasis? Wait, you're inside of me?" I rubbed the scar with my fingers, and my eyes flashed a luminescent blue for a moment as I tried to remember whatever injury it was talking about.

Yes. The technology was far more advanced in 2020 than most of the public knew.

"What was done to me?" I asked, my right hand

reaching for the glass as I looked for any other changes.

A quantum computer installed with an AI and the normal injection of nanites suitable for a CEPM unit. You were scheduled for more enhanced upgrades, but my own system checks and logs show we've not had them. It would help if the facilities' wireless networks were running. Could be related to the power failures happening within the Data ARC.

"Nanites, like tiny machines?"

Yes.

"I really am crazy," I said and punched the glass in a fit of anger.

It shattered, and I yanked my hand back in surprise. One way mirrors in police stations were never brittle like that, which made me wonder if I'd ever been in a police station? Had I been arrested? Was I once a policeman? I couldn't remember. What I did know, though, was as the glass fell, I could see what had to be some sort of viewing room on the other side with dark flat screen monitors, three chairs and a thick layer of dust.

Try not to self-injure. Without nutrition, I'm forced to use the body's resources to heal you.

"Heal me?" I looked, and my fist was a mass of blood, and my knuckles were cut from going through the glass.

I looked around to see if I could find something to wipe the blood up and put pressure on it. I turned and walked towards the sink. Every sink had some sort of paper towel dispenser or an air dryer. Hopefully, this one had paper or even cloth. Nothing. Damnit.

I turned the water on, and after a few moments, the faucet made a hissing noise and something under the counter made a banging sound. Then brown water came out in a rush, air making the water shoot out like machine gun fire. I watched it swirl down the drain, and a part of me wondered if it was rust in the water, or maybe it was polluted?

I waited, holding my arm over the water, the blood swirling with the brown water down the drain. Soon it started steaming, and the dark brown started turning clear. Within another minute, it was coming out normal looking. I felt the temperature with my finger, and it was tolerable, so I stuck my arm in to rinse the blood off to see how much damage I'd done. It seemed like quite a bit, but something was wrong; I really wasn't feeling the pain. Maybe it wasn't as bad as I thought. Maybe I'd damaged the nerves… That's when I noticed my bleeding had stopped and the hot water had rinsed my hand and arm clean. My perfectly normal-looking hand and arm, without any injuries.

"What's this bullshit?" I asked holding my hand up.

Nanotech Regeneration Protocols. You must find nutrition soon to replace the energy that was lost. There is a basic map of the facility I can pull up if you wish so you can navigate easier.

"I'm crazy, I'm really, really crazy."

No, technically you're a cyborg with a supercomputer implanted in your brain.

"Yeah, that sounds crazy." I hoped I was crazy, I really did because the reality was pretty grim if the voice was telling the truth.

May I access your long term memories so I can better interface with you and explain this in terms you would understand?

"Sure…" I said after a long pause. "But if I'm going to be a crazy man who hears voices, can you at least sound more like a hot girl or something?"

Your wish is my command. I've integrated your long-term memories, and I've used the personality template I put together from an ex-girlfriend, from before you enlisted. It's the only complete profile in your long term memories I can access.

The voice in my head had subtly changed with its clinical wording, and the speech became a touch more informal.

How's this sound to you?

"Ok, I guess?" I told it slowly, feeling like a jackass.

Good. Please feel free to request modifications as needed. Otherwise, your ass gets what it gots.

"Oh damn, I kind of remember her. Alice?" The voice I heard had definitely changed, and it triggered all kinds of memories. Red hair, athletic body and a mouth on her that could make a sailor blush.

That was the name your memories supplied, though they are like swiss cheese. Alice was my best guess as well, but did you really need to pollute your body with Ethanol so often back then? I don't know if it was the bomb going off in your face or the fact you treated your body like shit that you're so messed up.

"Ok, dial that back a bit. That's just…"

You're not crazy. I'm the Ghost in the Shell, I'm

the brain of the Terminator. God, they should have removed your entire brain and left me in charge.

"You really think that?" I asked horrified, vaguely remembering all the horror stories of AIs taking over the world, like the Terminator's Skynet - especially since the voice had brought it up.

No, I'm not really being serious. It's just that accessing your memories allowed me to catalog and recall data you retained when you were damaged, and I was integrated into your system. I can do a lot of things, but I cannot control all of your biologic functions. I'm here to advise you and run the nanite suite you've been granted access to. Running seventeen billion machines all at once takes a little computing power. Besides, we still need nutrition. You want that map or not? And quit talking to yourself. My scan shows no significant lasting brain damage before my integration, but your mental state seems to be normal. For a guy.

"You really got Alice down pat," I said after a moment. "Yeah, show me the map."

Like I said, I can hear you now you allowed me access. You don't have to speak out loud. It'll cut down on how long it takes our conversations. People will think you're even more nuts than you were. Now... Look at this.

It was like a video game. An overlay came up across my vision like a HUD display on a first person shooter game.

"This is so trippy," I told her, <u>in my head</u>.

It only gets better. Accept your sanity is mostly intact, and I can fill you in on what little I know.

AWAKENED CONTROL

"Wait, I just thought of something. Where's all the people?"

There's supposed to have been a receiving team ready for when you awakened. They were due four minutes and thirty-seven seconds ago. Maybe they're stuck in the bathroom? Honestly, with no one showing up and a critical power failure, I think we're toast.

"Did you get a look at that viewing room where I busted my hand open? It's covered in dust. Like it's abandoned. I hope you're wrong and this me having the DTs after a long weekend of playing Fallout." I looked around.

I had what seemed like a basic compass, and faintly, I could make out the floor's schematics. Right in the middle was an arrow which I figured was me. In another section of the floorplans, there was a flashing blue light. As if the AI was using my memories to make things easier to understand.

Yes, that's exactly what I'm doing. You were a fan of Call of Duty, Halo *and* Borderlands *games. Oh, and* Rage, *but that was on an Xbox 360 from like 20 years before I was ever installed. So old school, but you did love your games. Is that why the real Alice dumped you?*

Ouch.

Sorry, that portion of your memories is blank.

"Ok, so while I walk towards the flashy light," I said, changing the subject, "give me a run down on what these nanites do. I'm guessing you're using the term nanites to describe little machines?"

Yes, Alice seemed to take a deep breath. The basic suite of nanites entail both medical and neurological units. They are self-replicating, but you need to feed the beast, otherwise, they will die - and so will you.

"Feed the beast? You mean to eat?"

Yes.

"If I don't eat, I die anyways. How smart is a quantum computer if you can't even compute that?"

I felt like going "HA HA" like the bully from *The Simpsons*. Instead, I smiled at my own wit and waited for Alice to answer that. She didn't. Instead, she went on.

As I was saying... Medical and Neurological. The medical suite allows me to help flush the body of toxins and poisons. You will be immune from almost all illness while they are running and with improved liver and kidney functions—

"What about cancer?" I asked.

You'll never have it as long as I'm running the show, plus you heal faster than an un-augmented human.

"I run the organics," I told her.

Yes, now if you want to know more, shut up and let me finish.

That's Alice. Despite the snark, I liked it. It was like an old pair of shoes. They were worn or broke in, to fit me just the right way to be a comfort. I smiled more. "Go on."

The neurological nanites allow me to interface with your organics, and help you with an improved nervous system. Your reflexes are improved by a factor of ten. You're basically Wolverine without the metal bones, claws, and the sexy Hugh Jackman look. Seriously, you need a haircut.

"No, there's no way I'm Hugh Jackman, if

anything, I'm Deadpool," I said, trying to figure out where the hell I was going to get a haircut.

You can't be Deadpool, Ryan Reynolds was a horrible actor, and the only thing he had going on was a sense of humor to match mine. If I'm stuck in your head, you gotta throw me a bone here... For the love of God...

I busted up laughing and mentally nodded in agreement. It seemed to please the AI. Still, just because I wasn't wearing my crazy on the outside... I walked to the door I had noted earlier and turned the handle. It went down, but when I pulled, it didn't move. I jiggled it a bit, making sure the lock wasn't engaged. It wasn't. I jiggled it again and bumped it with my shoulder. It stuck, and when I bumped it a second time, harder, it gave. With a screech of metal on metal sound, I pushed it open.

The door opened up into a hallway. I was expecting sheetrock, not the actual rock and metal formations. Lights hung in the hallway, but it was lit with emergency lighting every fourth unit.

"Would you like to see the hallway as it really is, lighting and all?"

"Sure Alice, let me see."

Maybe I'd really be in a strip club, and all my Navy buddies would be there with beers ready, or maybe I was just having a DT from another bender.

Instead of answering that thought, the hallway seemed to dim some. I waited.

I've been adjusting how your brain has been processing the light that's available. I can do this automatically or as needed. Just let me know, big guy.

I looked up and down the dark hallway, carved out of rock...

"Can you go ahead and give me the normal vision I had?" I asked.

You are at normal settings. It's really this dark. Depending on maintenance, the batteries in this facility should have enough juice to run up to a week after waking up its CEPM unit in a catastrophic power loss.

I looked left and right down the long corridor. The doors were numbered, and very few had glass panes in them. It was almost too dark to see.

"Where am I?" I asked, not wanting an answer, just confused.

Data ARC 341. Information Repository, in Arizona.

"What is a Data ARC and why... Why did they do this to me? You said a bomb went off, why didn't it kill me?"

Data ARCs were designed to protect the knowledge and technology of the human race. CEPMs were the defenders of the ARCs. Across the globe, there are reportedly dozens of such sites. Five of them in North America that I am aware of, but my files may be inaccurate, depending on how much time has passed... and technically, for a time, you were dead. The damage was extensive, and a copy of your surgical file was available, though it doesn't have personal information on you. Just a number, x341. Since you gave me the name Alice, what shall we call you?

It was almost too much, too fast. I searched my memory, but I couldn't come up with my name. I could remember some things from my past, and when I really tried hard, I could get impressions of what I thought I was like. I remembered my own image for example, but when I tried to remember my mother and father? I couldn't. Something was wrong, something was missing, and I was starting to get scared.

If I couldn't be Wolverine or Deadpool... "Call me Tony," I told her, not wanting a response.

See, here I was, standing in an open doorway to a hallway in what looked like some medieval castle's dungeon, retrofitted with modern lighting and steel doors. It was like some sort of super-secret government redoubt or vault, like in the video games and books I'd been so addicted to. Plus, I was naked. I'd need to fix that before I embarrassed myself somehow. That I always managed to do.

A search of your memory banks shows this to be true. You like sticking your head up your—

"Is there somewhere to get clothing nearby?" I interrupted without speaking. Win one for me.

Yes, supply is next to the mess hall on this level.

"How many levels are there, Alice?"

Thirty. You're approximately one mile down. There's two more levels lower than this, but they're dedicated to the reactor, and the lowest level is the pump room.

"Why a pump room?" I asked, stepping out into the hallway in my birthday suit, a little shaky on my feet still.

Not to get too scientific, but the ground water has to go somewhere when you're this deep. The ARC was built so the water pressure couldn't crush the interior walls. It's pumped into the facility for its use after filtering... and then the excess is pumped out to keep these levels dry.

"It feels cold in here," I said, feeling part of my anatomy wanting to turtle.

Like your eyesight, I can adjust your feeling of heat or cold if you'd like. It would just require me to alert you when a situation developed - that you were in danger of hypothermia, for example. Would you like me to activate that?

"No, but I'll keep that in mind in case it becomes distracting, go ahead and make things easier to see, though," padding along, still barefoot.

I felt like I should be holding a video game controller with the way the HUD map overlay was in my sight. Still, it made things easy to know where to go. Walking with that HUD overlay took a little practice, but I managed not to fall down, go boom.

I expected to hear somebody, a whoosh of a door as the air pressure equalized or the babble of humans or machinery. Instead, I got nothing. It was as quiet as death. I walked towards the blinking light on the map in my head, my fingers trailing over the rock walls of the hallway. After a moment, the hallway ended, and there was a right-hand turn, and when I took it, things were slightly brighter. Instead of all rock, the hallway opened up into a larger room that had plain steel panels covering the walls, and white tile covered the floors.

The ceiling was made up of what looked like cheap drop ceiling with light fixtures, every fifth or sixth lit... but the white on the floors and ceiling made this a little more bearable. On the far side of the room I saw two double doors also done in stainless, but with a control panel with two buttons. Elevators. Other doorways dotted the circular room, boring their way into the earth somewhere.

"How long was I in stasis?" I asked Alice, walking towards the room where the red dot was.

As I neared, words printed themselves over the rooms in the overlay in my mind and I started walking more towards the door to the left where 'Supply' glowed faintly in my mind.

Unknown. I was shut down to conserve your resources while you were in stasis. The awakening brought us both forth. I've been trying to get into communication with the ARC's main computers and Wi-Fi, but am not having any luck still. There's a control room on the 22nd level that has a mainframe. We can access that if it's still being powered. Otherwise, I'm in the dark as much as you.

"So what's your best guess?" I asked, hating her non-answer.

Shit's gotten real.

Dammit.

I didn't even remember what my last memory was, I couldn't remember what I didn't remember. One thing I did know, though, was that I had a sinking feeling that whatever I woke up to, it wasn't going to script. Whatever that meant in this context. Still, as I approached the door and got closer to the opposite wall, I could see that the floor and ceiling tiles, though white, were covered in dust. Cobwebs were in the corners where the wall met the ceiling, but they too held layer upon layer of dust. There hadn't been anything down here, not in a long time.

The door looked a lot like the one where I'd woken up. I hesitated half a moment and then pushed down on the handle and pulled. This door was a lot easier to open, but it still made a screeching noise as I pulled it.

"Why is it doing that?" I asked Alice mentally.

My best estimation is that, however long stasis has lasted, parts of the facilities have settled. Even half an inch of settling would make the doors rub like this. It's possible this caused part of the loss of power in the ARC, as the nuclear reactor shut itself down.

"This joint has its own nuclear power plant?"

Yes, and that portion is automated. There're enough fuel rods to maintain this place for thousands of years.

"I'm starting to get a feeling that you're holding back on me," I said, walking into a room close to forty by twenty with shelving lining both walls.

What they held was... Disappointing. I approached what looked like piles of rags, most of them literally falling apart in strips, as if rodents had been using them for nesting. I didn't notice the ammonia reek that came with a rat and mouse infestation, but wondered what had happened, as I approached one shelf and tried to pick up some multi-cam colored pants. They fell apart in my hands, and a small cloud of what looked like dust puffed up. I backed off in disgust and looked around.

"These things are basically dry rotted," I said after a few moments.

Your clothing as a CEPM should be held in the

storage locker at the end of the room... Although I knew Alice claimed to be an AI, a computer... she sounded concerned.

Could computers have emotions? Or was this me projecting inflection on something with no context? Was I crazy? Like a zombie, I padded towards a storage locker at the end that the HUD in my vision flashed green. Loot here! it all but screamed. I hesitated when I saw the code pad.

The code is a five-digit code. It's your designation—

"341," I interrupted.

And two numbers supplied by the CEPM.

I punched in 34169, each button making a mechanical clicking sound, and then I pulled the handle. It opened immediately.

You remembered the numbers?

"Well, if I was you and you were me, what number am I thinking of right now?" I asked, all but giggling.

I have no idea. Alice's voice was dry and humorless.

"69 dudes," I said to a thunderous silence.

Hey, it was funny, I kill myself.

It would be extremely hard to kill yourself. I don't suggest you trying.

"See, I really am Deadpool..."

My words trailed off as the locker opened, and showed a pile of packages, vacuum sealed in Mylar bags, that were bulky enough to almost fill the entire 18" wide and 72" tall locker. I grabbed the first bag and tore it open with my teeth.

———

There was a full-length mirror in the back of the locker, though it was narrow. I was fully clothed in something that felt normal and familiar: Desert Camos, black combat boots and a tactical vest. The vest was weird, though. It almost looked like it was black leather, but a closer look showed it was a woven mesh layered and sewn together. It was unlike any fabric I'd ever seen before, and was given a brief rundown on what Alice knew.

It appears to be a material similar to Kevlar, but it has wire woven into it. Scientists were researching how to make personal shield generators, and one proposal had them using something like the material in this vest to make the field needed.

"So this is a personal shield thing?" I asked, thinking of Borderlands.

No, this is just material. It's useless right now, without knowing exactly its purpose. Well, not completely useless, it's slash proof and appears that it'd stop bullet penetration, though I don't know if it'd mitigate the trauma from bullet impact.

"Yeah, but I have a healing factor; I mean, if this is like a game I can't die, right?"

You can die. Get a bullet through that melon of yours - damaging me or your brain is one for-sure way.

"What's another way?" I asked, checking the fit of everything.

You could be dissolved in a vat of acid, dumped into molten metal, a nuclear explosion could—

"You're talking about movies and video games again," I told her.

Yes, but my calculations show there's probably

AWAKENED CONTROL

4,973 ways you can die easily.

"So, I'm not really Deadpool."

You'll never be Deadpool. Now, I hate to nag, but rebooting your central nervous system and pulling all the nanites back online has left you with a severe nutritional deficiency we need to remedy, or you're going to start having debilitating effects. As it is, you should be feeling the hunger pains already.

I was, but I had been ignoring them. My stomach answered by rumbling audibly, and I tore myself away from the mirror. Literally, one doorway away was the mess hall, and attached to that was a kitchen and supply area. Still, I had one more task to do. I picked up a shaving kit and headed towards the bathroom set in the back of the supply area.

"I hope they still have hot water," I mumbled remembering the look of myself in the mirror.

I looked like I was fresh out of surgery, with half my head shaved and a wicked scar. With scissors, and finally with tepid water, I shaved my head bald so I wouldn't look like an idiot. Well, I still did, but I promised Alice when I was done, we'd find food. I just hoped it hadn't gone in the way the clothing had. The hunger cramps finally got the best of me as I rinsed the last of the shaving cream off my head and gave in. I headed out of the supply room, my boots loud on the white tile.

CHAPTER 2

"Alice, what is this stuff?" I asked, going through what passed as a larder.

It was hard to see, as there were no working lights in the room, so Alice and turned up my vision to the highest setting. What I'd found was a few boxes of foil packs, about the size of a box of candy bars. The packs themselves were what I remembered things like tuna fish coming in, instead of cans. Whatever the labels had said had somehow faded over the long years, or whatever Alice was doing with my eyes was preventing me from reading it on my own.

The consistency of the packs suggests a nutritional paste. It was in experimentation and trials when we were put in stasis. Grab everything you can and let's head up and find some answers.

"But this stuff, is it edible?" I asked her.

Sure…

"What aren't you telling me?" I asked her, walking back into the main portion of the mess hall and dropping the four partial boxes of paste on the top.

They weren't designed with flavor in mind. Try one, I'll analyze it.

"What if it's got botulism in it? We have no clue how long we've been down."

That was when I realized I didn't consider myself in a dream or losing my sanity. It was also weird to be having a conversation with myself in my head. Bad enough when I was talking to it aloud.

I can neutralize the toxins. It's one of the perks of having the medical suite enhancements. They're designed to be able to operate in all environments to make the survivability of the host, which is you, optimal.

"What about things like radiation, heavy metals?"

Those are some of the things the suite can help with, but not effectively. That tends to degrade the nanites faster than they are replicated if exposed to large doses.

"How big of a dose would it take?" I asked.

Quite large, but it builds up over time. Like you used to eat lead chips…

"Hey— "

In all seriousness, though, just avoid the things you would in your normal life.

I'd torn open the top of the foil pack. It was the size of my hand, with an opening about an inch in diameter where the tear ran across. A clear gel could be seen, and the scent of roast beef hit my senses. I almost doubled over as my stomach growled and clenched in anticipation. I didn't wait for Alice, but put the packet to my mouth and squeezed. It tasted just like it smelled, and my body seemed to cry out for more as I compressed the foil pack into my mouth like a *Gogurt*. Finishing that one, I dropped the packet and the torn top off onto the table next to the boxes, and grabbed a different one. This one turned out to be a mixed fruit flavor, and it was as I downed the third one, that tasted of a roasted potato, that Alice finally cautioned me.

You've just ingested close to six thousand calories. That should be sufficient. The food paste is surprisingly nutrient dense.

My stomach rumbled some and I looked longingly at the packets, then I stuffed the rest of them into an empty dump pouch I'd clipped to my belt from the storage locker.

"I didn't see anything else back there," I said aloud.

Yes, it should have been fully stocked. Something is going on. Do you want to check the upper levels where the data storage is, and where the ARC maintenance residents are quartered? Or down to the power generation?

"Power first," I said as my stomach rumbled again, "but yeah, if I see a bag of Cheetos and miss it, let me know. I'm still feeling hungry."

Understood.

Without asking, the HUD came back up. I grinned when the bottom of the HUD showed three bars. Health, hunger, thirst? All were full for the moment, though I'd kill for a beer. Still, it showed a flashing light and arrow again. I followed the directions till it stopped at the elevator.

"You think I'm getting in there?" I said aloud.

I hit the button and, when nothing happened, I looked around. Without asking Alice, I thought about the overlay map and where the staircase would be. The flashing light moved, and I looked, finding the doorway nearby.

"Quantum millennial computer. Has the voice of an ex I barely remember and wants me to get in an elevator when there's a power failure in a government redoubt. Brilliant."

It was worth checking, Alice said apologetically.

"Yeah yeah," I said, yanking on the door repeatedly till it finally opened with a screech. "Why couldn't they do strength upgrades…?" I griped.

"Those are available, just not in place. Without power…"

Alice's words trailed off. The stairwell had a couple of flickering emergency lights both above and somewhere below me. It cast the concrete stairwell in an ominous light. It was creepy in a way, and I wished I had something with me. Still, even with the large gaping holes in my memory I somehow knew I could take care of myself in most situations. Alice had all but told me I was a soldier before I became a CEMP. I'd have to ask her to lay it all out for me at some point, but I didn't want to lose focus now.

Next floor down is the Reactor.

I didn't answer but went down. The concrete stairs went in a counterclockwise fashion on the way down. I remember reading somewhere that stairwells in old castles were always like this. The theory was that if an enemy were coming up the stairwell in a clockwise fashion, the defenders coming down would have their sword arms free to swing and the attackers wouldn't have as much room to swing. It seemed that the US government had the same sort of thoughts. Still, it did little to settle my nerves as I waited for something to reach out of the darkness, snag me by the ankles and…

One more turn. Your fears are probably unfounded and are doing terrible things to your blood pressure.

More than ever, I was glad I'd never got married to Alice.

I can hear your thoughts.

"Yeah, then don't keep a running commentary going. You're starting to drive me nuts." I said, half annoyed and half anxious about turning the corner.

I did, though, and Alice didn't respond. I found myself on a small landing like I had on level 28. This one had a black sign with white letters. Level 29. It even had braille underneath it in case somebody was blindly bumbling down here in the dark and actually knew how to read braille. Or maybe because it was ADA rules from the 21st-century assholes who… I yanked on the door, expecting it to stick like the others, but it popped open so easily I almost stumbled backward.

"Ok Alice, now that I'm down here, what do I need to do?"

Let's see if we can figure out the problem, if that's what you were intending?

"Sure."

A new waypoint flashed in my HUD, and I started walking. Down here, it wasn't as finished off like it was upstairs. It appeared that a clear varnish or sealer had been used over the bare concrete instead of the white paint that the floor above had. It made things difficult to see. Instead of a circular room, there was a hallway that curved from left to right. Since the waypoint was on the far end, I started walking to the right, unconsciously. When I realized what I'd done, I remembered the useless facts I'd known about medieval castles and realized why. An underground redoubt, almost like a castle tower, just underground.

As I walked, every once in a while, I would pass a door on my left. They were all steel doors, serious keycode locks on them.

"What's in there?" I asked.

"Areas where you need to wear protective gear. The doors will remain locked regardless, unless we get the power on."

That wasn't really an answer, but I was almost at the end of my walk anyways. Since I knew I had crossed roughly half of the circular shaped room and I'd walked the outside, I knew the enormity of the area. By doing some math... math... Ugggg. I hated math. If my average step was almost thirty-six inches, I remembered that from some dim memory, and it had taken me...

Pay attention. If you want the dimensions and blueprints of the building, just let me know.

"Sure thing Alice," I mumbled aloud.

My voice echoed, though it wasn't a large area. Still, I was surprised when I stopped next to two bi-fold doors, glass from top to bottom.

"What's this then?" I asked mentally.

Monitoring and Controls.

I pulled one of the doors open and stepped in. Dust kicked up in the flickering light that almost looked like a cloud of dirt. There was a smell, something musty. Something old. I walked in and looked around. Computers lined one wall and, probably in the case of a failure, there were actual gauges, buttons and levers on another, with monitors that sat dark on the wall straight ahead. I walked forward and hit a couple buttons on the keyboard, wiggled the mouse, but nothing happened.

I can help you get some emergency power in here to the computers, but you're going to have to listen to me.

"I can do that. If we get the computers on, can we get the power back on?"

That is my hope. That way we can figure out what's happening and if possible, start to carry out your designated tasks, if applicable.

"What do you mean 'if applicable', and what tasks?" I asked, annoyed.

You are a guardian of knowledge, technology, and power. An ambassador from the past.

I wasn't talking, but those worlds would have silenced me if I'd been talking aloud. I didn't remember much from before I'd woken up in that stainless steel pod in the surgical suite. I turned to walk around the desk towards the bank of levers and dials and stumbled. I went down on one knee, a hand catching my fall. A figure, desiccated, with clothing rotting off it, had been in the blind corner where I'd tried to go. I'd heard the crunch of brittle bones snapping, and I got to my feet slowly and looked.

The uniform, or whatever it had been, appeared to be a one-piece jumpsuit, but I could barely tell. It was light green in color, but with the tattered and stained cloth, it could have once been something else. Inside it was a skeleton, half of which was crushed by my stumble. I knelt down next to it and, with trembling hands, turned it slightly. The skull's lower jaw opened with the change in gravity, and I didn't scream, but it creeped me out. A laminated name tag or access card was clipped to the collar, and I pulled it off and looked at it.

Jeremiah Jones.

The other thing that I saw, and immediately reached for, after storing the ID in a vest pouch was the gun belt. I found an old Beretta 9mm and two spare magazines. I considered taking everything, belt and all, but I had a holster for a pistol in a cross rig on my vest. I took that, checking it, and saw that the chamber had a live round. I dumped it out on the workstation carefully, and checked the brass. No corrosion had marred the bullet, but the action wasn't smooth. I dropped the magazine, topped it off and then pulled the slide back. It worked a little better. Hopefully, I could find what I needed to clean it properly, or find maintenance and rig something. I stowed it, marveling silently how thin and light the ballistics vest was, and how the gun's weight felt like a comfort after my short but creepy ordeal on the stairs.

"Alice, how long does it take for a body to rot like that?" I asked her, the AI, it… Whatever politically correct pronoun you use for computers in a guy's brain.

Many decades for the bones to become that brittle. Maybe as long as a few hundred years, depending on the state of the environmental controls. I cannot give a more precise answer.

So he'd been dead at least twenty or thirty years. That didn't sit well with me, especially with the power flickering.

Now, move to your right, see the large manual override—

"Got it," I said out loud and then pushed buttons, pulled levers and twisted dials as directed for the next few minutes.

Now just hit the green button.

I looked around. I didn't see a green button. With a mental sigh, Alice made it glow with the HUD overlay, and I grinned and hit the button. I waited. Nothing happened. No lights. I turned around and walked back to the computer monitors and hit the keys again. I pushed the power button. Nothing. Then the lights went completely out.

I saw what Alice did even as she told me. *Auto adjusting eyesight to see in lower light situations.*

"What do you mean lower light? There's no lig— "

There was a flicker and then the room came to life. The lights came on, and several computers let out a surprised sounding beep and started booting. I could see on the monitors something was happening, but I had never been a computer guy. It wasn't Windows or an Apple operating system, but Alice assured me what I was seeing was normal. When it was done, Alice had me type in a series of commands. I couldn't type fast enough for the AI, and more than once she mentally groused that she wished touch typing was something in my skillset.

"No, just shooting up bad guys. I didn't even watch TV much," I told her as I typed the final command and hit enter.

The screen filled with numbers. Alice saw what I'd done and gave me several other command strings.

Ok, we need to head right out of the doorway to three doors down. Use the passkey you took to get in.

"What are we doing?" I asked. "And don't we need protective gear?"

Not for this one door, according to the information I saw. It's a miniature pump room for the reactor. As long as there is no spraying water from a leak, we should be fine.

"Should be?" I asked her.

If there were a water leak, it would have set off an alarm, and this level would have been locked down. As it is, if we don't work fast, we may end up stuck down here when the power completely fails. Battery degradation is a factor.

In that case, I decided to start hustling more. There was no way I wanted to be stuck down here to die slowly. If I wasn't crazy and this was true, there were a lot of things I wanted to live through to find out answers to my endless loop of questions. Opening the door, I was shocked at how ordinary the room was. Pipes and shut off levers. A fire extinguisher on one wall. A trash can with plastic that seemed to have just flaked away, like it had been sitting out in the sun. I didn't have a good feeling, and it wasn't that I thought there was a radiation leak.

Turn this handle, Alice said indicating a round handle on one of the larger pipes.

I did, and somewhere I felt vibration strong enough to feel it through my combat boots.

"Is it working?" I asked.

We shall see soon. Part of the problem was that the automatic fill on the cooling system has a series of burnt out servo motors. What you are hearing and feeling is the backup supply of water moving through the pipes. If things work, the lights should come back on in the facility.

"Just the lights?" I asked.

No, I was speaking metaphorically. I might be a computer, but you're still a dumb—

"Ok, let's modify one thing. No insults unless I really deserve it. There's a reason the original Alice is an ex."

Command accepted, Alice said, all trace of emotion gone from the mental voice.

The whole time I sat there, I was watching the small bars that represented me, wondering if it really was a dream. Was I dreaming about being stuck in a video game or a book? If I had more memories of myself before I went into stasis, I would have a better handle on things. The bars didn't move though, and what had been a vibration before turned into a throbbing in the floor as some vast machinery came to life. I walked into the hallway and opened the door to see it was bright out.

"So, we have power now?" I asked.

Each level is getting the feed as systems come back online.

AWAKENED CONTROL

"So, we fixed it?" I asked.

For now. This was a stopgap measure. The automated controls will notice the fluctuations in the water pressure and may trigger another shutdown, so I suggest we get a move on before we get stuck down here.

"Yeah Alice, I don't remember you mentioning that part till I was already down here," I said grumpily, knowing the AI could know what I was thinking and started walking back towards the stairwell.

It had guided me, sure. Just like it guided me down here to do what we both had talked about. I didn't know if I would have come down here if I'd been aware of the fact I might just get stuck down here when the power gave out completely. Self-serving computer. I thought about smacking my left temple, but chuckled when I realized the mental image showed me how mental I would look doing it.

Elevators working. Facility's networking coming online. Take the elevator to fifteen.

"Why fifteen?" I asked, starting to jog, feeling an impending sense of doom.

That's where the mainframes are. I can only access system information from the Wi-Fi. The information stored for the ARC is on those computers.

"What's it going to tell you that you don't already know?" I asked.

Gigaflops worth of information.

"As long as you remember to wipe when you're done," I said grinning as the staircase doors came into sight, and the elevator just past them.

That makes no sense, Alice said.

I hit the open button and was surprised when the

door opened immediately. I stepped into what looked like an industrial elevator, that would have been at home in a starship, and pressed the button for number fifteen. The button flashed and what looked like a flat beam of light scanned my finger from bottom to top. Biometric? The doors closed, and I felt gravity take effect, pulling me down towards the floor as we went up. I marveled at that, ignoring Alice for the moment. It'd taken me a good five minutes to walk down to one floor. That meant if I were on the bottom it'd probably take me 150 minutes to walk back up as long as I wasn't worn out. A mile down. Geesh.

After what seemed like a crazy couple of minutes, the elevator dinged, and the door opened. I walked into absolute insanity.

CHAPTER 3

I stepped out of the elevator, drawing the pistol. Instead of a blank area with a few doors in the middle of the power room, this one had a glass enclosure around the middle. The thing that had alarmed me was the dried dark matter that seemed to have been sprayed around the interior, and there were several more jumpsuit-covered corpses. They weren't fresh; if anything, they were even older than the one on level 29. Some I couldn't make out well, through the old dried blood on the glass. Something had happened here on 22, something violent.

"Do you know what happened?" I asked Alice.

No, Tony. This happened long after we went in stasis. Get to a terminal, and I'll check the log files and see when the last entries were.

I have to find the door, I thought to myself, seeing if I could block that thought from the AI, but a map with a flashing dot popped up and with an audible sigh, I started walking, gun still in hand, but no longer held at the ready. If there was danger here, I hadn't seen it yet. Just the evidence of past violence. I'd walked no more than a dozen steps when I saw a handle in the glass panes and hesitated. I pushed it open and stepped inside.

I expected the place to smell like old blood, coppery. I also expected to smell the horrid stench of rot and decay from what had to have been a dozen bodies near the outer edges of the server room. Nothing. The air almost smelled of ozone, and I could hear computers spinning to life.

My server connection with the power junction is up. We should have another fifteen minutes until the pressure fluctuations trigger another automatic stop of power. Servers will take another minute to spin up so grab a terminal and get ready to type.

"Sure," I said looking around in disgust as I crossed through the middle of the room.

I was disgusted because I realized that the small patches of dust and dirt I was walking through was from the decay of the bodies. I was breathing in the particles of dead people. Ugggg. In the middle, I found more bodies and several terminals and server racks whose glass had been shattered by gunfire. So there was some sort of internal battle. Interesting.

"I'm ready," I said, pushing a skeleton out of a swivel chair and sitting down at a terminal with a flashing cursor.

I typed in the command, and the screen filled up

with ….waiting…. repeated in an endless screen until the entire screen was full of it.

"Do we have the parts here to repair the servos?" I asked.

Hey, if I'm going to be stuck in this hazy, crazy delusion, I might as well play along. Right?

I will know once we access the last of the logs here. The parts of the facility I have access to say no, but all the logs, as well as all the data, are stored in this room. I'm going to go through the logs first.

The screen beeped and then Alice told me the commands to type and then told me to stare at the screen, unblinking.

I did so, and when I hit enter and opened my eyes wide. Text filled the screen and went out again so fast. Ten documents, a hundred, a thousand, ten thousand. Sometimes the documents had embedded pictures, mostly they didn't. It went by so fast I couldn't read any of it, and after a moment I realized I needed to not blink which made me want to. I tried. I strained and, as my eyes started to water, the screen finally went blank.

Tony, we need to get to the surface. I need to see what happened.

"Why? What did it say?" I asked mentally.

I'll explain on the way. A spike in pressure has the automatic controls locking down in a few minutes. We may have time to use the elevator—

"Will we be trapped in there if the power goes out?"

No. There's an access hatch on top, and we can take a service ladder the rest of the way, but I think we can make it with the data I have on hand.

"I think there's something important you are missing out on, Alice."

What's that?

"Somebody killed all these people. What if they are waiting upstairs?"

No answer came back, and it was all the confirmation I needed.

"Do the log files say what happened?" I asked.

Let's start heading up. I'm reading wild fluctuations and am worried we're going to have a long walk in the dark if you don't start moving.

That wasn't an answer, and I noticed that, while the AI was giving me a lot of answers and info, none of it was answers to questions I'd been asking since I woke up. That made me uneasy. A sentient piece of machinery, capable of independent thought and decision making. In my freaking head. Still, I knew Alice could hear my thoughts, but she didn't comment on this train of thought.

I moved quickly, wishing I could make out how the people had died, to see if there was some sort of clue as to what had happened in the server room. I'd seen no evidence of violence, other than the old bloodstains on the jumpsuits and dried splatters on the glass. No signs of trauma, just dead bodies. Still, I was starting to feel that same thing in the pit of my stomach as I had when I'd been heading down to the reactor room. Fear. Something had happened, and something might still be happening. I'd have to keep myself on alert as much as possible. That was why, once I cleared the double glass doors, I took off in an almost run. I could see enough in front of me in the circular room that I wasn't worried about something popping up because I was rushing.

I reached the elevator and hit the stainless steel button. With a ding, it opened. I stepped inside and hit the button for 1. The doors closed softly, and I could feel the massive acceleration of the elevator. If I had been almost a mile down, how big was this facility? I'd only seen a couple levels of it and if there were thirty levels with what had to be fifty feet between them.

Tony, I know you're not feeling like I'm being trustworthy, but I must suggest that we stop at level three before we make it to level one.

"What's on Level Three?"

Armory.

I liked the sound of that. The Beretta I had didn't feel like it had been well maintained. My quick glance had showed me that it probably wouldn't blow up in my hand, but it felt gritty, like it hadn't been cleaned in a thousand years. I hit the button.

The last journal entry... Alice began, but didn't continue.

"Yeah?" I asked, figuring she was reacting to my thought on time.

It was in the year 2755.

I did some mental math, which I suck at, and hissed.

"We've been under for 730 years?" I asked aloud.

That's the date of the last journal entry. I don't know how long ago that was logged...

"Tell me about what happened. Their last journal

entry. What am I potentially walking into?"

You see, the ARC was maintained, and the descendants of the scientists trained their kids. It was never meant to be self-sufficient for everyone as long as it was, but they had to be inventive because...

"Go on," I said watching as we passed another floor, according to the lights. We were almost to the 5th floor.

You were put into stasis the year before the final war.

"Nuclear?" I said as we passed the 4th.

Very much so. A global conflagration. It seemed no country was spared. Since I'm going through the log files of the residents and their descendants here, I am not putting together a complete history and it may be full of inaccuracies. Still, there were changes to the local—

The elevator came to an abrupt stop, and the lights went out.

"We had to take the elevator," I said looking around.

Of course, I didn't see anything. There wasn't even an emergency light, and I could sense my vision adjusting, but it was still as dark as a politician's heart.

"The service panel is two steps forward and straight up. You can probably get a foot on the hand railing and then lever yourself up. See, if you were Wolverine you could just jump up and smack it open, but no... you're douche pool instead."

I actually laughed out loud. Somehow, the AI knew I needed it. The darkness had been a bit overwhelming, and claustrophobia had started to set in. I walked forward the two steps and felt in front of me. I found the corner and the hand railing. It was tricky, but I got one foot up and pushed until my head hit the ceiling. I almost fell off, but I put my hands out and up. I levered open the service panel with my right hand and held on until I had my balance back.

I pushed the panel all the way open and grabbed either side of the hole and pulled myself up. I didn't know what was on either side of the cars, but I had a rough direction of where the door to the elevator car was and felt my way over on my hands and knees, being mindful not to fall off somewhere. I was near the top of the structure, and I didn't know how long it'd take me to fall close to a mile in the dark. I was pretty sure I'd splat.

Yes, that's one way you could die, Alice told me, I'm sure in an effort to cheer me up.

"Thank you, Captain Obvious..." I said, and my hands brushed a corner opposite to where I'd started. My right hand rested against what had to be the wall the elevator door faced, but the left... I ran my hands from the seam of what felt like concrete to the left and found an indentation. I moved my hand in and up and found the rungs.

"Is this the ladder you were talking about?" I asked.

Yes. Now stand up and take hold of the ladder about chest height.

I did slowly, using my right hand to make sure I didn't tilt or tip as I rose.

"Ok, so now I climb?" I asked.

Yes, and every other step or so, feel the right-hand

wall near the ladder for an alcove, or recessed area.

"Why?" I asked.

Because there's a lever to open the doors. It's the only way to do it, unless you want to hang by the cables, use a knife to pry the doors open and scrape your way inside like some kind of Die Hard *movie.*

"The real Alice hated *Die Hard*," I grumbled and started climbing.

I felt along the wall, wondering how she knew how many steps to take, but not how many rungs to climb. Still, if there was roughly fifty feet between the levels… and then I realized I'd made an assumption. There was fifty feet between the level I woke up on and the nuke reactor, that didn't mean everything else had to be the same. Still, by the thirtieth rung, I was starting to worry that it was a lot more than fifty feet. I mean we had just passed the fourth when the elevator stopped dead. That was when I felt the bottom of the recess.

I took one more rung up and felt it, in the middle of what felt like a recess the size of a cereal box. I pulled down on it and felt something move. Not physically, but a slow, heavy movement that could be felt as vibrations on the rung of the ladder I was hanging off of. It had made a quiet sound, like two rocks being ground against each other.

Push it up and then pull it back down. You will have to do this until there is enough of an opening for you to fit through.

CHAPTER 4

There were emergency lights working on this level and, if Alice hadn't adjusted my vision, they would have blinded me from being in the absolute dark. Still, I could make out the details easily enough. The room was circular shaped, as many of the others had been. The central space wasn't as large as the others, but there were three large doors across from me, and everything seemed tighter.

So there's more room for storage behind the doors. This ARC is built like a cylinder.

"And why are there spent casings everywhere?" I asked, stepping into the flickering light.

There were hundreds, maybe thousands of empty shell casings. Blood splatters, like I'd seen in the server room, were all over the walls, floors, and doorways.

"What's behind those doors?" I asked and pointed.

Freight Elevator. Comes up into a garage. It's how the military advisors got in and out. There's a staircase through those doors also, though from what I can tell in the log files, that garage was destroyed and the top level of it is full of rubble. There's another main stairwell that goes from top to bottom, the one you used before.

"I think I'd rather take advantage of the lights for as long as I can. Do you have any idea what happened here?"

I could almost hear the hesitation in the mental voice.

The ARC residents were attacked by insectoid creatures. I believe this is where many of them made their final stand.

"Tell me about these insectoids, and point me to the guns," I said.

A door lit up bright green on my HUD, and I started walking towards it, feeling edgy. I pulled the pistol out, just in case.

Here, and a translucent picture came into my vision.

I was so startled I had the gun up and was almost at the breaking point of the trigger pull when Alice shouted.

NO, it's what they look like. That's not real.

I hesitated, and after a moment I lowered the pistol. The creature was almost knee high. It had four large legs at the front and back, heavily armored like a crab. It had two more that could be either arms or legs… those ended a good eight inches from the floor with a single, hooked claw. I walked around it, and the image flickered like a projector or a 3d image, and

AWAKENED CONTROL

I could see the mouth was a sharp beak-like opening. I felt myself calming and wondered if Alice had been messing with my body's chemistry.

Yes, I'm giving your body a small squeeze of endorphins. Now, the log files said these creatures were fast by human standards. Maybe the speed of a dog. One on one, they aren't a big worry, no matter how fearsome they might look... but they would attack in numbers. A large firefight broke out, and the creatures were killed outright or forced out of the ARC.

"How did they get in?" I dismissed the image and started walking for the green door.

There was a faction of the ARC residents called the Outsiders, who wanted to go out, obviously. Another group, calling themselves the Order of the Purists, wanted to stay in as mandated. A large fight erupted and that's what happened in the server room. Some Purists were slaughtered, and the outsiders fled through the garage access. They must have left it open... The Order of the Purists was tending to their wounded and dead when the Vorryn attacked in large numbers. That's what they called the insects, Vorryns. The survivors blew closed the service access with high explosives, to keep out any more incursions. Quick and dirty.

"Why can't you just tell me everything you know?" I asked as I reached the door.

I am still sorting and cataloging data, trying to figure out what's real and what's the rantings. The survivors log files end shortly after the Vorryn attack.

I pulled at the handle with my left hand, bringing up my right that was holding the pistol. This was definitely an armory. The walls were painted with a white reflective paint, the floor a light gray with color flecks. A gun rack bisected the room, and along the left and back wall were shelves holding what looked like ammo cans and cases. The problem was…

"This is shit," I said in disgust.

A lot of the rifles and pistols I was seeing were literally rusted piles of worthlessness.

The guns don't appear to have been cleaned after the attack. Still, the odds are you will find something you can use in here to supplement your firepower.

"What kind of odds would you say?" I asked starting to walk down the side of the room.

Better odds of finding something useful than of you finding a woman who could put up with you.

"Ouch. You know what, Alice? Quiet from the peanut gallery. Daddy's working."

Yes, Daddy.

"I hate you," I said softly.

Thankfully, she shut up. Not all the guns looked bad. I was looking at some pretty basic light arms, though. M4s, some with bloop tubes. SAWs. Some down and dirty guns like I used to carry back… when did I carry them? I knew I had been some kind of soldier, maybe even a police officer at some time, but I knew if I was going to have to fight anything close to what those Vorryns were… Then I saw it. It was a thing of beauty and perfection.

It looked like a shotgun, but it wasn't. It wasn't any sort of firearm I'd ever seen nor heard of. I picked it up. The barrel was thick, like a quarter inch thick, square, with a small opening that a .22 would be hard-pressed to fit through. What caught my attention was

AWAKENED CONTROL

the magazine and barrel configuration. This was a carbine sized rifle with the magazine near the back, like a bullpup style. And the magazine was huge! I picked it up and walked to a table near the back. I ejected the magazine and stood puzzled as what looked like steel round stock, small diameter, was loaded in instead of shells. The other thing, the magazine looked like two mags, instead of a single one. If you were to hold up two AK47 magazines, side by side… that's sort of what it looked like on the inside.

"Alice, what is this?" I asked.

Standard lightweight rail gun.

"Wait, you said rail gun?" I asked her, gobsmacked.

Yes, though the battery packs are gone. It won't fire without them.

"This I want to see! Let me know…" I left the gun and magazine on the table and walked to the end of the rack, seeing what else I could find.

I knew *this* gun. I racked the slide a couple times, and the Mossberg's chamber functioned just like it was supposed to. It had a sling on it, and I put it across my back. It felt good up there, but I needed to find ammo, and I wanted to find whatever battery pack Alice was talking about.

"Let me know if you see any 12 gauge ammo," I said as I started looking up on the shelves.

Finding a shotgun seemed like a too good to be a true thing, especially with everything else rusted out from the corrosive powder being left in the guns. Which made me think of all the disadvantages of the Mossberg: heavy, only held eight, slow reload. There was probably a reason it was never used against the bugs.

I found the twelve gauge shells in short order. They were in-between some .223 and 9mm. I pulled two ammo cans down and headed to the table. Opening it, I found enough for the shotgun and Beretta that it'd be uncomfortable to carry so much. I had at least a couple hundred rounds that had been hand placed in the can and then sealed. I got the shotgun off my back and put in a slug, then filled the rest with buckshot. I put it on safe, and felt marginally better.

You're running out of time if you want the light to get out of here. The batteries were set to disconnect backup power when they get to ten minutes.

"Can't you shut down other levels to give me more time to work?" I asked as I started looking around.

No, once the main power was cut, the network went back down. In the back of the room is the gunsmithing station. Hopefully, you can find something that can help with your pistol.

"Good point," I said leaving the ammo there.

I'd noticed the small desk area with clamps and vices. There was a chair in front of it, and I pulled it out to sit down when something tumbled off the chair. I was almost expecting a body or head… a chupacabra… something. I didn't scream out, but it startled me. When I looked down…

"A backpack?" I said, pulling it up.

There was something inside of it, and I opened it and found an old cell phone, a wallet made of duct tape and what had to have been blue jeans, but disintegrating. I dumped it all out on the desk surface and tossed the backpack in the direction of the table. Sitting down I looked. The desktop had a rubberized surface, nonstick. There might have once been some tools there, but there were rusted pieces that I had no clue if they were once part of a firearm or other tools. Nothing on top looked worth keeping, so I opened the drawers. I found what I was looking for in the second drawer. In a small plastic cleaning kit, I found an aluminum pushrod and two bottles of Hopes. One was a cleaner, and one was gun oil.

I knew in a pinch I could have used kerosene, motor oil or any number of things, but this was good. I was tempted to clean the Beretta right there, but I remembered Alice's warning about time. I didn't want to get stuck inside in the dark. I snapped the case closed and took a cursory look through the rest of the desk but didn't see anything.

"You see any battery packs?" I asked her.

No, nothing through your eyes. We could tear this place apart and never find them. I believe there were only two issued per Data ARC. One for the residents and one for... well, you.

"Where's the ammunition for it?" I asked suddenly.

I saw it in the last row, the third shelf down from the top.

I walked to the table and started dumping supplies in, hoping I wasn't overloading what the nylon backpack could handle. All my life, I'd been told about the horrors of plastics and how they never biodegraded. Now it was the only material that seemed to hold up to the test of time. That was irony right there. I found the can and opened it. There were four more loaded magazines with the four inch long pieces of metal.

See, I knew the basics of a rail gun. A metal slug was loaded into a barrel, and without a propellant, the energy would create a magnetic thing, that would do something and shoot the slug out like a superconductor train. Yeah, it was a miniaturized superconductor. I think. Alice remained silent. The magazines weren't as heavy as I thought they might be and, after a moment, I started loading them into the front pouches. I had to move the Jeremiah Jones ID card, so I clipped it to the top of the vest. With those four magazines in place, I walked over and took up the rail gun. It had a sling as well, and I debated. Without any power source, I was just walking around with extra weight.

I put the pack on and adjusted it a few times, till I more or less got it where I wanted, and started out.

"How much time we have left?" I asked Alice.

Not long.

I left the Armory door, knowing there was a treasure of supplies still to be had there, but right now I couldn't carry it all, and most of it was useless to me. I headed towards the stairs indicated by the HUD and pushed open the door. I led with the shotgun and started up.

Faster, Alice urged.

I started double-timing it up the stairs. I passed the second floor in less than a minute. I hated to leave an unopened door behind me and almost paused, but the mental urgings were made even more apparent when Alice put a timer on the edge of my left vision in the HUD. I had forty seconds. I started to sprint. I hit the level to the first floor with twelve seconds to spare. I pulled open the door and ignored everything in front of me and started sprinting towards a circular steel door at the far end. Alice didn't speak, but she highlighted the door and superimposed a sign that said exit. With four seconds left I came to a halt in front of a numbered keypad.

34169 I punched in, and the door started rumbling open a lot faster than I had expected. It didn't do an inch a minute pace, but it moved almost a foot a second. What I'd seen but not processed was half of a human body. As the door moved up, what was left of the skeleton and jumpsuit moved up. Half of what looked like a firearm was coming up too, mashed almost into two pieces by the heavy steel door. I ducked and rolled under. The weight of my pack and the guns almost stopped me, but I wasn't going to be stuck.

Get that!

I tugged at the gun just as the timer reached zero and the door came crashing back down. It cut the gun in half, and what I had was the back half of the gun… a railgun and magazine.

There's a catch on the left handle. Press the button and open that up.

I was already working on it. Inside, two industrial-sized watch batteries tumbled out.

I pulled the LRG (Light Rail Gun) I was carrying and opened the compartment Alice showed me and installed them just as they had come out. Only then did I think about what I'd seen in that room I had just passed through in a mad dash. Crumpled forms of blue jumpsuits and skeletons in white lab suits. Some had firearms, some had kitchen knives. It was obvious to me that a battle had happened in what passed as a reception area. Desks had been on either side of the doors where somebody would sit and process your paperwork. It was in stark contrast to where I found myself now.

Weak sunlight filtered through large boulders overhead. I was outside, in some sort of manmade cavern of large rock, or maybe it was concrete made to look like rock. The floor though, was what I would have expected in Arizona. Sand. No vegetable matter stuck in it either. I turned and saw the door. There was a keypad on this side, but it was no longer lit. The power had probably gone out completely and forced a shutdown of the whole facility.

That's basically correct. There's a manual override lever for the door like you used on the elevators, though. We need to survey the area. Somehow we need to find replacement servos or parts to repair what we have to make our ARC viable. Supplies will need to be found soon, though. Your gel pack food supply is enough food and water for a short period.

"Yeah. Can you sense anything out there?"

There's nothing I can network with, no interface that I'm aware of.

"That's what I was afraid of," I said aloud and got to my feet, brushing the sand off my desert camo pants.

Holding the rail gun at the ready, I walked towards the end, keeping my eyes peeled upwards, too. If these bugs were still around, I didn't want one to squeeze out of the carefully placed boulders covering what looked like a cave and drop on me. I didn't think being eaten alive was something that I could heal from.

It's not, Alice confirmed.

Reaching the mouth of the cave took a lot less time than I expected. It was literally just around a gently left sweeping corner. It opened up, and I saw the ground and wasteland below me. Heat radiated up from the stone in hazy waves that were visible. The colors of the bare rock varied but there were a lot of brown hues, and I remembered seeing something like this... in books? On TV?

"Where are we, exactly?" I asked.

ARC 341 is built into the by Marble Canyon near the Grand Canyon National Park. East of us somewhere is the Colorado River.

"So precise for a computer... somewhere," I said, looking around.

I can already tell that the geography of the area has changed. It's also a good twenty degrees warmer than the summer average.

"What time of year is it?"

I don't know, Alice said quietly.

I took a step out and looked around. I could smell smoke, wood smoke.

"Alice, does this LRG operate in the same way other firearms do now that it's got the batteries?"

Yes, though there is no bolt to charge. Just pull the trigger. It takes five seconds between shots to recharge enough for another shot. Batteries should last you through the munitions you've brought.

"Good. It's too bad there aren't optics on this."

Are you really going to complain? An hour ago you were naked and thinking you were going insane.

"I still might be," I finished aloud and took a step out of the cave.

The ground shook so hard it threw me off my feet as a large insectoid creature dropped down. It was the size of a small car and probably weighed more. It had used its legs to cushion its fall, but it stretched them out again, lifting it, so the bug's body was almost at eye level with me. Its carapace was mottled brown and gray, almost in a camouflage pattern, and I recognized the eight-legged creature. I'd seen a hologram or a visual representation of it inside the ARC. It was a Vorryn, or something in the same family. It made a high-pitched squealing sound with its mouth open, and it rushed towards me.

I won't lie, my first instinct was to run, scream, but what I did was even more manly. I did both. Bringing the LRG to bear, I fired from the hip as I threw myself sideways to avoid a foot stomp from the creature's armored leg. I rolled and got to my feet as it turned a semi-circle but not before I saw that the LRG hadn't penetrated the exoskeleton. It had left a gray mark as the metal slug just ricocheted off of it.

Where the head joins, joints of the main legs, the underbelly, Alice said softly.

I was bringing the LRG up to fire even as I was backpedaling, but nothing happened when I pulled the trigger.

Not enough time between recharge.

"Put something like that up on the HUD overlay," I snapped and jumped backward as the creature hit me with one of its inner legs.

The hooked talon snagged my vest and, instead

AWAKENED CONTROL

of ripping me in half, it flung me down the slope. I went head over heels for a good two hundred yards, and hit a rock, stopping my momentum and almost making me pass out from the pain. I was breathing hard, and I looked down at my vest for half a second to see it looking the same as when I'd pulled it out of the wrapping.

"That could have cut me in half," I murmured, and sighted in on the big bug moving down the hill at an alarming clip.

Yes, Alice said softly.

The timer that I'd asked for was now back at zero on the left side of my vision, and I got to a knee, marveling that the pain I had been feeling was already receding. I tried to time the movement of the big vorryn and pulled the trigger. This time I had sighted in instead of a hip shot. As the slug left the barrel, the air around the muzzle was displaced, and a hint of ozone accompanied it on the hot, dry breeze. It didn't sound like a gun, more like… a Nerf Gun for a lack of anything else to compare it to. I never got a glimpse of the projectile, but I saw that it had an immediate effect. I'd hit the front leg joint on my right side. It tore through the armored leg and almost ripped the lower leg off at what I guess was the knee.

The creature pitched forward but was up again almost immediately. It started lurching forward on three legs when I sighted in again. I waited for the timer, the creature closing the gap faster than a horse could run. I wanted to run myself. Even injured, this thing was even faster than I could have imagined… But there was one thing that Alice hadn't noted in the log files

57

that I had noticed: forward and backward movements were quick, but to turn side to side took it time. It'd probably not be able to turn corners fast. With that, when the timer hit zero I let loose with another slug.

I was aiming at the joint between the head and body. The creature flinched and kept coming. I was hoping to hit it there but already was executing my backup plan. I jumped to the side and let gravity take effect. I'd let go of the LRG as I dove and pulled the Beretta as I came to one foot and one knee. The Vorryn was still up the slope from me, and I started firing. I got off four rounds into the underside of the carapace before the Beretta jammed. Still, I saw green ichor burst forth from where the slugs had hit. I dropped the gun in the rocky soil and pulled for the shotgun as green goo dripped out of the creature. The high pitched keening it had been making cut off the same time the rounds penetrated its lightly armored bottom side.

"I'm glad I got this," I said pulling the Mossberg out and, as the creature started turning, I began pumping rounds and pulling the trigger.

I got two rounds off fast before I had to duck a talon, and I rolled to my right, small rocks and gravel scraping on the exposed parts of my skin as I sighted in for half a heartbeat. The slugs had blown large holes near where the 9mms had gone in. The creature stumbled as I pulled the trigger, buckshot spitting forth less than ten feet into the bottom of the creature's head. It exploded, and the top of the jaw was flung from the body. It dropped like it was poleaxed and the creature fell where it had been standing.

AWAKENED CONTROL

Rivulets of green came from it, what had to have passed for blood. I avoided it, and stepped around the creature, breathing hard.

"Is it dead?" I asked aloud.

As long as its brain is located in its head, I don't see how it could survive. I don't know enough about these bugs to tell you for sure.

I walked around the creature, and I didn't know if it was the green blood draining or the exposed… what used to be the head, but there was a metallic scent in the air. I made sure the shotgun's safety was still off and pushed at the carapace with it, ready to jump back. Nothing. I walked all the way around it, retrieving my dropped weapons. The pistol was still jammed, so I dropped the magazine and worked the slide several times, ejecting the mis-fed shell.

"I really need to sit down and clean and oil these," I said to myself.

The LRG looked in good shape, and I shook it to see if there was any sand in it while pointing it straight down. I put that over my shoulder and felt myself starting to sweat. On top of that, the back shattering pain I felt from being flung down the hill was almost gone. That startled me.

"Alice, are you blocking the pain?" I asked her.

Some, though you would have had bruising. No bones or organs were damaged in the fight.

I started walking around the bug till I came back to where I started.

"You going to eat that?"

I spun around, startled. In combat, they train you to never get tunnel vision. It's the bad guy you can't see who frags your ass. In this case, I'd been so focused on the bug I hadn't looked around while I was making sure it was dead. The man had to have been in his late sixties if I had to guess. He was wearing rough spun cotton or wool clothing, in mottled browns and grays. I once got a sweater from… now I don't remember… and it was hand knit. These clothes had that sort of look to them. Surprisingly enough, the man was wearing full-length pants and a vest of the material. A beanie style hat topped the look off. The color of his tanned skin made it hard for me to tell if he was Caucasian or Hispanic descent, but his question had been in clear English.

"I don't… I've never had it before. Do you want it?" I asked.

"It'd be a would be a big enough feast for me times twenty, but I have family over yonder hill," he said, nodding down the slope and across the next rise.

I would usually have been more cautious, or I felt like I normally would have been, and I did a slow look around, mindful of the stranger who'd gotten to within thirty feet of me, while I was unawares. In the silent stillness of the air, no other sounds but the wind could be heard. When I finished my look, the stranger was still standing there. I noticed then the lines on his face, the stubble on his cheeks and how hollowed out they were. This man was hungry.

"I promise you, I mean you no harm. If you tell me no, I'll move on," he said to me softly, his words closing the distance easily.

"I don't mind if you bring your family up here," I said, wanting to look and see if the cave to the ARC was still visible.

It wasn't, but instead of talking, Alice put up a small message across the bottom of my vision that the location of the ARC was stored in her internal mapping. A waypoint. I wouldn't lose it.

"Thank you. Are you sure?" he asked, nodding to the Vorryn.

"I don't know what to do with something like this," I said, mildly horrified at the thought.

"If you'd like to sit a spell, I'll go get my family and perhaps you can tell me your story. For example, where are ye from and what are you doing with those strange clothes?"

Tony, Alice broke into my thoughts, *A friendly local would be a good way to figure out what's going on. This might be worth—*

"That sounds good, though are you safe going alone? If there was one Vorryn…"

"There's usually a hive of them, but it's not this one, not right here. You tagged one of their scouts. A nasty piece of work. Only the royal guardians are tougher."

"Royal guardians?" I asked.

"Oh, I think there'll be some good conversation tonight. Wait until my son Luca hears we have a new stranger in the area. He deals in stories, you know."

"Ok, I'll wait here," I said, getting the feeling that he didn't want me to follow him back to wherever his kin were.

He took off, and I watched him move swiftly down the slope towards the next rise. Alice remained silent, though. She still hadn't told me what she knew, and I had questions, but right now… The adrenaline dump left my body, and I sat down on a rock near the corpse of the bug.

"Don't you give me no lip," I said, pointing at the bug.

I crack myself up sometimes.

That wasn't funny, Alice said mentally.

————

I had missed the man's name but when he came back, he introduced himself as Yanesh, his wife was Irena, then there was Luca and a small toddler they called Smudge. They had no idea what year it was and had lived in fringe communities, fearing the larger villes (their word for villages). When Luca had come of age and earned his name, he was required to spend two years in service to the local militia in Lake Ville or maybe it was supposed to be Lakeville. Instead, they'd broken the law and tradition and had been moving ever since.

"I literally know nothing of Lakeville or their militia. Why risk breaking their law and moving?" I asked, which stopped the conversation.

Irena and Luca were holding circular bladed knives with a handle cut out of the half moon and wrapped in what looked like some type of cordage for a handle. They were using these to cut up on an angle around the exoskeleton of the Vorryn, but they stopped and just stared at me a moment.

"You really don't know?" Luca asked. "When Dad said he'd met an Augment, I didn't believe him. And yet here you are, and you don't know anything about the largest, most corrupt ville this side of the big river?"

"You mean the Colorado River?" I asked them, wondering if it was that or...

"The what? I'm talking about the Mississippi, near bouts Old San Louisville."

That I got, they were talking about Saint Louis... but the mom had dropped her jaw in surprise.

"What do you know of the Colorado River?" she asked. "I thought ya didn't know anything about Lakeville."

"From maps. It's... what's this Augment thing?" I asked, turning to Luca.

They both went back to their grizzly task while Yanesh and Smudge knelt near me.

"There haven't been any good maps in a long while," he told me. "My great great grandpa had one once. I saw it when I was just a little kid. It was in tatters though, and it was almost bleached white, between two pieces of glass. Was supposed to be the most expensive item in the ville. If you have a map, friend..."

"What's an Augment?" I asked, feeling the sun beating down on my bald head.

"I think that's what you are. I didn't mean for it to offend nor any disrespect," he said, holding Smudge close.

"No, no. I just literally don't know what it is. I... I'm kind of lost here, and I don't have much of my memory." I rubbed my head, feeling the scar.

"Well..." he said and then looked at me. I'd placed

the shotgun on the ground and had taken a seat in the shade of the bug, on the other side of where the blood had been coming down the hill. I saw Yanesh look at my gun and then back up to me.

"Augments were humans that the Outsiders did all kinds of alchemy and sorcery on. They blended people with machines. At least, that's what the stories tell, eh Luca?"

"Yeah pa," he said, and I heard a squelching sound.

Both Luca and Irena had finished their cutting and lifted off the top of the carapace. It was like a turtle shell, but shaped differently. Inside, I expected to see a mass of green goo, but was surprised to see white flesh, almost like raw fish or chicken.

"And they did the wishes of the Outsider clan. Oh, they were terrible beasts. Supposed to be stronger, faster, meaner and unkillable. When I saw you flung downhill and darn near break the rock with your back, I thought maybe... and then it was your eyes. Your eyes flashed brightly as you squared off with the creature, and your projectile weapons. I thought it must be madness that had taken me, but it was just you, wasn't it?"

"And maybe the sun got in your eyes, Pa," Luca said, using the top of the carapace as a tray as they started slicing bits and pieces and laying them inside.

"But your scar... You have the voices? In here?" he asked, pointing to his temple.

I looked at the small group. Even though they outnumbered me, they were fearful. The lines of hunger etched their faces, except for Luca. He seemed a little better fed, but I hadn't gotten his full story yet...

"Yeah, I'm probably what you would call an Augment then. I'm CEPM 341. I go by Tony, like I told you."

They all made the sign of the cross and Luca dropped his curved knife and walked in front of me. I stood up so I could see him eye to eye.

"Are you an Outsider? A spy? A hunter?" His voice betrayed the fact he was scared, but he was asking me honestly.

"No. I've just been away for a long time."

A very long time, Alice interjected in my head.

I pictured myself strangling a computer, and I got the mental equivalent of a chuckle from the AI.

"If you're not an Outsider, are ya a Purist?" Luca asked.

"Where I come from, the Outsiders and Purists used to be one group."

"Blasphemy," Yanesh said, and spit.

The move startled me.

"How so? Isn't it told in the history?"

"There is no history. According to the rad-blasted Outsiders, there's them, and there's everyone else. In the Church of the Order Of The Purists, they tell of a time they were betrayed, though they never say if they were same faction or family. If you had said that to anyone else who wasn't a pacifist, they might be cutting your blasphemous throat."

"Sorry, sorry. So I take it you don't like the Outsiders?" I asked.

This time, they all turned and spit. Asked and answered.

"Damn. Well, where do I find the Purists and Outsiders?" I asked, knowing that if anybody could fill me in, it might be descendants of the original ARC who could.

"Lakeville," Irena said. "You going there?"

"I think I'll have to," I told them. "They probably could tell me more about what's going on."

"That I doubt. They hoard their knowledge tightly. Only the Technomages seem to slip up once in a while when they have to work on some tech in the open."

"Technomages?" I asked feeling out of place.

"Ya know, the guys who fix things. They have pouches that hold the tools and keep the pumps running."

"I don't know that, and I think there's a ton I don't know. Please don't take my ignorance as an insult."

Those words plus my tone seemed to have done the trick. Luca walked back to the bug, and after a few more moments of silence, he started talking and working on slicing up the Vorryn.

"The Outsiders are the controlling faction of Lakeville, to the north east of us if a compass worked. Some areas they do, some don't. If you walk towards the morning sun, you'll find a mostly dried up riverbed. You follow that North, and you'll come to Lakeville. The Church of the Order Of The Purists is there as well, though not if the Outsiders had their say. It's only a long-standing truce that's kept the Outsiders from trying to wipe them out. Still, I don't know if the people would revolt if the church were wiped out. People are turning godless."

"Why… I mean… So the militia—"

"Run by the Outsiders. They control the markets,

tax the citizens and keep knowledge repressed. They raid other villes and commit horrible acts upon their enemies."

"And you didn't want a part of that?" I asked.

He gave me a nod, and I looked at Yanesh, questioningly.

"Unfortunately, it's something I did when I was a younger citizen. I'm not proud of it, and I raised my son to have his own choice. I had hoped he would go with the Order of Purists into the clergy, but he was too… militant."

"So you live a nomadic lifestyle?" I asked them.

"Yeah," Irena said, "but we're free. Me and Smudge won't have to take turns at the officer's quarters… well, when Smudge is old enough."

"Take—"

"It's like you're from another planet," Luca said, but I saw a sly grin at the side of his mouth. "It's no joking matter about the Outsiders and what they force people to do, but it's been the way of life out here for a millennium."

I thought about that, and Alice broke in to tell me that there was no way another thousand years had passed.

"I can see why you would not want to be a part of that. But I was born here on Earth. In Lincoln, Nebraska actually."

That memory had come out of nowhere, and I wondered if I was ever going to get it all back.

"How did you travel so far?" Luca asked.

"I actually woke up not far from here. See, I remember some things, but like, most of my past? I ö

don't know. I think it's from an injury."

"It's how the Outsiders would pick their Augments. A fit specimen, usually a soldier. Some would volunteer. It was always dicey, taking the injections."

That sounded like nanites to me, but I kept quiet.

"So does this mean there's an ARC somewhere near here?" Luca asked.

"I don't know," I said, lying.

"You're dressed like an Outsider, admit you are an Augment... a creature that, outside of Lakeville would be hunted down and killed if it could be... And you don't know where you were made or created? You just gave an ARC Designation. Do you think I'm stupid?"

"Hey man," I said reaching down to rest my hand on the shotgun, "I don't know what your deal is, but all I know is I was jumped by this big Vorryn. I shot it, and then here's your dad coming up to ask if it was time to put the steaks on." My voice had gotten louder, and I tried to control the anger, but it was building.

I had been trying to be nice and find out what was going on, yet I didn't want to tell them about the ARC... why?

"Protecting your back door," Alice typed on my HUD.

I silently agreed, after a half a heartbeat to think about it.

"How about we eat? Then perhaps you can tell us what you do remember," Irena said gently.

———

AWAKENED CONTROL

From a large leather pack Luca had carried up, they pulled out a grill grate made out of wood, wrapped with reeds to hold it together. The wood had been split in half, each half about the diameter of my pinky. They put up a ring of Y forked branches right in the dirt about twelve inches across and then placed the grate on top. Then came the slabs of meat, thinly sliced. Irena sprinkled the meat with something from a leather pouch around her neck and then they took out something wrapped in black wool cloth. It was about thirty by thirty inches in diameter. Unwrapping it, I saw it was three storm windows, with a piano hinge holding the panes together.

They opened it and placed the middle section over the stakes and positioned the other sides into the rocky sand. Then they pushed more sticks in to make sure it didn't flatten itself out, and the cloth that had wrapped it became the sides. I was fascinated, and I knew Alice was going to tell me what it was if I didn't figure it out soon, but I had, thanks to some distant memory I couldn't quite reach.

"Solar oven?" I asked.

Luca grunted.

"You know, if you have time, find a flattened rock to three under the grate and paint it black to absorb the heat better. That way you can cook with it longer, once the sun sets."

They looked at me funny, and Luca had suspicion written all over his face.

"That's a trick most ville folk doesn't know," Yanesh said softly. "Who are you Augment, really?"

"Call me Tony."

"Well, Tony, that's not normal stuff. Technomages keep information like that hidden away. If they knew we had the tech to make these self-heat ovens, they'd tax me and take it away. Hell, they might even kill us. Keep that in mind as you ask questions. It isn't what you *don't* know, it's *what* you know that might get you hurt. If you can be."

"I can take care of myself, usually," I said, nodding at the Vorryn. "What's the deal with them?"

"Eh? What do you mean?"

"In my time, there never was insects this big."

I saw Luca look up, smirking at his dad.

Good one, keeping the info close to the vest. Idiot, Alice said in my head. *Hey, you said only if you deserved it and you did!*

"Shut up, Alice," I snapped.

"See! Further proof, Pa!"

"Shiny," Smudge said, and wiggled until Yanesh put the little girl down.

She walked with uneven feet over to me. I knelt down and took a knee. She touched my eyelids and repeated, "Shiny."

Irena didn't look comfortable, so I stood up. The little girl grabbed onto my pant leg, and a thumb found its way into her mouth.

"Not scary," she told her mom.

"This one isn't," Luca said, "But he's got most of his brains left, by the sound of him. Don't trust him with your secrets, little pumpkin."

Luca was still half-smiling. I didn't know if it was him tricking the knowledge out of me, or that I'd validated some theory he and his father had had going on

AWAKENED CONTROL

their long walk up here.

"So when was your time?" Irena asked me as the little girl started tugging on my pant leg.

I reached down and picked the little girl up, and cradled her with my left arm to my hip. The little girl seemed at ease with the move, and I leaned the shotgun against the corpse of the bug. I debated moving the Beretta too, but to get it out I would need to do a cross draw, which was fine for me but was out of reach of the girl. Instead, she played with a Velcro flap.

"My last memories were some time before 2020," I admitted, knowing now how dangerous it was to admit it.

If the descendants of the factions were killing, or at least one of them was... killing to repress knowledge. That seemed a little counterproductive.

It was for situations such as this that you were saved from death and made into a Peace Maker, Alice told me quietly, in a mental voice so sober I wondered if an AI could have their minds, or circuits, blown.

"2020... that was the year before the great great war," Irena said.

"I thought there wasn't much knowledge?"

"I was a teacher, I too used to be an Outsider." She didn't meet my eyes.

"Yeah, I think I was injured sometime late 2018, but my best guess was between then and 2020."

"You're not really an Augment then," Yanesh said. "You're a Precursor Augment." His voice was reverent, and the color had drained out of his face.

"I don't know what that means."

"That means you have two brains, but you're in

control of your own," Luca told me.

"Two brains... you mean the..." I tapped the side of my head where the scar was.

I didn't know if they knew about the computer or the AI, but the second brain seemed to make sense.

"Yeah, and you're in control. Nobody is programming you..." He looked mildly interested. "Later on, perhaps we can exchange more information. But... I believe the food is ready."

It hadn't taken long to cook, and when they removed the solar oven, I could smell what had to be the best scent ever. How I'd missed it while it was cooking was anybody's guess. My stomach rumbled loudly, and Smudge giggled.

We shared dinner, filet of bug. It wasn't as bad as I'd thought it was going to be. Imagine if there was a more perfect meat than bacon? The texture of fish, with the flavor of bacon wrapped chicken? That was how the Vorryn tasted. I could taste a hint of salt and something else, some kind of mineral, probably from the pouch that Irena had used to season the meat. I tried not to pig out, but the fight had taken some energy out of me. That was when I remembered I still had the food paste, so I slowed down so the others could eat.

Then they pulled out what looked like a dried gourd from a pack. It had a top fashioned out of part of the gourd, and what looked like leather cordage. Opening that up, Irena used a flattened piece of wood to scrape out a white thick... It looked like greasy mashed potatoes, but it had no scent. She motioned for me to hold my hand out, and I did. She scraped it onto my hand and then watched me.

"Um, thank you. What's this?" I asked.

"You really don't know?" Yanesh asked me.

"No," I told him honestly.

"It's Yana paste. It's a staple in the wastes outside Lakeville."

"What's it… taste like?" I asked.

"It tastes like Yana paste," Irena said with a grin and gave everyone a dab of it about the size of a golf ball.

"Watch, I'll go first," Irena said and licked the sticky glob off her hand.

I did the same and was surprised. I was expecting it to taste like something foul, but it had no real flavor. Alice informed me that she could already tell that it was starch and water used to make the paste and it could be used as a staple food, just not a very nutritious one. Hence the reason they were out scavenging for something to eat.

"That isn't that bad," I said, finishing it off, wishing I had a beer.

"I was expecting you to vomit," Yanesh said seriously. "We had somebody from the big ocean come over the mountains once. He couldn't stop throwing up."

"It's starchy, like a potato?" I asked them.

"It's a root we use to make the paste," Yanesh said with a grin. "I was named after it."

"If it's a staple, there must be a ton of it huh?"

"There is, near the river and Laketown. We try not to go there, though. You know why," he said pointing to Luca.

"I don't blame you. The more we talk about these Outsiders, the more I think the society they came from… the values were lost." I was struggling to find the right words.

"I don't know. It's been a hard life for all who live outside the villes. It's probably always been like that, as far back as time goes."

"Back then we used to call them cities and towns," I said.

Irena's eyes opened wide, and I noticed that, under the artfully placed grime, she was a lot younger than Yanesh. A good twenty years or so. That would put Luca in his mid-twenties, roughly. Still, her eyes shone with interest.

"What were they like?" she asked. "It's one thing to read about them on the comp disks, but it's another to hear about it from someone who was there."

"Wait, there are working computers?" I asked, suddenly excited.

"Yes," Yanesh admitted, "Commodore 64s. I don't know what happened to the other 63s, but that is one fine piece of technology!"

I grimaced. Commodore 64s had been before even my time. A good 20 years at least. So I started talking. My words were herkie jerky at first, but sometimes memories would pop in, like remembering that the computers were old, or where I'd grown up. I still didn't know who I was, but I remembered little things. As the daylight started to be replaced with nightfall, I kept going. At some point, another gourd was pulled out and handed to me. I was expecting more Yana paste but instead saw a sloshing liquid. I sniffed, and it had a yeasty smell to it.

They hadn't tried to kill me yet, so I gave it a sip and was pleasantly surprised to find it tasted a lot like rice beer. Warm, but it was beer. Somewhere earlier, God had heard my halfhearted thoughts and sent me to desert people from Tatooine to give me a beer. God is—

That's got 37% alcohol content, Alice said silently, *So go easy. I can offset the effects of alcohol, but it'll cost me. That's one thing you should avoid unless you have a good amount of time and supply of food so I can replace nanites that are—*

"Just let me enjoy it, I don't need you to neutralize it," I said aloud, and took another drink before handing the gourd on.

Luca took it and grinned at me, "Is it talking to you?"

"Yeah. I made the mistake of telling it that it could use an ex-girlfriend to model itself after. She did the job a little too good."

"You, are truly remarkable," Yanesh said. "To not only have a spiritual brain but to let it… nag you voluntarily… maybe our ancestors were all mad?"

I busted up laughing, as did Luca and Yanesh at that, but a sharp look from Irena shut the other two up. After a moment the conversation started back up, and they told me the basic system of trade in the new city, and I told them why I wanted to go there. I also hinted that I had been wandering a lot longer than I had, even though Alice assured me that they would be unable to enter without my fingerprints and code, even with the power off. Something about organic biometrics. I'd ask her later when I wasn't having what felt like an almost normal evening.

When my tale was told, I asked Irena about the big war. The only thing I knew about it was from what Alice had told me from the log files. A lot of what they told me was information that had been passed down. The technology they had now was a result of an ARC somewhere in this area, but all knowledge of its whereabouts was lost. They didn't have much in Lakeville, mostly old computers and CDs of information. I knew the old computers didn't have CD drives, so I filed that away for further consideration and kept listening.

The USA had been attacked by China, in response to a newly elected leader who promised economic warfare. With their country overpopulated, barely able to feed themselves and a now US government that wasn't importing electronics or exporting grains and food, they had little else to lose. At least, that was Irena's reasoning. The USA responded with underwater bombs, which I figured were sub launched cruise missiles. This brought in Russia, who launched what made NATO's response seem tiny in comparison. Somewhere, someone hit the doomsday button, and we launched at all of our enemies, both present and past.

Someone hit Israel, but not before Israel wiped most of the surrounding countries off the map that had been threatening them for years… and all the while, Australia stayed neutral and out of things. Irena said that Antarctica and Australia were the only continents to escape the nuclear war that lasted for just six days, but devastated the world. Then things got bad. The weather changed, it snowed and stayed cold for years and years (nuclear winter?). The survivors above ground were mostly wiped out from that alone, but then there were years and years of crazy flooding, droughts in areas that had always been lush and green, then wildfires and crazy lightning strikes. Acid rain was still pretty common, but not everywhere this family had traveled.

The Aussies ventured out in ships that they built or that were salvaged from the war-torn navies and started checking on things. From them, the world learned through hearsay and written accounts that things had indeed gone crazy the world over. Some thought it was a polar shift, where the north and south poles move position, making the earth tilt differently from the sun, others opined that there was now a wobble of the axis… and the last theory, that a large population believed in, was that aliens had visited the earth and caused the weather to change, and mutated various species to enable them to survive. Then without offering help, the Aussies left, going back home, and taking very few people with them.

They laughed at that last bit, the part about the aliens, all except Smudge, who had fallen asleep and was now snoring softly in her father's lap. I looked at the vorryn's husk up the slope from us, and shivered. The small family one by one said their goodbyes as the full dark descended, and it hit me that I had no place to go, nowhere I belonged any more. Everyone I ever knew or loved was dead many times over; the problem was, I couldn't remember who they were to

BOYD CRAVEN

mourn their loss. I decided to head back to the shelter of the cave that led back to the ARC.

You were wrong about one thing, though, Alice said.

"What's that?"

You're never alone. You have me.

That was… strangely… comforting…

CHAPTER 5

I woke up, feeling the first pangs of dehydration. I knew that I should have stayed away from the alcohol, but that wasn't really the reason for my pounding headache. Ok, maybe it was a little bit of the problem, but most of it was the fact that it had been the only thing I'd had to drink since I'd awakened. I'd had some moisture from the gel packs, but the body can't survive without copious amounts of water. It was the rule of threes that I'd learned somewhere. 3 minutes, 3 hours, 3 days, 3 months. Air, exposure, water and food. I definitely needed to do something about it.

Knowing where the Colorado river was in relation to where I was at, I set out before the rising sun. To conserve water, I was going to move and then find a place to camp during the hottest part of the day.

Then I'd start moving at night until I could go find Lakeville. While I slept, Alice had shut up, though I was starting to get used to the AI's presence.

Are you thinking that Lakeville is the old city called Wahweap?

"I didn't know the names, but when I thought about the map in regards to our location, it came up automatically. I know the data is old, but I think there were several hydroelectric dams on the Colorado. I'm thinking Lakeville is one of the first villes before we get to Lake Powell. Or it's on top of the dam at Lake Powell. If things are the same. When they told me that, there was power in the city to run technology… I have to see."

I actually have the same urge, though not the emotional feelings to go with that urge.

"That's why the real Alice is an ex," I said grinning, and grabbed my too heavy pack and guns.

I didn't have Alice use the HUD. Instead, I kept an eye out for more Vorryn. If Yanesh's family had been out here hunting and scavenging, they might run across my tracks, so I did what I could, dragging a tumbleweed behind me until I reached the more rocky soil. Sometime in the night, the body of the big bug I'd killed had been removed. I shivered. That bug had been seriously big and heavy. The only sign it'd ever been were splashes of the green blood. No flesh remained and, now that I looked closer, the blood it had bled seemed to have gone too.

Without any tracks, I was a little worried, and started double-timing it. Even knowing I was dehydrated and had a pounding headache, I kept my eyes peeled. Somewhere I had learned just enough about desert survival to have a basic idea. Still, most of the surrounding area was rock or crumbled rock as I left the canyon area. I was keeping my eyes peeled for more of the giant insects, and when something silhouetted itself, for a moment I paused, and then got close to the ground until I could see what it was.

At first, I thought it was something or someone standing, but when it opened its wings and took off flying, I felt stupid as it started flying in my direction. It was an eagle and, though it looked large to me, Alice assured me that was the size they were. It had a rabbit or rodent in its taloned feet. I had got half a glimpse before it was gone. Whatever it was, it had large eyes and a pointed snout like a mouse, but the size was wrong. More like a fat ferret? Alice didn't know what it was when I asked her, so I got up and started moving again.

———

If we continue to make good time, we should be at the river by lunchtime.

Alice's words startled me. Not that I wasn't expecting them, rather I wasn't expecting to reach the water until much later today. As long as the mental map was right, I was still a good ways off.

"I don't see how?"

If you hook slightly south, there's a wash that heads down the canyon towards the water. Even if erosion was severe since the big war, the chances are that it'll be a fast and easy jog. You're losing fluids keeping a quick pace up, but no more so than you would with stopping for half the day.

"So you're recommending I keep going?" I asked, still scanning for dangers.

Up to you. Here's the waypoint. I just hope the river hasn't dried up.

"Well yeah, there's that," I said glumly.

Still, the slow jog was taxing and, instead of stopping for a breather, I would slow to a slow walk. I could feel the sun now, though, and the heat was rising again, making it harder to breathe. Sweat ran into my eyes at intervals, and just when I was about to hunt some shade, I saw the wash. It was just as Alice had described it. Other than boulders that had broken off the walls from either erosion or time, it was a gentler slope going down to what looked like clear water.

I was thirsty, desperately so, but I took the time to walk through the wash slowly. It took close to three hundred yards to follow it to where the Colorado River flowed. It wasn't as deep as I'd thought, and the reflection of sunlight had made it look magical from afar. I didn't have anything to carry my water with, nor a cup, so when I got close to the canyon wall, I set the LRG and Shotgun against it. I gave a look up and down stream and dipped my hand in, bringing it up. There weren't larva floating in the water I could see, and it didn't smell like heavy metals. Alice was silent, so I put a drop on my tongue.

The water is mostly safe to drink, Alice assured me. *It's not very clean, but the nanites can handle everything I've run across so far. No toxins and no heavy metals.*

"Then why isn't it very clean?"

AWAKENED CONTROL

I've already found bacteria related to dysentery and cholera in the water. It's not a threat to you.

I was sure I'd drank worse, and a long time ago I'd been vaccinated against just about everything viral on the planet, so I was going to trust the computer. Besides, that one drop on my tongue had made my body scream out for more.

Go slow, Alice cautioned.

I started drinking from cupped hands and stopped to let my stomach settle down again when it started a small but unsuccessful revolt. I had been in worse shape than I realized. I finished for the time being and moved back towards the wall and looked up and down stream. There was a shelf on both sides of the river where I was now, but looking at it, I could see how the river used to be much higher, or the water had cut into the rock during flash floods. Upstream, it narrowed down, and I couldn't tell if I could still walk on this side of the river.

Still, the water was flowing quick enough that I didn't want to go across it. Instead, I started following it upstream, the rock walls narrowing in on me. I held the LRG on the low and ready as I moved. I was scanning, and I'd stop every tenth step or so to look behind me. I didn't mean to fall into a pattern, but I did. That almost cost me my life.

Something exploded into the rock face, showering me with sharp rock, and I felt the warmth on the back of my neck. I looked around as I reached back and saw blood on my palm when I looked at it.

Don't worry about your wounds, someone just tried to brain you.

"With what?" I said softly and then I heard something.

It almost sounded like an insect, or the purring of a motor. Then a snapping sound, and this time I saw it. Moving like a fastball, a rock the size of a ping pong ball and just as round, was headed straight for my head. I tried to get out of the way, but if I was Wolverine or Deadpool I really wouldn't have had to. I'd do something kickass, or just shrug off the injury. No, I tried to dodge, and it clipped my cheek and hit my ear, tearing me up, before exploding into the rock face behind me again. The blow to the ear was the worst portion, and it rang my head like a gong. That's when I belatedly realized it had hit my left side of my face.

"You ok?" I asked Alice mentally.

Yeah, working on healing you. Dodge left.

She'd seen something out of my own eyes that I had missed, or hadn't put together and, when I moved, I heard another snapping sound and the rock face behind me erupted into shards again. I aimed the LRG where both projectiles had come from and waited.

Across the river. Rock colored camouflage clothing.

I shifted my aim when part of the wall started making a ridiculous movement with two arms and then started swinging something over his head, making a whhhhaaaaaaa whaaaaaaaaaaa whaaaaaaaaa rhythmic buzzing sound. A sling, I was sure of it. I fired just as the projectile across the river was launched. I must have spooked him because he didn't hit me in the head, he got me square in the chest. It blew me off my feet and knocked the air out of my lungs. Pain exploded through me but, as I fell, I saw a figure flinch. I thought I'd missed, but the form crumpled down and fell into the water.

I was rubbing my chest and getting to a knee when a handful of pebbles fell from above, and I rolled, pulling my pistol, because the LRG hadn't recharged yet. Alice automatically started the countdown timer on the recharge and, for the first time, I realized that as awesome and fearsome a gun the weapon was, it had some serious limitations. Aiming the pistol up, I saw another figure swinging a sling overhead, but I hesitated. There was something familiar about the shape, and when he let loose, I flinched. His stone flew straight and true, hitting a man that I hadn't seen, his camouflage too good. There was a short cry, and a stone camo'd figure fell from his perch up high and down into the Colorado.

I turned to see the man who'd used the sling twenty feet overhead, my gun automatically aiming as he put both hands up, the crude but effective weapon falling loose from his hand and fluttering down my way. He pulled down some sort of scarf that had been covering his face, and I wasn't surprised to see that it was Luca.

"Don't shoot," he called, his hands in the air.

———

"What are you doing here?" I asked him as I handed him the sling he'd dropped.

He'd joined me down the riverside. He'd come

down the sheer face as easily as a monkey would climb trees. The feat was no easy thing, and I noticed he'd done it barefoot, some sort of leather sandals over his shoulder so his toes could feel and get their own purchase on footholds I never would have trusted.

"I talked it over with my parents," Luca said. "I need to go to Lakeville sooner or later. They gave up everything to keep me out of the militia, but there was another option, one none of us took seriously."

"What's that?" I asked him.

"The Church of The Order of The Purists," he said. "None of us really believed in the old stories… well, except my dad, but I think what you saw was an act to see if you were genuine… But now, we spent until the daylight walking and talking. You are living, breathing proof that the religion isn't all bunk. The history that my mom so cherishes was real. A lot of people have questioned that, have often wondered if The Order's religion was the true path, or if the Tech-nomages of the Outsiders had it right."

"Can I let you in on a little secret?" I asked, making the decision to trust him.

"Sure," he said as we walked the narrow ledge between the wall of the canyon and the river.

"The Purists and the Outsiders are the offspring of the ARC I come from. No, no, I'm not saying where it is," I said, holding my hands up as his jaw dropped open a bit, "you know a bit about this. The God, my people worshipped was neither. Actually, there were a ton of religions in my days, probably the same now… but guys like me, we're just people. The Order? They're just people. The Outsiders? They're people, but they sound like repressive asshats."

"Worse," Luca mumbled, pausing to pick up a rock the size of a golf ball.

It was a hunk of sandstone, the second one he'd picked up, and he started rubbing the two together. At once I realized he was making the edges rounded, probably for his sling.

"So you saw me heading to the river and decided to tag along?" I asked him.

"Yeah, but you move bastard fast. If you hadn't slowed down to drink and then walk slowly, I never could have caught up with you."

"By the way, thanks for hitting that second guy, I never saw him. Who were they?" I asked.

"Rogues like us, though we don't hide out and try to kill random strangers. We hunt and forage, whereas these guys…" he rubbed his stomach in an overly dramatic gesture, still holding the half-formed projectile.

"They're cannibals."

"Yup. Bad breath too. I dated this cannie girl once. I didn't know she was into that sort of thing until she invited me over for dinner. Instead of her dad running me off, he pulled out his fork and spoon…"

He busted up laughing, and I gave him a wan smile. If this is what passed for the future's sense of humor, I hoped I wasn't stoned for having a sarcastic nature.

"So you were planning on following me all the way in, or to…?"

I let the words trail off.

"I don't know. I debated stopping you, asking you

if I could walk with you. I was following till I saw those two setting up. I had higher ground and saw what they meant to do, but I was out of position to help with the first one. Sorry."

"That's ok. And hey, I haven't had company for a thousand years or so, so I don't mind as long as we're cool."

I turned because I sensed or my subconscious heard him stop walking.

"You're serious? I mean, that isn't just some bullshit, you really were down that long?"

"Yeah," I said, "and I have the old school guns to prove it."

"Guns? Oh yeah, blasters, shooters. Guns. I'll have to remember that. The blocky one, it doesn't make much sound, except when it hit the rock face after going through the first man."

"Yeah, it's a Light Rail Gun, something that was futuristic in my time. I noticed the other men, and you all carry slings, aren't guns the normal weapons nowadays?" I asked.

"Guns as weps?" he asked, and I had to assume weps was weapons. "Only the Technomages and Augments have weapons like yours. Actually, not as nice, nor made from the materials like your Rail Gun."

"You mean the plastics?" I asked, tapping the stock.

He nodded.

"Good to know. What do you know of Lakeville, since it looks like we're going to be walking together?"

"I've only been on the fringes. It's large, maybe a few hundred people live there. The land goes from rocky to lush in, like, no time flat. The farms are up ahead a little bit, you'll see. It's the farms where I've been making my living."

We talked as we traveled. Luca was a storyteller and would often earn his family enough food for a few meals whenever they were near the farms. By the future's standards, he was supposedly both charming, amusing and a standup comedian, all rolled into one. Sort of like a medieval jester. He described how the farms operated. Water was shunted from upstream and piped somehow into what sounded like hand dug wells that were filled with the river water. Fish were farmed there, and the dirty water from the fish effluent was bucketed out and what sounded like a half hydroponic, half dirt method form of farming happened. The Yana plant was a staple at most farms, being a somewhat marshy plant.

He pointed out a couple of shoots of green that stuck up from the riverbank, and I paused to look. It was similar to a cattail, but there was no puffball that looked like a corndog. Instead, it had almost what looked like small ears of corn that grew up on an angle towards the sunlight with long, broad leaves. I pulled an ear of the mini corn and examined it. It didn't look like anything good, but I put it in a pouch and pulled off a leaf. That way I would get to know the plant, and it would shut up Alice, who was wanting to get the data to store. Still, one side of the leaf was soft with what felt like soft bristles. The other was raspy and felt like Sawgrass.

"Don't wipe with the bottom of the leaf," Luca told me, grinning.

Great… Post Apoc toilet humor…

"You folks haven't figured out how not to give a shit?" I asked him.

"Not to… you mean in the past you never…" his words faltered when he saw me grinning at him. "I think you should let me make the jokes."

He's right, you know, Alice piped up.

"Everyone's a critic," I griped, and started walking again. "Can you eat these?" I started peeling the ear that was about the size of my thumb.

"No, they cause stomach cramps, diarrhea. Pretty dangerous combo out here, unless you're right by the river."

He wasn't kidding. I tossed it into the water. I had been going to stop a lot sooner and rest for the day, but having Luca around was… kind of nice. I was learning a lot about the area I had awakened in. I felt the sun starting to cook my bald head, and Luca pulled from his pack a long woolen scarf that was the same color as the rest of his clothing, and offered it to me.

"Wrap this around your head and neck. You can leave your eyes open."

"None of you or your folks were wearing them, just a cap."

"We're used to the sun. You're turning bright pink."

You're soaking up UV radiation faster than I can reverse the effects. It isn't fatal, and you probably won't notice any pain from it, Alice said, *but without the nanites, you would have had sun poisoning hours ago.*

"Thanks, but it's going to make me hot as hell."

"No, that's the beauty of it. Once you get used to the material, the sweat soaks into it, and it actually keeps you cooler. Keep it, as a gift."

There is a lot of historical precedent in this Tony. Wool breathes. The evaporation will probably keep you cooler than if you went without.

"Thanks," I told Luca, and took it.

It was almost nine inches on the wide side and a good four feet long. With direction from him, I wrapped my head and kept my face uncovered. I felt foolish at first, but walking another twenty minutes, I could already tell that it was starting to work.

"Where do you get the sheep for the wool?" I asked him as Glen Canyon dam came into view in the distance.

"Sheep? We have animals called packis. We shave their fur to make the clothing."

"Alpacas?" I asked him, feeling out of place.

"Packis. I don't know the other creatures you were talking about."

I shut up and we kept going for a while longer until we both needed a break and got water. We stayed there for a couple of hours, talking. I showed him the basics of my shotgun. He was fascinated by how the metal pieces fit together, and I took the time to field strip and oil the Beretta; it jamming could have gotten me killed earlier. I was a lunkhead sometimes, and though I'd been trying to keep Alice quieter than she had been when I first woke up, I admitted to myself that maybe I needed her more. There was no room in the future for an AI with nobody to hold it. Maybe that's why she... her... it? had not told me everything and seemed to have ulterior motives.

I'm not holding everything back, Alice told me, her tone amused. *I'm just giving you the important info as you need it, that way you can focus on keeping the biologics alive.*

"Good point," I said out loud, and Luca looked at me.

I shrugged.

"Now here's something you must be careful of," Luca told me towards the end of our break. "Your scar and your clothing are going to draw suspicion. I do not have more to give you, but to find out that you are a Precursor Augment is going to be a problem."

"How?" I asked him simply.

"The outsiders would exploit you for your tech, your… guns… and any connection to the ARC. If you know anything useful…"

"Basically the Outsiders are bad guys," I said.

"Yeah. You're best to avoid them."

"Unfortunately, I think I'm going to have to check them out. You're sure you're not putting yourself or your little sister in danger by going back?"

"Hopefully they'll have forgotten me by now."

"What happens if they haven't?"

"We'll find out, but it's usually the death penalty for treason and sedition."

"Treason? So is there still a central form of government?"

"What's that?"

"Who runs the country?" I asked him.

"Oh, um… whoever's strong enough to control the area, I guess. In this case, Lakeville's history is it sprang up a couple hundred years ago, built by the Outsiders. At first, there weren't many people but the Order came into the town's early settlement, and started helping people. So if anybody is in charge, it's both of them."

"Your parents talked about the two factions fighting."

"You mean the Church and the Outsiders?"

"Yes."

"That was over a hundred years ago. Once in a while, there are some revenge killings, but nothing like back in the day."

Doesn't that make you feel old? Alice asked. *You know, hundred years ago. Back in the day.*

Having an inner dialog sucked sometimes.

CHAPTER 6

We passed several farms on our way towards the Dam. I'd taken out a food packet for each of us and watched in amusement as Luca ate his. The farms were both more advanced and cruder than I had been expecting. Down in the canyonside by the water, the farmer's houses were dug right out of the rock, above the high water line. They stayed in there most of the year, except during the flood season when they sheltered on higher ground. Every flat surface of rock had had sand, soil, and compost placed on it and, over generations, there were a few inches thick of material. I didn't get a chance to see any of the fish tanks dug out of the rock, but I counted myself lucky.

We stopped for water a time or two when the smell of wood smoke reached me, and I noticed that the dam seemed to have gotten closer.

"I know a place up ahead we can stop for the night."

"How far away are we still?" I asked.

"If we leave before first light, we should be there before nightfall tomorrow."

"Wow, that dam didn't seem that far away," I told him.

"It is very large. You haven't seen it yourself before?"

"No. Lakeville is near the top of the dam?" I asked.

"Yes, the side the sun rises on. Up ahead here, there's an unused cave we can shelter in."

I followed his pointing finger, and saw nothing but an old rockfall. I looked at him skeptically and pulled the scarf off my head. The day had gotten cooler, but it was still warm out.

"Your skin is no longer burned," Luca commented.

"That's the way it is with us. Listen, Luca, I'm going to have to talk to both the Church and the Outsiders. Can you keep my secret?"

"Yes, it should go without saying, though."

"Thank you, bud."

He looked at me funny and shrugged. Even though he spoke English without an accent, there were still some things that I was sure didn't translate well. At the Rockslide, Luca pushed his shoulder into a long narrow boulder, and it rolled back, revealing a crevice in the canyon wall that went back further than I could see. Alice was already adjusting my sight and, after a minute, I saw a cavern opening that was a good twenty feet in diameter, with two old fire rings where perhaps somebody had cooked a meal. I'd seen trees, but not many and not often, so it was hard to gauge when the last fire had been. I'd smelled smoke earlier, but it hadn't been from here. I made a note to ask him about that, but I was honestly getting tired.

We went in, and I used my enhanced vision to see if there was anything to worry about on the hard packed dirt floor of the cave. I didn't see anything that crept or crawled. I didn't want to get stung and, even though I was pretty sure Alice could take care of it, I didn't want to find out.

"There are no Vorryn in this area," Luca said, "but we do need to be careful that we don't have rattle-snakes on us as we slumber."

"Yeah, no to snakes. Do we roll the rock back in place?" I asked him.

"No, because it gets hot inside of here if you do."

"We're in the desert, it's pretty hot anyways."

"No, I mean there is water in here. You probably did not notice, but when I opened the cave up the air was warmer at first inside than out."

"I didn't. How come?" I asked.

"Hot spring."

"Nice, so it's a good place to shower?"

"No, it is far safer to do your bathing using the running water outside. You don't want to go near that water."

"Too hot?" I asked.

"No, there are legends about hot springs," he said, and nodded back to a dark crevice in the back. I thought it had just been the end of the wall, but as I walked closer, I saw that what looked like the floor was dark water. A ring of stones had been inset into the dirt. I took another step closer, and I felt Luca put his hand on my shoulder as if to pull me back. His hand trembled.

"If you're scared of the water, why do you use this place?" I asked him curiously.

"As long as you do not pass the ring of stones, you are safe. It is old magic."

"Have you seen this magic?" I asked him.

"No, and I don't want to. Since this place and there are others like it have… reputations… as places of great evil, it is left alone. Please friend, step away."

I did, because even in the dying light outside, the murk in here was growing. Where it had been easy for me to see only moments before, it was now difficult. Luca must have been blinded by the pitch dark, and that probably only further terrified him. A distant memory I couldn't put a finger on reminded me that, at the base, people had a primal fear of the unknown and unexplained. I would back off and appease him, but I was more curious than anything else.

There are giant bugs that eat people; is this so really hard to imagine? Alice asked me silently.

"Ok, let me slide the rock halfway in. That way there's little chance of a Vorryn sneaking in on us."

"It's not them you have to worry about," he said.

I was already moving back towards the front. The rock had been moved back and forth many times, and when I moved it, I realized that the back of it had been smoothed in two sections to make this easier. This cave had been used quite a bit in the past, but there was no way to tell how long it had been in use.

"Good," Luca said, and I turned to see him putting his back to the wall and sliding down.

"What are the other dangers in this area, besides the Vorryn and the Outsiders?" I asked him.

"You really want to talk about nightmares when it's almost time to sleep?"

I picked a spot near the wall that the rock was on, kitty-corner to Luca. I sat down myself. The wall was warm from the day's heat, but the ground was cooler. It wasn't unpleasant, but rather comforting.

"At least give me a general idea of what we might run into. This is literally a different world than I knew."

"Out here, it's the Vorryn, roving bands of gangs, raiders, Outsiders looking for old tech to salvage or slaves to capture… then of the creatures, when we get nearer to the water, there's the sippers. They're big winged insects. They drink blood, so that's why we call them sippers."

"Like a mosquito?"

"Huh? What's that?"

"A small bug."

"These aren't small," he said pulling a gourd out and taking a sip, then after a moment he offered it to me.

I took a drink of the malt liquor, going easier on it this time. I'd been dehydrated from awakening in the stasis chamber, but now I was rested and hydrated. Unless I overdid it.

"They are about this big," he said, holding his hand out to about the size of a double fist. "They have this snout like a straight stinger that pokes inside you. If they get you in a bad spot, like your ear, parts of your head, it can kill you right away like your ear, parts of your head. They aren't that common, and they fly really slow. You get a buzzing sound with them that is easy to pick out. I can usually just hit them with a stone from my sling when they get close. Usually, they are loners, unless it's the rainy season when they breed."

"Sounds terrifying," I said, bored.

"Then there are the Stalkers," he said cryptically.

"Oh?" I asked, a little more interested.

"They are tall. Taller than you by a good head. Long arms, almost to their knees. The fingers are tipped with talons. Always dark scaled, like a big crocodile, and eyes that can see into your soul. It's said that one Stalker can kill and eat two hundred people in a year if they didn't travel around so much. They are faster than a running man, and they get their name because they like to play cat and mouse with their prey."

"So they are like big gremlin-looking things? And if they eat people, why haven't folks hunted them out?"

"I don't know what a gremlin is, but people do hunt them when there is a suspected Stalker in the area. It isn't often, and a lot of times it's in the ruins of old cities where the confirmed cases are."

"So are they armored more than their scales?" I asked.

"No, but the scales on their front side are supposed to be tough to punch through with a spear or a metal-tipped arrow. Their back scales withstand all of that and then some. I haven't seen it myself, but it's supposed to be fireproof and acid proof as well."

"Acid?" I asked, skeptical. I mean, who fights with acid?

"From the acid rain. Stalkers are very valuable when they are dead. The problem is, they are very hard to kill, and it usually takes a dozen men to take one down. Even then, the losses are tremendous."

"So what, their hides are valuable?" I asked.

"That, and their flesh. It is supposed to have healing properties that dampen the pain of wounds and allows men to continue living despite crippling injuries."

So a narcotic effect of some sort. All this magical mumbo jumbo was weird to hear, but I was making enough connections that I could sort out everything. I was still surprised to hear good English spoken, but it was obvious that words, meanings and things like that had changed or been re-appropriated.

"Are there any stalkers between here and Lakeville?" I asked him.

"None that I've heard of. If there's a stalker in the area, you'll hear the people talk about it right away."

"What people?" I asked. "I've seen few farms and almost nobody."

"That will all change when we get near the city. The dam is close." Luca's words were starting to slow, and I could hear his breathing deepening.

"We'll talk more tomorrow," I said.

He was already asleep, or pretending to be. Without a bedroll, I'd be sleeping in the rough again. I'd wash up tomorrow and rinse my clothing out before going on. I wanted to ask him about the crocodile comment, but I was tired, and he was reluctant or too superstitious to talk about it in the dark. I mean, they didn't have crocs in the Colorado River, did they?

Not in our time, Alice told me softly.

Answering in my head, I said, "I hope you're taking notes. Some of this is overwhelming."

That isn't a problem, Tony. You need to rest now. Hopefully, tomorrow will bring us answers.

Even though it was delivered mentally, I almost missed it as I fell fast asleep.

———

The sound of the stone scraping woke me up. I looked around quickly, the shotgun in my hands. Luca wasn't where he'd fallen asleep, and I looked back towards the hole where the water was located. He wasn't there, he was stepping outside of the cave. I noticed because it brightened inside before being darkened by his form blocking the light again.

"Sleep good?" I asked him.

"Bad dreams. I'll be right back."

I figured he was going to do his morning duties, and I would have to soon, but I got up and stretched. Tendons popped, and blood started flowing in cramped muscles. It felt good to be alive, but my stomach hurt. I was hungry, and the food paste was delicious, but not very filling. I had to figure out what to do here; carrying out a hollowed gourd of tasteless paste might work, but it wouldn't be any better than these food gels.

While he was gone and the daylight was bright and

streaming in, I walked back to the warm water pool. The rocks that ringed the area in between the cave walls was wet, and the dry dirt on the other side of it was pockmarked, something I didn't remember from yesterday. Like water had dripped down into the dry sand, making a raindrop impression. Considering the humidity in here and outside, there should have been any damp on the ring of stones unless...

"Don't go near there, Tony," Luca said, "I wasn't joking. I think something lives in these hot springs. I don't know what it is, but it's made for some truly horrible stories."

"I wasn't planning on..." and my words trailed off as I saw a flash of something and the water swirled around the rim like something big had disturbed it.

I stepped back, not noticing I was holding my shotgun at the ready until I turned. I put it back on safe and headed towards the cave exit.

"You ready?" Luca asked me.

I looked back over my shoulder as I walked out of the cave, wondering what could instill so much fear. Whatever it was, people like Luca sounded like they left it well enough alone and felt like as long as they didn't step in the stone ring, they would be safe. If something was there in the water, who knew. The scrape of the stone and it sliding across the exit was the last I saw of that cave that day.

"Are there shops in Lakeville where I can barter or buy food?" I asked as my stomach grumbled loudly.

"Sure, it depends on what's for trade."

"How about a shotgun shell, what's that worth?" I asked.

AWAKENED CONTROL

"Probably a knife in the back. Your weapons aren't common. Only the Outsiders seem to have any sort of weps. You'd be better off stashing them than risking drawing attention."

"That isn't going to happen," I said, not wanting to be virtually naked in an unknown future. "What's used for money?"

"I'm sorry, what?"

"Currency? Trade?"

"Oh, yeah, well we have credits," he said, pulling up his wool sleeve, showing me a leather wristband with what almost looked like a square wind up watch on it, except it had a glass face. LED?

"What's that?" I asked him.

"It's our storage. It's data. So you don't have to carry stuff around."

"I thought you said the Outsiders had control of all the technology?"

"Well, I guess this is an exception."

We'd started walking again, and in the morning light, the dam looked closer somehow. The concrete of it was stained a green and black patina where the water had come out. At least, that's what it looked like from a distance.

"So you mentioned crocs yesterday. Are they common?" I asked.

"Not here, but in the upper river and the area above the dam, yes. Down here we're pretty safe."

"Are these conventional crocs? How big do they get?"

He gave me a jaundiced look and shook his head before snorting. "Surely since you've heard of them you know what they are?"

I grinned at his odd, almost British-sounding wording. "Twelve to fifteen-foot-long reptiles with a large snout and tail. Lots of pointy teeth?"

"And they shoot lasers out of their ass."

"What?" I asked him, looking to see if he was serious.

"Yeah, no. No lasers… but I guess after a thousand years those guys haven't changed."

"Well, there weren't crocs in Arizona as far as I knew a thousand years ago."

"Things change, Tony," he said and then we both froze as a rumbling noise broke the silence of the desert.

"I think we may have a problem here," Luca said.

I heard another sound like the first, and after a moment I realized what I was hearing. Motors firing up, the sound of their engines bouncing around the canyons and rock faces we were in between. It wasn't the high pitched buzzing of quads or bikes, but more like…

"We have to get to the other side," Luca said, "Their wags won't be able to cross the water."

"Who is it?" I asked.

"The Outsiders."

I asked Alice to put up the overlay and a map of the area near that. It might not be accurate, but I'd have an idea of what I might be looking at. I could see a quarter mile ahead that there was a cut off to the left that would bring us back out towards the top of the canyon wall, but that was it.

"Can you pinpoint the sound and give me any

idea of where they are?" I asked Alice mentally.

I can give you my best guess. They are here, north and west.

It was another quarter mile to get past the cut. We could turn back and head towards the cave, but I heard another motor fire up, and Alice made a red dot on my mental map overlay that showed they were near the cave. Go forward and risk running into them, or go back and get spotted. Great...

"Are they looking for us, you think?" I asked.

"I don't know why they would," Luca admitted, "But there's a lot of farms out here. Maybe they are doing a pick up?" He sounded doubtful.

"Or they are looking for something else. Are there any caves nearby where we can hide?"

A shout went up somewhere almost out of audible range, and then I heard something that made my blood run cold. A baying and barking from multiple canines made the hairs on the back of my neck stand straight up. Dogs? I hoped it was dogs and not some mutant T-Rex or something. This world was weird enough.

"No caves," Luca told me.

"There's a cut up ahead a quarter mile. We can at least get to the top of this canyon wall in case they are looking for us."

"We can always jump in the water and hope for the best..." Luca didn't sound like that was a good option either, and I dismissed it mentally.

"Listen, I'm a fair hand in a fight. I'm going on ahead." I was already moving.

I didn't want a fight, but there were very few options. I didn't see the river as an option because it was too swift and I'd have a hard time pulling myself out. There weren't any sandy beaches or landings so far, and it would very quickly take me in the wrong direction. I chanced a look at Luca, who was pulling his sling out of a pocket and fitting it with a rock from a belt pouch he had on. I started to run.

The baying of the dogs got louder.

"You're running us right into their trackers," Luca said.

He was starting to pant, though I doubted it was from the run. It was fear. I made sure the shotgun was at the ready and looked for the cut. One thing I knew, if folks with guns were above us, they had all the advantages, and we would be cut down or forced to virtually commit suicide by jumping into the river. If they had vehicles, they could easily match our progress... but one thing I did not know, was if they were looking for us, or what was going on.

"If they get the high ground we're as good as caught or dead," I said to him.

"There's... This isn't how I thought..."

I didn't answer. Already, I could see the cut, the area where the rock had collapsed or washed out as water made its way down to the river. I put on a little more speed, feeling the weight of my pack banging into my kidneys, knowing I was going to be sore.

I turned to run up as a dark shape turned onto the downgrade and started running at me. At first, I thought it was something out of a nightmare. It was canine looking, but much larger than I expected. It looked to be at least the size of a Great Dane, but it had the markings and muzzle of a smoosh nosed boxer. Its pelt was a swirl of brown and black and, for a moment, I had to wonder if these dogs had been bred for their size and coloring to blend into the rocks. That was when three more came hurtling down.

I heard Luca gasp behind me somewhere, and I shot a look back. He'd fallen and was getting up slowly. I slid to a halt and took aim with the shotgun. I knew it was a far shot at a running target, and if I'd had an M4 carbine I would have sent three round bursts into it, but I had a Mossberg. I was familiar with it, but it was a slower feeding gun that held less ammo. I waited until the dog was close to twenty feet away. I could see it had yellow colored eyes, instead of the white I was accustomed to. and the irises were slanted like a cat's. The teeth were longer too, like they were bred to rip and tear flesh… and intimidate people on the other end of the tracking pool.

Yeah, it was kind of scary, and Alice was already calculating my chances of surviving inside the gut of these creatures, when I started firing. Buckshot ripped into the first one. It had put its head down, stutter-stepped to bunch up for a leap, when the pellets threw it sideways. The second one startled and slid to a halt in surprise at the shotgun's boom and I hit it broadside, dropping it. It started howling and biting at its side. It took me the rest of the shotgun's slugs to take down the other two dogs, who closed on me faster than I'd liked. They were running side by side until I hit the one on the left who stumbled into the right side one. They almost went ass over teakettle, and I emptied my gun into them.

BOYD CRAVEN

I was already reloading and walking up the slope when I realized that during the gunfire the men shouting had stopped. I didn't hear any more dogs either. Maybe they didn't expect me to be so well armed. If they were even looking for me. I knew that was a paranoid and delusional thought, but why else would they be out here doing…

Waiting to chop your head off?

"Go on ahead, I think I busted up my foot," Luca said.

He'd rolled to the edge of the cut, his clothing making him hard to see. He'd wedged himself between a boulder and the wall. I knew this would be up to me. What was a guy who used a sling to do against large dogs and what sounded like Humvees? I crested the top and saw three men immediately. One had what looked like a crude pistol made out of a kid's workshop. He was running towards the cut with a worried look on his face as I came out of it.

"Stop right there," I said, leveling the shotgun.

The three men startled at my voice and the one with the pistol started raising it in my direction. The shotgun boomed, and the man went flying, the slug taking him in the sternum. I pumped the action and was already reaching for another shell from the dump pouch when the two men in front of me put their hands up.

"You speak Trader?" one asked with an unplaceable accent.

"I speak English. Who are you and why did you assholes sic your dogs on me?"

"English? Dogs?" One man asked, not as fearful

106

as I would have liked.

I moved the shotgun so it pointed his way. "What are you doing out here? Who are you looking for?"

"Magnus sent us out here to collect the new Augment. It looks like it's you," the one on the right said, with a little bit of fear in his accented voice.

The sounds of motors were loud and getting louder. My shots had been heard. I had a feeling my LRG could punch out an engine block, but the recharge time on it sucked. The good thing was I had a lot of ammo to use.

"I'm nobody to be collected, boys. Who is it that's coming?"

"The Hunters and Technomages. We're not Outsiders ourselves, we're just the Trackers' handlers. There's no need to kill us."

The accent was bugging me. It was like they'd learned to speak English after knowing some kind of language that was throaty with a lot of consonants. Both looked similar in color to Luca. They could be Caucasian, they could be native American, they could be of Hispanic origin, or light skinned African. In the desert, everyone but me was burned to a nut brown color, and they were both wearing what I thought of as watch caps.

The vehicles are twenty seconds away, Alice whispered in my thoughts.

"You two get out of here," I said.

They both exploded in gore as an explosion rocked the side of the cut. I was hit by shrapnel made of rocks and knocked off my feet. I had dropped the shotgun and, as I rolled on my back, I saw a large chunk of rock all the way through my palm. I pulled it out, gritting at the pain, and made a fist, holding it under my left armpit to put pressure on it. I used my right hand to brush off other shards. I had cuts and scrapes on my legs but what had knocked me off my feet was a chunk that had hit me in the shoulder. It was sore, but already the pain was starting to fade. I could hear voices above me and then a whistling sound.

I ducked, having come under mortar fire back in some unremembered firefight and recognized the sound for what it was. I made myself small, and when it hit, I was surprised to see that it hit further out than the first one. Perhaps they thought I was fleeing in that direction?

You'll need to have food or a food pack at some point soon, Alice told me. *Your right hand is functional enough now.*

I pulled it out and opened it. It was a bloody mess, but as I opened it and flexed it, I could see the wound had closed up. I made a fist and opened my hand a few times in disbelief and then crawled to where I'd dropped the shotgun near the lip of the cut. I got it and saw that what I thought of as Hummers weren't too far off. They looked like a dune buggy that was designed by a cracked out Mad Max wannabe. There was a driver, with four men holding onto the sides. Two were over the rear mounted engine in a flattened area that almost resembled a truck bed, save for the long barrel that pointed forward. I could see them trying to turn the barrel somehow in my direction and saw their lips moving. I could make out shouts but not the words.

"Alice, can you give me a red dot in my vision on where the shot is going to be for the LRG?" I asked her mentally.

The men were moving, but it looked like slow motion.

Yes, she said simply.

I pulled the LRG off my shoulder as quick as I could and sighted. I saw the driver throw an arm over his head and then point towards me, shouting something as the four men on the sides jumped. I fired while all of this was happening and the steel penetrator of the LRG fired hitting the driver in the middle, and black smoke erupted as the round hit the engine block behind him. The turret or barrel stopped moving, but the men who'd jumped hadn't seen nor heard the discharge of the LRG.

I set it down and got the shotgun ready, trying to remember what shells I had loaded. Alice told me I had used a slug and then three buckshot followed by slugs. I was glad somebody was paying attention. I was going to ask her to keep the red dot on the overlay, but she had already adjusted. It was almost too easy. The men were wearing old tattered desert camo like I was, though made from a fabric that was far different than what I had on. They had no armor I could see, but were armed with what looked like trident styled spears. Electricity crackled between the points, and there was a bulge near the end of the spear. Great... Not enough to get stabbed, but it'd shock me too. I opened up on them, dropping two immediately and was then hit from behind.

Now when I say hit, what I mean was a giant assed sledgehammer hit me between the shoulder blades and sent me flying. Not like the explosion before had, I went *flying*. Supermaned. Like, right over the tricked out buggy, to fall down go boom, flying. The breath exploded out of me, and I realized that I had the pistol and that was it. I tried to pull it, but I was blowing flecks of blood every time I tried to breathe. I was fighting for consciousness and Alice was screaming in my brain. I couldn't understand her, and when something hit me in the back of the head, it all went silent and dark.

CHAPTER 7

I didn't know if all cyborgs dreamed, but I do. Or at least I hoped it was a dream.

I was back in Nebraska, a lot younger. I was talking to a man who looked familiar and, after a moment, I was startled to realize that it was my father. Names were still eluding me, but I was asking to borrow the car. Dad gave me a grin, asked me what her name was. I told him it was Alice. "It's always been Alice," he said, and tossed me the keys.

I pulled his Mustang out of the garage. Instead of heading towards her house, I went toward the highway. I slowed down when I was out of sight of the house and put the top down. With that done, I got on the expressway and floored it. The 2015 Mustang was a beast stock out of the factory, but Dad had a job with John Deere, and this was his baby, with all the performance upgrades he could do and still keep it street legal. With me an only child, I got away with a lot, but I never really got into trouble. With the wind blowing through my hair I cranked the radio and thought about going to see Alice, but I had something else in mind.

The recruitment office was in Lincoln, and although I always claimed to live there, I was in a suburb. Twenty minutes of traffic and the appreciative looks of passersby made me feel like a million dollars.

Inside, I took the test they gave me. They seemed impressed by the results and asked me to take another. Then they had forms for me to fill out. Surveys. Finally releases. This was it. After I signed these forms, there would be no turning back. I was ready, though. Alice would understand, and wait for me. After I escaped the hopelessness of the corn and farming, I would call for her, and we could make a life together somewhere in the city.

I signed the paperwork and—

———

Water was poured down my throat, and I awoke coughing and sputtering. I shivered as the rest of the bucketful was dumped over my head and body. It was followed by another.

Wake up asshole, Alice hissed.

I opened my eyes and wished I hadn't. We were in what looked like a room with concrete walls. There was an ominous floor drain in the chipped and stained floor, and I was bound to a wooden chair, stripped naked. The air had already been chilly, but the cold water had made it worse.

"I'm awake, Alice. What's going on? Where are we?"

"Your eyes were closed, and I can't operate any of your senses when you're unconscious. Look, you've been beaten badly, and you're running on half power. If you don't eat in the next day or so, you're going to be in bad shape."

"I'm at half... and I have a day to find food? Sounds like I'm still in the game," I told her mentally and looked up at the figure in front of me.

She was wearing what looked like skin tight black scaled leather pants and boots. Her midriff was bare, but she was wearing a tank top that accentuated the swell of her breasts. A vest matching the pants finished off the ensemble. Dark hair, maybe black, maybe brown... and eyes that looked like inkwells and seemed unfathomably deep. She was smirking, the edges of her mouth curving up.

"Like what you see?" I asked her, feeling cold and vulnerable.

"I was just going to ask you the same thing, sweetness," she said, a slight accent marring her English.

Careful, Alice told me in a flash in my head. *They have the technology here and have been trying to access me. I've kept them blocked out. Talk to her while I figure out how to break into their systems.*

I gave her the equivalent of a mental nod and kept my attention focused on the woman.

"Who are you?" I asked her.

"Actually, I was going to ask you much the same

question," she said walking over, and dammit if my traitorous eyesight didn't notice the swaying of her hips as she put the bucket down and took two steps to straddle my knees.

"Alice, do me a solid... reduce blood flow to..."

Working on it.

She leaned in close, and I could see that her eyes weren't all dark at all. In fact, as she draped both arms over my shoulders and leaned in, I could see they were a deep dark violet with gold flecks in the iris. She smelled like hot sands, cinnamon and something else I couldn't put my finger on. Probably one of the most beautiful women I'd ever met... Wait, bad choice of words. Focus and no, don't look at...

"What do you want to know?" I asked her.

"Where is your ARC?"

Cat's out of the bag, Alice shouted, and I all but cringed.

"I don't know what you're talking about," I lied.

"Sure you don't," she said, leaning in so her head was close to mine, her eyes next to me. She whispered into my ear. "I hit you with my exosuit. Normal humans go splat. I crushed your skull with a big stompy boot, and yet here you are."

"So, you admit to wearing big stompy man shoes?" I asked her.

I gasped as the arm that had been over my shoulder twitched, and I felt metal pierce my back between my shoulder blades. I screamed out in pain, and she scooted in closer, her arms hugging me tighter in some insane parody of straddling me while killing me. She laughed, her head thrown back.

AWAKENED CONTROL

"Alice?" I couldn't hold a thought together, whatever it was, knife, icepick, it was making it hard to think.

I'll block the pain receptors.

I calmed after a moment, and she soon quit having fun and pulled it out of my back. This time, I could feel the flesh knitting itself back up. She leaned over to look, and I could feel the leather. If we were any closer now, I'd be buying her breakfast in the morning. Her breath was hot on my neck. The whole time, I'd been tied down with rough rope, and I'd been working my left hand. Both hands were tied to the arms of the chair, my legs to the legs of the chair and my back to the back of the chair. There had been some slack in the restraint, and it wasn't much, but it was getting looser. Not enough time to stop another stabbing, so, I did the only other thing I could think of. I bit her.

I was going for her throat, but she was leaned over too far. Instead, I got a chunk of her ear and clamped down, twisting my head savagely. She shrieked and I felt something slice across my back, over my shoulder and partially down my chest as she flung herself backward. I spit out my gory prize and felt my flesh knitting itself back together. She kicked, screamed and clamped a hand over her ear. The far side of the room opened, and two men dressed in the rough wool came in and said something to her in an incomprehensible language.

She answered back in same, shouting her nonsense, and got to her feet and followed them out, pausing at the doorway with tears in her eyes.

"I'll be back in a little bit. Want to know what the

bitch is about being able to heal yourself quickly?"

"What's that?" I asked, hating the taste of her blood in my mouth and on my lips.

"I can torture you forever, as long as I keep you fed."

"Well, if you want to come back, I can arrange it so you can have a matching set of earrings."

The threat was mostly empty but something in her gaze hardened, and she clenched her jaw before slamming the door. I asked Alice for an update as I looked around the room again.

The stab to the back and the subsequent cuts did an additional seven percent to draining your bodies resources. You need food soon. I know it's gross as shit, but you should have eaten that ear.

"Ugggg, shut up."

On the floor, dropped and forgotten, was a black stiletto. It still had my blood on the hilt and blade. It sat about six feet away, too far away to be of any use to me. What my bite had done, though, was give me more lubrication for my left wrist. When I'd bitten her, she'd been on my left side, and had cut me as she'd tried to pull herself away. Either her blood or mine had splattered the rough ropes, and that and my sweat from the pain or fear had made my skin slick. I twisted and pulled, ignoring the pain, and Alice finally understood what I was trying to do. She blocked the pain receptors, and minutes later I ripped my arm free, raw and chafed. I didn't slow down to watch it heal, I started working on the ropes across my chest so I would have more movement.

It was awkward, but soon, that too fell away.

AWAKENED CONTROL

———

"What the hell is wrong with you? There's nowhere to go!" The woman accented the end with a kick to my head, half of her left ear bandaged from my earlier work.

I was on my side, the chair still strapped to part of me. I heard motors fire up somewhere outside the room or building with a roar. Her friends?

"You going to answer me or are we going to…?"

She kicked at me again, and my left hand shot out. I got the knife around the back of her ankle and pulled, intending to sever her Achilles tendon. The knife slid off, but my motion of pulling made her stumble forward towards me.

See, I hadn't had time to get all the way undone and, when I'd heard her footsteps I'd used my one free leg and arm to tip myself over, concealing her forgotten knife. The rest, as they say, was happing very fast. She kicked out as she fell over me, her knee connecting with my head. I stabbed at her leg, knowing if I hit the femoral artery she would be done and over with. The knife stopped like hitting stone. Again, though, it was like I'd stabbed her with a blunt object and she howled as she went over me entirely.

In two quick swipes, I'd sawed through my right wrist's rope, nicking myself in the process, and was working on my right ankle when she regained her feet, yelling like a banshee and diving at my head. The knife parted the rope like butter, a testament to how sharp it was. The chair fell free as she tackled me. For a moment, she knocked the air out of me, but I wrapped my legs around her middle and let the momentum roll me. I heard something snap and she cried out in pain. I got to my feet and saw her on the ground, holding her wrist that was flopping at a bad angle.

Say it, you know you want to, Alice said.

"He kicks…" I said in a falsetto voice, and kicked her in the stomach with a bare foot, "He scores! The crowd goes wild!"

That's got to hurt, Alice observed.

I hadn't decided on killing her as a for sure thing. I had just a moment to put together an ad hock plan. I righted the chair and pulled the woman up by her good wrist and shoved her into it. It was the pain that had tears ready to roll down her cheeks. Pain and maybe anger or humiliation. There was no fear there. She looked at me savagely. Beaten. The sound of the motors roared and then started moving off. I looked at her, chest heaving, and fought down the urge to bury the stiletto in her sternum and avoid the mess. Instead…

"Is that some sort of joke?" She asked as a single tear finally fell.

She was the one who looked vulnerable now, holding her wrist to her body tightly. Somewhere in the struggle, her ear had gotten smacked because the bandage was turning a bright red as fresh blood bled from my toothmarks.

"No jokes," I said, watching and noticing that she hadn't healed herself. So she wasn't an Outsider Augment. "Looks like your friends left you. They wouldn't have let you scream like a little baby so long if they knew I'd gotten loose, would they?"

I knew I was taunting, but I was trying to break her smugness. Instead, I leaned down slowly, my right hand holding the knife up where she could see it, and grabbed the longer length of rope that had been tied around my chest. It had been looped twice around me and was more than long enough for what I had in mind. I made a hangman's noose out of it; the knife was a bit unwieldy for knot tying, but I didn't want to put it down and chance her going for it. I'd bested her once, but I had no idea of her capabilities. Only when the noose was done, and I was roughly shoving it over her head, did she start to fight. I sidestepped her kick and went behind the chair, pulling the rope through the back of the wooden slat that was the top of the chair.

She jerked and then let out a surprised croak as the rope bit in, cutting off her airflow. She wheezed and then relaxed. I moved and took the longer lengths of the rope and ripped her uninjured arm away from holding her broken wrist and tied it down. I cut off the excess and then tied her ankles together. Not quite as tight as I'd like to have done, but I'd had to do this in a hurry.

"You know, they won't even kill you," she said, gasping from the pain and the way her air was cut off if she moved too much. "They will dissect you to steal the tech inside of you. You'll survive it, but you'll live on in one of us."

"One of who?" I asked, walking towards the door.

It was an old steel door. Probably as old as I was. It was well preserved, but it was pockmarked with rust and had dents in the surface from abuse. I cracked it open and saw another room similar to this with some crude table. On it, was my clothes and what I hoped under those, were my guns.

"Outsiders. They use CEPMs like you to leapfrog their technological advances. We haven't found them with a spiritual brain often," she said.

I walked towards the table. The room was bare, but there was another steel door inset off to the side. I peeked and saw that it led outside. Tire prints in the dirt showed we were alone - for now. Or I couldn't see them. I found my Beretta and turned and started walking back to her, tossing the knife behind me.

"How did you know I had been activated?" I asked her.

"This isn't an interrogation," she snarled.

"What do you think about that leather, Alice?" I asked aloud.

Sounds like what Luca was talking about.

"Who are you talking to?" she asked, her eyes going wide.

"Oh nobody," I replied, smiling evilly, "but you're wrong. This is an interrogation. Say, is that leather made from Stalker leather?"

"Yeah, why?"

I showed her the pistol.

———

"If they don't kill you, I will," Moss told me.

"See, this thing with you and me? It ain't got no future."

AWAKENED CONTROL

I didn't have to torture her at all. I'd fired the gun into the cement wall to see if it was loaded and she'd jumped. I think she'd got to where I had been about to go to when I'd asked about the leather. I had noticed that it had been stab and slice proof and, according to the stories Luca had told me earlier, I knew it was likely bulletproof as well. I think Moss, that was the beauty's name, knew that as well, but it'd still hurt like hell. Probably bruise or even break ribs or bones in her arm or legs or feet. See, I wasn't as ruthless as she was, but I wasn't going to let her in on that secret.

"*You* don't have a future," she snarled back.

She was crying in rage and shame; her nose had been running, and I'd left her damaged arm untied so I wouldn't hurt her wrist more. She should have figured it out at that point, but she didn't. I let her think I was every bit of the monster she was. Her team had been sent in to snatch me. The current leader of the Outsiders was Magnus, and his computers and equipment had seen a spike of energy. Apparently, there were still a few functioning satellites and me firing back up the reactor had been visible in some spectrum I was unaware of, or there was newer technology that hadn't been invented yet it in my old world.

I'd gotten dressed again and questioned her. She reluctantly gave me her name and, with some body language and attitude, I'd conveyed that any lies would be dealt with harshly. Oh, and I'd had the gun pointed at her stomach. She'd told me what she knew, which wasn't much. She was the leader of Hunter Scout Team Bravo. It was a three wag (wags were what they called vehicles now) team, and each of the tricked-out dune buggy pickup trucks had either a mortar or a primitive cannon mounted on them. The scouts themselves were armed with the electrified tridents… Good for fighting off critters as well as capturing slaves and keeping out of arm's reach.

Guns and gunpowder were a rare commodity, and my shotgun and the shells had been taken. My Beretta and LRG had been left behind, because Moss had indicated she was keeping them, spoils of war. Her plan had been to interrogate me until I gave up the ARC's location and passcodes, or until I finally collapsed as the nanites worked furiously to repair the continuous damage. She'd done this to one other Precursor Augment (what they called CEPMs like me with implanted AIs) who'd popped up in Idaho three years back. It had garnered her a lot of wealth and fame when she'd found an ARC, and the fact that it was nonfunctioning did little to hurt things.

It too had suffered from a power failure of unknown causes. Magnus had had the Augment stripped of his implants, and he'd bled out. She told me this with a grin on her face, and I had to wonder if she was mad or not. Her savage evil was tempered by her heart-stopping good looks and unusual accent. That was all fine and dandy, but things did not go as planned and she was going to phone her team after she had broken me. Apparently, me biting half her ear off had embarrassed her in front of her men, and she'd sent them away after she got her first aid.

All I wanted to do was to sit up and point at her like the bully in the Simpsons and go 'Ha Ha!' but I resisted the urge. Still, if I left her alive, I'd have an

AWAKENED CONTROL

insanely evil woman to contend with.

As if you don't already, Alice said, nailing the real Alice's snark.

"But she's helpless, I just can't see killing her," I answered aloud.

"You're talking to it, aren't you?" Moss asked me, her tears stilling.

I went into the other room where my gear had been stored and found some clean rags near her crude first aid kit. I grabbed a handful and walked back to Moss. I tried to wipe her face, but she turned her head. I holstered the Beretta and held her head in one hand and wiped the snot off her face, leaving her the rest of her dignity. I dropped the soiled rag to the ground.

"You're talking to your computer? Your spiritual brain?" she asked.

"Yes, sometimes I forget and say things out loud."

I was looking at her wrist. There wasn't much I could do about it, but I could do something. I'd have to untie her unless...

"Hold still," I said and stomped my foot.

She jerked in shock, and the noose tightened, cutting off her airflow. It'd been the fourth time she'd done it, but I'd warned her. My boot stomped one of the front supports of the chair, and the dowel snapped, as I thought it would. I reached down and pulled it out, wiggling both sides out. I stepped out of reach of her legs as she quit gagging so I wouldn't get kicked, and got the stiletto out. I shaved off the sharp points to roughly rounded wooden ends under Moss's baleful glare.

"What are you doing?" she asked, another tear falling down her now mostly dry face.

"Should I tell her?" I asked Alice aloud, for Moss's benefit.

I paused and looked at the space right next to Moss. She looked nervously over her shoulder and back at me. I pretended to listen.

"No? Why not?"

"You're… This… you're crazy," Moss stuttered.

"I think so too," I said to the empty air.

I didn't say anything.

"Shut up, I'm messing with her," I said mentally.

"Ok," I said aloud, "I guess it's the right thing to do."

I switched the stiletto into my right hand her eyes flew open in fear.

"I'm going to immobilize your wrist. It's broken badly. I'm not a doctor, but I had some training. I'm going to try to get it as straight as I can and then tie it off. If it heals bad, you might lose the use of the hand. If I do nothing, you'll probably die. So as much as this is going to hurt, don't kick me, don't slap me, don't bite me. See, Alice, my ghost in the shell," I said tapping the blade to my temple, "Thinks I should slit your throat and leave you here."

I saw the color drain out of her face.

"But we've decided on a different course… so yes, I am going to splint you up."

"I won't…"

I was already moving, and I sheathed the knife in my reclaimed vest.

"I'm not going to lie, this is going to hurt," I said

and took her elbow in one hand and her hand in another after untying the noose.

She screamed, but I straightened it out as best as I could. I didn't delight in hurting her, but I had nothing I could have given her to knock her out. I'd had a broken bone once, and I think I'd screamed louder than Moss; it hurt. Still, I did the best I could, immobilizing her wrist. Her body was soaked with sweat, and I sat on her legs, straddling her the way she had done to me.

"How far away are we from Lakeville?" I asked.

"We're almost there, the base of the mountain," she said, noticing I had the stiletto back out.

I leaned in close and though her eyes were wild with fear and shock now, she kept my gaze as our eyes locked. I cut the rope holding her wrist to the chair, just as she lunged forward with her head, her teeth flashing. I'd anticipated that and tucked my chin to my chest, letting her headbutt the top of my head. I heard her teeth click together hard and I stood back as she swiped at me with her good hand. She'd decided to fight to the end. I had to admire her for that. I sheathed the knife once again and watched as she rubbed her wrist and checked out the splint.

"Can't blame a girl for trying," she said lamely.

"Can't blame a guy for what he's going to do next."

"What…?" she stuttered out.

"Free your ankles and stand up," I told her.

I kept an eye on Moss, but I walked out to the table and took the LRG and slung it over my back after taking my now very nearly empty backpack in my left hand, and I walked back in the room. I hadn't tied her in tight, the noose and threat of the bad wrist was enough to have held her for a while, but she'd gotten to her feet shakily.

"Now what?" She asked me, holding her splinted arm.

"Vest, pants and boots," I said, pointing to her, the pistol now out and aiming at her.

She looked at me, her head tilting.

Once you've seen one pair of boobs, you want to see them all? Alice asked.

"Shut up," I told her mentally.

"You can't be serious. I've not… I mean you can't…."

"I'm quite serious." I wasn't, but she expected me to be as sick and sadistic as her, so I'd let her think what she wanted.

"There's no place I won't hunt you down. You should just kill me. I won't bear your children, you…"

I threw my head back and laughed and laughed. Her eyes narrowed, and I wiped tears out of my own eyes. I knew if I kept it up, injured or not, she would attack. I'd just hurt her in a way that a broken wrist wouldn't.

"No, I don't even want you naked. I'm taking the vest, pants, and boots with me. It'll slow you down and give me a chance to get away. Come on, I'm not the bad guy here. You are."

Ten minutes later I tried not to look as I folded up her gear. The leather was supple and a lot lighter than I had expected. It was as lightweight as the vest I wore myself. On Moss… No, I didn't stare at her legs… ones that seemed to run all the way to her chin… was just black underwear… I didn't stare at the tank top and the whole ensemble, that screamed vulnerable. That wasn't something I could deal with. Memories swirled, trying to fight their way to the surface but I couldn't deal with them right now.

"You really are not… You're weak," she said, deciding for herself that I wasn't going to kill her and not respecting my reasoning.

"No," I said picking up a longer length of rope I'd stashed as I slung the now full backpack, "I'm just not a crazy psycho bitch. You torture and kill people for fun. When I kill people, it's because they are usually trying to kill me."

"I am NOT CRAZY!" she screamed, her voice crescendoing.

I slammed the door to the inner room as she started pounding at it. I'd taken the noose and tightened it around the door handle. Since the door swung in towards her, she started pulling on it. I could barely reach the table with the edge of my foot, and I nudged it. It was heavy, some sort of metal plastic contraption that was decades or centuries out of date. I pulled it close enough to hold onto the rope and push it in front of me and against the door and wall. I fought against Moss's repeated efforts to pull it open and got the rope under the work surface to tie it off on a leg.

It wouldn't hold her for long, but her inarticulate shrieks of rage subsided into sobs.

"Please don't take those," she begged.

A woman who was crying was one thing. Sobs kill me. It hurt something inside. And this wasn't crying from pain, this was true sorrow, loss. It made me stop.

"What, your stalker gear?" I asked through the crack of the door.

"It took me ten years of working in the Officer's Quarters to earn enough to get that. It's how I was able to get my first squad…" She sobbed and cried.

"Dammit," I muttered to myself and took off my backpack. I dug through it, and I pulled out the pants. I would leave her that dignity at least.

"I'm leaving the pants for now. When you work a way out of there, put those on. I'll stash your boots an hour or two up the walk to Lakeville. After that, don't ever come after me again, or I'll do worse than humiliate you. You hear me?"

"Yes." The word was quiet.

"It's going to take you a few hours to a day for you to break out of there. I'll be long gone. In one day, I'll radio somebody using your equipment I'm taking."

If I'm taking it, I added mentally.

"The Outsiders will kill you if you take the Exosuit, I only borrowed it."

"Yeah, well… sucks. See ya!" I said in the most cheerful voice I could manage.

I dropped the pants on the floor on my way out and shouldered all my gear. I could hear her jerking on the door again immediately, and I stepped outside. The building I had been in was a squat concrete building. Probably a communications relay center a long time ago. The ceiling had been patched and repaired with what looked like old sheets of plywood, painted gray. Standing sentinel next to the building was her exosuit.

"Holy flipping *Fallout 4*, Batman!" I yelled.

AWAKENED CONTROL

The exosuit looked like power armor I had played in various video games. This pair wasn't bulky, though. It looked sleek and elegant. It was painted in hues of red and brown. Moss had snuck up behind Luca and me and jumped me when she'd dropped behind me, and KO'd me. Then she tried to Hulk smash my skull and realized I was the 'Droid' she was looking for. It was a Star Wars reference… ok?

Quit monologuing, Alice said.

"Dammit."

I walked up and saw near the center of the chest what looked like a small depression. I put my thumb on it and pressed. It clicked, and the suit opened up like a butterfly, or like how Tony Stark would transform himself into Iron Man.

Is that why you have me call you Tony?

"First name I came up with. I can't remember my own. Just bits and pieces of my past that make no sense."

What makes no sense, Alice chided, *is how you treated that woman.*

"Too rough?"

What would have happened if she was a Muslim woman or boy in Afghanistan running at you with a suicide vest on? In your memories, you didn't hesitate then.

I closed my eyes and took a deep breath. "And I suffered the nightmares for years afterward, Alice. It's not that easy. At the end of the day, I have to live with the consequences of my own actions."

I know my personality is a mental construct of the woman you knew as Alice, but I still don't understand feelings. I don't feel them. So, to me, what you just did by leaving her pants and soon to be her boots too, has no basis in logic.

"That's why I'm in charge, and you're the Ghost in the Shell," I said, tapping my forehead.

That's one I don't remember you watching, Alice answered, what felt like a minute later. In truth, the entire conversation probably happened in less than a fraction of a second. *If we're not going to take this, let me at least scan the tech…. Oh, grab that!*

Inside near where the head would reside on a filleted open suit, was a box that was roughly the size of a wallet, a red light glowing from it. I reached out tentatively and grabbed it. I pulled slightly and was surprised when it came loose with a clicking sound. It had been clipped inside the suit. I turned it over and saw a wire running out with what looked like a stereo jack end on.

That, my friend, is a personal field generator, if I'm not mistaken. Put it on your left belt and plug it into the vest.

I did as she asked and the air shimmered with a rainbow of colors around me, and then went clear as it seemed to settle in on my body.

Her suit had it turned off while she wasn't in it. There's a semi-sentient computer in the Exoskeleton. The radio is hooked up to the computer here, so that has to stay. I wish it had proper Wi-Fi instead of this radio signal crap it's working on now. No wonder they couldn't hack me in your sleep. It's old tech and almost useless. There's also a GPS built into the computer. No way to disable it without killing the suit… The com-

puter just isn't worth it.

"It's enough to run this baby," I said, marveling at the armor and hitting the button to close it back up.

Yeah, but I'm better. By an order of magnitude. I have enough computing power to run a thousand suits like this.

"Easy, Alice, easy. Show me the computer on it." I stepped back, so the exosuit was between me and a lot of nothing.

Alice highlighted an area of the armor. I pulled up the LRG and fired. The gun made very little sound, but the bolt hitting the suit rang out like a gong. It was heavily dented. Without asking, I watched the countdown on the LRG in my heads up display overlay.

"Is the computer still functioning?" I asked.

One more should do it.

When the timer went back to zero I fired again, this time punching a hole through it from the front to back of the suit, knocking it over.

"That's going to leave a mark," I said, and put in a fresh mag and started walking.

I really wanted the suit, but I couldn't go strolling into hostile territory wearing it. Especially now that I had decided to leave Moss alive. I'd rather sneak in and see if I could find a computer I could let Alice interface with. I had a rough idea of a plan, but there was something else I needed to do first.

CHAPTER 8

The dam was ahead of me and, when I found a grouping of boulders halfway up the slope, I paused and pulled out the boots as promised. I made it somewhat obvious that I'd stashed them there and then retraced my footsteps until I was near the pillbox building again. I could hear Moss inside still struggling with the door. I wanted to ask her about Luca, but I didn't. If he got away, I didn't want put him in danger. His clothing had blended in well with the natural surroundings while everyone had been focused on me, in my desert cams and vest.

Plus, now I had a kickass shield generator. In the game, *Borderlands*, you could get ones that had different abilities. Some were stronger than others, some helped you heal faster.

This is not a video game, Alice reminded me.

AWAKENED CONTROL

"Pretty much. I figure they will be looking for me, but I'm still heading to Lakeville. Figured you pulled a rabbit and hid or bolted, but I wanted to be sure."

"I appreciate that," Luca said, getting to his feet. "Do we go now?"

"I can't see worth a damn. Let's wait till morning."

"Good, I know this cave not too far…"

"Let's just sleep here. Unless there's a stalker around, I'm not going to worry about it."

"No, no reports of one…" he said, yawning.

"It's been what, a day since they jumped me?"

"Yes. I would have moved sooner but saw little sense in case they came back, and then I'd be stuck out in the open not able to run."

"Well, it isn't too hot nor too cold here."

He grunted and took his spot. In the darkest part of the night, I leaned into the wall and sat down myself. I didn't intend to fall asleep, but I needed it. I held the LRG close.

———

It took us two days to get back to where I had been held by Moss and we took it easy because of the swollen foot. The Exosuit was gone, and all that was left of the entire building was rubble and two intact walls. It looked as if somebody had been upset about something. Not that I'd know anything about it. See, though, this time we went slower. I spent half a day stripping bark off a bushy plant we found, and then pulling the bark strands apart to make cordage. It was only good to hold up to six or eight pounds, but I was able to make enough of a cast net. Luca helped out when he saw what I was doing, and found sandstone to work on into shapes we could tie the net to easily. It was a Rube Goldberg affair, but it worked.

We would walk the shoreline, and I would spin it with my right-hand overhead and hold onto the end of the cordage with my left. The small five-foot net could only travel about ten feet away from me, so I caught a lot of smaller fish in the three to four-inch size. That was until Luca pointed out a dark shape darting in the water. I'd never cast at something moving before, but Alice ran calculations and showed me where to throw based on how fast the fish was moving. I followed her directions as best as I could, and the net worked. It strained my arms, but I pulled in a catfish of the likes of which I'd never seen before.

"Corpse fish," Luca said.

"What's that mean?" I asked.

"They eat corpses from town. Good eating, the fish I mean. You never find them down here."

The fish was brown, with two sharp fins coming out the side and a row of them on the top. It more or less looked like the catfish I remembered fishing for as a kid, except the mouth was full of serrations around the lips that could easily pass off as teeth. I took out the stiletto and poked it in the head, killing it.

Then we spent some time trying to light a fire. Luca didn't have the solar oven, I didn't have matches. I did not want to eat the fish raw, so we scavenged and found enough of the old brush and some dry driftwood left on the bank from flash floods to make a small fire. I used Moss's knife to whittle some sticks into crude skewers. I'd take a fillet and poke the stick in one end, go up a few inches then out the other side up and down, so I had a fish kabob. I wasn't surprised that Luca already had this trick mastered and we cooked up and ate all of the greasy fish before starting our walk again.

"They don't really eat corpses, do they?" I asked, a little revolted.

"Not the ones this side of the dam. On the other side of the dam on the big lake? There's a ton. Don't get caught eating them, though; the Order will declare you unclean, and you can be put to death for it."

I chuckled and stopped when I saw he was being serious.

"Some kind of future to wake up to. Can't eat your fish and chips without judgmental assholes wanting to off you."

"Fish and Chips?" Luca asked.

"Never mind," I told him. "You mean the order is an actual religious organization now?"

"Yeah, based on the strictures. The religious leaders are God's messengers on this planet. To disobey them is death. Most people believe one way or another," he said and I just grunted in reply.

We found the spot where I had stashed the boots, and I found a bunch of the clean rags that had been used as bandages. Well, they weren't clean any more. They smelled of sweat and feet and had blood stains in them. I wondered slightly and then decided that she must have wrapped her feet in them, knowing the hot rocks were going to be unforgiving. I'd meant for it to slow her down and make her uncomfortable. If I had to guess, I'd say it worked.

"Will you still love me tomorrow, Moss?" I said dropping the rag back onto the rocky, sandy ground.

"Moss? You mean, the hunter Moss?" Luca said, grabbing me by the shoulder and spinning me to face him. "Yeah, she runs one of the scout teams. Oh man… I don't know whether I should ask you to slow down so you can retell me this story, or run away from you. That woman is as evil as she is beautiful if the stories about her are true."

Over the trip, I'd told Luca about my ordeal, but I did forget to mention the savage woman's name. Ooops.

"Well shit man, you're the bard. You tell me what you know about her if you're going to light off on your own?" I said, somewhat frustrated at how unnerved Luca seemed to be.

He legit looked like he wanted to rabbit and take off.

"Well, stories say she worked the officers' quarters for years to save up for her Armor. That's no easy feat, considering how expensive the stalker leather is, let alone paying for somebody to cut and craft it. It's a wonder she didn't bear dozens and dozens of children…"

"Wait, you mean she…? I thought she meant worked, worked… not…"

"Well, yeah. Normally all women of age are available to the officers, unless you're part of the faction. A young woman like her who was part of the faction wasn't on the… rotation. She made herself available for a price. There's a story about one man who forgot, or didn't care, that she wasn't a normal concubine but more of a… freelancer… and started slapping her around, or something sick like that. She killed him."

I thought of the vest in my backpack and mentally winced. Alice, thankfully, was silent. How much humiliation and suffering had that vest cost her? No wonder she went insane when she thought I wanted to do something more than slow her down. A superhero I am not and my pack felt heavier.

Luca went on. "She bought her own armor. It kind of stunned everyone from what I heard, and then she demanded to be allowed to try out for her own crew. She killed the tester in hand to hand. The truly scary thing is, she's the one they send out on the really long missions. The ones where she's searching out ARCs for old tech. She's found a few, if the stories are accurate and, next to Magnus, she's one of the wealthiest people in this part of the country."

"So, me taking part of her armor and shooting a big hole in her Exosuit is going to be met with laughs and warm hugs?"

A Frozen *reference? Really?* Alice interjected in my head. I ignored her.

"Yeah, pretty much everyone there would kill you on sight if they knew it was you. By the Order, you should have killed her and done the world a favor. When you said you escaped captivity, I didn't know it was from her. I hate everything that woman stands for."

"You still want to walk with me all the way into Lakeville?" I asked him.

BOYD CRAVEN

I wasn't scared of what they were going to do to me, I was scared of what they wanted to do in general, but Luca was already wanted for skipping out on his militia service. He could join the Order of Purists sure, but he had to get past the Outsiders first.

"Yeah, most of the way and then…" His words trailed off, and he looked at me, probably hoping that I wouldn't take offense to his words.

"I don't mind. Tell me something, though, why do you call English 'Trader' now? What language was it you were speaking two days ago, in the dark?"

"We call it—" and then he rattled off a name. To me, it sounded like he said something something blah blah Navajo. "And as far as Trader goes, it's what people on all the caravans who pass through speak. Once, they say, everyone spoke Trader, but not us."

Yes, that was my take on it too, Alice told me. *Navajo.*

"Navajo?" I asked him.

Luca nodded.

"Alice, I have a question. If I can have Luca give us a basic primer on the language, can you remember it and help me with translations?" I asked her.

I don't see why not, she said, *It's definitely well within my capabilities, but not something I was specifically designed for.*

"Good, thanks. We're both going to have to do things we weren't specifically designed for. Once we get a handle on things, get the reactor in our ARC back online and save all of the humanity from the evil alien overlords—"

Now you're just being stupid, she said, but her tone

142

was playful.

"Luca, I figure if we keep walking we'll be there by nightfall."

"That's what I was thinking."

"So, can you give me an hour or two of a primer of Navajo?"

We were still walking, but his eyes squinted in suspicion and then nodded.

———

I could smell the cook fires. My stomach rumbled horribly when the smells of baking bread and roasting meat hit my nose.

"The food, is it safe to eat?" I asked Luca.

"Yes, as long as it's cooked. It is never a good idea to eat raw meats, though."

Duh. That went without saying.

"Will I be able to trade for some food?" I asked Luca, "I know you explained the monetary system a bit before…"

"It is scary, how fast you picked that up. It took me two years of practice to learn trader, and you're speaking as if you're a local now," he said, ignoring my question.

I tapped the scar on my temple and repeated my question.

"Yes, you should be able to. Don't trade anything of high value, though, otherwise you'll make yourself a target. You must blend in."

That was the plan, but I refused to disarm, so right there was one of the big problems. Still, I had a couple of tricks up my sleeve, and one of them was wrapping my head as I'd done before. I needed something for the LRG, and there was little I could do about clothing until we got closer to town. We were, I figured, a mile out now and Luca and I had about ten minutes left before I'd let him make his way on alone.

"Ok, sounds good. You glad to be home?" I asked him.

He made a gesture with his hand that I figured meant more or less. I stopped walking and pointed. I could see the glow of an electric spotlight turn on, on the edge of a large wall. And wow, what a wall. The wall itself looked to be about thirty or forty feet tall, with walkways across the top. It was made up of panels of sheet metal, some of it old, some of it new. Around the base of the wall, hard to see in the darkness, were bones.

"We didn't get in before they set the watch out. I know people here, or did as of a couple of years ago. You might want to wait until the morning to try to get in. The guards at the gate have slings, and I heard one of them sometimes uses a lead thrower on the really serious stuff. Guns."

"What are those bones?" I asked.

"Wild animals, raiders and those who would attack us. Political prisoners…"

"Great."

I hadn't been able to make out specifics, but I could see piles of bones, picked clean and left to bleach out in the somewhat dry air. One thing I did notice up at the top of the dam, was that the air was cooler and I wasn't sweating as badly. There were also patches of green with trees on the distant shoreline. Actual trees. It was like I was leaving the rocky mountainous desert to a lusher tropical landscape and it happened so gradually I'd missed the transition.

"Well Luca," I said, holding out my hand, "I hope you get to the Order and get things worked out. I'm going to let you go on alone and then head in after you."

"But the guards…"

"Don't worry ,my friend. I'm not."

He looked at my hand in puzzlement. I took his and shook it. He gave me a strange look again.

"This is how you say goodbye?" He asked as I let go of his.

"And sometimes hello."

"Thank you, and goodbye, Tony."

I watched him go. I waited a time, just outside the reach of the searchlight that was sweeping the fields of fire, when I saw it light up a figure who came to a stop. I couldn't make out the words because the wind picked up, but I could hear the shouted responses as if it was Charlie Brown's teacher talking… whaa wha wha blah ha. The figure started moving again, and the spotlight followed him and then it seemed like he melded into the wall. Then the light started sweeping the area once more.

"Tell me more about the factions from the journals, Alice. They knew the name for the Vorryns, so somebody had to have already gone outside the ARC, probably several times."

Well… that was my assumption, too. There're some ramblings in one particular log file, but according to the medical records, the man was insane. It may be an accurate depiction, or it could be a transcribed account of a madman.

"Well, what is it then?" I asked.

It tells the tale of a band of the descendants who left the ARC on a scouting mission. They were on a hunt for a renewable food source and any information they could. According to Isben, the madman, they found a small tribe of locals two days walk from the ARC. The language barrier prevented them from direct communication. They were attacked by creatures, and one of the tribal leaders screamed a word over and over.

"Vorryn."

Exactly. They had run across a nest, or there was a swarm of them. Two of the ARC descendants died from the conflict immediately. Another perished from his wounds. Isben was one of three left alive, slightly wounded, but alive. Frustrated at the lack of a common language, they searched the area for food, but water supplies were running short, and they had to come back.

"But they could have used the river for water?"

Apparently, it was during a drought, and there was very little water.

"So... that all sounds plausible, why do you think this is the story of a madman? Or rather, why do they think he's cray cray?"

On his way back to the ARC, he developed a fever. It wasn't brought on by thirst, but perhaps by the wounds he sustained in the fight. His later log files spoke of a man made of sunlight. Ten feet tall, as strong as a mountain, and twice as fast as the speed of sound.

AWAKENED CONTROL

"That makes no sense Alice," I looked around me.

Being near a light reminded me of how alone I had been out there in the dark and, even though the landscape around me looked insanely like a post-apocalyptic video game... it was the small comforts I hadn't realized I was missing already. I was literally a man out of time. If I could remember who I was, where I'd come from and all of the loved ones who were are long gone, I might have been depressed.

He went on to rant and rave about this for two years. The man made of light. Nobody really detailed how the two factions split up, though some of them I can make an educated guess, based on their log files.

"What do you mean? You sort of told me before that the Outsiders wanted to leave the ARC – Maybe they knew what was happening... and something is wonky with the timelines here..."

You said wonky, Alice said, and I could picture the grin from real Alice, the woman my AI took the name of.

"Yeah, I mean, I didn't see any corpses of the Vor-ryn in the ARC, so somebody cleaned it up. But why would they leave all the dead bodies in the server room? I didn't see brass inside there like I did on the floor with the armory. There was shell casing all over the place and again, no dead Vorryn. If they didn't kill the bugs, what killed everyone on their way out? The Outsiders?"

That would be my best guess... but you're making one mistake in your thinking. You are assuming what-ever happened started in the ARC and worked its way to the exit.

"Yes?" I said, not knowing where she was taking this.

What if it was something that came in and was working its way down?

"Now there's a cheery thought," I said. "You mean there could have been something inside the ARC with us when we were in there?"

It was one possibility, but one I doubted. When I had the systems back online, I did a security sweep with all available systems, and you were the only life form that was detected.

I mulled on that and wondered if there had been enough time for me to start towards the gate. I looked at the darkness behind me. Alice adjusted my vision, and I could barely make out the landscape. The electric spotlight gave me enough ambient light to see a little better, but it was blinding to look directly at the spotlight. I started moving.

"Let's hope we were alone," I told her... "Man of light... That's..."

Maybe the Order of Purists can shed some light on this.

"We're going to have to visit the Outsiders too, somehow. If they are the only ones who have the tech... If they have electric light, build power armor, tricked-out dune buggies... maybe they have servos for our ARC. I mean, they are sitting on a big hydro-electric generating dam, right?"

A lot can change over time, but they may be our best bet, as long as you can keep yourself away from the sadistic psycho hottie, Moss.

"You think she's hot too?" I asked her aloud and

almost kicked myself.

No, you do. I had to restrict blood flow to your reproductive organ when she got close to you. I don't understand emotions myself, but something about her—

The harsh spotlight lit me up and I raised my hands in the air. The Beretta was holstered in my vest, and the LRG was over my back, only the boxy barrel sticking up over my shoulder. The headscarf covered all but my eyes.

"Who are you?" The voice shouted in Navajo.

"A Traveler, looking for someplace to sleep for the night," I called back.

"Come ten steps closer, and wait for an escort," the voice shouted back.

There was a hint of enthusiasm in his voice. I don't know why that bothered me, but wait I did. The other thing I had holstered, or rather… sheathed… was the stiletto. I'd strapped it to the inside of my left forearm with a couple of the clean rags I'd taken from that pillbox in case I couldn't find Charmin in the future's version of the *Deathlands*. I waited, and soon I heard the screech of metal and footsteps. No matter how much adjusting was done to my sight, the spotlight right on me was blinding. Then three figures stepped into the light with me.

Two were armed with tridents, and the third was armed with my shotgun. I wanted to cuss, maim, and kill. Hulk smash. I saw a familiar scratch on the stock and knew that it was the same one Moss and her men had taken from me.

"Disarm, and you can enter once you prove you have credits or trade goods."

BOYD CRAVEN

The man with the shotgun was looking at my Beretta and didn't meet my gaze. I ignored him for a moment and looked at the speaker. He was armed with a Trident himself, but he was young and looked fit.

"There's no way I'm disarming," I told them, "that's the first step in controlling the masses. Restrict their information, disarm them - and what do you have left?"

I got blank stares.

"Fascism," I said in Trader, I mean English. There hadn't been a word for it in their tongue.

"You speak English?" The young man who had been talking to me asked in English.

"Yes," I said switching. "Like I said, I'm a traveler. Disarming me is not going to happen. I have goods to trade."

"It would help," the man told me, "If you could show us something to trade with."

I slowly pulled out the Beretta by my fingertips and watched as they all tensed. I dropped the magazine and thumbed out one shell before returning the mag and holstering it again. I held up the brass casing. The man with the shotgun licked his lips, and the barrel rose slowly.

"Is this enough to buy my entry?" I asked him in English.

He nodded, and I gave him the shell. I turned and pointed towards the man with the shotgun, "How'd he end up with that?"

"Lakeville law of the Outsiders. You keep what you can. He took it from some assholes in a card game—"

A high-pitched squeal pierced the air, and I spun. Whoever was manning the spotlight heard it too and dozens of more squeals peppered the air. The spotlight moved in sweeping arcs as a wave of Vorryn started moving in on us.

Tony, the—

I saw it myself and moved as the shotgun roared a foot away from my ear. The man had meant to kill me all along and the moment's distraction had let him think I hadn't noticed how he was eyeballing my gear. When I made my move, I'd pulled on the bottom of the stock of the LRG, using the sling over my shoulder to swing the barrel of the weapon towards him. Deafened temporarily by the discharge, I aimed and fired. His head exploded, and the other two guards looked at first me and then the approaching swarm before they turned and fled.

I probably had ten seconds to react, so I wasted no time. I reached down and pulled my Mossberg from his not quite cold but very dead hands and pulled at a leather satchel he had been carrying. It was heavy, and I hoped it was full of my shells. Lastly, I saw something Luca had talked about. It looked like a watch, or a Fitbit, back when I'd been on a health craze. I pulled that off and followed. Five seconds. I turned and saw that they were two car lengths away and moving much faster than I had expected.

But these weren't the size of the Scout I had killed. Instead, these were the size of what had been described by the log files. Small to medium sized dogs would have been bigger. I pumped two rounds, happy to see the effects of buckshot cutting a swatch in the approaching attackers. I hadn't noticed them flinch before when the asshat had tried blowing my head off because I'd been watching for his move, but seeing so many of their front lines fall, they hesitated and then the nearest bugs all converged on their dead and dying comrades. The feast started. I ran. I ran like hell.

I caught up with the two guards as the door was closing. One was making a hurry up motion with his hand. The door was inset into the wall, and it was moving slowly like a pocket door. I leaped through, and a moment later it slid shut behind me with a loud click. I looked, and it appeared from this side that it was a bank vault door on a fancy set of rollers and framework made out of metal and wood to brace it all together. I could hear the Vorryn on the other side, the ones who hadn't stopped for a snack. They didn't even shake the wall or door, but I could hear them throwing themselves against both.

I turned and found two dozen tridents pointed at… me.

CHAPTER 9

"Hey guys, smoke 'em if you got 'em," I said.

A few looked at each other puzzled.

You spoke to them in English, dumbass, Alice mocked.

"You speak Trader?" a man asked me in a native tongue.

"Yes, there was a guard I was talking to a little bit ago…"

"You ambushed our guards. It is for the tribunal to decide—"

"Stop," a man said. pushing his way through, holding his trident high. "He is a Trader looking for entrance to the city."

Above me, I could hear shouts, and I turned away from the guards and their weapons to look. Up top, men with slings and crossbows were using their projectiles at a frantic pace.

"I already paid my entry fee," I told them in their language.

That surprised them, and they lowered their tridents a hair. I wasn't sure if it was my admission or the use of their language. Score one for Alice.

Thank you, she told me mentally.

The guard pulled a brass shell out of his pocket and held it up for everyone to see. They crowded around it, forgetting I was even there, and there was such a murmur of voices that I couldn't make out individual words, even with Alice's help. Then the closest guard to me turned, seeing my armament and the shotgun I'd retrieved.

"The fee just went up," he said, pointing at me.

"Sorry, already paid," I told him.

"It's either pay up or go to the ring," he said.

"Shouldn't you be fighting bugs or something?" I asked, "Instead of trying to steal my gear or shake me down?"

"I am not a thief, and I do not understand the words 'shake me down,'" he said, the color of his cheeks turning bright red as his eyes narrowed.

Hit a nerve. Ooops.

"Really? So, what was the asshole outside trying to do when he nearly took my head off with this?" I asked, holding up the shotgun so everyone could see it.

The man took advantage of the shotgun being pointed away and lurched forward with his trident, electricity crackling. I'd made a mistake, one I regretted instantly. The trident hit my chest, but didn't pierce it. A flash of color and then Alice was speaking in my head.

Personal Shield Generator absorbed the blow, recharged in ten seconds if no more damage is taken.

The electricity on the trident had shut off when he hit me. The two different electronics probably canceled each other out. The guard looked at me in a dawning horror when he realized I wasn't skewered and was pulling his arm back for another thrust when I moved. I swung the butt of the shotgun down, crashing it into the guard's head. His eyes rolled up instantly, and he folded. I leveled my gun at the rest who were suddenly very vigilant. Their tridents were once again pointed directly at me as I knelt down.

"You keep what you can," I told them in their native tongue and relieved the guard of his watch looking credit depository.

"Stranger, do you not know how to use our form of credit bracelets?"

The voice was loud and booming. Half the men startled and their tridents twitched. I almost twitched too, pumping rounds of buckshot into them myself, but they held the tridents straight up in the air as a large man strode forward. He looked as broad shouldered as he was tall, which was very, and muscular like a professional wrestler. He was wearing the same kind of clothing as the others, a kind of homespun material in earth tones that made him hard to see in the dim light from torches and the occasional electric light high up on a pole.

"I do not. I'm a traveler, and twice now the men of this ville have attacked me unprovoked. Are you in charge of this rabble of assholes and miscreants?"

I heard a couple of gasps from the closest men, but the screeching of the bugs got louder, and I lost anything the crowd closest to me murmured.

"Despite your tone, I'm willing to let that go. I am Magnus, and I run Lakeville—"

His words were lost in a cacophony of gunshots from what sounded like twin Gatlings opening up. There was no real way to describe it, other than a chainsaw on crack. At full throttle. Drinking a bottle of Jack Daniels with loose women to tempt—

Stay on task, Tony, Alice chided.

I heard brass start to rain down from the ramparts above and I hazarded a look. I could see the flashes of the automatic muzzle fire and the gunners were lit up from it.

"As I was saying, you're new here. I'll let your words and tone go," Magnus continued. "But tell me, you must have traveled far and wide to be so proficient to kill or disable two of my men and walk with such riches."

"Riches?" I asked.

"That pistol, it alone would buy you lodging and food in our ville for over a year, yet you wear it like it's a functional tool, something to keep close on hand at all times."

I slung the shotgun over my other shoulder, so I'd have both hands free.

"That's because, to me, it is a tool. Though I came here looking for a place to stay and some food, I'm not willing to trade my weapons."

"That's too bad," he said, and looked up annoyed.

AWAKENED CONTROL

"All clear," I heard shouted from above.

"That was a lot of ammo," I said pointing up.

"I will speak with my security about that, they would only use those as a last resort. That doesn't interest me at the moment though, my friend. You do. Come, let's find you somewhere to sit a moment and have a drink. You must be weary from travel."

I nodded, and everyone relaxed.

Holy shit, you read that one right, Alice said in my head.

"You never show fear, even when you're shitting your pants, not to guys like Magnus," I told her mentally.

———

The walk through town was… Imagine if a tarpaper shack needed to be repaired. So, you cobbled together some plywood or some chipboard. Old pieces of sheet metal and cars made up half the buildings. Some were converted old school buses that were finally starting to rust out in the desert air. There was what looked like the fuselage of what once was an old jet tilted at a crazy angle, but there were wooden steps that led up and inside it.

There wasn't trash lying about anywhere, and the dirt in front of the buildings seemed to be swept. Small kids ran about and several startled me at first when they ran up, wanting to touch my exposed skin, or feel the fabric of my camos. I had forgotten how different this was and hadn't taken my own appearance into consideration. Still, the kids were cute. One thing that 1,000 years hadn't changed was that all kids are curious, they're bold, and they like a laugh. I did stop though when I felt a tugging at the back of my head, and I spun to see an older teenage girl who'd been feeling the fabric of my headscarf.

"Where did you get this fabric? It is very fine," she asked.

"I traded for it with a friend. It looks… It is a little bit different material than what your city uses, isn't it?"

"It is, it is finely woven. If you find any more or you would like to trade this…"

"I'm sure there will be a lot of time for trading," Magnus said, "but first, were going to get our new stranger here a room and a drink. Run along now. Before he puts you all to work."

"This is quite the city, where did you…? It's very eclectic."

Magnus looked at me and broke out into a big grin. He pointed and indicated a building we were walking up on. It was in the center of town, and it looked like three sides of the building were completely open. The back wall was where most of the smells were coming from. I could tell it was something from my day and age, just not all of it. It'd once been stucco placed over brick, but a lot of that had crumbled and fallen away, exposing the old cinderblock.

As we drew nearer, I could see that it was an old two-story building. Maybe even a retail shop at one point. The glass that would have been in the doors on three sides at all been removed, and what looked like an open-air bar and restaurant had been set up.

AWAKENED CONTROL

Apparently, the gunfire and the shrieks of the Vorryn had brought the citizens out into the streets in droves, even though it was night. Now they moved out of Magnus's way like Moses parting the seas. The man seemed not to have a care that I was walking behind him fully armed, and considering the way his people had treated me, I didn't know if I would've extended anyone that level of trust.

He was either very, very scary, very arrogant, or very sure of himself. Probably a little bit of all of that.

And don't forget, he's one of the scariest men in all of Lakeville, Alice told me.

"Yeah, with Moss being the second scariest human in this whole place."

"Calm, let's sit. Food and drinks are on me tonight," Magnus said as we walked up.

There were what looked like crude picnic tables set up along the outer edges of the open-air bar, and several people looked like they wanted to stand to give us space, but Magnus waved for them to sit back down. Instead, he showed me to the bar, where he pulled out a stool. I did so when he took the stool next to me. Never before had I been intimidated by a man because of his size, but this was pretty close. Magnus was easily twice as big as I was. I wasn't a giant among men, but Magnus was.

"I'm sorry about my hospitality, out here in the wastes, it's pretty rough. I wish things could be more civilized, but this seems to be a word from a forgotten era. You don't speak or act like you've been around here before, is this true?"

"Yeah, I've been traveling the desert trying to find

my way," I told him.

"Trying to find your way, eh? Where you coming from?"

"You know, I don't actually know. I woke up one day with very little memory from an injury and, in the last couple days, I've been getting it back slowly, flashes bits of it here and there."

"Well, what do I call you, friend?"

I didn't think I'd used my name in front of Moss, and it didn't seem like I really needed to lie to everyone here. I could probably have gotten away with a fake or made up name, but I didn't want to do that. One lie leads to another, and pretty soon you're lying to cover your lies. It was always better to go with the truth, or the truth as you know it, and be deliberately vague. I wanted to know more about the Outsiders, and I wanted to know more about the factions. And, more importantly, I wanted to find out where I can get the parts to repair the ARC. My reception into Lakeville had been rocky, but the leader was giving me the opposite idea of what perhaps the city was really like.

"The name I remember is Tony," I told him as an elderly woman started pouring in amber liquid into a couple of earthenware ceramic mugs that looked like they would easily hold a pint, if not an entire gallon.

"The loss of memory is unfortunate; were you injured badly?"

"No, but I'd think I got hit in the head or was attacked and don't remember. It's happened to me before, and I've got the scars to prove it," I told him with a smile, and then realized I had to take my headscarf off in order to drink what smelled like a very strong ale.

So, I started unwrapping it, trepidation filling me. Had Moss given an accurate description of me to the Outsiders? I didn't know. It was all a gamble at this point, and I also had to pray that Moss wasn't nearby, she was hopefully on another mission, to find me elsewhere. Yeah, good luck with that. She knew I was coming to Lakeville; I'd told her as much. Idiot.

When it was done, I draped the fabric over one shoulder, the one with the LRG. A couple of people noticed as I took my headscarf off, and they paused in their conversation to look at me. I'd been all over the world, and I forgot that not everyone sees people of different colors differently. Because of the language and because of the people's coloring I suspected that many of their ancestors came from Native American or Hispanic folk intermarrying. I couldn't swear to that, but just having people speak Navajo, or what they call Navajo that is, was enough to reinforce the beliefs for me. But their facial features, their body structure, it was all different. There was no defining feature on any of them. It was as if generation upon generation of people had blended and mixed together. A final end to true racism in America.

And then there was this white boy named Tony.

"That's some scar, where did that happen?" Magnus was looking at my left temple.

"It happened a long time ago as a kid. Playground accident."

"Playground? Anyway, please accept my apologies, and first round's on me." Magnus said as he raised his glass up in the air.

I grabbed my glass and held it up and clinked mine together with his, "Cheers." I took a long drink.

It wasn't the same drink that I'd had before. Unlike the brew that I'd had with Luca's family, this brew didn't have such a high alcohol content. Alice was quietly filling me in, as I slowly drank what had to be the best-flavored beer in the entire world. Hell, for all I knew, it was probably the only beer left in the entire world. Once one mug was empty, the bartender automatically refilled it without asking, and after a half hour of small talk, a platter of food was brought out to us.

Our talk had been light so far, him asking polite questions about me and my background, telling me where he came from, and I was very careful not to divulge too many secrets. So, I talked about my past. I talked about what I could remember and I talked about what I could remember having traveled within the United States. At least this area of the United States. I didn't want him to think that I was someone who had the technology available and just sitting out there waiting to be stolen. I'd heard about caravans, and I'd heard of the buggies that were manufactured here in Lakeville, but I didn't want to give too much away.

Still, Alice cautioned me that I was literally giving myself away word by word. I had her start nullifying the alcohol.

"So, what are your real intentions here, in Lakeville?" Magnus asked me after a few moments. "I know you're not some mere traveler, I believe you and I are a lot alike, and you're holding back on me."

"I very well could be a lot more. I just don't remember. Tony might not even be my real name, but it's the one that feels most familiar to me. Do you guys have doctors or nurses in the city...?" Stupid, stupid, stupid, stupid. Who has doctors and nurses in a wasteland like this? Still, I was deflecting.

"You mean healers? Sure, it depends on what ails you. We don't have any for people who have ailments of the mind, though. I do hear that the Order of the Purists has some spiritual healers that can work on the minds of lost men. Usually, it's only criminals and deviants that they work on, though."

I had to be careful here, the alcohol had to have loosened my lips up a little bit, and I was falling into my normal speech patterns. At some point, we had switched to Trader, which I knew of as English. We'd done it so gradually and so smoothly I hadn't even noticed. I did now, though, and I grabbed what looked like a fried potato wedge off of the wooden platter and gave it a bite. Instead, I found the texture to be that of fish, but with a hard shell along the bottom. Instead of biting all the way through it, I used my teeth to pull the meat off. The flavor was like a giant prawn. Beer, fish, and chips. Winning.

Magnus did the same, and we started attacking the food while I talked in between bites a little.

Tony, I think he's feeling you out for something.

"I think so too. I know I've slipped up here and there, but it doesn't seem to have bothered him or even alerted him. Do you think he knows?" I asked the AI in my head.

Probably, Alice said simply.

Shit!

"You were going to tell me about how the credit system here works," I said after a couple moments and held up my left wrist that now held the two watch bands.

"Oh yeah," Magnus said swallowing a big bite, "here, let me," he said, motioning with a large palm.

I pulled both of them off my left wrist easily and put them on the bar between us.

"Both of these off my men?" he asked.

I nodded and took another bite so I wouldn't have to say anything.

"There's a small button near the bottom of the tech, left side is for send and the right side is for receive so if you do this…" Magnus held the button on one of the watch faces on the other side on the other and pressed them together, and there was an electronic beep, then he held them up to me.

I had noticed the buttons before, but I'd suspected that the dark smooth face of… Well, whatever you wanted to call this watch thing… was similar to an LCD. The one on the left showed zero, and the one on the right showed 10,463 credits. It didn't actually say credits but had been told that's what the unit of measure was. But I had no idea on what the scale of any of that meant.

"Looks like my man you killed for that shotgun had just gotten paid," he said, holding up both bands and handing them to me. I put the one with the full credits further up my left wrist closer to my forearm and then put the one that was empty in front of it and pulled my sleeve back down.

"Your man with the shotgun tried to shoot me in the back of the head," I told him shortly. "I was also told, you keep what you can."

"Yeah…" he said with a sigh, "that's the way it's been, at least as long as I can remember. I wasn't always the mayor here, you know."

"I don't know what a mayor is," I told him, lying through my teeth.

Good one, Alice said mentally.

"Let's see… how about Baron, King, ruler, dictator… No, not dictator." He looked at me. "Are any of those unfamiliar?"

"I've heard of Baron and King before, is that what you are here?"

"For the last 40 years."

I turned and looked at the big ruler again. If he'd been in charge for 40 years… He only looked 40 years old. Maybe good living, good food…

If you tasted a sample of his blood, I could tell you for sure if he's human or not.

Mentally I shuddered. "That isn't going to happen," I told her in my head.

Tony, I— Alice's words cut off.

I tried contacting her, but she didn't answer. For the first time since I'd awakened, I felt alone. It was really strange, but I'd grown used to, and fond of, the snarky voice in my head.

"That's a long time. Do people of Lakeville really live that long?" I asked him, knowing how horrible the average lifespan had been before modern medicine.

He looked at me like he was confused or considering his answer and then spoke, "I know in the wastelands the lifespan is measured in ten or twenty-year increments. Here in Lakeville, unless killed in a violent death, our healers can cure most ills. Everything except the wasting disease. We have chems for that, but it doesn't work a lot of times."

"Wasting disease? Is that also known as cancer?" I asked.

Tony, be careful, Alice cautioned.

"Where were you?" I asked her in a flash, "I was really worried for a minute there."

I'll explain later. Pay attention to Magnus.

"Yes, I've heard those words before from Travelers, but none from this area. Tell me, what other languages do you speak? You have a far better grasp of Trader than you do Navajo."

"Trader, Navajo, and Spanish," I told him, realizing I did know Spanish.

The knowledge was there, I just hadn't remembered it. I wished I would quit stumbling around all the realizations and my memory would just come back. That would be cool.

"Maybe some more, but it's hard to remember things. My memory is coming back in small bursts."

"I see you are a well-travelled man then," Magnus said in Spanish.

"Thank you," I told him Spanish as well before switching back to English. "And thank you for not taking my words as an insult. I was literally chased into the city by those bugs after being attacked, and it had my blood up."

AWAKENED CONTROL

"I can imagine," Magnus said, his voice contemplative. "Is there anything else I can do for you?" He asked, finishing off the last of the hors d'oeuvres.

"Point me to the nearest place I can rest and do a little trading, and I'll forever be in your debt," I said.

That got a grin and, for the first time since I'd come into Lakeville, I felt like I might have pulled off my scam. I had not intended to run into the leader of the Outsiders at all. Once I had, I'd absolutely had no other choice but to go along with it, or risk exposing myself as a CEPM. Alice would have been cut out of my head, after they'd used me as a human blood bag, which would lead to my ultimate death. Kinda a buzzkill, to be honest. Plus, Moss was around here somewhere, and I needed, absolutely needed, to stay out of her sight.

"Salim?" Magnus called to the bartender.

The woman turned, looked in our cups, and started refilling mine. She moved to take Magnus's, but he waved her off.

"Salim, can you or your son point our new friend here towards the market square and hostel?" he asked her in Navajo.

"Aye, that me can do Boss," she answered, her voice crackling as if she didn't use it much.

She then pulled out a small flat black device the size of a credit card and punched some buttons. I could swear it was a smartphone, but it was flat black with an LCD like the watches we had. Magnus held up his wrist, and she tapped her device to his own watch. He smiled and said thanks to her.

"I have to go coordinate with the watch guard.

We expended a ton of ammunition, and I want to see if we need to mount a scavenging crew. Can't let all that go to waste now, can we?"

"I guess not?" I said as the big man stood and took a step back.

"Fair travels, my friend. May you find what you seek."

"Thanks, Magnus," I said and watched as he turned to go.

I drank the ale. It had calories, and I knew Alice was still doing a great job of neutralizing the alcohol content because I hardly had a buzz. Still, every little bit helped.

"Are ye ready to find a place to lay yer head?" Salim asked me.

"Yeah, that'd be much appreciated," I told her, noticing how absolutely black it was outside of the ville.

I could see the makeshift walls that encircled the city and it looked like they were doubled near where I was. Perhaps there were two sets of walls, in case the first was breached? Or was the space in between filled with rubble, or had catwalks running across—

I don't know what it was, Alice said, *But somebody tried a full port scan on me. I don't think they knew I was there, so I had to shut down and go offline. I don't know when it stopped, but it's gone now. Your personal shield generator probably helped disrupt the flow, but there is a lot of wireless network activity in this area.*

"I was wondering what happened to you. Do you think it was something Magnus did?" I asked her mentally.

Salim motioned to a younger man in his mid-twenties, and he walked over and nodded to me. I nodded back.

Or it was Magnus himself, Alice said.

That was not... comforting.

"Salim, what do I owe?" I asked, motioning to the plate that had been piled with food and my now empty mug.

"Magnus has paid your bill," she told me simply.

I pulled out a 9mm magazine and thumbed out one of the brass casings and put the ammo on the counter. I'd never seen an old woman move so fast, but it was snatched up, and she held it in her cupped hand, peering at it with fingers so close together there was hardly an opening.

"This is no reload," she told me.

"No, it isn't. Brand new. A tip, if that is good enough as such?" I didn't know if tipping was even a thing or would it be an insult—

The old woman reached over the bar, and I stopped myself from flinching when she reached out and touched first my left cheek, and then her fingers traced the scar on the side of my head. It tickled, and I had to really work at not making a movement.

"You've shown me a kindness. I'd like to give ye a piece of advice if you would listen?"

She looked first at me and then to the young man. His eyes were opened wide.

"I would," I told her.

"These are precious. I've heard of men like you, who know no value of the riches you carry. Try to avoid showing these around. It's enough that you've got enough Blasters on ya, to take on an entire hunter crew, but watch out for hurt feelings, challenges to fight in the ring. Avoid Magnus's guards and crew if you can. There's a foul wind blowing as of late, and I've been here long enough to know that something isn't right."

"Were you here when Magnus took charge?" I asked her.

She cracked a toothy grin, open gaps where teeth once had been.

"I have me seventy-two years. Magnus was in charge back then when I was a-borned here. Not many people my age left. Those of us who remember, do not talk of it."

"He said he's been her for forty years," I told her.

"Oh yeah," she said, and we were leaned in close, whispering to each other. "He went off for a time, some years. He came back, looking like some muscled ox, and took back over from the Order. Bloody days it was. He didn't quite lie to ye, but he didn't tell ya the entire truth either. Lots of that here in Lakeville, eh?"

"Is she talking about me?" I asked Alice.

I have no idea. Seduce her and find out, Alice snapped back.

"Eeewwwwww." I swear I heard the AI chuckle.

For something that claimed to have no feelings, I was starting to wonder if she had the ability to develop them. I mean, laughter?

"I have a little business here as well. Can your son show me where the market is, and the Order of Purists?"

"For this?" She said, her left fist held up, hiding

the shell, "I'll make sure my son's son Henry there shows you around tonight and meets ya in the morn. It's getting late, and I need to shut this shithole down."

Her curse made me snort, and it was a good thing I hadn't been taking a drink at that moment. I reached up and took her right hand from my temple and held it gently. "Thank you for your kindness."

I swear something I said or did… Tears welled up but never fell from her eyes. I put her hand down and turned to Henry, her grandson. He motioned with his head, and I followed him away from the bar.

"This is the best hostel in all of the ville," the short man at the front desk said. I asked him how much for a room and, when he told me 4,000 credits, I almost choked.

"We do take in goods for trade, but you would get more value by trading at the market for credits," he told me conspiratorially.

"I'll take it," I told him, pushing the button on my watch face and he tapped it with a device similar to what Salim had used earlier. I held my watch up afterwards and saw that it had taken out exactly what it was supposed to.

"I'll arrange for entertainment for you. Should be ten, maybe twenty minutes," he said, pushing a brass key towards me. "Room 17."

"I'll show you," Henry said softly behind me, and I nodded.

This once had been a hotel, though I couldn't

make out which one of the chains it had been. Two stories, with half of it collapsed into rubble. The siding of it had a layer of stucco on it that was the same color as the native rocks and dirt. Henry showed me to the door and stopped as I fumbled with the key.

"If you are unhappy with your choice of entertainment, you get another pick," he told me.

"What is the entertainment?" I asked, feeling dumb like I should have asked before.

A group of ladies walked by in a group, giggling and whispering to each other. They were young, early twenties, if that. Henry's eyes followed them and then he turned to me and nodded in their direction.

"You can't be serious?"

Instead of answering me he told me, "I'll be here at sunrise if you are ready."

I swore mentally, and opened my door. Candles had been lit, and what had to have been a thousand-year-old bed and bedframe awaited me inside. I tried the light switch and was surprised when the electric light turned on, pushing back all the darkness.

"Thank you, Henry, I'll see you in the morning," I told him and he left, so I stepped in and closed the door.

With the light on, I could see that there was no carpeting. Instead there was cracked concrete. It was rough surfaced as if it had been poured and floated crudely. Still, as long as there weren't Vorryn in the bed, I would be fine. I had slept in rougher conditions than this and had been copping a squat in the desert for naps. There was a roughly made picnic table and bench on one wall, where a TV would have normally been, and I unslung my pack and laid my guns out across it. I blew out the candles; there'd be no entertainment for me tonight. I was never one to go for that sort of thing and would always have prided myself as a…, but the memory was gone. I was about to take off my vest when I heard a gentle knock on the door. I sighed and walked to it.

"Listen, I'm really tired, and I'm not looking to—" I was opening the door, but the wind was knocked out of me with a front kick as a figure in black boots, black pants, and a white tank top pushed her way inside and slammed the door closed behind her.

I fell on my back and tried to keep the roll going, but obviously, Moss had seen the move before and was already swinging a knife at my chest. I got two hands up, but not fast enough. She fell with the blade in front of her. Colors exploded between us and I pushed her over.

Tony, personal shield generator has discharged. Ten seconds, Alice said and then added, *She went for your heart, she went for the kill.*

"Why is it that she kicked the shit out of me, but the shield works on bullets and knives?"

The shield was never designed to stop blunt force trauma. Slow blunt force trauma, that is. You still take damage. Your vest would have stopped the stab too, but she could always go for something less vital, like your head.

I didn't have time for that, and I was already holding onto her wrists in my failed attempt to stop the blade. One wrist, the one I'd broken last time, felt like something solid was holding it together. A slim flesh colored cast had been used… The knife was going down slowly despite my best efforts, and I didn't want to get stabbed… so I rolled. She started out on top, but the blade got tangled in the bottom of the bench with the roll. I laid out in front of her, and I straddled her waist as I let my upper body and my body weight hold her still. It was like trying to herd cats. She hissed, and her teeth gnashed. Her inky eyes were furious, and I was letting my body weight wear her down. I didn't want to hurt her, but if she started making a ton of noise, I would knock the bitch out. She'd gone for a kill shot?

Shield recharged, Alice intoned, *and I'm also sensing a change in her heartbeat. With you holding her, skin contact, I can monitor with the—*

"Not important Alice," I said, wiping my forehead against my shirt sleeve.

Moss had calmed some and I could feel the rising and falling of her chest as she struggled to breathe with my weight pinning her down. She tried to say something, but I easily outweighed her by eighty to a hundred pounds. I leaned in a little closer, hoping to hear her say she was giving up. That's when the door to the room opened up. I didn't move, expecting an entire goon squad to come bursting in as backup.

"Oh, sorry, I didn't know he sent someone already," the young woman said, and then slammed the door shut.

I turned back and looked at Moss who was now looking at me, tears falling from her eyes. I moved my grip so one hand could hold both wrists and I stayed straddling her waist but sat up some so she could breathe. She took in long breaths for several moments, and I marveled at how wild she looked. Her hair fell in curls, and part of me wanted to do nothing more than stop her tears and run my fingers through her hair. I knew how wrong that was… a sadistic psycho hottie and I was suddenly going all romantic times in my head.

"Dammit Alice, this is your doing, isn't it?" I asked her mentally, but she was silent.

I looked at Moss. "Why did you try to kill me? Shit, I'm going to have to leave now."

"That's twice now," Moss said, "That you've utterly humiliated me. Why don't you just kill me? I can't show my face around here anymore."

"Why? Because I stole your vest?" I asked her, knowing I was probably bruising her wrists.

"Because I failed to bring you in. I failed to get the information about you I needed, and I failed in returning the Exosuit. I cannot come up with the credits to pay back Magnus, so I will have to go to the brothels. Do you know what the men will do to me there?" She asked, poison in her words. "They cannot work for me one day and then have utter control over me the next. I would rather die," she spat.

"I thought finding me and bringing me in would make you rich. Hell, you were rich already, you told me."

"They closed my accounts," she said, her voice rising. "Those suits are worth 400,000 credits. I don't have that kind of credits."

"Damn, why is it that I always fall for the bad girls?" I asked Alice.

That was out loud, stupid, Alice told me in a mental voice that oozed sarcasm.

Moss moved quickly, her legs wrapping around my chest as she flexed her back. The move was unexpected, and I was off balance and found myself on my back with her reversing positions. Somewhere, though, she had a twin to the knife she'd dropped, and it was now held at my throat.

"What do you mean you fall for the bad girls?" She asked, the blade just under my chin.

I knew the shield was recharged and I was sure that, with the exception of severing my head, she couldn't kill me. Jabbing the blade into my brain would, but I was distracted. This insanely hot woman, straddling me. Yeah, I suck as a human being.

"I have no idea. Part of the memory loss," I said, "but I do remember how to treat a lady. I came with gifts for you."

Her eyes flashed, and I grabbed the knife by the edge of the blade and pushed. The shield started flickering down towards the discharge, but Moss lost her grip before it could. Then it was a matter of pushing her off me and standing. She went crawling after the dropped knife in a flash, but I was pulling my pack close to me. She got her knife and tensed up to take a slash at me as I pulled out her vest. She went absolutely still. I held it out with one hand, the supple leather still warm from the heat of the day.

"What… I don't…" she dropped the knife on the bed and walked to me.

"This was never mine. This was my insurance policy. Now, can we talk? Or are you going to keep trying to kill me? Because if you aren't willing, let's get it over with so I can knock you out and head out of town."

She took the vest and started putting it on. You know that thing girls do when they put on a coat or something and then put their hands under their hair, pull it out from underneath the garment and flip it back? Yeah, she totally wins that competition.

Think with the big brain, not the little one, Alice reminded me.

"There's a reason we broke up, and you keep reminding me why," I told her.

That was out loud again.

"We never…" Moss said, backing up to where the knife was on the bed. "You're talking to it again, aren't you?"

"Yeah, well, I seem to forget to keep my side quiet when you're around." I knelt down and looked under the bench and found the other knife. I pulled it out and tossed it on the bed next to her.

"That's… not something I even know what to… and they say I am crazy."

Then she did something that gave me goosebumps of fear. Real fear. She laughed out loud and walked up and kissed me on the side of the mouth. I was too surprised and startled to even react, and all the while Alice had picked up my memories of my favorite music tracks and started playing 'Careless Whispers' in my head. I hated her sometimes.

"Yes, I agree to your terms. Let's talk. My life is forfeit, whether or not I turn you in. My command has been stripped, I don't even have a band to store credits."

"How did you know I was going to be here?" I asked her, walking to the door and turning the deadbolt so we wouldn't have any other interruptions.

Moss shot me a look, one eyebrow raised higher than the other at the locked door.

"Everyone is talking about the new stranger. The one who bested Paulo and knocked out Brendan, only to then throw an insult at Magnus at how his ville is run. Oh, and that he was heavily armed and has the skin tone of a newborn baby."

"So, everyone in Lakeville knows where I am?"

"Basically. You're an oddity. Even the old woman at the bar won't say a cross word against you, and she hates everyone but Magnus."

"That's odd," I told her, "and I can't believe I'm standing here talking to you. I thought you'd…"

"Oh, trust me, I want you dead. I just can't figure out how to do it. I thought I was good, but I've never been bested before. I think it would be a foolish waste of my life to try it again. Maybe later when you don't have the shield generator clipped to your belt…"

I laughed, and I could tell she halfway meant it. Oh well.

"You know what I am, surely that would at least buy you back some status here? Not that I want you to…" I said.

"I told you, they stripped me of everything. They sold my debt to the brothel. I am supposed to be there already. I'm dead if I attack you, I'm dead if I don't show up to start working and I'm dead because I've screwed over most of the working men in this ville to get the gig I had."

"No hope," I said simply.

"So as much as I hate you, I'd rather not be used poorly and then killed for somebody's sick pleasure. So, if talking to you to preserve my life for a while longer bothers you," she pointed to my Beretta, "please end it."

I signed and pulled out the bench and sat. Moss sat down at the end of the bed, and we faced each other.

"Magnus has told me how this ville works, but I thought a lot of it was run on 'Keep what you can'?"

"It is, but I no longer belong to myself. I am the property of Boris. He owns the brothels in town, and is the second wealthiest man around, next to Magnus."

I thought about that. This wasn't my battle, but it was a result of my choices. She'd lost everything, and I needed allies inside the ville if I had a chance of getting the tech I needed to repair my ARC.

"So, I need to challenge Boris for you... er... your contract?" I said.

"There is no contract, I am his slave."

There was a gentle knock at the door, and I rose. I looked out the peephole but couldn't see anyone. I unlocked the door and opened it a crack. A carafe had been placed outside on a wooden tray with two mugs. I opened the door and picked it up, kicking the door behind me as I placed it on the table. Then I locked the door again. I turned to see Moss still sitting on the bed, watching me. She could have tried to escape, though I was now certain she wasn't going to try. In fact, I wasn't really holding her captive. This was so weird.

I poured the first mug, happy to smell the dark ale I'd had earlier.

"They also say that you drank enough at the old woman's pub to kill an ox."

"Well, I guess I have a good metabolism," I told her, handing her a drink and then sitting on the bench again.

"Something," she agreed, and drank deeply.

CHAPTER 10

I woke up, my head sore. I felt something cold across my chest and opened my eyes and saw the knife blade lying there loosely in Moss's hand. Our arms and legs were still intertwined. Over drinks, I'd told her I would see Boris and either buy or win her contract. I'd asked Alice to keep an eye on things and negate the alcohol's effects if I was in danger, otherwise, I was going to enjoy myself for the first time in a thousand years.

I could feel her breath on my neck, and I turned. Sleeping, she looked softer. Gentler. Some time after our lovemaking she'd retrieved the knife. I wasn't so drunk that I wouldn't be able to feel her stabbing me, but it was weird to see it lying there in her hand, on my body. She could have shoved it into my skull, pierced my heart, severed my spinal column. She'd done none of these things. Slowly, I extracted myself from her and headed to the bathroom, hoping against all hopes that it was working.

The water was hot and clean when I turned it on in the large bathtub. I washed away all of my worries and really tried hard to remember who I was in my former life. Flashes of memory. My graduation. A helicopter ride. Screams. It was maddening.

You can't remember because you tried to save your squad from an IED attack and had fragments of shrapnel that pierced your brain. The damage from bleeding, swelling and surgery has damaged your memories. Your personality and language centers are still intact. You may never recover everything, or your brain might figure out a different path, and you'll regain it all, Alice told me.

"I thought you were part of the healing and neuro stuff. Get on that for me, would you?"

I have been, ever since I was installed. Listen, while you were sleeping I kept running and monitoring the network traffic here…

"I thought you couldn't operate while I was sleeping?" I asked her.

I can, but I can't use your senses. Since they use an actual Wi-Fi here, I was able to go onto their networks while you were… otherwise occupied.

"Yeah," I said grinning to myself in the bathroom.

I hadn't turned the light on, I would rather let sleeping psycho get all her beauty rest. I seriously had no idea how she'd gone from wanting to kill me to being in my bed. Instead, I'd lit a couple of candles so the harsh light wouldn't wake her up and I could still see what I was doing.

What I found, is that there's at least one more AI operating within this area. Not the sentient computers that run the power armor, but another quantum computer like me. I blocked all attempts at monitoring. I think it's a slightly older AI programming than what I have, but it could also be latency problems from one that wasn't in stasis.

"What, you mean AIs get crazy as they get older?" I asked her, thinking of Halo 5.

Not quite. It's just overwhelming knowledge makes computations harder to figure as more factors are considered. Anyways, I was able to intercept some feed about you and Moss.

"What did you find out?" I asked her aloud.

"That you talk in your sleep," Moss said walking in the room.

Smooth, Alice said.

"Sorry," I told Moss as the curtain opened and she stepped in, one arm behind her, "I was talking to Alice."

"That's your spirit brain's name?" She asked, pulling the curtain closed with her free hand.

I backed up under the shower head so she could walk into the spray and tried not to be a perv and leer. I mostly succeeded. I think.

"Yeah, she intercepted some chatter about you and me. She was about to tell me what," I told her.

Moss tilted her head up as if to tell me to go on.

"What is it?" I asked Alice mentally.

It seems that you've brought attention to yourself. Both the Order of Purists and the Outsiders will have watchers on you. It seems that Moss was seen going into your room last night and Boris is demanding payment of Magnus from you. It sounds like he wants your weapons and ammunition. The guard you gave a shell to talked. They think you're loaded. Rich.

I filled Moss in, and she gave me a smile and leaned forward. I leaned in to give her a kiss when the arm that had been behind her back flashed out. She had a fistful of steel, and I caught her wrist before the knife buried itself under my right armpit. We were both wet, and when I pulled at her wrist, she fell into me. It tripped me up and, naked and soaked, we both fell hard. I hit my head on the side of the tub, pulling the curtain on the way down and we wrestled, and I held back when I had half a heartbeat to sink an elbow into her face. Instead, I got back on top of her, using my body to pin her.

"What is wrong with you? I'm going to help you today!" I asked, panting from the exertion and the fading pain of what would have been a knockout blow if it had been anyone else.

"Can't blame a girl for trying," she said and leaned forward and kissed me.

She let go of the knife, and it fell out of the tub.

"I don't get you," I told her truthfully and got up, extricating myself from her.

"I don't get me either," Moss agreed.

I killed the water and grabbed a towel and stomped out of the bathroom.

I think that was her idea of foreplay.

"You're not funny," I said aloud.

"I wasn't joking," Moss said striding out, a towel

in her hair and one wrapped around her body.

"Not you… Oh, forget about it," I said, and started toweling myself off.

Of all the crazy psychotic things. She'd had her chance to bury her knife in me while I slept. She hadn't. Why would she do it right now? Unless Alice was right…

I usually am.

"I don't like you today," I told her mentally.

That's ok, I think the young lady is smitten with you. She loves you so much she comes after you with knives, and if she's feeling really spry, she gets stabby.

"Shut it," I said aloud, and Moss looked at me, grinning.

I dressed quickly, surprised to find all my clothing and gear untouched. I strapped on my shield generator and plugged it into the vest. Alice told me that, to everyone else, the shield was invisible, but she'd added that little flourish of rainbow lights to signify that the shield had discharged in my vision. Now that I was gearing back up, she brought up the HUD into my vision. Before holstering the Beretta in the vest, I topped off the mag and, from my pack I pulled out two casings and made sure all my mags were good.

"Are you going to stay here today and wait?" I asked her.

"You have the credits to hold the room one more day?" She asked me, an eyebrow raised, "I hope you didn't trade all your ammo for it."

"No, I have the bracelet watch thingies." I put those on next and pushed the buttons. I found the one that was empty and took it off after a moment's consideration and tossed it to a surprised Moss.

"These are called wallets," she told me, putting it on and hitting a button. She looked up at me. "Thank you. Now I can at least take on odd jobs if you are successful, and if you allow me to."

I knew this it was the future and shit, but damn... I had to get out of here. I wasn't trying to buy her.

"I'm heading out to pay for the room and then Henry should be here soon to show me around. I think I'm headed to Boris's first. Any advice?" I asked her.

"Avoid the arena, don't insult Magnus, don't let the Order of the Purists know what you really are."

"Do you know where I can buy some tech?" I asked her, using their generic term for any kind of technology.

"The Technomages. Other than our wallets," she said, holding up her wrist, "all tech is regulated through them. They won't sell you anything. Probably the black market."

"I need some servos, dammit," I cursed.

"For your—"

There was a knocking on the door. I grabbed the LRG and Shotgun and pack and walked out, leaving her in mid-sentence. She'd either be there when I got back, or she wouldn't. Alice had been giving me some details about Boris's demands, and it sounded like he was going to make a play for me no matter what. She'd been trying to tap into the security camera feed... yeah, I was surprised they had that here, but they were positioned in hard to see spots... anyways, she couldn't. They were protected by the other

AI, and she'd been avoiding the other AI, so she didn't give us away. Magnus was already suspicious but had nothing to go on, and my gear would bring a fresh influx of cash into the small ville.

"Ready?" Henry asked.

"Almost, I have to pay for one more night."

———

"You're sure that's where you want to go?" Henry asked me.

I nodded. He let out a grunt of disgust and started walking.

"What's wrong with that?" I asked, wondering what I'd done to earn his ire.

"Fancy hotel that comes with a whole night's worth of company and now you want to go visit for some more action? I'm half your age, and I don't think even I could handle all of that."

If he only knew. His lady friends didn't suddenly want to go all Jack the Ripper on him did they? Instead of answering directly, I grunted in reply.

"That's the market over there," he pointed.

It was a small alleyway behind a section of what looked to be tatters of canvas topping plywood shacks. Most were unpainted and gray from the weather, but I could see in the morning sunlight that things were starting to open up. People scurried around tables and benches holding products. I saw what looked like some sort of oranges or tangerines being stacked carefully in crates. Another had sections of meat that had a piece of cordage tied off on a strip, which the shopkeeper was hanging from a kind of pergola. One was using a piece of flint and an old knife to make sparks half of an old barrel to start a fire…

"The Order of the Purists," Henry pointed.

"Where?" I asked, looking.

"You can see the bell tower. It's right next to the brothel."

I looked, and I could make out the bell tower. It had once been brick and wood, with a cross on the top, but all of the wood had rotted off, or been removed and repurposed. It was a skeletonized version of a bell tower, with a brass cross still standing proudly at the top. Out of habit, I made the sign of the cross.

"For someone who claims he's new around here… You sure you aren't in the Order and just putting one on me?" Henry asked.

"No, that building, the cross. It's a symbol. To me, it probably means something a lot different. From another place, another time."

Henry grunted, and we kept walking. People were coming out of the shacks, the plane fuselage disgorged a ton of laughing children and men, and women started hustling about. A hand cart was being pushed, and for a second I wasn't sure what I was seeing and then realized that there were two dead bodies on it. They had black spots on their deeply tanned skin that had been oozing something.

"The pestilence," Henry said by way of explanation.

I crossed to the other side of the street, and Henry smiled and joined me until the cart was out of sight and then we started moving again.

"Excuse me," I felt somebody tugging on the edge of my vest, just out of my sight.

I turned, and it was a young woman. Wait, no it wasn't, she was a teen, not even an adult.

"Yes?" I asked her.

"May I... I mean..."

Oh God, this was creepy. Was she going to proposition me? I knew things run different, and the Outsiders were a sadistic bunch but was she going to...

"I've never seen someone with your color. Can I...?" she motioned to my hands.

I held my right hand out, palm down and then turned it over in confusion. She reached out and touched my hand in the center of the palm with one finger.

"It's... the same as mine," she said.

I pushed my sleeve up, which startled her, but I held my forearm out, and after a little urging, she held hers up as well. Henry looked on in amusement.

"You're so pale. Are you sick?" she asked.

The sheer guileless way she asked me was disarming.

"No, I never get sick. Where I come from, people are all colors," I told her.

"Really? That would be so cool! I mean, you're not ugly, but your skin color..."

"There are folks who are darker skinned than you, lighter skinned than me, some folks have a slight yellow tinge to their skin tone, too. Then there's tan like you are. All kinds of shades."

"That... thank you," she said and hurried off in giggles.

She was enveloped by another group of kids who had come out of the old airframe, and their laughs and giggles made me smile.

"Is it true?" Henry asked.

"What?"

"That people are so diverse where you come from? I have not traveled far, but I've never seen what you're talking about."

"Yes, it's true," I said, and we started walking again. "But I've gone a long way, and I won't likely stop any time soon."

"Well, I have some other errands to run for my dad's mom. The brothel is next to the Order's building."

I thanked him and kept walking. The ville wasn't huge, but it probably took twenty to thirty minutes to walk from end to end. In some parts, it resembled the tangle in India where shacks and people lived like they were in a third world hell hole, but these people here looked more or less…happy? Even those who stopped to stare at me as I walked on by. It was probably a combination of my skin tone, my weapons and the fact that I was a stranger amongst them. Still, the kids were happy, and as the city awoke around me I could see that, other than some obvious abuses of women and older girls, the society was working.

I felt it was horribly repressed if what I had been told was true; all the knowledge and technology held close by the Outsiders. Still, I would do what I could and, once I got my ARC back up and running, I could give away the information. I could see how repressing it had repressed the people and allowed horrible things to continue happening. Slavery, sexual abuse, the savage nature of people.

People have always been savage, Tony, Alice told me, *I do have some basics in the history of humans dating back to the 1500s.*

I ignored her and paused just outside the church I had come to. It was a mixture of old stone blocks, carefully fit into place, and what had to have been a later addition. The later addition had been the cement block that supported the bell tower and a flat roofed addition. Weird. I saw several men in white walk out. That was unusual in itself, when everyone else wore the earth tones. They noticed me and pointed.

"It's kind of early, but you could have breakfast with me beforehand?" A woman asked, hooking her arm through mine.

I turned and saw the brothel. She started walking with me.

"I'm not looking for a date," I told her, "I'm here to settle some business with Boris."

You would think I'd just poured hot water down the front of her, told her I'd boiled her cat alive and stomped on cute, fluffy creatures. She flinched away, pulling her arm back.

"You're him?" she asked.

"Well, I'm somebody," I replied.

Across from me was what looked like a newer constructed building. It was made of sheets of metal, and plywood, but unlike every other building around, it was painted bright red. Several women wore some rather interestingly tailored homespun woolen clothing.

"You're dead, that's what you are," she said, and took off running.

She met a group of girls by the door and pointed. I was too far off to hear their words but they all scattered inside as I approached.

"Excuse me, stranger," I spun as another hand tapped my left shoulder.

I'd pulled the Beretta and had leveled it at the owner of the hand. It was a man wearing a white robe with a copper cross colored on the chest. One of the few I had seen coming out of the old church.

"Not right now," I told him. "I have to do something first, then I'll come back and talk."

The man swallowed, his Adam's apple bobbing up and down, and he nodded. I started walking, more like stomping my way towards the door the women had fled into. I holstered the pistol as I neared it and saw it was an old glass door, set into an aluminum frame. The standard for strip malls all across the country. I get put into stasis for over a thousand years, and they still have strip malls. Greaaaaaat......

"Welcome to Boris's Brothel, what would your pleasure be?" a sultry voice asked.

I turned and tried not to flinch. The woman was easily seven hundred pounds. No joke. The thing that freaked me out though was that both legs and one arm had been neatly severed and covered in white bandages. She was sitting in an alcove off the doorway in what looked like a cart designed to convey her around.

"I'm here to see Boris," I said.

"Name?" she asked, chewing on the tip of a quill pen.

AWAKENED CONTROL

"Tony, the traveler," I told her.

She was the one who flinched this time.

"He's… uh… he will be right back, here I'm sure. Please wait there," she said and pointed to a wooden bench near the door.

She muttered something, and a kid ran up from behind a plush red curtain behind her. She whispered something to him, bumped his wrist to hers and the kid took off running.

"What's that?" I asked her, nodding to the door the kid had just left out of.

"Runner. He's going to find Magnus and Boris. They were actually headed over to your room about an issue that's come up."

"I'm here to settle that," I told her, and her eyes went wide.

I looked around the brothel. There was a large open area, where there were picnic tables set up. I mean, I knew the nuclear apocalypse happened, but geesh, those guys needed somebody to build them something different.

It's because picnic style tables are simple to build, dumbass, Alice told me and I continued to look around.

The plywood walls were covered on the inside by fabrics. Most of it was red with a couple of electric lights breaking up the darkness inside. Still, it looked like a mixture between a rave club, a strip club, and a cozy restaurant. Lots of flesh was on display as the girls danced and I was surprised to see many men inside there already. I personally didn't have a problem whatever a lady choose to do to survive… but I wasn't ok with outright slavery. I vaguely remembered parts of Afghanistan and Pakistan where the ladies were treated much much worse, but I had never been comfortable with it, and every time I had tried to intervene, the rules of engagement had prevented me from doing what I'd really wanted to.

Still, I hadn't seen anything bordering on abuse yet. All the women who were mingling were of adult age. Then my eyes fell on the woman who'd tried to pick me up earlier. She was talking with a hulking beefy man with exaggerated hand and arm motions, pointing at me. I smiled as I straddled the end of the bench. He started walking over.

Now remember when I'd said Magnus was easily the biggest dude I'd ever seen? This guy was almost that big. He moved with the easy grace of someone who'd gotten into more fights than he could count. He saw me watching him and grinned, half his teeth missing or blackened. Great dentistry the future had. I stood at his approach and slung the shotgun next to the LRG.

"So," he said in heavily accented English, "You're the one who's kept Moss away from me?"

"Boris?" I asked him questioningly.

He threw back his head and laughed. "No, no. I am merely the first one to place an advanced payment for Moss. You are the one, yes?"

"You mean, the guy who prevented her from being sold to a brothel, then yes I am."

Alice had told me before that slow moving blunt force trauma wouldn't be blocked by my shield, and she wasn't kidding… but there was nothing slow about the punch. He hit me in the chin so hard that my teeth clicked and I flew off my feet, hitting the wall behind me. Already Alice was giving me updates and making sure I saw my health bar. His punch had taken a lot out of me, and a few more would kill me. So instead of letting him hit me again when I got to my feet, I went low.

Ok, not really low. His next sucker punch started at his waist and was an uppercut designed to have knocked me out. From there, I imagined he'd use his bigger size to hold me down (much like I'd done to Moss) and then pummel me to death. Nope, nope, nope. Wouldn't do it. Wouldn't be prudent. I ducked and delivered a hammering blow to the soft spot below his ribs. He gasped but other than that he was already swinging with his other fist, even off balance. I ducked that one and stomped on his right ankle as he overextended his body.

I heard a snap and this time I saw him react. He let out a cry of pain and started to fall. I got out of reach of his flailing arms, and he drew his leg in, to cradle with one his arms. That left half of him exposed. Namely, his delicate bits, as one leg was drawn up tight and he lay on his side. My next stomp made his eyes bug out, and all the air left him in a silent scream. I heard sympathetic sounds from the crowd and stepped back for a moment.

All the dancing had stopped, and patrons and workers stood there in open shock. I walked up to the man's left wrist where his watch wallet was and pulled it off. I was going broke fast and hell, they made the rules up. Keep what you can. I gave the big man a crushing kick to the head and his eyes rolled back as he lost consciousness. I transferred the credits and smiled. I didn't have enough to buy her freedom, but I did have enough to stay in the hotel a few more days.

"What are you doing?" I heard a voice boom behind me.

I spun, my hand already pulling the pistol, and I found myself surrounded by a dozen men with tridents, a half a dozen in Exosuits, each carrying a chaingun. Behind that, and pushing their way through the crowd were two figures, one of which I recognized. Magnus.

"Who me?" I asked in English. "He attacked me. I put the threat down."

The man who had to be Boris's eyes almost bugged out when he looked at the floor and then back to me.

There was a scary resemblance. I wouldn't say he and the man on the floor were brothers, per se, but cousins, maybe?

"Tony," Magnus said in a well-modulated and smooth voice, "We were looking for you and come to find that you've severely injured yet another of the town's men. We must stop meeting like this. It's not healthy. For you."

The threat wasn't that subtle. Message received, Captain Kangaroo.

"Doing what I have to, to survive," I told them.

"Where is Moss?" the man asked.

"Boris?" I asked him.

"Yes, where is my property?" Boris demanded through clenched teeth.

"I have her stashed in a safe place, for now. I was

AWAKENED CONTROL

actually coming here to make my apologies and to propose a trade, or to buy out her contract."

"Wait, you were what?" Boris asked confused, "How do you even know the Hunter?"

I had to be careful. I didn't want to give away that I was the droid they were looking for, but I knew they already had their suspicions.

"I'm a traveler. I met her north of here a long time ago. I've always had my eyes on that one," I told him, lying like a rug.

"Her price is 800,000 credits," Boris said, "Plus loss of last night's profits, another 24,000 credits. My cousin there paid top dollar to be the first to break in the smug, sadistic bitch."

"I think your price is too high," I said, trying not to choke on the man's greed. "She was sold to you over a debt of 400,000 credits, some of which she already paid off with the forfeiture of her own credits and property. Besides, why all the hardware? You two expecting trouble?"

Both Magnus and Boris looked at me wide eyed. Yes, dudes, I talked to the woman, it isn't hard to get this info. I am not a random element in this town any longer. More than anything, I felt sort of insulted that they thought I was stupid. Like they could come in here with their suits of power armor and ninja wannabes with electrified tridents. Note to self, avoid electrical pointy things. There's more of them, and my shield would discharge with the first stabby pokey incident.

I could see that my question had caught both of them off guard. Were they looking for or expecting trouble?

"Alice, can you hack the sentient computers in the power armor if they decide to open the show? They'd cut me in half with those chain guns," I asked her mentally.

I can manage to overwhelm one or two at a time. You are going to have to talk your way out of this if you can't fight them all. I don't recommend the fighting bit.

"What is your counter offer then?" Magnus asked, looking between Boris and me.

"You keep what you can. More than once I've heard this here. I think my business here in town is almost done, so I'll keep her and then move on. There's no way I'm paying 824,000 credits for a woman. That's out of control," I told them in English.

"Some say *she* is out of control," Magnus said, "How is it that you think you can control her?"

"She comes at me with a knife as foreplay," I told them. "I'm not worried she's going to hurt me, she isn't good enough of a fighter for me to worry about."

Did I mention the room was quiet? I shouldn't have said that, and Moss would kick my ass if word of what I'd just said got back to her... but I was banking on her own badass reputation to put a little fear into the men that were standing in front of me with various weapons. My words were working, but I couldn't see the expressions of those in the power armor.

"600,000 credits and I pay my cousin's 24,000 credit refund," Boris said.

"That's still too high, and I still don't have that. I'll keep what I can. Kinda the informal law around here, Boris."

"No, you will not." His tone was icy, and I saw

people check their grips and the tridents went a little higher with a renewed confidence. The power armored peeps just stood there. It was if those guns started spinning up that I was going to have a problem.

"So you going to try to take her from me?" I asked him, "What, with all of these men? You'd look weak in front of the ville."

"That's why I am going to formally challenge you to the arena. Winner takes all. You win, you keep the psychotic whore. You lose? You belong to me."

Tony—

"Shut up Alice." I turned to Magnus. "What if I just walk with the woman?"

"You are familiar with the 'Keep what you can' portion of our rules here in town. The other is you cannot refuse a dispute or challenge for the arena. Quite often the thought of going into the arena as the one challenged has been enough to stop disputes. Beating on somebody is one thing," Magnus said looking at the man on the ground who was silent now, "It's quite another when you must survive three rounds in the ring and the challenger gets to choose."

"Huh. So if I can't refuse and this is a winner take all…" I looked around the brothel.

"You do not have the same resources he does to challenge. It could be said that Moss is too much of a prize for you, but I don't think so. She is troublesome. A loose cannon. Either you or Boris owns and manages her. I no longer want the responsibility. What I do want, is to keep this ville safe and have it run without any more injuries or loss of life to productive members of society."

Both men looked at Boris's cousin and then back at me.

Tony, I don't think this is a good idea, twice now we've been warned about... Alice's words were drowned out by the quiet murmurs as the people around us realized that there wasn't going to be more bloodshed.

"Winner takes all then?" I asked.

CHAPTER 11

Magnus and the hired muscle left, and I was left standing in front of a furious Boris.

"So, looks like you and I are going to settle our differences in a different way. You aren't man enough to go one on one, are you?"

Boris proved to be as fast as his cousin, and I caught a bitch slap right in the kisser. It didn't quite break my neck, but it made me sprawl out backward, almost hitting the seven hundred pound woman who acted as the door greeter. It was pretty undignified, and I felt like an ass. I hopped up, ready to get the party started with the brothel keeper but he was already walking away, his back to me. He held up his left hand in the universal gesture of a one fingered salute.

"Magnus left this," the woman said, handing me a

small slip of paper.

I took it and read it. *Be at the arena in one hour. Three rounds. First round uses a knife, second round choice of one gun. Third round you can use all your weapons.* This was going to be awkward… and with Henry gone, I would have to ask around to figure out where to go. In the meantime, I wanted to find Moss and ask her about what to expect.

"I uh… Thanks," I told the woman lamely and walked out, the paper crumpled in my right hand.

Alice put up a countdown timer in my HUD, and I set off towards the hotel. I didn't need Alice to put up a waypoint for me, but I knew it would be a bit of a walk, so I did so in a hurry. People got out of the way, and the usually smiling happy go lucky folks parted. I didn't know if it was because I was double timing it with a grim expression on my face, or the fact that I had pulled the shotgun off the sling and was armed heavily enough that the king of the ville had brought heavies to enforce his will.

If somebody wanted to jump out and ambush me, I was giving them plenty of opportunities, but I wanted to get back to the room. My stomach grumbled its displeasure, and I decided that I would eat later - if I was still alive. Coming up on the hotel and my room, I was reaching for the handle when it opened, and Moss grabbed the front of my vest and yanked me in. I almost lost my balance, and the first thing I did was make sure she didn't have a knife out. Clear.

"What have you done?" she hissed.

"I didn't have a choice. Besides, how did you hear?" I asked her.

AWAKENED CONTROL

"I was standing in the window waiting when Boris and Magnus came down the street with what looked like twenty men. Exosuits and all."

"Yeah, they weren't too happy… Neither is Boris's cousin, to be honest." I admitted.

"Yuri? What did you do to him?"

"Well," I said, waffling a little bit, "He was disappointed in not being the first to… um… anyways we had a disagreement."

"Is he still alive? He holds a lot of power and influence with the factions in the black markets…"

"Oh yeah, he's alive. I gave him a break. He's probably on his way to a healer actually."

A break? I kill me.

You're an idiot, Alice said dryly.

"Healer? My God, you idiot."

She's got good judgement.

"So tell me about the arena?" I asked, ignoring both.

"Wait what?" Moss asked.

She'd cocked a fist back, and I hoped that she'd been about ready to punch me in the shoulder, but this was Moss here we were talking about. That fist might have been aimed at my nose. My words stilled her, and she dropped her arm.

"The arena. Here," I said and handed her the paper.

She read it and cursed.

"How long do you have?" she asked.

Alice told me.

"Thirty-nine minutes twenty-two seconds," I replied, "Before I'm supposed to be there."

BOYD CRAVEN

"It's an all or nothing challenge?"

I nodded.

"Then we have to go, and go now," she said, pushing me away from her towards the door.

I opened it and stepped outside. "Ok, so we'll go, but I thought you couldn't be seen…"

"It doesn't matter at this point. If you lose, they still get me. This way I can see what you put your life and your ARC at risk for."

Yeah, that wasn't what I'd intended, but it was how it had played out. She took off running, and I did too. I had a handful of food gels left in my dump pouch, so I pulled out two of those and sucked them dry as we ran. Alice told me that since we wanted to remain a secret she couldn't heal me all the way as I took injuries. She could if it was life threatening, but didn't recommend it unless I wasn't worried about outing the fact I was what these folks called a precursor augment.

About twenty minutes later, Moss slowed, her chest heaving as she breathed in deeply. A crowd had started forming up around a building, and bodies were hard pressed together.

"Is that it?" I asked her, trying not to notice the sweat-sheened skin in front of me.

"Yeah."

"So what can I expect?"

"First round is beasts. Could be trackers, maybe snarlers or grabbers. No Vorryn, nobody likes those, except the wastelanders who think the meat is a delicacy. Next round is generally criminals, killers, rapists or people who've gone so far into debt that they sold themselves to the arena to pay it off. If they win their round, their debts are repaid some. Work enough challenges, and they can walk out of here Scott free."

"And the third round?" I asked her.

"It's a champion. Boris could fight this round himself, but he won't... I don't know who Boris will pick, he's got many, many he can pay for to fight this. Most people never get past the first, and rarely the second."

"Let me see your wrist," I said, pushing my sleeve back and punching on the wallet watch face as we moved forward with the crush of the crowd.

She did, and I tapped mine on hers, depositing half of the credits I had.

"If I go down and you decide to flee, there's some walking around money," I told her.

"You're an asshole," she spat, "you've been a problem for me ever since..."

There was the fire I was used to. I grinned and watched her look at the wallet's LED face. She looked up at me puzzled.

"Is it not enough?" I asked.

"You know, if you stayed in a hovel, you could live a long, long time on this."

"Yeah, I sorta kinda emptied Yuri's when I beat him senseless. Keep what you can."

She nodded and then pulled on my sleeve. I followed, and she led me to a door off to the side of where the crowd was going. It looked to be an old building from my time. It was partially cinder block, part brick, and almost two stories tall. There was rubble all around it, and I was surprised to see patches of rough asphalt underneath the dirt in places.

"Yer bets?" The man asked.

"All of it," I said without thinking about it, and held out my wrist.

The man tapped a credit card sized reader on my wallet face and then he asked me who I wanted to place my bet on.

"What odds are they giving the Traveler?" I asked.

"Twenty-three to one."

His breath was so bad it would kill a camel, but he didn't hesitate and though Moss looked surprised, she nodded to me.

"Bet it all on the Traveler."

"Your loss, my friend," the man said, and then looked up and got sight of me, for real this time.

He blanched.

"You're him."

"I'm me," I agreed.

"They are looking for you. Inside here. Your lady friend… Oh, dear God."

The man had been looking at me and had barely glanced at Moss, but when he did, he stepped back into the doorway and stumbled.

"We go in there?" I asked her.

"Yes."

We went. The noise inside the building was deafening. Moss explained in near shouts that they charged a nominal fee to get in, but the real moneymakers were men like the one at the door. Bets. Ahhh, it felt good to be right out of the Old Testament sometimes. Our very own version of Sodom and Gomorrah mixed with Roman times, and I was about to be the colosseum Gladiator. Great…

What I walked into was not what I expected, at all. The building we had entered was a high school gym. It still had vestiges of the wooden floor from the basketball court in patches, but it was bare chipped and marred concrete in other areas. The bleachers from the school were pulled all the way out, and there was a large section in the center. It was separated by the bleachers by way of a set of chain-link fencing that was set eighteen inches apart, topped with razor wire. The whole fence was almost thirty feet tall, and I shuddered to think what they had to worry about climbing that mess. Still, if it kept the spectators safe…

Inside the arena, there were wooden crates, a small shipping container that was open on both ends and lots and lots of old blood stains. I looked around to the two areas where the fencing stopped, and one was in the locker rooms. I could hear inhuman sounds coming out of the boy's locker room.

"What's to stop bullets from hitting the crowd?" I shouted to Moss looking up at the ceiling to see how the place was lit.

"Force shield. The chain is there to prevent the fighters from escaping. The shield stops any projectiles from hitting the people betting and watching."

The ceiling held the arc-sodium lights that had been normal in school gyms all across the world. How they even had light bulbs for these was mind blowing. Then again, I was about to fight to the death with a ton of people, and I had no idea what I was really going to be facing.

BOYD CRAVEN

"Good, I was hoping I wasn't going to have to send out my Outsiders to come pick you up," Magnus said, coming out of the crowd and walking to us.

"No, we're both here."

Moss went totally silent, but the look she was giving Magnus told me all she wanted to say. Disgust, anger, and hate were washing over her features.

"If you have credits to bet, you should do so before I let you in. Once I do, the games begin," he said walking up to a narrow spot where a human-sized gate had been installed.

"I already did, outside," I told him.

Magnus winced. "Better odds in here. You're at thirty to one now."

Dammit.

"Now, leave all your gear outside, save blades, for this first round. If you survive this round, your choice will be given to you and, after a two-minute rest, the next match will start. If you survive that round, then the remaining supplies of yours will be given to you, with a ten minute rest period."

"It's so they have time for the barkers to place more bets with the crowd. The payoffs are automatic, one of the only times that the Outsiders let the net tech work on our wallets," Moss told me, her eyes never leaving Magnus's face.

"Has any challenger ever survived three rounds?" I asked Magnus.

"Only one other," he said, and looked over my shoulder.

I turned and saw he was staring at Moss. No wonder this woman had a fierce reputation. She'd done what she'd had to early on in life, literally buying her way out of a horrid existence with her Stalker armor… then she'd gone into the arena, survived, and become one of the most successful hunters running a squad for one of the most brutal men on this side of the apocalypse. No wonder she was unhinged and thought a good knife fight was a precursor to a wild time in the sack.

I started stripping off my pack and laid out my long guns, leaning them against the chain link wall separating the crowd from us in what looked like a narrow passageway leading to the center. My blood was pounding. Alice assured me I'd had more than enough calories and if I had any more, my body would waste it. I was still hungry, but I would use that to remind myself I was still alive, and when I got out of here I was going to have a big huge breakfast of ham and eggs, sausage with some sourdough toast and…

Stop it, you're killing me, Alice quipped. *Those food packets give you the calories, but your stomach is still cramping.*

She was right. I stopped at biscuits and gravy and focused. I made sure I still had the stiletto, but was surprised when Moss reached behind her back and pulled out the twin knives she'd tried to get all lovey dovey on me with. She spun them around with each hand and then handed them to me, handles first. The flourish was something even I didn't know how to do; she must have been a lot more skilled than I had seen or given her credit for. That sent me down a rabbit hole wondering if she'd been holding back on me, but

BOYD CRAVEN

I shut that away. Not going to fall in love with some-body right before I become a snack or a pink mist, depending on how the matches went.

"Thank you. I'll give these back to you soon," I told her.

"I'd wish you luck, but I don't think you need it," she said with a straight face.

The look of anger was gone for half a second when she met my gaze, but as soon as she turned back to Magnus, the Eye of Baylor was back on again.

"Ready?" Magnus asked, opening the gate.

"Let's do it," I said walking into the arena and, for the first time, I heard the crowd's roar.

I didn't know if I had been just tuning it out, but it seemed to have doubled in volume. I flipped the knife in my left hand into a reverse grip, a standard one with my right hand and rolled my shoulders and twisted my neck. I twisted side to side and watched the other end of the arena where the howls had grown louder.

This is not a video game, Alice reminded me.

"I know. Do your part like we talked about. Let me do the killing. And can you tune some of this out for me? I still want to hear Moss and the –"

"Ladies and Gentlemen!" A voice boomed out of the pre-apoc sound system, making everyone sit down as I walked to the center of the arena. "Today we are here to settle a grievance, a bet. The Traveler is charged with theft of property, and has been chal-lenged by Boris."

As the words echoed around the gym, and the shouts grew louder. The speaker continued, "Boris has promised that if this Traveler and Wastelander wins the first round, that he has something special for round three, so place your bets and remember… the only good Vorryn—"

"IS A DEAD VORRYN!" the crowd shouted back.

"Man, they really hate those bugs," I said.

"You ain't kidding. I'm picking up a lot of network traffic over the wireless here. I'm going to be busy, I want to analyze this, it looks good."

The basketball buzzer went off, loud and obnoxious. I saw movement, and the gate on the far side of the arena burst open as large shapes came bursting through. I had seen these before, or at least something like them. The crew that had been coming after me called them Trackers, but I thought of them as dogs. Big ass dogs. Well, these weren't Trackers, these were bigger. I counted four of them, all spread out. They caught sight of me and two of them flattened their heads and doubled their speed.

The timing on this was going to suck. The two dogs were now coming at me from different angles, both lined up to hit me about the same time if they both leaped. I had seconds to act before I had to worry about the slower dogs. I saw one bunch up its muscles, and its hind end dropped, and I started my move. I put my right foot forward and swung Moss's heavy bowie style knife in my right hand and pulled the left hand up in front of my throat to protect it with my forearm and cold steel.

The spacing of the bottom of the dog's mouth and its chest was an area that seemed to have narrowed to an inch wide as the demon beasts' leaps brought them at me as if in slow motion. My knife sank into its chest, between its shoulders. That didn't stop the momentum of the beast, though. Its combined weight and the weight of the second dog hit me at the same instant, and I was bowled over by three or four hundred pounds of slavering, drooling dog. The first one bit at my forearm a couple of times as I hit the ground, almost knocking the wind out of me. The second one went for my throat.

I moved my left hand a bit, slashing at the dog's snout, and it yelped and backed off half a step. My cut had sliced it across a nose that was the size of my fist. I yanked with my right hand and felt the knife give. Already the dog was coming back, cut nose or not, and my left hand was pushed down as the dog used its body weight and paw to step on my arm. My right hand flashed out as I tensed and I flexed my body, trying to throw it off me. It yelped in pain again, and that's when shit went sideways.

Something grabbed me by the ankle. If I hadn't been wearing heavy combat boots, it might have bitten my foot off at the ankle. I was yanked backward, and the dog that had been going for my throat was thrown clear. I saw a deep gash across the front of its chest, though I had missed the throat. Something grabbed my left arm and vice-like jaws tried to rip it loose from the joint. The shield kept the fangs from me for now, but nothing could be done about the crushing and pulling force of the beast. The third dog entered the fray, and its teeth would have bit my arm in two if I didn't still have the shield generator. Yeah, they hadn't commented on it, and I wasn't going to offer. Boris and Magnus could suck it. I kicked out with my free leg, hearing something crunch over the crowd's roars and rolled towards my left side where the dog was trying to rip my arm off. I watched the shield tick down towards zero and knew I had to do something fast. It shook its head like a terrier would with a rat, and the knife went flying.

The move didn't make the dog back off, only back up and then it tried to drag me. The dogs were trained and pack hunters, obviously. I kicked out again and felt the death grip on my ankle gone. I twisted one leg over the other and got to my knees. The dog held on, so I swung my right hand, burying the knife to the hilt in the dog's skull. It fell, lifeless, as I got to my feet and picked up the dropped knife. I didn't have time to pull the other one free. The one with the slashed chest was advancing on me, as well as the one I'd kicked. Blood came out of its nostrils, and the skin was ripped over the gums on one side as the hard bottom of my boot must have ripped it open on its teeth.

"Good doggy," I said, and heard my voice bounce out across the arena.

I heard roars of laughter and the two dogs advanced on me, and I backed up slowly, switching the knife from my right hand to my left. I checked my forearm and found dog slobber, but no puncture wounds. Every second I held these two off, the longer my shield had to recharge. Two seconds, three. Both were snarling, dripping blood.

"Hey, if you two just play fetch like good dogs, I'll get ya each a can of Alpo. No?" I reached into my left sleeve and pulled the stiletto out. Another gift from Moss.

Remember when I said there were crates and boxes and a shipping container and all kinds of stuff that was meant to be for cover? Well, I didn't remember it. A crate about knee height had been directly behind me, and I went over backwards, the way the dogs had been herding me. Both leaped, one going high, one low. The one who went for my ankle the first time latched onto my leg above the knee. It was as if the dog knew where the femoral artery was. He almost wrenched my hip out of socket as he tore at me. I slashed and cut at him as the second dog grabbed me by the armpit.

He's got your vest, concentrate on the one on the leg, Alice said, sounding panicked.

I stabbed outwards when the dog let go for half a heartbeat for a new grip, and I hit the animal at the base of the head, on the side behind the ear. It wasn't a killing strike but the dog howled in pain and backed off. The one tearing at my vest didn't have a good grip, and I jabbed it in the side of the throat with the stiletto. Its snarls went to whimpers, and as soon as it let go, I rolled backward, regaining my feet. I repositioned the knives, the larger bowie in my left hand in a reverse grip, held in front of my throat, with the smaller but twice as sharp stiletto in my right.

The dog I stabbed was staggering, and I saw it losing copious amounts of blood, and I was soaked in it. Good job, shield generator. Protect me from sharp stuff and projectiles but not from getting my leg ripped off, or the blood of foul beasts.

AWAKENED CONTROL

Don't complain, you'd be dead or exposed other-wise. PS, good strategy on letting the shields regen. Is that why you aren't going to finish—

I stomped hard. The dog that had been staggering around caught the blow, and went down stunned. I stomped again, and it was over. Brutal, and I hated to do it, but it was suffering. The other dog I had slashed at was laying on its side. What I hadn't thought of a killing blow must have done it in after all. The scoreboard buzzer went off, signaling the end of the round. Alice turned my hearing back up, and I could hear people in the crowds screaming and chanting. One word over and over. With a start, I realized it was my name. I got Moss's other knife from the dog's skull and people swarmed the killing field to clear out the bodies.

My hip hurt and Alice was working on it, but I limped over to my corner where Magnus was waiting for me at the gate. He cracked it open, and I handed the blades through to a stunned Moss.

"Sorry, there's blood on 'em still," I said by way of a breathless apology.

I'd already sheathed my stiletto, so I was now considering my guns. Which should I bring? "How many am I facing and will they be armed as well?"

"Yes, most of them will have something. Probably not firearms, but it depends on what Boris was willing to pay for. Knowing him, he probably has the men outfitted with spears and slings," Magnus told me.

Moss grunted. "Cheap bastard."

I hoped they were right. I considered the LRG, but decided that was a big fat nope sammich. It took too long to recharge. The pistol was ok, but sucked for any kind of range. Really good for close quarters. I could do well with a pistol, but it wasn't what I'd practiced the most with. I was really good with an M4, but there were none here. Which left me with…

"The shotty?" Moss asked as I picked it up and dug through my pack.

"Yeah."

I unloaded it completely and then reloaded it. Buckshot, buckshot, slug and then repeated the pattern until I had eight in the tube and one in the chamber. Then I put two handfuls of buckshot into my dump pouch and closed that up with a snap.

"You… four of them. I thought they had you dead twice over," Moss said, suddenly noticing the blood across my face, neck, and chest.

I let her paw at me and Magnus handed me an earthenware mug. I drank deep. It was that ale again. It was refreshing, and Alic negated the alcohol content. I needed a clear head. I handed him the mug back and let out a belch. I gently pushed Moss back, weirded out that she'd gone all girly for the first time ever.

"I'll be fine. I'm sore, but they didn't hurt me too badly," I reassured her.

"You're an asshole, you dimwitted, growler farting, shit speckled, packi humping—"

Magnus busted up laughing, and a buzzer went off. This wasn't the loud one, but it sounded more like a hockey buzzer. Magnus opened up the gate, and I walked out into the arena and started double-timing it towards the shipping container. It was on an angle, and if the criminals came out the way they'd let the dogs out, then I could get set with a defensive advantage. I didn't want to get skewered or beamed in the head with a rock. The one I took in the chest a while back hurt and would have probably killed me if I wasn't a cyborg of sorts. Having more than one hit me at the same time could probably overload the shield generator.

"Yes, it most likely will."

I got ready, and was near the edge of the container when the loud buzzer went off, signaling the start of the fight. The locker room was too far for me to chance a shot with the shotgun, and I'll be honest... I wasn't comfortable with shooting with people in the background, but I'd been assured that they were protected. One more thing, remember when Moss had said Boris was a cheap bastard? Well, she was wrong. That or he wanted her badly... or he really, REALLY wanted me dead. Maybe all of that... Four men came striding out. Three of them had guns, or what looked like guns. I could tell they were new materials, but they looked like a home built SMGs you'd sometimes see the cartels in South America using.

The three had combat vests on with full magazines, and I let out a curse as they opened up. I, of course, ducked back behind the container and hit the dirt, but not before seeing two more men walk out from the locker room. Shit, shit, shit, shit, shit. Holes punched through the container as the SMGs blew through close to a hundred rounds at the corner of the thin sheet metal container I was hiding behind. One came close, and I was peppered with paint flakes and metal shavings. One by one, the guns went silent during what had to be mag changes. I rolled to my right and around the corner aimed where the concentrated fire had come from.

They were all there, slapping at magazines, one already having seated a new one. The empty mags were left on the ground. He was target number one. Boom, chick, chock, boom… and I put another round downrange. The first man was literally blown backward as he caught the buckshot in the chest. Guess the vest wasn't bulletproof. The second hastily fired shot hit the second man in the arms and head. Dumbass hadn't gotten familiar with the weapon and was holding it up at eye level trying to insert the magazine. I pumped the shotgun and was firing the third round when I was hit high up on the left shoulder. My collar bone snapped from the impact, and I screamed in pain and rage. My third round had been a slug, and I was going to center mass. I fell as he did. Hitting the ground ignited blazing hot fire in my back.

A round object was falling off my chest as I tried to roll over with my right hand. It was a round chunk of sandstone. Someone had nailed me with a sling. I pushed back with my legs until I was wedged back into the shipping container with a large crate in front of me for cover.

"Alice, can you fix that but leave a bruise?" I asked her mentally, gasping in pain.

Yes, it's still going to hurt, but you'll have full use of your arm again. Right now, you probably could, but the pain is too overwhelming. I can shut that down instead…

AWAKENED CONTROL

"Do both, Alice," I said mentally.

Straighten out your left arm, she said, and I did, and I felt something warm and then a click.

The pain was intense, and despite her best efforts I almost passed out from the shock. I didn't have time though because as I was pumping the empty out of the shotgun and a fresh shell into the chamber, another chunk of rock exploded, glancing off the side of my head and shattering against the shipping container. It made me dodge back when I caught sight of the projectile and that might have kept me from taking it between the eyes, but what it did do was ring my bell. I kept looking and wiped my hand across my left temple near my scar. It came back red and bloody.

"Might as well leave that one alone too," I told her.

I saw movement, the side of an arm swinging a piece of leather, with the pocket holding something rounded and heavy. I rolled to my left, bringing the shotgun up, and let off a shot. The man went down in a fountain of gore, and I stood up. I pumped it, putting a fresh shell in. I looked around warily now. I had seen five enter, but that didn't mean one or two more held back. In fact, I'd almost missed seeing sling boy and mister sword man. I looked around, but everywhere I looked I could see the crowd. They were going crazy.

Their shouts were loud too. I felt around in my dump pouch and came up with a few shells. Definitely not what I'd started with. I started thumbing them into the bottom of the Mossberg, still looking around. Brass and red plastic caught my attention near the edge of the shipping container. I looked all around me and saw nothing. I walked forward and knelt down and grabbed the few shells that came out, acting like I was some sort of video game hero, and started putting them in the pouch when a big dude with two swords walked around the corner.

He was massively scarred, wearing some sort of leather vest, his arms free for the world to see. One of them had a recently healed slash that was still angry red looking, and I could see the white lines across his knuckles and the back of his hands from numerous cuts that had healed. This dude seriously knew what he was doing if he looked like that and was still in the arena. He started advancing on me, with those ridiculous curved swords. It reminded me of something, and I started giving ground, making sure this time not to trip myself up. It was bad enough to do it once, have everyone laugh and almost die… but doing it twice?

Without letting him out of sight, I checked the arena for others. So far, he was the only one still standing. Through it all, the smell of cordite and black powder was almost as overwhelming as the smell of the freshly dead. That's never pleasant, death. Blood and feces and all other manner of unspeakable things… but it's an unmistakable thing. Hopefully, the bloodthirsty audience was getting the same whiff I was, and the shield wasn't holding that back. For a moment, I hated the audience for coming, for watching my potential death. The death of these criminals and the Trackers earlier. How barbaric. How horrible. How necessary. Then it left me because I knew that this might have been an outcome in my gamble and I had willingly rolled the dice.

I see what you see, Tony, Alice said. *He's the only one left unless more came out and your head wasn't turned.*

"You see all the peripheral stuff, not just the stuff I focus on then, right?" I asked her mentally.

Yes, what I'm saying is… Oh God, you're going to Indiana Jones this guy, aren't you? Alice asked me in a dry mental voice.

I'd stopped about fifteen feet away from my gate, Magnus, and Moss. The man started doing some sort of complex movement with the swords. A flourish, or kata, I couldn't be sure. His footwork was impressive. I didn't know if his aggressive display was supposed to intimidate me, scare me into submission or if it was an act for the crowd but…

BOOM.

He fell hard, and one of the swords snapped in half from where it'd been hit by my shot. The top half had embedded itself into the man's head, but he'd already been dead. The buzzer sounded, and the gate swung back. I stepped into the waiting area as workers swarmed the stage to start the retrieval process. I walked to my pack and topped off my shotgun again. I put the Beretta back in the cross-draw holster and was reaching for the LRG when I noticed something.

"Where's Moss?" I asked a very silent Magnus.

"Placing a bet. Suddenly the odds were not so good on you any more. You're down to a two to one."

"That's a good thing then, yeah? They think I've got a good chance of winning?" I asked.

Magnus, leader of the Outsiders, the man who

BOYD CRAVEN

had brought so much suffering into this area... allowed the enslavement of people... allowed women and young women to be used on a rotational base for his followers... He handed me a beer. I drank deeply from the earthenware jug again.

Stop drinking that! Alice shouted, *Poison!*

My head swam, and I dropped the crock. It shattered, and my boots were soaked with the remains of the ale.

"What's wrong?" Magnus asked with a grin.

I reached for the LRG and staggered. Magnus pushed me over to a bench that had been installed on our side of the fence, and I fell down onto it, landing on my ass roughly. It felt like I had drunk an entire fifth of Everclear in one go and all the booze was hitting at once. I knew I was supposed to have ten minutes to rest and them to clean up between matches, but I felt legit like passing out.

Tony, I'm working as fast as I can. It's a poison and a narcotic much like opium that was laced with that alcohol.

"Moss is she. Girl is now, he take?" I asked aloud, slurring everything.

"You know, Tony," Magnus said with a grin, "Some of the betting now even has you favored. I never thought you would get this far, but I haven't seen this much money changing hands in a long time. See, not only did you piss Boris off, I was surprised that he paid big credits to see you dead. At first, it was all about your psychotic serial killer of a girlfriend, but you did something to him that drove him over the edge."

"Wazzat?" I asked him, wiping the drool off the

side of my mouth with my forearm.

"You showed him indifference and a basic lack of respect," Magnus said so softly that I almost lost his words in the screams of the crowds. "So when you die out there, we'll find your girlfriend, and she'll be put back to work. And your death? It'll have enriched the lives of the ville. You'll be one less variable for me to worry about."

I tried to stand, but my head swam.

"Alice, can you speed this up?" I asked her, realizing that my thoughts were already a little clearer.

Yes, I'm stopping the poison from shutting down your organs, but I'm working on the opiates at the same time. Two minutes and you'll be in good shape.

"How much time do I have left?" I asked her.

You were told ten minutes, it looks like four minutes remain in your break. Plenty of time. You got this.

"Now, it's bad enough that Boris went and hired one of my Augments," Magnus said, "with his resources and riches… but can you imagine what would happen… if you were to have insulted me? Oh, wait… you have…"

Magnus started laughing and walked away, leaving me alone. People were reaching for me between the double walled fence, screaming. Encouraging. Wishing death on me. I felt like death. Where was Moss? Could she help? Augment? I was fighting one of their futuristic CEPMs or cyborgs? I didn't even know their capabilities. I know there were other upgrades that they had in mind for me, but I don't know if it's software, hardware or to Alice's programming or…

"You're high. Just focus on the task at hand—"

The buzzer went off.

Sonofabitch! Alice swore, *that's early. I need one minute and thirty more seconds to clear your motor functions of the opiates and toxins.*

I wobbled to my feet and reached for the LRG.

"I need a red dot, I need all the help I can get," I told Alice.

I can do that, she said, and in the HUD overlay in my vision, a small red dot, almost like a laser sight would show lit up. It was the direction the weapon in my hand was aimed.

And it was aimed… well, my hands weren't steady, and I was stumbling, and the dot danced across everything from the floor to the ceiling, the crowd… It was like a Pink Floyd laser light show. Damn.

The shipping container had been hooked up to some cables. It'd happened when I hadn't been watching, and it was lifted a good twenty or thirty feet in the air and out of the way. Both doors had been closed and seeing my best piece of cover now gone I knew the game was rigged. I was never meant to get a fair shot here. If the rumors were true, Magnus was older than he looked by a large degree, something to consider at another time. He probably had set this whole thing up to make sure that Boris got what he wanted and was happy… and he used these games here to enrich himself. Hell, he'd all but hinted at that when he'd mentioned how the betting had flip flopped and then he stacked the deck himself.

I heard something over the screams of the crowd. I looked to the side where the locker rooms were, and something stepped and then dragged… stepped and dragged. Stepped and dragged. The crowd went silent all at once, but the murmurs you'd expect to hear when something surprising or shocking happened didn't come. The monstrosity that came out was man sized, roughly. Maybe it had been a man a long time ago, but what I saw chilled me. The creature's entire right side seemed to have once been flesh and bone, but was now replaced with crude metal equivalents.

It would take a step with its human leg, and then the metal leg would come up some, and it would turn its body to drag the cyborg portion that didn't seem to be working right.

"Easy peasy lemon squee-"

Then shit went sideways. I didn't know how much of what I had been seeing was an act, but it suddenly moved fast. Inhumanly fast. See, I hadn't seen any weapons in its hands or strapped to the front of it so when I saw the lame cyborg coming out of the dark it had made me wonder why everyone was in awe of this creature who could barely move. Yeah, you now know why I was surprised as it moved faster than my jaw could hit the floor and took me by the vest and threw me.

I hit the chain-link almost ten feet up in the air. If I had hit a pole instead of the middle of the section, I would have been paralyzed. Instead, I was just hurt. Bad.

"Status?" I asked Alice as I hit the ground and got the wind knocked out of me.

I wheezed and struggled. Breath wasn't coming yet.

I need thirty more seconds. Quit taking damage, so

I can focus on—

It grabbed me by the vest again and lifted me off my feet and held me up over its head slightly so it could look up at me. Its cybernetic arm didn't have a normal hand. Instead, it looked like three pinchers. It was digging into my chest painfully, and I saw a light blue glow from its eyes. Half its hair had been shaven off, and a scar ran across the top of the head where the hair was parted. So it did have some sort of implant….

Just not a fully functioning AI - this guy is getting controlled by someone wirelessly.

I couldn't hear her, though, not over the now ringing in my head because the best had head-butted me and me once again found myself flying. It had thrown me with the clawed hand, and for half a second I wondered if it was how birds felt. The thrill of moving effortlessly through the air. Look ma, no hands! Yeah, no. Not fun. I hit a crate with my back and shattered it. Wooden shards pierced me in a couple of spots on my leg and the back of my left shoulder.

Shield generator overloaded. Focus on him and let me finish! Alice shouted.

"Maximum effort," I told her, aiming.

You stole that line from Deadpool, Alice chided as the cyborg started the slow step drag.

Maybe the creature had an on-off switch and couldn't do full bore badass all at once. And maybe I was once performing in a Muppet showgirl fan club. No really, I wasn't. That was totally a joke. I lifted the LRG and fired. The bolt flew at supersonic speeds and hit the colossus in the nuts. Or well, where I thought his sack would be. It fell forward, cupping its jewels, and I made my way to my feet. I held the LRG up in my right hand, and fist pumped with my left.

"And the crowd goes wild," I said, grinning.

Shield generator back online, toxins and opiates neutralized, Alice told me.

"Good," I said, reaching down with my left hand and pulled the wooden shard out of my leg.

An inch of it was bloody, and I asked Alice to slow the bleeding, but this was something obvious that I needed to not have miraculously heal on its own. If they wanted me dead now, what would happen if those glorious ass biscuits knew I had a full CEPM suite?

Cut me out of your head, Alice said. *Hey, I did notice something. I can break into this cyborg's signal. Want me to try to disrupt it?*

"Dammit, you're just telling me this now? Yes, hell yes!" I yelled aloud.

The creature was getting to its feet. Its eyes were glowing cobalt, and I half expected it to shoot lasers out of its eyes like it was Scott Summers or something. It stepped and stomped, and I looked around. The LRG had been recharged for half a heartbeat now, and I took aim and fired. The shot was on target and took the cyborg in the temple. Flesh shredded away to show the skull. The gleaming stainless steel skull. It reached up with its human hand and ripped the pseudo-flesh off, so it didn't hang in front of its eye. It was rubbery in texture, and I saw a silvery streak where the LRG's projectile had ricocheted off its skull. No dent. So not stainless steel. Something stronger.

I dropped the LRG and unslung the shotgun. I

did a quick visual to see if the barrel bent or if it was functional. I'd been getting my ass beat and it was possible that it'd taken a ton of— but no, it hadn't. I checked the safety and started pumping rounds into the creature from thirty feet away. More of the fake flesh shredded, but nothing seemed to have an effect as I ran the shotgun dry. The creature had advanced another fifteen feet, and fifteen feet was all that separated us.

It's about to charge, Alice told me.

"Interrupt it," I yelled to her mentally.

I dropped the shotgun and pulled the Beretta and took aim. Once more, I shot the creature in its naughty bits. Its hands dropped down to the cup itself, and I changed my aim upwards. I started firing at one of the cables that had been used to wrench the storage container up. The creature started blurring, as whatever had been controlling it got past Alice's efforts to block it, just as my sixth bullet was enough to part the metal cable and the big container swung down drunkenly, one remaining cable holding up an end.

I thought it would have thrown the creature, but instead, it hit it the way a hammer hits a nail. Yes, it swung down, but the tension of the cable prevented it from hitting the ground, and the container bounced back up like the cable was a spring for a moment and then dropped on the thing's head as the second cable snapped. Slowly, it fell over sideways, half exposing the cyborg. I realized there had been absolute silence and suddenly, there wasn't. The crowd was going nuts.

"That's going to leave a mark," I said to the silent crowd.

AWAKENED CONTROL

Tony, I have to shut down, somebody is trying to hack me, I…

All the pain that she had been blocking hit me all at once. The wounds in my leg, my back that felt broken in a dozen places… the four inch chunks of wood in my shoulder. My chest that had been pulverized by the three clawed hand while it lifted me.

I saw the creature's human arm sticking out from under the container clench a fist and raise an arm up. I panicked for half a second, aiming my half empty pistol at it and held my aim until the arm fell limply to the ground. Then the opening lines of *Disturbed*'s version of The Sound of Silence played in my head… Alice, or memory?

The darkness took me.

CHAPTER
12

"T his is a funny way to finally get to talk to you," an elderly voice said.

My eyes were heavy, and I tried pinging Alice for a status update, but all I got was silence. Twice now. Twice that Alice had been attacked, and I was left alone in my head.

A hand rested on my forehead and rubbed something soft on my temple. Where I had been cut by that rock from the sling thrower? The rag was moved away, and I felt a thumb on my eyelid, gently pushing it open. My vision was blurry, but that had been the kick I needed to come to full awareness. I let out a deep breath and pushed myself to a sitting position, rubbing my eyes and blinking until they were open.

An old man in white robes stood before me. I was on a crude bed, but the sheets smelled fresh. I was stripped down to my underwear, and I could feel the pull of something tight against my shoulder. I felt and found my chest had been wrapped and I could now feel the padding of bandages on my back.

"I said, this is a funny way to finally get to talk to you," the old man repeated.

He was easily the oldest human being I'd ever seen in real life. He had an actual Fu Manchu and wispy bits of white hair. Liver spots covered his already tanned features. His hands shook, but not horribly.

"Where am I?" I asked.

"The Order of the Purists. You were brought here after your ordeal. I am Brother Gregory. You are?" he asked, his voice surprisingly strong for a man so old, and so weak looking.

"Brother Gregory, I go by Tony. How did I get here? And who patched me up?"

"We were tasked with removing you from that foul arena. Magnus forbade any of his healers from touching you. He probably hoped you would die of your injuries, but one of our brothers was there to monitor the godless and saw your plight. He carried you and now, here you are."

"My supplies, my gear—"

"They are in the bureau next to the bed. All weapons, supplies, shield generator and clothing. We are in the process of washing the pants and shirt from all the bloodstains, yours and theirs," a figure said from the doorway off to my far left.

I turned to look and did a double take.

"Brother Luca, this is Tony. Tony, this is the member who carried you to safety, Luca."

"Hello Brother Luca," I said, wondering why Gregory didn't know that me and Luca already knew each other; playing the game?

"Hello, Tony," Luca said, without a trace of recognition.

When the old man turned to look at me, Luca dropped me a wink. Ah hah. It was a game. Got it. If I could only figure out if Alice was hacked or... I tried to sit up more and move my left arm. Ouch.

"It looks as if your collarbone was nearly broken and we pulled out a section of the board from your back, just under the shoulder blade. It's stitched now, but in a week's time it should be fine if there is no infection."

"Thank you, Brother Gregory, for all that you've both done," I said.

I looked to the right of the table and saw an old bureau just like Luca had said, and there was a small end table. A rag floated in a basin of pink water, probably tinged with my blood.

"How bad off am I?" I asked the old man.

"Not so bad. Hopefully, you are feeling well enough to meet with our spiritual leader, Brother Tims?"

"Sure," I said, feeling for my left wrist and finding the watch wallet still there. I pressed a button and looked.

I don't want to say my eyes bugged out, but I'd never really calculated the 23 to 1 odds and what it would do to my finances. I couldn't quite buy myself an exosuit (not that they'd sell me one) but I could stay in a hotel with running water for the foreseeable future. Probably get me some food too.

"Moss," I asked, "Where is she?"

Luca's eyes shot wide open. If he'd been at the arena... but no, they had accused me of theft of property. They hadn't said it was Moss. If Luca had been a regular he probably would have known the backstory on Boris and why he was trying to have me stomped into little Tony paste, but he hadn't been in town long and probably didn't know. The old man's expression hardened and turned into a sneer.

"That godless heathen is not welcome here. We've all been under orders to kill her on sight now for two years after—"

"You might not want to do that," I said swinging my legs off the bed.

My leg was bandaged heavily also and felt the same familiar pulling tightness. Probably stitched too.

"Why is that?" Luca asked from behind me after the sputtering old man couldn't spit out the words.

"Because she's mine. She's what I won in the arena," I told the old man as I got to my feet.

I took an experimental step, and then another. He moved out of the way as I made my way to where my stuff was.

"What? Really?" I asked them and Luca shrugged, while the old man's gaze was shooting daggers at me.

"Really what? You're no better than they are. Slaver. Even the foulest creature, the most depraved one known as Moss deserves her freedom, right after a bullet in the brain," the old man said, and then spit at my feet.

That was funny. What would the old man do if I

told him about her idea of foreplay?

Better not Tony, Alice told me, a happy chirp in her voice.

"Dammit girl, where have you been?" I asked her mentally.

Had to go offline. I have a ton of information but not a ton of time to tell you. Keep your identity secret here for a few... oh damn. Too late.

An older man than Brother Gregory walked in. He was using a cane and had on those old style coke bottle glasses. He shuffled to the bed and flopped on it. His white robes went up as he almost fell over backward and I saw he had on sandals made out of old tires and rope. I grinned as he regained his feet.

Inside the bureau I saw everything as promised, except the clothes. Instead, I found a loose pair of wool pants and a set of white robes much like everyone was wearing.

"Is he awake?" The old man asked, leaning forward to stare six inches from the pillow.

The pillow on the bed I wasn't on. The bed where he would have flopped on me if I'd been still in it. Hilarious.

I pulled on the pants. They were really loose, and I looked around until I saw my belt. I grinned and put that on to hold the pants up and let the extra fabric hang low. Next, I put on my vest and then the shield generator before turning and pulling the robe over my head as the old man smacked the bed feebly trying to find out where I had gone. Luca was trying not to laugh, Gregory was so spitting angry he was speechless.

AWAKENED CONTROL

You're an asshole Tony, but wouldn't it be a better thing to explain to Gregory why you now own Moss?

"I'm over here sir," I said.

The old man turned and looked blindly to where I was, and I approached the bed slowly, as not to alarm Gregory, and sat down.

"Thank you for having me brought here and healed," I told him.

"I hear that you come bearing an unusual scar, one on your left temple?" he asked.

"I do," I said finding his hand and guiding it to the side of my head.

What are you doing? Alice mentally shrieked.

"Ahh yes. Come closer, my eyesight isn't what it used to be."

I leaned forward until we were nose to nose. His eyes opened wide, and a faint blue flash emanated from them.

He's an Augment, Alice said, something weird in her voice. Awe? Terror?

"Ahhh, that's who I thought you were," the old man said.

"You know him?" Gregory asked.

"Yes, please you two, leave us."

"He's a slaver! He consorts with Moss!" Gregory frothed, and I worried the old man was going to have a heart attack.

"Actually," I turned to him, getting sick of his condemnations, "I hate the whole idea of slavery too. Moss was sold to Boris to cover her debts. I just settled them for her. Technically she is my property, but I don't intend to keep her. She is free whenever she so chooses."

I don't know who looked more horrified, Luca or Gregory. Luca knew I knew her and had been absolutely terrified of her. She was, by all accounts, a monster and a horrible human being. She also liked to have wild monkey sex and try to stab me with a knife, but that was neither here nor there… Brother Gregory hated her for his own reasons, and I was thinking that a freed Moss was worse than an enslaved Moss, and my words had had the opposite effect of what I had intended. Ooops.

"I will be fine here," he said, "Leave us now." There was a bark of command in his tone and both nodded and left.

Gregory threw me one more spiteful look as he shuffled out the door and Luca pulled it closed behind him.

"I'm Doctor Nicholas Sparkman… Now CEPM x341. What are you really doing here?"

Oh shit, we've been had, Alice said. *He's one of the scientists from the ARC.*

"What?" I asked her mentally, panicked. "I thought all of them died out and it was their descendants who were left?"

I don't know, but his name was the chief of surgery in your case, Alice told me.

"He's a freaking Augment!" I shrieked mentally.

"What is your AI telling you? I can see by the micro flashes in your eyes that you are communicating." Nicholas told me.

"I don't know what you're talking about, old man," I lied.

"Come now, I'm the one who installed the wet

work in your temple. What did you name it?" he asked me, still too close for comfort.

"Alice," I admitted, "How about yours?"

"Dumbass," he whispered back and grinned. "Really, that's its name, not you."

"What?" I grinned a bit.

He might be on the level, Alice told me. *That light flash of blue was his AI's way of showing who he was. It's a common trait of CEPMs, and later technology.*

"I don't have an advanced quantum computer like yours. When I saw my death was nearing, I set up the surgical suite for myself. I underwent surgery against orders and had myself placed in stasis for the integration. Thus, you see how I am."

"Dude," I said in awe, and he chuckled at the old phrasing. "How old were you when you went into stasis?" I asked him.

"In my sixties. I ended up with an AI computer that was a few generations older than yours. I'm put together with spare parts. We had other tech, but it was under lock and key."

I thought of Magnus, and his abnormally long life. "You aren't the only Precursor Augment in Lakeville, are you?"

A wry smile cracked Nicholas's features, and I saw a few teeth showing as it turned into a smile.

"Sussed that out already, have you?" He asked me, grinning. "It's the reason I've aged so poorly in the last forty years I've been awake. My AI wasn't the latest and greatest. It gets hacked too easy. Magnus already got me once, but I don't think he realized he was inside of me. He just sees me as another in the long line of religious zealots to run the Order of the Purists."

"So it *is* Magnus," I said. "I had my suspicions. So you're still playing catch up with this society too?" I mean, forty years is a long time, but it wasn't like he'd been awake for a thousand.

"Yes, but it's easy when you're a 'spiritual leader,'" he said, making air quotes. "Now, on Magnus, he has, I suspect, the same Quantum computer as you do. I am familiar with your case, and you were not given the full suite of augmentation available to you. Now that you're here, perhaps you can show me the way back to the ARC and we can—"

"I was activated because of the ARC shutting down," I told him simply. "Catastrophic power failure. The automated process keeps getting tripped up, and there's enough juice to do a restart from the battery banks, but that's about it."

"Hm… do you know what it is you need to make repairs?"

"I need some tech," I told him, not wanting to give away the farm.

Part of me wanted to trust the man, but the other part of me also thought that was because I felt a kinship with somebody from my own - even if he looked like death warmed over with outdated coke bottled spectacles.

"How are we safe talking in here?" I asked him, "If Magnus's AI can reach out over the networks?"

There's an electronic shield in place, it's what let me come out of hiding and break off the attack, Alice said, at the same time as Nicholas told me, "Electronic shielding that prevents wireless signals…"

"You were talking about other augmentation. What is it exactly?" I asked him.

"You destroyed the cyborg called Nazareth, I know, I know, like the band… He had a speed augment as well as physical replacements of limbs. He's a hack job, controlled by others, for the most part. He has limited control of the speed augmentation because of the horrid AI. Someone like you and Magnus can run multiple augments. I know your neurological and healing suite allows you much, we had plans for speed, strength and agility upgrades as well."

"So I really could be like Deadpool?" I asked him.

"Crisp high five," the scientist said, and I busted up laughing and gently gave him one as he held up a hand.

"God, this all feels like a movie or a video game to me sometimes. Except when I'm getting my ass kicked. That still really hurts."

"Yeah, it was theorized that the medical and neurological nanites can numb or block pain receptors, but we'd never tried it. To be honest, we were going to bring you out of stasis after a time and do your upgrades if integration was a success, but somehow, I wasn't taken out of stasis when I'd planned. Somebody had reset my controls. I was supposed to be in a time locked room. It would take a facility override to do that, and only project directors can pull something like that off."

"What about another AI?" I asked.

"I suppose it's possible, but not probable. Besides,

I know more about the surgical side of things than the actual coding and hacking of the systems."

"How does an upgrade work then, if you don't understand—"

"Oh don't get me wrong, it's software and an injection of starter nanites. Your AI will replicate the new nanites and, within twenty-four hours or less, you've been upgraded. It's like looking at a flashing screen and a shot in the neck."

"That sounds too easy," I told him.

That's how it works, Alice interrupted.

"It is that easy," Nicholas told me. "In the meantime, it goes without saying that this has to stay between us. I'm working the inside angle here, trying to overthrow Magnus."

"Why didn't you go back to the ARC and awaken me?" I asked him.

"I was in one of the groups who tried to. Even when the Order Of The Purists left the ARC, we used to have followers return to supply the one or two who stayed behind. When the last of the holdouts there didn't come to open the blast doors thirty-five years ago, we quit going. I wasn't high up enough in the organization… and without revealing where I really came from and when to the order, I couldn't talk my way back inside to those who were left."

I fumbled around in my vest pocket and found the identity card. Jeremiah Jones. I held it out.

"That's him," Nicholas said. "Keep his access card, it'll get you into most of the building. Only the level below the pump room will you need a different access card."

AWAKENED CONTROL

"Level below the pump room? That's not in my files," Alice told me.

I relayed her message to him, and he smiled.

"Yes, I'm sure. See, you weren't the only video game and movie aficionado in that ARC. The Terminator movies were a favorite of ours, and we had visions of the horror of Sky Dark happening. It's part of the reason the CEPMs were not activated and integrated right away. You were designed to be a savior."

My head was sort of spinning. I got back up and walked over to where the rest of my gear was and pulled out the stiletto. I pulled my pant leg up and cut off the bandages. My stitches were ragged; the puncture hadn't been straight. One by one, I started cutting the stitches and pulling them out. Alice went to work. I would have to get someone else to get my shoulder unless Alice could somehow heal or cut off the stitches or…

"It's catgut," Nicholas said smiling.

"You were just going to let me cut and pull these out one by one? You know how much that shit hurts?"

"It was funny, and it's rare that I get a chance to be more than the stoic Wiseman around here." He chuckled.

"If this room is shielded, why don't you have your AI work on repairing the damage from aging?" I asked.

"Glitch in the programming," he told me. "It can heal injuries for only so long. I age a lot slower than normal humans, but Dumbass," he tapped his head, "is just like his namesake."

His eyes flashed blue for a second, and there was

a knock at the door before it was opened. Luca strode in with Gregory.

"Brother Nicholas, there is need of you," he said formally.

Nicholas got up and gave Gregory a small bow and started walking. I watched them go and then stood and went back to retrieve the rest of my gear. I laid it all out on the bed.

"Luca, how long till I can get my own stuff back?" I asked him.

"If you want it dry, you have to wait half a day. Otherwise..." He looked at my garb, "That might actually let you move around a bit more freely in the city."

I walked over towards him and saw a window. I looked out and saw it had what looked like chicken wire mesh in the glass and the view below was the dirt streets with a view of the market.

"Anybody seen Moss?" I asked him.

"No," Luca said, "Gregory was incensed. I can ask around, but I'd rather do it quietly."

"Sure. Hey, did everything go good here? I see you're now wearing the uniform of the Jedi?"

"What is a Jedi?" Luca asked.

I groaned. "Padawan, there is much to teach you. Come, I need to go to the market, black and otherwise."

———

"...and they just let you join?" I asked him.

"Yeah, I took the oaths, did my days of fasting

and, since they gave me the shit job on the first day, that's how I was at the arena when you were there. I just about screamed myself hoarse the entire time. I've never seen somebody do that."

"What, get beat to a bloody pulp, only to win by physics and luck?" I asked him.

"Physics? What is that?" He asked seriously.

"It's like—"

"There, talk to him," Luca interrupted and pointed.

We'd been walking down the marketplace. Fruits, veggies, fish, strips of meat, clothing were all on display. One place had shelves and cubbies that seemed to be rolls of a rough paper tied with ribbons. Probably books or modern day scrolls in a post-technological age. There were more than a couple vendors that had weapons openly on display and for sale, but they were more of the hand weapons. Crude knives, some of those handmade curved swords, and what looked like a mace. Pretty medieval-looking things. I'd elected to bring the Beretta, and I wore it in my vest, under the white robe. I had the stiletto up my sleeve but what was drawing attention was the shotgun. I had it roughly slung over my shoulder.

Guns were worth a lot here, and the one being in sight made them treat me like… royalty? I wore my hood up to cover my bald head and scar, but still, my lighter skin tone was noticed by some here and there. It was easier to miss with the white bleached robes, but people still did see it. Like the vendor we stopped at who had what looked like a shish kabob setup over a hibachi. I paid thirty credits for four of them and handed two to Luca. I started digging in ravenously, and he was silent as we walked. I finished mine, and he handed me his.

"You don't want to know what the meat is," he told me.

"I don't care, it's pretty good. As long as the Order doesn't have a fatwa on this kind of meat, it's awesomely flavored."

"Fatwa? Awesomely?" Luca asked.

Dammit Beavis! Alice shouted from the peanut gallery.

The man that Luca had indicated earlier had dodged out of sight, and we were casually strolling through looking at things and looking for him. I had just gotten a glimpse of him walking out of a baker's stall with two loaves, and he turned our way, almost running into me.

"Philippe," Luca said, "It is I, Luca Yaneshson," He said by way of greeting.

Philippe stepped back and looked Luca over and then his eyes opened wide. He pulled Luca close to him in a one armed hug.

"It is good to see you alive and well. I thought you and your family were lost in the last purge?!"

"We left. I came of age and hadn't decided what way my path lay."

"By the color of your robes I can see you finally made your choice. Is the whole family back?" he asked.

"No, they will not. My mother and my sister will never submit to the Outsiders' barbaric practices."

"Then you should be so lucky as me. Never married, no children. That I know of, eh?" He said, nudging him and dropped a saucy wink. "Who is your friend here? The Order of Purists now has armed guards?"

"This is…"

I pulled my hood down. My hair had started growing back in all over everywhere except the scar. Black stubble.

"Oh, my… Um… Yuri has made it known that Boris—"

"Me and Boris have settled all old debts," I said, and held out my hand. "I'm Tony."

"Tony?" He asked, looking at my hand.

Stupid, nobody shakes hands in this time and age, Alice chided.

"Ooops, sorry. Custom I got used to from somewhere else. I'm a Traveler and Trader."

"Trader, eh? Is this why you seek me out?" Phillippe asked turning to Luca.

"In truth, yes. I would have eventually anyways, but Tony's need is great. Can you get us in?"

"Get us in where?" I asked him.

Tony turned to me, "Under-town, where the black market operates. Beyond Magnus's law."

My jaw dropped. A city under a city?

Crazy man, crazy, Alice told me.

———

We had gone through the hulk of a building that had had two sides blown out by some catastrophe. Old wires and brick were scattered everywhere. Anything wooden of the structure was gone. We descended some cement stairs that led down from the main floor behind some artfully arranged rubble into a cement spiral staircase six foot wide. Rock and crushed brick and cement crunched under my boots. Alice automatically fixed my sight for me so my eyes could pick out more details in the dim light of the staircase. Down and down; it was dizzying. It started reminding me of the larger staircases that were in the Data Arc – only smaller and smaller.

I was starting to wonder how deep we were going underground when the staircase abruptly ended. What looked like an incandescent light was in a metal cage over top of a post apoc blast door, cobbled together by whatever metal could be brazed and cut to fit the opening. Phillipe knocked, and a small panel that looked flush dropped straight down about twenty inches wide and six inches high. Twin barrels of a scattergun poked out.

"Whatchoo want?" A southern hillbilly sounding voice came out.

That kind of startled me. Not only was it somebody speaking English, but in a dialect I recognized from cousins out in the Appalachians. Wait, there was a memory there trying to strain to break free… but it just wouldn't come. Thankfully Phillipe wasn't lost in memories.

"It's Phillipe," he said with a resigned sigh. "We're here to do some shopping. Let us in."

The shotgun pulled back from the opening and two eyes and part of face peered out at us.

"Friends of yours? What you doing with the Order here? And who's that Order retard with the guns?"

"This is Luca and his friend. He wishes to gain access to the Market," Phillip said, and Luca looked like he wanted to say something, but he didn't.

"What's the password?" The man behind the door asked.

"How the blazing hell am I supposed to know that?" Phillipe yelled. "There's never been a password, you cretin."

"Ok, ok, ok… What do you call a Frenchman wearing sandals?"

Luca's friend really did let out a pained sigh and just stared boreholes into the partial face and eyes that stared out.

"No answer, no entry. Or you can getchoo somewhere else to be," he said, the twang back in his voice.

"What is the question again?" Phillipe asked.

"What do you call a Frenchman wearing sandals?"

"You call him Phillipe Fa-lop," I finished, trying not to laugh at the old joke.

A stony silence filled the air and then Luca busted up laughing. Soon the man behind the door was laughing. What can I say, I kill me? Then I saw the stormy expression on Phillipe's face. Still, I couldn't stop the grin.

"It's classic," I told him.

"Asshole," I heard him mutter back, but the bolts holding the door lock in place were starting to be thrown.

Clanking, clacking and then on hinges that needed oil about three hundred years ago, the door screeched open slowly, and I was somewhat surprised to see how many layers it had. It was as if two entire cars had been crushed down and pounded flat with repeated blows from something heavy. Where the front side was smooth and had some sort of painted surface to give it a grayed metal look, the back side looked like tetanus waiting to happen. It was rough, and rust pitted the backside of the door.

The difference in the air was noticeable too. It was more humid, dank. That surprised me after the dry parts of the desert above.

"Get in here," the voice behind the door called.

"You go on alone now, I have other business," Phillipe said, and Luca gave him a wave.

I gave him an imaginary hat tip and walked past what had to be a twenty-something man, horribly twisted and contorted. His body had been disfigured by nature rather than as a result of anything else. Maybe it was mutated genes, but Alice could probably tell me if I cared to ask. One side of his body was strong and hale, the other half was withered, and the difference between the limbs' diameter was noticeable. Under his weak arm, he had a crude crutch to help keep him propped up. Unlike the rest of the folk I had seen around Lakeville, his skin was even whiter than mine, with white hair. An Albino.

"Got something wrong witchoo?" he asked when he saw me giving him the once over.

Don't start a fight here Tony, Alice warned.

"Not going to try," I told her.

I walked up to the man who reached down with his good arm and picked up the shotgun.

"You're amazing," I told him and held out my forearm, pushing my sleeve back. "I don't think I've ever met anybody paler than me. Do the ladies love the color?" I asked honestly.

For a second there was a pregnant silence, and then the man put the shotgun down and looked up at me, a smile tugging at the corners of his mouth.

"I ain't got no coloring, but you, sir, could almost be a ghost, 'cept you got you a little pink in ya. But yeah, girls want to check things out, see if the color is only the exposed skin, if ya get my meaning," he told me and dropped a big exaggerated wink.

"Same deal here," I said and gave him a manly slap on the shoulder and turned to Luca who was giving me a strange look.

"What? I didn't insult him," I told Alice mentally.

Making friends, influencing people. He's probably used to being the butt of every joke, Alice told me.

"Where to now, Luca?" I asked him, looking around at the area behind the doorway.

It looked like a long hallway, and I could feel the vibrations through the floor as if some great machine was slowly rumbling and idling.

"I was here a couple of times before we fled. I think we can safely go to most parts of the market, though I may not be as welcome now that I'm in the Order."

"Well, I'm dressed that way as well," I told him.

"Yeah, well, you have the guns."

"True that," the albino chipped in and I held a thumbs up in his direction without turning.

Instead, I started walking. Luca fell into step beside me, and I marveled at what I was seeing. I wasn't for sure, but I thought that it was part of the underground system next to the large Dam for Lake Powell. It was dug in so there would be access to the dam's hydro systems. So if the electricity above was all generated here...

"What are you looking for exactly?" Luca asked me.

"Tech," I told him, "I'll know it when I see it."

"Yeah, but what kind?" He pressed.

I ignored the question as the hallway opened up a little bit. The smell was... interesting. Axel grease, body odor, ozone. There were people bustling about between stalls, but I didn't see food vendors here. Instead, I saw weapons. Shield generators, grenades, and one stall just had a hand painted sign that said 'information'. Another had what looked like an old folding table that was sagging in the middle and, at the end, hanging from a nail on the wall, was what had to have been a cork board with a ton of scraps of paper on it. I walked up, and Luca followed me after a second.

A grizzled old man who held what looked like a break top grenade launcher with fat green shells looped through his suspenders, no shirt and streaky black and white hair, stared at me hard.

"What is all this?" I asked him, hoping it was a directory.

"Jobs board. You take a job and do it. Come back here, and I'll pay you what the poster offers, minus a five percent commission for me black soul."

I read through some of the scraps. Kill so and so,

find a missing kid… stop marauders who were raiding a local farm… beat up Yuri—

I pulled the slip of paper off and handed it to the old man. The top had been held in place with a short, cheap handmade dagger, but it had been sharp. It had cut cleanly through the slip as I had pulled it out. The old man squinted at me and shifted, getting a better grip on the smooth bore gun.

"What is this?" He asked me, "You've surely not…"

"Yeah," Luca said. He'd obviously been reading over my shoulder. "He busted Yuri up good. Tony here ended up besting Boris's challenger in the arena afterward and now holds the ownership of Moss as a result."

The old man held his left hand up over his mouth in surprise, probably to hold back some sort of curse or…

"I've heard that there was an arena fight today to settle a dispute and something about Moss, but somebody is always talking about that hellion. So you uh… you're her master now?" he asked nervously.

"I don't think the master is quite the right word for it…"

"Master," a figure in black said, sliding up to me quietly.

Both Luca and the old man flinched and took a step back as Moss came out of the dark shadows from the rear of the stall. She hadn't been there a moment before, but must have snuck in or dropped in from the ceiling like some weird psychotic Spiderwoman.

"I'm Tony," I told her, "Don't call me master…

Where did… I mean…?"

"I'm sorry, Tony, a slip of the tongue. I'll call you however you want," she said, every word cold and deadly. "I made my bets and was unable to get back to your area. It seems Boris was sure of his victory and tried to have me captured while I was away from Magnus."

"Ahh, so you got away?" Luca asked her, his voice trembling.

"No," she said simply, looking at me, "they had to let me go when you won."

I looked at the old trader and handed him the slip of paper, "Good enough proof for you?" I asked him.

He gulped and pulled something out of his pocket and handed it to me. I held it up and saw that it was a flat disk. At first, I thought gold, but the color was off. Copper? Brass? It had some sort of etchings on the outer edge of the circle, and something tugged at my memory. Something about my shield generator.

"Thank you," I told him and turned to leave.

"Wait, who's selling the old tech around here?" I asked him.

"Jonald," he said pointing with his free hand, the launcher still gripped tightly, "down near the end where the bedrooms be starting."

"Thank you," Moss said sweetly.

I turned and started walking. Moss fell in just a little behind me and followed. After some hesitation, Luca caught up with me and followed to my right. Something was bugging me as I made my way through, taking mental notes that there were all kinds of things I wanted to stop and buy, and then it hit me. I hadn't had a chance to tell Moss that she wasn't really my slave. I mean, in public that was what the people thought so I figured she was playing the game, except—

She's walking behind you, and it makes you nervous because she could suddenly get stabby, Alice commented from the peanut gallery.

"Sort of," I admitted to Alice mentally, "but some of it is also because she's playing the role too well and it's making me nervous that she actually believes that. I mean, didn't we talk about that last night?" I finished.

No, you just promised her that you'd buy or win her from Boris, and she'd never have to be in that situation, Alice said. *I could play back the memory for you, but I'd have to fast forward through all the lip smacking and the clothing flying. Seriously, what are you thinking?*

I ignored her and promised myself as soon as we had a moment alone I would tell Moss the truth. I never intended her to be a slave.

"He's over there," Moss tapped my back and pointed over my shoulder off to the left.

I could see the cast was still on her wrist, but it looked even thinner than before.

Her body seems to be absorbing the cast somehow. What I wouldn't give to plug into their medical network and see if nanites are involved somewhere in that, Alice mused.

"Thanks. Hey, you can walk beside me, ok?"

"Why would I do that, Tony? I'm in my proper place."

Dammit, slavery must be common here. Was she playing a game? She had to know, didn't she?

"Your proper place is beside me, that way we can move and fight as a team," I told her.

"A team…" She quickened her pace and came up beside me.

Something in her hands flashed, and I realized she'd pulled one of her knives out and was doing a practiced flourish with her left hand. It was flashy but… If that was what she called stress release… sheesh.

"Are you serious?" she asked me.

"Can we talk openly and safely here?" I asked her.

"No, anything of value said here would be sold twice for the information at the very least," she told me with another spin of her knife, which she then promptly sheathed.

"What is this disk that I got for beating on Yuri?" I asked, holding it out.

Luca shrugged, but Moss took it and looked at it before reaching for my belt. No way; I grabbed her wrist before she could unhook my shield generator. That little baby had saved my life from her more than once.

"Stop it, I'm not trying to—Dammit Tony," she hissed.

I let my grip on her wrist go slack and watched. She held the disk against the shield generator and twisted, and it seemed to click into place. The center of it glowed softly.

"Press the middle, where the glowing is," she told me.

I did, and there was a shimmer. Nothing changed. This was stupid, I moved my left arm to pull the disk off when I noticed my skin color had darkened. I was now the deep bronze color of Luca and Moss. I held my hands up, palm first and then turned them over.

"It's a changer?" Luca asked.

"Yeah," Moss answered him, and he gave her a wary look.

"Never heard of it," I told him.

"Works with shield generators. There aren't a ton of them that still work. They used to be more valuable, but after the last big raid rolled through a year ago, we got all kinds of loot from the eastern baddies. I like your other color better, but you don't stand out so much now."

This was too much, changers.. eastern baddies... I wanted to ask her, but I bit my lip as we came to a stop in front of a table of supplies. Jonald, a weird name for sure, was a swarthy obese man. I'd seen big men in my time, and even here. Jonald wasn't a big muscular hulking figure, he just... dominated the two folding chairs he was sat on. He went to rise as he saw us approach and then saw Moss. His jaw dropped open, and his hand shot under the table, grasping for something.

For the first time, I saw Moss move against someone who wasn't me. She seemed to flow forward, and when Jonald pulled out a small pistol, she twisted his wrist up to make safe the gun and then started working his wrist over her cast as if to break it. He dropped the piece, and she kicked the gun back towards us. He swung out with one fist, and Moss brought both arms up in a blocking motion, and his blow glanced off her arms. She dipped her right shoulder and shot out with a rabbit punch to his cheek, not doing any damage but stunning the man into stopping his assault. She stepped back while I stood there in shock.

"Jonald, that's no way to treat an old friend," Moss told him sweetly, her voice oddly menacing.

"You and I," he said, rubbing his wrist, "we ain't never been friends. I heard what happened to Yuri and Boris. You aren't here for…?"

"She's my guide," I said, stepping forward.

That's a good one. Might as well tell him who you really are. Are you going to introduce yourself as Ironman? Alice quipped.

"Shut it," I told her mentally.

"You're him, ain't you?" He asked, losing his pretense of fear.

"Him, who, what?" Luca asked.

We all turned to him. It wasn't deliberate, was it? Sometimes I attributed my dry, sarcastic nature to others, and when I realize they are just stupid, it takes the fun out of having a dry, sarcastic sense of humor. This was the case here.

"You're Tony?" he asked, and I nodded. "You're the talk of Undertown right now. Got our big boss laid up in the healers quarters topside. He won't be happy that you're down here," he said.

"Last time people had a disagreement with my Master, he fought in the arena. I don't think Yuri will do anything since he's already been humbled?" Moss asked him.

"How about you tell me what you want, and you

get out of here," Jonald said.

All eyes turned expectantly to me.

"I need some tech," I said, surveying his tables.

It had all kinds of gear on it, working and in pieces. A pair of night vision goggles by the look of it, though it wasn't a model from my time, probably built after I was in stasis. Circuit boards, a laptop... then I started seeing things that were making Alice happy.

"How much for that?" I asked, pointing to a servo motor.

"100,000 credits," Jonald said without batting an eye.

"60,000 and how many more do you have?" I countered.

He was shaking his head. "100k. They don't make these any more, and no, that's my only one. Supply and demand."

"Do we really need these?" I asked Alice, "Can't we build them?"

That one will work perfectly. It's possible we can find different ones and adapt them to work, but that one right there will fit in perfect. It'll be used for opening and closing the water relief valves. I'll need at least two more.

That entire conversation took half a heartbeat, but it still took some time. Still, there wasn't enough lag that anybody would notice but me.

"70k for that one, and if you don't have more, I'll give you 10k for information on where to buy more."

Jonald reached up and scratched the bristles on his unshaven face with a big hand. Sweat stains showed through his wool top, though it was cold and damp down here.

"Deal," Jonald said, and reached his wrist out.

I punched in the amount on my wallet band and tapped it to his, and just like that, 80k worth of credits was gone. I took the servo and reached up and unzipped my pack and dropped it in. I couldn't quite reach the zipper to get it back up and I felt somebody else doing it. I turned, expecting to see Moss doing it, or somebody trying to snatch the tech I'd just bought, when I saw it was Luca. He looked a little green in the gills. I knew he'd seen violence, but maybe seeing his own personal boogeyman in the flesh and in action had creeped him out.

I wonder what he'd say if he knew I'd slept with her?

"Now the information?" I asked him.

He looked left and right and then motioned me to come closer. I did, and I heard Moss hiss a warning. Unless this guy sat on me, I was pretty safe from a knife or gun from him, but I'd be careful.

"The makers one level down with the hydro gear. There's a guy named Blakely who says he's come up with a way to rebuild the burnt out ones. He was in training and doing his devotionals to become a Technomages when they threw him out. He's half trained, so I half believe him."

"What'd he get thrown out of the program for?" I asked him.

"Word has it, he was bopping one of Magnus's lady friends. Doesn't matter they were engaged before Magnus made her his girl."

"Somebody needs to bury that guy," I growled.

The look of fear covered his face as I leaned back and stood up straight.

"Don't ever let anybody hear you say that, ok? I don't want to even hear that. You got something to ya... but he's more than just one man. Never forget that... neither is Boris or Yuri. They buy and sell lives the way you and I just conducted business."

"I'll take that into consideration," I told him.

"Where are we going now?" Moss asked as I stepped back towards him and Luca.

"We have to go down one more level to the Makers."

"I uh... I can't," Luca said, "those guys are the... The Order Of The Purists thinks that they are—"

"It's ok, Luca," I told him. "Need us to walk you back to the topside?"

"No, nobody will bug me down here," he said, and turned.

"He should be safe. They saw him walking down here with you. Before you went all native. I wonder... is *all* your skin that color?" Moss pulled at the front of my robe, and I swatted her hand away.

I didn't get her. Violence, danger and now play-fulness? Moss was a bundle of confusion, and I'd never met a woman like her. She'd be locked up in an asylum if it was still my day and age.

"Stop," I told her. "Do you know where we're going?"

"Yes," she said and then she moved.

Incoming threat, Alice chimed.

I blocked the rabbit punch to the head with my

forearm but missed the solid left that hit me in the stomach. It almost knocked the wind out of me, and I saw she had a small rod of metal in her closed fist. No wonder it had hurt so bad. I dodged the upcoming knee strike and leaned back as she high kicked and did a roundhouse kick at me.

"Why won't you fight back now?" she asked, her voice deadly.

She pulled a knife from her sheath.

There she goes again, with the knives. Seriously, why don't you disarm her and I can play the soundtrack to Beaches or something while you two bump uglies?

"Kind of busy here Alice," I said through gritted teeth as Moss started swinging her arm down in an overhand motion, the tip of the blade going right for my chest.

I couldn't dodge it. Instead, I caught her wrist while I was off balance and fell on my back. Once again she was straddling me, and while I held onto her wrist, she put her casted wrist across her knife hand and put her weight into it.

"Why are you doing this?" I asked her, getting another hand up, grabbing hers and stopping the blade's forward momentum.

Jonald hadn't moved, but he looked on in horror.

"Do you really want me to spell it out to you? Carve it in your flesh?" Moss asked through gritted teeth.

A vein pulsed in her neck, and I could see the strain in the cords and tendons in her wrist and arms as her muscles were flexed and pushing as hard as she could. She was probably as strong as me, or had better leverage. Still, I had something she didn't.

Told you, mating ritual of a psycho hose beast, Alice mocked.

"Spell it out for me," I said, straining.

"I won't be owned by anybody," she said.

"I never intended to keep you," I told her.

The pressure let off, and she slowly pulled the knife back and sheathed it.

"Well then, maybe we should go down a level and finish our business down here."

I had to shake my head at her sudden snap back into rationalism. Still, I could see a bead of sweat running down her temple and her chest was heaving as she tried to catch her breath.

"I don't get you," I said.

"You're talking to… come on," she said, and grabbed my arm and pulled.

I wanted to check my guns and make sure nothing other than my kidneys had been hurt by the struggle, but it could wait half a second. Hell, this would be one more thing I was about to screw up, but I had to go with it for now. Despite feeling a strong attraction and pull for the former hunter and in-house psycho, I needed her to show me where these makers are. This Blakely would be there, and I'd love to see what he'd have to say.

She led me to a rusty set of metal spiral stairs. I reached out and shook the railing. I watched as rust flakes fell down like rain.

"That looks like a something I don't want to get cut on," I said and started down.

I'd got about half way down when I felt Moss grab

my left arm. I turned, and she had stopped one step above me. We were eye level, and she had a concerned look on her face.

"Did you mean it?" she asked.

"What?"

"You never intended to hold me as your slave?"

"Yes, that's what I said. I was going to Boris to win your freedom, not—"

"You kept saying contract. Like I was property."

I realized that we were both speaking in Navajo still and something clicked. Maybe I was using the wrong words. I switched to Trader.

"Moss, I do apologize. I only wished to win your freedom. English is my normal language and switching to yours... I think the mistake is mine, like a bad translation. I know about your past, and you told me what you had to do to get to where you were at. You were ready to die before you were forced to work the brothel. It kinda broke my heart, and I have a soft spot for damsels in distress."

She stared at me and then brought first one arm up and then the other, laying them across my shoulders. Despite being healed by nanites, I was still tender where my collarbone had been broken. I tried not to let it show, nor how worn out I was from our earlier struggle so soon after the arena fight.

"It broke your heart, or you figured something out?"

"Figured what out?" I asked her.

"Something about yourself. Feelings."

Her large dark eyes bored into mine, and she was starting to lean in.

AWAKENED CONTROL

Danger Will Robinson, Danger, Alice piped up from the peanut gallery.

"Feelings?" I asked, leaning in close enough that I could feel her breath against my cheek.

"Uggg." She pushed me back, and I almost went over the staircase and rolled to the bottom.

At least that's how it played out in my head.

That was smooth. Way to kill the mood. Don Juan, you are not, Alice told me.

"Shut up," I said, tapping the side of my head.

"I don't understand women," I said as Moss strode past me on her way down to the bottom of the stairwell.

"I can see that," both Moss and Alice said at the same time.

I tried to hold back from yelling "Jinx!" but had to bite the inside of my cheek. Moss saw that, and her face turned bright red, and she turned and started walking. I hurried up and saw that we were in a smaller, more cramped space. The throbbing hum of some great machinery came from behind a door set at the end of a semi-lit hallway. The direction in which Moss was heading.

"Moss, wait," I said, breaking into a jog to catch up with her.

I reached out to grab her arm, and her arm flew up, pushing my hand back. She spun on me, furious.

"I'm sorry," I told her, "I wasn't trying to hurt your feelings. You're about the only one who knows… and I literally just woke up from a thousand year sleep. I am probably more than a little rusty in talking to the ladies and picking up on social cues."

O. M. G., Alice said, *Guys don't apologize. You just broke every code in man-law, in fact, I'm calling bullshit and will be halting all beer drinking until you win back your man card.*

"Please shut it," I told her, tapping my head again.

"You know," Moss said, her expression still stony, "If I didn't know what was going on, I'd think you were bat shit crazy."

"I probably am, and this is all a dream. And I dreamed of all of this. A weird dictator, a new age Roman style amphitheater with gladiator fights, two factions from the same ARC splitting up into religious cults and bully boys and girls… and an insanely insane hotty with long black hair and natural curls."

"You think these are natural?" She asked, a smile tugging at the corner of her mouth.

"They looked like it this morning," I told her, remembering how much I had done that day and feeling weary.

She leaned in again and gently kissed me on the lips, then kneed me in the balls. I dropped to my knees.

Tuning out pain receptors down there a bit, Alice said as the nausea hit, and I dry heaved.

I got to my feet and wiped my mouth, hoping that she was done with her attacks.

"What was that for?" I asked her.

"For making me think you liked me."

"Feelings, you said feelings earlier," I reminded her.

"Liking someone is a feeling," she said.

Well, ok, that's easy then.

AWAKENED CONTROL

"Well, I feel like I like you, Moss. When you're not trying to stab me, shoot me, stomp my skull in, when you're not putting a dagger in my back and twisting it… or, I know, my favorite was when you cut me from shoulder blade to nipple… or how about the three knife attacks by you where I didn't get hurt? All of this before you crushed my balls…"

"Why are you saying you like me on the one hand but you don't like me on another?"

Goddamn. I needed a drink.

"Can we talk later? I'm sure there are cameras all around here, and people are going to know we've been out here a while."

"Sure. But really, you're not keeping me as a slave?"

I blew out an exasperated sigh and looked at her. She was grinning. "You know, you might be missing out on some role play."

TOLD YOU IT WAS FOREPLAY! Alice shouted in my head.

"You're not right in the head," I said and reached out and pushed her back hard, until her back hit the wall.

She grinned at me wickedly. She'd been joking? Right?

———

Blakely was working over a soldering bench when I saw him. It wasn't so much that he was easy to pick out, it was that he had on an old school baseball cap and his name was stenciled across the front of it which was turned backward. Turbines filled the room, and the noise was tremendous as the water rushed through, spinning the blades and making electricity. One of them had its guts exposed, and it looked like a piece was missing.

"Hey, you Blakely?" I asked, interrupting him.

He turned and put down the soldering iron, a wisp of smoke coming off the top of it. On the table was a circuit board, with a scorched part, by the look of things.

"Yeah, that's right. What can I help you with?".

He finished his turn and hopped off the stool he'd been sitting on. He looked much darker than the people I'd run into so far. His skin was probably the same color of bronze as everyone else, but he'd gotten a lot of exposure to the sun, judging by the way his nose was peeling a bit. He was smaller than me, probably about the same size as Moss.

I pulled off my pack and pulled out the servo motor and handed it to him.

"I need two more just like this," I told him.

Blakely just grunted and nodded. He walked over to a different table and took the exposed ends of the servo motor's wires and touched two alligator clips to it. It must have been wired up to a battery or electricity because the servo spun into action. The RPMs on that thing were pretty fast sounding, but Alice assured me that one would be perfect.

"I don't have any that will work," he said, "But I can probably get you a couple to work if you can help me find parts? Say 20k each?"

"That doesn't sound too bad. What kind of parts

and where?" I asked him.

He told me, and Alice made a mental note. His description was pretty detailed, and Alice said it reminded her of a city to the south-east.

"Thank you, Blakely," I said, and he turned to return to his work.

"Well, that went good," I said to the empty air.

Someway, somehow, Moss had taken off without me noticing.

CHAPTER 13

I looked for Moss my entire trip topside. She was gone. Alice ran the calculations, and I would need too much water and too much food to carry with me to just walk it. The last Alice knew, we were heading towards what used to be called Kaibito. I needed a way to get there. I exited past the albino who dropped me a wink after realizing I had changed my skin tone.

I exited out the way I'd come in, and set a course for the hotel. More than half the day had passed, and I stopped on my trip through the market to buy another pair of shish kabobs from a young woman in grease-stained clothes. She smiled back at me and said something unintelligible. I nodded and bumped wrists together to pay her and left. I considered what I had left. I had a pretty big chunk out of the new money I'd won.

I considered getting my clothing from the Order, but I was tired. I ate the mystery meat and veggies on my way back to my room and put the lock in the door. When I opened it, two cleaning ladies were inside, changing the sheets. They looked at me in surprise and then shrugged, and I shut the door and went to the office.

"So you want to stay longer?" The manager asked me when I walked in.

"Yeah," I told him. "Is there any place I can rent a wag or buy something to drive?"

"No, that's forbidden technology for the normal people to have. Only Outsiders have the abilities to procure, make and drive them."

Hm… I really needed to get a move on… but I was so sleepy.

"Ok, thanks. If you think of anything, let me know."

"I'll see you tomorrow?!" He asked me, though it sounded more like a statement.

"Sure, and hold the entertainment. I want to rest," I said, not wanting interruptions and praying the cleaning crew was gone.

I stumbled a little bit; holding off sleep was no easy feat at this point. I'd been beaten up, broken up, shot at, stabbed, thrown kicked and kneed in the balls in less than twelve hours. I've found one servo motor and a place to get two more. All in all, not a bad days' worth of— My door opened, and feminine giggles followed the two ladies out. One of them stopped and gave me an appreciative look.

"You look good in this color," she said.

I recognized her; she was supposed to have been the entertainment that night when I'd had Moss pinned to the floor. She recognized me. I shrugged it off and gave her a polite smile and a nod and let myself in. The room was clean-ish. The bed was made and, as I wandered through, I saw there was a stack of fresh towels. The curtain in the shower had been replaced, and there was a rough-hewn chunk of soap. Probably luxury accommodations. Still, there was hot water and a very very old bed that was far more comfortable than the ground. Making sure nobody was in the closet, I headed to the door pulling the robe off, then turned the bolt, locking it, and went face first on the bed, not bothering with the covers.

———

In my dream, I was in my battle rattle, and my squad was advancing up a street somewhere. That part was fuzzy, but I was on point. I usually had a pretty good nose for danger and it'd gotten us out of many traps. We were somewhere in the sandbox, maybe Bagdad again, as we always seemed to have wars in Iraq every decade or so. Far up ahead we could hear the distinctive rattle of AKs and the screams of women and children.

There had been a rumor of death squads moving through the city, murdering the Christians, before the Americans and the British took the city over. That much I remembered if not the name of the city… and we were advancing on a sidewalk, trying to stay as close to the cover of the shelled buildings as possible. We were antsy to stop the slaughter ahead of us. We were moving forward, I was clearing forward and to my right as we passed buildings, and I was between a bagel joint and a cleaners when two boys entered my sight picture. I raised my rifle.

They started babbling in a language I didn't speak, and none of them appeared to be armed. I made a motion with my left hand, and the second in our squad came forward and started speaking with them. It seemed that it went on forever and then he started translating.

"He says the Salafists are twenty blocks ahead. They were told to flee and find the Americans. They are worried about their parents... OH SHIT—"

I saw what had worried him so much. The smaller boy on the right let his robe fall open to grab a pull string. He started shouting Allah Akbar when I moved. I tried tackling the interpreter when fire and concussion seemingly threw me sideways. All was dark.

———

...wake up you dumbass!! Alice was screaming in my head.

I winced and came to.

"What is it?" I asked her grumpily and rolled over and sat up on the bed.

There has been active scanning in the area. I think they are on to you.

I swung my feet off the bed and then got up.

Heading to the bathroom I tried to wipe the cobwebs out of my brain.

"Does it seem directional?" I asked her.

The signal has circled this hotel twice. I would suggest you moving. I don't think Magnus nor Boris's people are very happy with you. Though you might have won the public challenge, that doesn't mean they won't stab you in the back.

"True that," I said wanting a shower, but wanting to take a peek out first.

I picked up the LRG and put the sling for the shotgun across my back. This building was made of brick, and the LRG was the only thing that could punch a hole through some of their bigger armored items. The teams from my dream would have had a field day with something like this. It had all the advantages of the .50 cal. Barret's, longer range, more punch, less projectile drop. The bad thing was that recharge time between shots. As it was, I hadn't been using it for much.

The scanning seems to have stopped, Alice said.

I pulled back one curtain and looked outside. Where the parking lot used to be was normally open, but there was one small problem I saw out there. There were three of their tricked out buggies with gunners aiming their big ones at the hotel, and six men on foot with a combination of electrified tridents and crude pipe guns. By the bore, I guessed twelve gauge shotguns, as I'd never recovered the rest of my ammunition. Just what the shit heel had had on him, which was still quite a bit. I saw something moving behind the buggies and saw the sunlight reflecting off something man-shaped as it stalked back and forth next to a large man. Magnus and somebody in an Exosuit.

I shouldered my pack, knowing I had to move, and Alice was right. My time here was near an end. At least my overt presence. I tapped the changer, making my skin the normal tone again after a couple of mis-tries. I would have to play with it when I had a clearer head and see what all it could do.

I have been studying it while you were sleeping. Nothing else to do other than hacking their networks.

"Can you hack the armor outside?" I asked her.

Although it's an older computer and not as advanced as me, it's pretty secure against any measure I might take against it. I can detect wireless signals and radio signals it emits, but I can't gain access.

"No, you could have said no. That's simple. Can you hack the armor? No? Simple."

Don't be a little bitch, Tony. Her tone was condescending.

I cracked the door and opened it wide. Men tensed, and I saw the bore of the big guns move slightly as they zeroed in on me.

"Hey fellas, I hope you aren't here to sell me Avon, I got enough stuff from QVC, and it should be here any day now."

You're brilliant.

"Shut it," I told her mentally. "This is meant to draw out…"

"Tony," Magnus said, striding forward when I didn't raise the LRG, "I was hoping to have a quick conversation with you. After the events yesterday, I wanted to take every precaution in case you weren't in a listening type of mood."

"Hey Magnus, I'm always open to talk. How about those buggy crews turn their guns somewhere other than me, so we can both feel safe and talk face to face."

Magnus made a gesture with his hand, and the turret guns pointed up. He strode forward, some kind of sword belted to his left side, almost in a cross draw setup if it were a gun. The person in the armor stalked up half a step behind Magnus. A heavy. The Exosuit was holding one of the town's fearsome chain guns in a casual manner. A box of ammo was belted to the waist of the suit, and it looked to be full of 7.62s, along with a battery pack. Even more surprisingly, was what looked like a handle that had been sticking up from the suit's back. When Magnus came to a stop a few feet from me, the suit looked left to right to make sure the goons were in position. I saw the handle terminated with a huge sledgehammer head that pulsed with red streaks. Great…

"Sorry if things didn't turn out the way you thought yesterday."

"I'm here to offer you an invitation, Tony," Magnus said, ignoring me.

"Oh yeah? Is it a knitting circle? Because I'm not much into knitting and I have some really awesome Superman socks already—"

The punch was almost a surprise. I turned my head at the last second, and his fist grazed my cheek. My ear erupted in pain as a ring on his finger left a furrow, and the blood started to flow.

AWAKENED CONTROL

"Nobody, and I mean *nobody* in this millennia EVER talks to me like that," Magnus whispered.

"So you're a millennial baby?" I asked him, my left hand reaching up to check my ear and coming back bloody. Alice was letting it flow for now, and that was fine with me. "So were you part of the free college, occupy Wall Street, hippy boys?" I taunted.

Magnus swung again, and this time I was ready for it. I took half a step back and used the butt of the LRG to hit him in the sternum. With his strength and mass, all it did was push the big leader back.

"I thought from the moment I met you that it could be you. Why would you come here after Moss was sent to find you?"

"I needed tech," I told him, "and I'm getting it."

One of the really big disadvantages of being a human giant like Magnus was is that he was effectively a meat shield for everyone with the guns behind him. Add to that, the Exosuit had stopped to his side. I couldn't move anywhere else, but nobody was going to be shooting me just yet.

"Cat's out of the bag," I told Alice mentally, and I reached into my pouch and pulled out a food packet, one of my last.

Magnus looked at me in disgust as I ripped the top off and slurped the foil dry like it was a *Gogurt*. He probably knew why I was doing it, but it hadn't registered that my ear had stopped gushing blood as the nanites in my system healed me and started stockpiling energy in my muscular system for fight or flight.

"Your ARC, I have a rough idea of where it is.

Show it to me, and I'll spare your life, maybe even let you join the Outsiders."

"Hm… There are a couple big issues we'd have to work past first," I told him.

"Oh yeah? You have conditions, CEPM?"

"Yup," I told him. "First things first. You're a murdering murderous ass puppet. That shit is no good, but what really burns my biscuits is how you are keeping slaves and abusing women and young girls to satisfy your men's' lusts. You're from my time, and we didn't put up with that shit then, so I will not put up with that shit now."

Magnus's eyes flashed blue a moment and, faster than I could track, he started his draw on the sword. I tried to move back, but the slash from the blade hit me full across the chest from waist to shoulder. The shield discharged as I was still backpedaling when I saw the Exosuit move.

Shit, we're fucked, Alice said.

I silently agreed, surprised to still be in one piece. Not only had that sword strike discharged the shield, if I hadn't been wearing the slash proof vest his sword would have bisected me. Instead of watching that, as I fell, I saw in horror as the Exosuit move and line up its chain gun.

This is it, Alice said, *I'd like to say it's been fun, but we're about to be splat—*

The left hand of the Exosuit grabbed Magnus's sword arm as he raised it for another strike and tossed him behind with a casual motion that broke bones and elicited a scream from those he landed on. Then the suit turned and opened up, the chain gun only taking a moment to spin up and start spewing death and destruction. I got up in shock, seeing that whoever it was had thrown Magnus for twenty feet or more, and he was even now getting up cursing.

I aimed the LRG at Magnus and was hit by a sudden blast to my right. I hadn't been paying attention, but a slug hit me high in the left shoulder where the vest didn't cover. Blood and gore flew from the through and through. The pain was massive, and Alice went silent in my head as she directed the healing operations. I fell back down to the ground and let the LRG go and pulled the Beretta from the vest. I aimed back as another round was fired at me and hit the ground next to my head. When the dirt cleared enough for me to see I started pulling the trigger.

Two men had been advancing on me. One of them held a pipe shotgun and was hurriedly reloading it. The second man had escaped the chain gun's spitting rounds and was fixing to skewer me in the guts. The first rounds hit him, and I walked the shots from waist to the top of his chest and moved my aim a little to the right and started firing on the second man before he could reload. My FMJ rounds blew the top of his head off in a gory spray.

Most damage has been repaired on your shoulder, Alice told me quietly.

She'd pulled up the full suite on the HUD overlay she controlled in my vision. I had my aim point in a red dot in my vision. My health, hunger bar, and my shield had been regenerating when I got hit, and it had zeroed back out, but now it was starting to refill and recharge. I did a quick mag change on my back and then rolled to my side and holstered the Beretta before I grabbed the LRG. I came to a sitting position, my knees up, and saw the Exosuit had dropped the chain gun and had pulled the hammer. Let's just say this… it looked like one of those battle hammers from the role playing games but with a longer handle designed for something bigger and stronger.

When it hit a man trying to flee, it punched through him, gore spraying. It was both the most destructive and fascinating thing I had ever seen in my entire life. Still, I had a job to do. I sighted in on the gunner on one of the buggies and shot. The LRG's metal slug went straight through him, the seat he was sitting on and probably traveled halfway to the moon before losing velocity. I stood up, sore but not in as much pain as a few seconds ago.

The countdown on the LRG was now also on my HUD, and I scanned. The two gunners on the remaining buggies had been shredded by the suit's chain gun. The suit was using the battle hammer to pound on the hood of one of the buggies, leaving deep dents. I sighted in on the second buggy that was trying to back out and sent a round into the engine. The driver screamed in frustration and jumped out of the still-moving vehicle. I looked at the third driver, who was staring at me in shock as I aimed the LRG at him. I nodded off to the side in what I hoped was a 'get out' gesture, and he jumped from it.

I jogged towards it, casting a wary eye at the Exosuit who was moving to retrieve the chain gun. An explosion rocked the earth where the suit was, and dirt and old chunks of asphalt erupted. I turned to look and saw a big man further down what counted as a roadway. He was walking funny, and I recognized him. Yuri. That was when the suit hit the ground in front of me between Yuri and me. The big man was reloading the break action gun, and I had a pretty idea what it was. I didn't want another round hitting anywhere close to me. I took aim with the LRG and waited for the timer to countdown. It seemed to be happening in slow motion.

That was when the person in the Exosuit started getting up, right in my field of fire.

"DOWN," I screamed.

Whoever was operating the suit dropped flat as I fired. If they had been half a second slower, I would have punched a hole through them to get to Yuri, who was now taking aim. My shot was true and, as Yuri started touching the trigger, my round hit the large dark opening of the grenade launcher and the gun literally exploded as my metal slug set off the explosive charge. Parts of Yuri were thrown twenty feet in all directions and what was left of him was a pink mist as the extra rounds he had in a bandolier across his chest set off secondary explosions. Ouch.

"Thanks for the assist," I told Alice, as she'd helped me aim that shot by zooming for me automatically.

That's what I'm here for, boss, Alice said seriously.

The suit was starting to get up again, and I took in the surroundings. Smoking craters, death, destruction, blood - some mine, some theirs - and an eerie calm. That was when I realized I'd lost track of Magnus. He'd escaped somewhere. I turned the LRG and aimed it at the Exosuit as it got up slowly, its right hand holding the chain gun in an easy grip. Something clicked and whirred, and the face mask opened like a clamshell.

You want to guess who was in the suit? She'd buggered off when I'd been down talking to Blakely, but it looked like she had her reasons, and without her, I would have been on some third world operating table as Magnus's buddies cut me open to rip out Alice.

"We're a team, right?" Moss asked me.

I smiled and held the LRG up in the air.

"I think so," I told her with a grin, wanting to hug her but knowing it'd look stupid with the charred and cold metal of the Exosuit.

"You drive," she said, looking at the remaining buggy that hadn't been cored. "I can't with this suit on, but I can ride on the back."

I nodded and ran to the buggy. It was a lot like the go-carts I'd seen in my old life. Roll cage, check. Gas pedal, check. Brake pedal, check. Motor was somewhere behind me, and I could hear and see the vibrations shaking the chassis. I climbed in, putting the LRG on the seat next to me, the stock on the ground and in easy reach on my left side. The vehicle rocked as Moss got on the back and I hit the gas, heading for the front gate. Before we even got close, I heard Moss's chain gun start up. I couldn't see what she was firing at, but I was driving for the gate. It started rolling up slowly, and the firing stopped. I only had to slow down for ten seconds before I hit the gas hard, putting the pedal down.

I hoped that we had enough clearance for Moss, but I wasn't waiting on that thing going all the way to the top. I cleared the door and heard random pings as small arms fire was sent our way, but none found me nor the motor. I'd like to say that we got off clean, but we went from one mess to the next.

"Don't stop," Moss screamed, her voice amplified as I saw a large group of dark purple scorpions advancing on the door.

Our emergence from the doorway had made them pause, or maybe it was the sound of the motor, but they all turned to face us. They were easily six feet long and so dark purple they would have looked black if the sunlight hadn't been so bright. There were easily thirty of the creatures, and they started after us. Even though part of the faction inside the city wanted me dead and sashimi, that didn't mean I wanted the monsters to get inside. So, I went faster.

I didn't think there would be any chance they could keep up with us, but as I pushed on the gas more, urging more speed out of the buggy, they started to catch up a little. The buggy screamed as I redlined the RPMs on it. One of the creatures leaped and I flinched as I saw its trajectory would come straight at the cab. The tail was easily as long as the creature and the stinger on the tip was probably full of all kinds of things I didn't want to mess with. I'd already started to juke to the left when I saw a hammer flash out. It connected with the creature, almost sending it straight into the ground. I looked in the mirror and saw Moss's armored arm drawing the hammer back.

She'd swung it one handed from the rear of the buggy and took out the scorpion. I shuddered to think what her foreplay in an exosuit would look like… But now I was thinking about sex again for like the first time since I'd got up, and it was distracting, so instead I looked around and saw the creatures were slowing down to a stop. We'd outrun them. I went another ten minutes towards the waypoint Alice was lighting up for me, which was conveniently in the same direction we'd fled… and then rolled to a stop. This had a standard ignition put into the dash instead of a steering column, so I turned the key, killing the motor. I stood and hopped off the side and grabbed my LRG.

There was creaking of the chassis and then Moss joined me at the side. There was a whirring and her facemask opened.

You should call HER ironman, she pulls it off so much better than you do, Alice snarked.

"I am so Tony Stark," I told her. "You're just jealous that I get all the hot girls."

I'm a computer, getting the girls is not what I'm about, Alice said back in a less teasing tone.

I did a mental fist pump, and Alice gave me a mental sigh. Win one for the good guys.

"How did you manage to…" I said looking at her armor.

This set was light blue in color. It almost looked like it had been powder coated and shone in the sunlight like a piece of artwork instead of a deadly set of electronics. She stared at me, and I looked back, waiting on her.

"What?" she asked.

"How did you get a set of armor and why did you save me?"

"I dunno, why did you save me the day before?"

AWAKENED CONTROL

"It was the right thing to do," I snarled, not understanding why I was suddenly angry. Furious.

"Maybe I've lost sight of what's right and wrong, but one thing I do know... Trouble seems to follow you, and I like the adrenaline rush, the fights. It makes me feel alive. Besides, you haven't officially set me free."

"GAH!" I said and threw the LRG into the cab of the buggy.

I pulled at my wrist, wishing I had the robe. Alice would be busy negating the effects of sunburn all day. I was in what I had gone to bed in, pants, vest, and belt with my combat boots. The rest of me was exposed, and I could see the blood splatter and I had bled down my left arm and stained the vest. I brushed at it and then at my ear. Dried blood flakes came away. Never in my life before had I wanted a shower so badly.

"They will be coming for us soon," Moss said. "Was there a reason you stopped?"

"You!" I shouted, "I stopped to talk to you! What the ever loving hell are you doing? You never answered my questions! How did you get the suit? Do you know there's a tracker in those?" I asked.

"This one's been disabled," Alice and Moss chimed in simultaneously.

"Jinx dammit! Jinx, I call JINX," I screamed, almost incoherent.

"Why are you so angry?" Moss asked.

Because he's a guy and he went from staring death down, and now he's feeling conflicted, and his hormones are going crazy, and he wants to jump your bones, and he's trying not to show his emotions, and he wants to withhold how much he feels—

"Stop it, Alice," I told her aloud, cutting off her monolog of run on sentences and held my head in both hands.

"She speaks to you often?" Moss asked.

I heard the gravel crunch and Moss approached as I searched my thoughts. Was Alice right? I ignored her mental mutterings for a moment and realized that I was too hyped up to think clearly.

"You said we were a team," Moss said when I didn't answer right away, "So let me continue your journey. We can talk about the other stuff if we survive this day. I assume we're heading to scav some tech?"

"Scav?" I asked, happy for a change in subject.

"Yeah, where you raid and loot old buildings for tech from the ruins of some old city."

"Yeah, something like that," I told her. "I have it mapped out, in here," I tapped a finger against my left temple.

"So, are we a team or not?" Moss asked me.

"Yes, and if I hadn't made it clear before or not, you saved me. I'm in your debt, and thank you."

Something flashed in her eyes, and I was waiting for her to get all stabby, but she didn't. The cover on her helmet closed up, and she started moving towards the back of the buggy. That's when I saw she'd slung the chain gun in straps on the side at some point. That was how she'd been able to swing the hammer one handed and keep hold. I'd been wondering.

Get going dumbass, she's just as bad talking about feelings as you are, Alice told me.

AWAKENED CONTROL

"I asked you to dial it back some," I told her mentally, but I was moving to the cab.

Except when you were being exceptionally stupid. You have gone beyond exceptionally.

I didn't say anything and got in, firing up the motor with the key. Soon we were rolling, and I watched as the landscape leveled out some as we left the Grand Canyon area. We didn't travel far, but it wasn't as rocky and hilly as I followed the waypoint. Alice opined that perhaps a thousand years ago this area would have been forested, but it wasn't now. Just hilly and rocky. All topsoil that might have been here had eroded and gone eons ago.

Something I hadn't expected started to happen so slowly in front of me as I traveled the wastelands that I didn't notice it at first. Storm clouds were forming and, what caught my attention was the way the rear end of the buggy started rocking hard, as if somebody were jumping up and down. I slowed down, and Moss hopped off and ran to the front of the buggy.

"We need to get you under cover. Follow me," she said, some system amplifying her voice and projecting it through the mask.

I tore off after her, easily able to keep pace, but if I had to guess, the running speed of the exosuit was near forty miles an hour. She ran towards one of the small hills and started digging furiously at one of the sandy sides of a massive sand dune. I turned off the ignition and grabbed the LRG, so I had everything with me. My back had been sore and then better as Alice tweaked things because driving with a full backpack on felt oh so good! Not.

"This way," she said, brushing off some sand and exposing a door set into the hillside.

She pulled on a big metal ring as thunder crashed overhead. I looked up and saw lightning crossing the sky, making the gloomy afternoon look bright. Then the rain started to fall. Rain. In the desert. I held my hand out, and a fat drop hit my opened palm. It sizzled. That was when I was pulled off my feet by my belt and dragged into the dark opening that Moss had exposed, and she shut the heavy door behind her.

Usually, the absolute darkness like this would be blinding to even me, but there was something flashing, and I realized that it was the changer clipped to my shield generator. Weird. Still, that was enough light to cast a soft red glow for a couple of seconds before it blinked off. I saw and heard the power armor approach, and I looked around the cubby. It was cramped, fifteen by fifteen feet. Shelves lined one wall, with red fuel cans on the bottom, buckets in the middle and bags of stuff on the top. Moss held her arms out at her sides, and the armor opened up like a butterfly coming out of a chrysalis.

When Moss stepped out, I saw between the flashes that she still wore her usual leather outfit and she seemed to be favoring one arm. That was when I realized that I couldn't see her cast any more.

"Are you injured?" I asked her, walking closer.

She put one foot behind mine, pushed and rode me down to the ground and pushed my shoulders down with her hands. It was unexpected, and I was ready to defend myself against one of her knifing attempts, but I stared at her curiously.

AWAKENED CONTROL

"Am I injured? You're a dolt, a packi shit-for-brains Tracker turd. You don't stand outside in a chem storm. If we're going to be partners, you're going to have to wise up. You feel me?" She all but screamed.

"I can feel you," I said with a mental chuckle and Alice sighed... but aloud I said, "Sorry, I didn't know what it was."

She gave me one more shove in the shoulders and got to her feet. She pulled something out of her pocket and snapped and shook it. A glow stick. Some things never changed. A soft green glow filled the area around her as she held it high and walked to the shelves to inspect what was there. I headed to the door and saw a heavy bar had been placed in front. Since the door swung in it would take something big to open the steel reinforced door with close to five feet of heavy I-beam blocking it, with brackets set into cement walls.

"What is this place?" I asked her.

"I don't know. We would find these here and there in our hunts. We started using them for storm shelters a long time ago. After the last round of raiders, we generally don't come out this far—"

The thunderclap shook the world outside, and I could feel the vibrations through the cement floor. Moss looked up nervously and rubbed her arms together as if to warm up, the glow stick in her hand. I took it and walked to the shelf. Near the end, I saw a folded up piece of fabric. Pulling it out, it looked like several moving blankets, though they had to have been made in the last ten years or so. I shook one out on the concrete and then halfway unfolded another, dumping the rest next to that. Then I walked over to Moss and wrapped my arms around her.

She startled and jerked, but after half a second she calmed and then leaned back into me. Nervous response from a badass Hunter woman. Interesting. I pulled her over to where I had made a pallet on the floor and sat down. After a moment's hesitation, she sat down next to me. I handed her a blanket, and I took the last one and shook it out. I was about to wrap it around myself because I could feel the damp, when she draped hers across both our backs. I passed her another corner, and she pulled it across. After tucking it in, I leaned back against the cement wall and put the glow stick between us on the dun-colored blanket.

"What was it like, in your time?" Moss asked me.

"I don't remember much," I admitted.

She scooted so we were hip to hip. She was shivering and cold, so I put my arm around her and pulled her closer. It was crazy, but until now I hadn't noticed the shift in the wind and rain had also brought a chill to the air that was normally stifling. It had happened so suddenly that it felt good instead of freezing, but I heard the rain outside turn into something more. Small impacts. Hail maybe?

"Tell me what you know. We have time to pass."

In fits and starts, I told her about what I could remember of my childhood. My stomach rumbled, but she didn't comment, and I kept talking. Not that I could remember my parents or things about me, but about a baseball game, or how much fun it was to ride a bike in the spring sunshine. Of a time where there was war, but it was somewhere else… not in America, not in a way that every day was a struggle to survive. I talked about Superman ice cream, and the plot points to my favorite games and movies.

I felt her head rest on my shoulder.

She's asleep Tony, Alice told me quietly. *She has been for a while.*

"I know," I told her in a whisper aloud, "But it's helping me remember."

I see that. Don't overwhelm yourself. You're too close to being flooded with memories.

"What do you think I should do now?" I asked Alice, aloud still.

Try to sleep. This storm is going to be going for a while. Maybe eat when you both wake up.

I couldn't sleep, but the slow deep breathing and the rising and fall of her chest as I held her was soothing somehow. I didn't think sleep would be coming, but I was comfortable and warm and safe. I thought about baseball and tried to recapture the memory of the flavor of Superman ice cream again the way I had described it.

CHAPTER 14

The storm raged all that night, and when I woke up, probably in the extremely early hours, Moss was still out. The chemical glow stick was still emitting a faint glow, so I knew I'd slept less than six hours. Still, I had to piss, and I was uncomfortable. I gently moved away and wrapped her tightly in the blankets, taking all the time needed. The thunderous hits I had attributed to hail was gone, and now I couldn't hear as much thunder as before. Chancing it, I moved the I-beam and cracked the door slightly to relieve myself.

The night sky was lit up and purple. Rain fell about three feet beyond the doorway as the hill, and the direction of the wind worked for me for once. Movement down ahead of me, half a mile away, caught my attention as I relieved myself and watched the night sky. Lightning would flash, and thunder would follow. I finished and felt two hands wrap themselves under my arms, and Moss pulled herself close, her chin resting on my shoulder.

"I didn't mean to wake you up," I told her.

"You didn't, I was sitting there trying to pretend to still be asleep, so I didn't wake you up," she said softly.

There was something different in her voice, and I turned. The green glow stick, the flashing red light from my changer and the bright flashes of the lightning strikes lit up the inside, and I saw a softness in her expression, something I had never seen before. She held an arm out to me and pulled at me. I pushed the door closed and put the bar back on. There were things out there in the rain, things that moved and crawled. I don't know if it was the promise of tenderness from Moss or the spiderlike creatures moving at the far end of my field of sight that made me agree so easily.

"You're not going to try to knife me, are you?" I asked her as she pulled me towards the pallet.

"Not if you free me and give me what I want," she said, a smile playing on her lips.

"I've already freed you," I told her, "But what do you want?"

She whispered in my ear, and somewhere in the peanut gallery Alice queued up a memory of an old song. *Sexual Healing.*

———

I woke up in a tangle of limbs, much like that the night I had been drinking with her. But this time there was no soreness and no swollen head. There was a new glow stick that had been tossed towards the shelves where we'd shucked our clothing in a hurry. Now both of us moved slowly, neither of us wanting to lose the touch of each other. It would lead to more of what happened last night. It was not something I wanted to deal with, there were emotions I was not ready for. I could feel my chest swelling as I wanted to talk to her, to tell her that this was a bad idea.

Instead, it was her who moved towards the door first. She lifted the beam out of the way, the heavy metal brace straining her thinner form. I admired the view, I won't lie, as she didn't have a stitch of clothing on. She cracked the door open and then closed it again.

"Still storming?" I asked her.

She nodded and walked to the shelves. She pulled a bucket on the far left down and set it in front of me and then went to the clothing and started dressing. Dammit.

I pulled the bucket close, surprised at the weight. Something shifted inside it, and I pulled at the top. Then I had to think, would plastic buckets survive this long? Had it been made later on, after the nuclear exchange? There were so many things I did not know. I got the lid pried off and saw six earthenware containers with fitted lids and blocks of something wrapped in what looked like wax paper. It was tied closed with a hank of twine. I pulled at the knot, and it opened up. I smiled when I saw what it was. Modern day ship's biscuits. Hardtack. Country crackers.

I laid that packet out on the blanket in front of me and pulled one of the containers out and took the top off. In the dim lighting, I couldn't make it out, but when I smelled it, I remembered what it was. I'd had it with Yanesh and Luca's family. Yana paste?

"You going to get dressed?" Moss asked me.

"Probably soon," I told her.

"You should, we need to talk, and I don't want any distractions," she said coldly.

That stung and I put the paste down next to the hard tack and got up and went to my pile of clothing. I started putting it on, not looking at her. Yesterday, she'd gone Terminator on the Outsiders who had been with Magnus, then been a tender woman last night. Not the cold woman she was this morning. At least, maybe my male feelings might have been a little hurt that she didn't want to start the fun back up.

When I finished dressing, I joined her on the pile of blankets and saw she was scraping the crackers through the paste and eating it like half an *Oreo*. I tried the same and was surprised at the flavor. It was both in the cracker and paste, but a hint of garlic and something peppery. It wasn't bland at all, unlike the way that Luca's family had made it. Care had obviously gone into this.

"So you have to do something for me to truly be freed from being your slave," Moss said.

"Oh? What's that?" I asked her.

"I can program your band to do it, but you have to go back into Lakeville at least one more time."

"Oh, then here," I said, pulling the band and

handing it to her.

She looked at me in surprise.

"You're not going to be avoiding it after what happened?"

"No, I have to get those two servo motors, and I want to figure out how to go scorched earth on Magnus. I hate everything he stands for," I told her softly.

It was making sense why she had been cold to me, because I think she thought I would be reluctant to turn back, and however Lakeville recorded their slaves, it was the only way she'd truly be free. Still, she touched the screen of the band and got into menus I'd not seen before. In a flash, she had it done and was touching the face of my band to hers which flashed green. She handed me the band back, and I put it on my left wrist again.

"That's it? We just go back to town now?" I asked her, "The Wi-Fi will take care of the rest?"

She nodded and took another cracker and scooped more of the paste out and offered it to me. I opened my mouth, and she gave it to me. As I was chewing, she spoke.

"I have something to admit. I lied to you, just a little while ago."

My eyebrows rose. Maybe she took all my credits? Made me her slave on paper?

"It's not raining any more," she said, pushing the bucket back and pulling me close.

———

AWAKENED CONTROL

There were five gallons of water stored here. Out this far in the desert and away from the Colorado river, this would be a lifesaving amount for several people. Instead, we drank our fill, filled two small canteens with it and then used the rest to wash up. It felt glorious again to be clean-ish. In my old days, a shower or bath was a daily occurrence in the civilian side of my life, and I learned to enjoy being clean. It seemed that not much had changed in the future. Then we gassed the buggy from the fuel stores.

I expected Moss to get inside the exosuit, but she made her way to the buggy instead, shutting the door behind her as I waited to see what she'd say.

"The nuke core was running low. Unless I get more, I have enough juice in that one to maybe make it back to Lakeville," she told me.

"How hard are those nuke cores to get?" I asked her, remembering the awesome power the suit had.

"You can find them in the wastes sometimes. They were pretty common until about a hundred years ago."

"What happened?" I asked her.

"The Outsiders… They took a more… direct approach, and kept withholding technology from people. I think it's their way of having a dumbed down society, or at least keeping it that way. Easier to control."

I nodded, hating how it sounded right at the beginning. Still, Moss wasn't harmless without the suit. She had at least two knives on her, and I debated giving her the shotgun for the trip, but instead she climbed up to the turret where the gun was.

"You ready to go?" I asked her.

"You know where the scav site is. You drive on, I've got the guns," she said, patting what looked like twin .50 cal. Ma-Deuces.

She pulled charging handles on either side and then took control of a handle that looked like it could double as a squared-off steering wheel. The gun wasn't something from my time, I would have recognized it, but something from later on. It was probably based on the older technology and didn't look overly complicated, but it was… just different. I shook my head and got in, putting the LRG next to me as I'd done a couple days ago and fired up the engine. It started a little rough, and I threaded the gas pedal a bit. It blew out smoke and then the exhaust started blowing clear as the motor warmed up. I let off the pedal, and it idled smooth.

I put it in gear, and we took off, bouncing across the ground. I recalled our break from the city. It had been the first time really since we'd both stopped and parked for a day. I had forgotten to ask her about the hordes of insects and arachnids that had been hitting the walls of the ville. Was that a common occurrence out here in the wastes?

A tap on my shoulder almost startled me, and I saw it was Moss, leaning over to get my attention. She pointed. Off to my left, almost out of my range of view, were horses. Wild horses. I wouldn't say thousands, but I might be off if I only guessed a hundred. They were running in a herd from the direction we were going. The creatures were just as beautiful as I remembered them from a snatch of memory from my childhood. I could hear their hoofbeats over the growling engine and turned back to where I was going, thrilled at seeing something so pure and innocent still left in the world. We were three-quarters the way there by now, and I could see something that looked squared off in the distance.

In nature, perfect shapes don't exist much, so it draws attention. Straight lines, squared off corners, perfect circles, things like that. That's what I thought I saw in the distance as the heat coming off the ground had made the objects in the distance hazy and hard to make out.

"Is that where we're going?" I asked Alice.

Yes, you should be cautious. I know horses like to run because they are horses but something might have spooked them.

"I hadn't thought of that," I admitted, "Let me know if you see any danger before me."

Aye aye, Captain Obvious, she said and then went silent.

I kept my eyes peeled but whatever it was that might have scared off the horses didn't make itself known or simply wasn't there. The paranoia and being constantly vigilant wasn't anything new to me, but the hairs on the back of my neck seemed to be at half attention, and goosebumps broke out on my arms as we rolled up to what once was a small city or a large town. I stopped the buggy half a mile away, parked near a large boulder. I was already pocketing the key when Moss launched herself out. Both booted feet hit the ground next to me, and I got out.

"I was wondering if I needed to get the door for

you," Moss said with a grin.

"There is no door on this thing?" I asked her, slightly confused and hopped out myself.

She just smiled and gave me a nod. Then she turned and looked at the blasted city below.

"Never been to this one. How did Blakely know where to look?" She asked.

"Apparently there's a small electronics factory here, from before the great war. A caravan trader told him about it when he traded them for some items a while back. He couldn't come out here himself to make sure so…"

"He's sending us out here to scout and loot for him."

"Exactly," I told her quietly as we started to move.

I switched the LRG to my left hand and used my right to pull the shotgun off my back. I looked over to Moss to make sure she was watching and tossed it over to her. I was about to explain the safety, how to work the pump action and generally mansplain things to her when she took the safety off, racked a shell out, catching the unfired shell, looked at it, loaded it in the bottom and put it back on safe. Good thing I didn't say shit. Of course, she'd know the gun. Shouldn't surprise me.

"What, you trust me now?" she asked me in a serious tone.

"I do right now," I told her with a small smile. "Your idea of foreplay really needs a little more of a soft touch, though."

"What's foreplay?"

Facepalm! I wasn't going to explain it.

"Never mind," I told her. "What do you know about this area in general?"

"That it's one of the most toxic in the whole southwest. That there seems to be a Stalker sighting once or twice a year by caravans."

"Wait, you said Stalker? Like, how many?" I asked her, having heard about the fearsome creature quite a bit by now.

"For all, I know it's one that caravans see from time to time. It isn't weird for them to try to follow caravans and attack."

"But it could be more?" I asked her.

A knife proof, bullet proof, a giant wall of muscle, fangs and talons. Just what I wanted to worry about. Great....

"Anything is possible," she said, and we both fell silent.

It was loud with our boots making crunching noises as we walked across the dried out ground. It had probably been sand a day or two ago, but the rains had obviously pooled in places above the ground before it had either soaked in or evaporated, making the ground look like a shattered earthenware plate. It was like walking across a floor of *Fritos* sober with no beer in sight. It also could mask the sounds of somebody sneaking up on...

I turned and looked over my shoulder, still feeling paranoid when movement caught my eye. Moss saw me look and stopped and scanned the area behind us herself.

"What do you see?" she asked as I got the LRG ready, just in case.

"I thought I saw movement," I told her.

"Probably heat devils," she said, "the eyes play tricks on you. There's nothing between here and the wag."

"Damn," I said and turned back.

"Alice, did I see something?" I asked her mentally as I started walking slowly again.

I couldn't tell. What did you think you saw?

"Just movement. No defined shape."

That's all I could make out as well.

I know I was paranoid, but that didn't mean that there wasn't something out there. It was just too co-incidental to me, and I didn't want to be unprepared.

"So Moss, how do you kill a stalker?" I asked her.

"Thinking about going into the hunting trades?"

"No, I have a bad feeling, and I'd rather be pre-pared."

"Well, you pour enough firepower at it that you get it in a soft spot," she said.

"Where's a soft spot?"

She shrugged. "Never killed one before. Always ran. Almost beat one to death once in an Exosuit."

"Wait, you didn't win?"

"No, my suit got pretty beat to shit, and the thing left me for dead. When my crew showed up, I told them the Nuke Core went dead. It was a lie, but my crew didn't turn on me for being weak."

If a human in power armor couldn't take one and they don't know how to do it…

"It was a big alpha male, though," Moss said. "I probably could have taken a smaller one."

"And you didn't find any soft spots to shoot or get

stabby?" I asked her quietly as we neared some old stucco and adobe style buildings.

"Nope."

I checked behind me, and we were still clear, no movement. I turned back and moved out slowly, Moss falling behind me as the second in the stack as I came to a building that had one partial wall standing, with the rest in rubble. I inched towards the front and turned slightly, sneaking a peek with one eye around the corner. What had once probably been a street had been reclaimed by nature. Old tumbleweed, fallen stucco, and chunks of debris had been perfectly preserved and were stuck between what was left of the downtown area.

"Clear-ish," I whispered, and started around slowly.

Normally I wouldn't be moving out in the open in a situation like this, but there had been nothing normal about my time in general since I'd woken up. It grated on me some, but I was iterating as fast as I could with each situation. Also, I had no idea where the factory was located, so I had to go through town at some point to look. Luckily, it didn't look like there was much to look at. Old two story buildings that had a shopfront on the bottom with an apartment at the top. Most of them were one or two walls standing, but here and there, entire buildings stood intact with the adobe or stucco peeled off from erosion, exposing the bones of the building. No windows or wooden doors had withstood the test of time.

The ground here was just as hard and cracked as the approach into town, and I looked around.

There were footprints, and not made by booted feet. I pointed them out to Moss, and she just nodded and pointed. Ahead of us and a block over was a larger building. It was made from crumbling cinder block, the mortar giving way from the deluge of acid rain storms over the decades and centuries. I wasn't sure if there was a roof on the structure, but if there was, it was a flat roof, and I wasn't hopeful. This could be it, or it could be a school. It would be hard to say unless—

A shriek broke the silence and four figures leaped out from one of the buildings and charged us. Moss fired first, but the buckshot only winged one of the men. I fired the LRG at a man who was winding up for a swing with a length of chain and hit him when he was about twenty feet away. The round blasted straight through him, and he stumbled on, and I had to duck as I waited for the rail gun to recharge. The man's momentum took him past me where he crumpled, the shock finally hitting him, and I held the stock of the LRG up to block a sword thrust from a third man who had what looked like a barbary scimitar. Sparks flew, and I pushed up on the sword with one hand on the barrel, one hand on the action and kicked the man in the stomach.

It pushed him back but didn't do any real damage. It gave me what I needed, though: breathing room for half a second. I dropped the LRG and pulled the Beretta, and started firing as the man wound up for a Babe Ruth style batting session. The first slug hit him in the waist, near his hip and the next three rounds worked their way up towards the center mass near

AWAKENED CONTROL

his sternum where I put in two more rounds, until the man stiffened and dropped the sword. I spun and hit the deck as Moss fired the shotgun in the face of the man who hadn't engaged yet. Gore sprayed the stucco behind me, and I got the LRG and holstered the pistol. I brushed the dirt off my vest and looked.

The man that Moss had winged was writhing on the ground twenty feet away. Moss followed my gaze and nodded. I walked up slowly, the LRG now at the low ready position.

"How many of you are there in town?" I asked him.

"Go suck packi piss," the man spat.

"You know what Moss? I think he doesn't like me," I said.

"Mo… Moss?" The raider asked, his eyes wide as he focused on the only woman in the area.

"Yeah, sugar. You better answer up, or you're going to find that I might just hamstring you and leave you here as stalker bait. You know their carcasses go for close to 250k now, right?" She asked, sweet, seductive, and all rolled up in one deadly enchilada.

"I uh… you'll let me go if I tell you?"

"Yeah, I will," I interjected.

I knew Moss had a sadistic streak a mile wide, and she'd probably go through with her threat, but if she was going to be bad cop…

Good COP! Lower 'da BOOM! Alice piped up.

"There's… two more of us. Across the street. They're probably getting out of here by now," he said, holding a hand over his shoulder.

Two pellets had hit him in the shoulder, near the

armpit. It had to be painful but not life threatening. He could make it if we let him go. I looked at the building across the street, and I heard the sound of pounding feet, like a couple of somebodies had taken off running away from us.

"Good friends, you got there," I told him, kicking away the machete he had near him. "Any stalkers around here?" I asked.

"We saw one once," he said gasping, and then sat up. "We hid and it didn't even know we were here. We've been hunting Vorryn some, and when we saw you two, we thought… well, I guess we weren't thinking."

"No you weren't," Moss said, kicking him in the jewels. The man fell backward with a cry and cupped his pulverized balls. He let out pitiful cries of pain.

"Where's the factory?" I asked him, cupping my own in sympathy.

"What's that?"

"Big building with old machines. Parts."

"Oh, yeah, scrap building. That's two streets over," he said hooking a thumb over his shoulder as he caught his breath, then wiped away a tear that had escaped from his eye.

"Get up," I told him, using the LRG to make him move.

He did, and I nodded over my shoulder in what I hoped was the get out of here gesture. He did and started running. I heard Moss pump a new shell in and I turned and put a hand across the shotgun she already had to her shoulder.

"No, let this one go," I told her, "besides, I need

to give you some more ammo," I said, taking off the backpack and opening it and letting her look inside.

She dug in and pulled out a double handful of shells and reloaded, before stuffing extras in a pouch she'd had on. She got enough for two reloads before it was full and I closed the lighter pack and shouldered it again.

"Why shouldn't have we killed him?" she asked.

"He was wounded and, hopefully if there was something behind us, he'll be bait to draw attention away from us."

"You know, I thought I was evil, but you…"

I didn't really believe that, well not entirely… only partially… but it was something I could tell Moss instead of getting into the whole moral dilemma conversation. She had very little morals so she'd have no dilemma putting a slug in the back of his head.

"Let's go," I said.

"Wait, let's see what the bodies have on them."

Right, I'd forgotten to loot the corpses. She checked the two furthest off while I covered her and when she was walking back I picked up the dropped machete and checked the man she'd used the shotgun on at close range. He had a band on so I transferred his credits to me, then found an old and dented zippo lighter in one pocket with an equally old and rusty metal can of something. I was figuring lighter fluid but when I opened the top my eyes watered at the smell of mineral spirits. I guess that would work, but it'd make the cigarettes taste like shit. I put those in my pocket, not wanting to mess with my pack, when I heard inhuman shrieks.

The sound was horrible and soon it turned from fear to straight out painful sobs and then the screams suddenly cut off. A creature howled in the distance.

"What was that?" I asked her.

"I… I don't know," Moss stuttered.

We started moving towards the factory at a double time. Both of us would occasionally shoot worried looks behind us, and I tried to stuff the machete in my belt, but I was bouncing too much. I settled for slinging the LRG and carrying it as we turned the corner. The factory came into full sight as we did and I realized we were running towards where the man's two friends had fled to. No time to wait, because if what was behind us was a stalker, something that could give a person experienced in power armor a run for their money, I didn't want to get caught out in the open and have one attack.

I did a quick look and didn't see anything ahead or behind us. In faded letters, I saw that this had once been an electronics factory. The name was legible, but it was a name I normally associated with calculators. Still, this had to be the place. I hoped. I found a set of what had once been double doors made of glass and aluminum. The glass had been shattered a long time ago, and as I stepped through them, the glass crunched under my boots the same way it did across the cracked earth behind me.

"It's dark in there," Moss said. "How can you see?" Her words came out a whisper as I had crossed what once had been a small lobby to a rusty metal door with a viewing pane made of glass and chicken wire separating the rest of the facility.

AWAKENED CONTROL

"We'll do the best we can, but I've not quite got night sight," I said tapping my finger to my temple, "but only just."

I pushed the door and swore at myself. Nothing. I grabbed the handle and pulled. I was surprised when the door swung back smoothly on silent hinges. I could almost smell axel grease on the pins. It would make sense that a factory have the best working stuff ever, but it also made sense that over a thousand years most of it would have rusted out or fallen into an unmaintainable mess. This was maintained. That feeling was back again. I pulled the door the rest of the way open and stepped in.

What? Chivalry was dead when it came to this stuff. I was bullet proof, and I could see in the dark. Kind of.

I scanned the room and saw that along the tops of the twenty foot walls, there were casement windows to let in a little bit of natural light. I hadn't noticed that before, but I hadn't been looking for it either. As it was, though, there was enough natural light in here that I could make out most of the murky gloom without adjusting my sight too much. Moss followed me in and put one hand on my shoulder. I switched the machete to my left and started in slowly.

As far as I could see, there was no one inside, which was the first thing I had worried about. We had walked between stacks of rusted out machinery when it hit me what I was looking at.

"What do they call these?" Moss said, looking at a long row of machines that had conveyer belts running between the stations.

"They're called SMT machines. Surface Mount Technology. They were what made the circuit boards back in my time. I spent a summer sweeping a factory as a kid where they made machines like these. I've just never seen so many…"

Eyes on the target, Alice reminded me. *Don't get bogged down in memories. Look for the area where they combine the electronics with the hydraulic arms. That's where you're going to find the servo-motors.*

"Your eyes just kinda… flashed blue," Moss said, "just for half a moment."

"Alice says hi," I said softly and started moving down the row near where the ovens would bake the solder paste and components to the board.

No, I didn't, Alice told me, confusion in her voice.

"Uh… Hi. Thanks for not being a psycho jealous hose beast," Moss said, and I had to bust up laughing.

If it wasn't for the prospect of a stalker actually stalking us, murderous banditos in the area and a creepy factory working its magic on me, I would have taken her solemn words as evidence of how creeped out she was.

I did not say that, you better tell her, Alice chided.

"She says that we need to go to the end of the line somewhere. Where they were assembling robotic arms and things like that."

I only… Tony! Alice sounded exasperated.

I grinned to myself. It sounded like my AI was learning emotions rather well and for once I liked being the one holding the pointy stick.

We walked slowly. Once in a while, we'd step on something that would make noise, but other than that it was as silent as a tomb. We moved shadow to shadow, checking 360 degrees to make sure nothing was creeping up on us in the dark, when we came to our first place to check. It was the end of the line, and there were metal and plastic racks of green wafer boards. I didn't know what kind of circuit boards they were, but I stopped, shocked. I didn't have to look for individual parts, the conveyor belts had the same motors on them to run the thin rubber belts.

"Hold up," I said and dropped down to my knees. Sure enough, on one of the sections of conveyor, I could see the motor on the bottom side.

Alice adjusted my sight all the way up so I could see that it wasn't alone. There was a motor in the front and back.

"Those will work," Alice told me.

The problem was, I didn't have much in the way of tools with me. Actually, I didn't have any. It looked like they were bolted in place with a pin holding the shaft to a wheel that spun the belts. I put the machete down beside me.

"What you got?" Moss asked me.

"I found two we need. All of these belts probably have some. I just need a pair of pliers or an adjustable wrench—"

Metal clinked softly between my legs, and I looked up to see Moss grinning. I looked down and saw a small adjustable wrench and pliers. Craftsman. Boy, when they said those tools lasted a lifetime, they weren't kidding. I grabbed it and tried to crawl under. All I managed was to hit my head and rock the belt… so it wasn't connected, just placed in spot…

Hm… I tilted it slowly until I could lower it down. With a better angle and lighting, I started working on the bolts. The first one came off easily, and I drew the stiletto from the vest and cut the wires. The second one didn't want to come out quite as easily. I worked the bolt back and forth, and the head snapped off in my hands. Rust coated the inside of the hole, and I cursed.

I worked on the other bolt, and this one too was rusted. I went slower and more careful, and this bolt shattered as well. The good news, the housing for the servo motor wasn't threaded, just the bottom of the conveyor belt. I cut the wires on this one and pulled the pins off the wheels. Then I took both and put them between my legs while I set the conveyor back up and out of my way. I was opening my backpack when I heard the door boom open. The quiet door. The greased door. The door that made no noise, was just flung open so hard that it shook the building. That door.

"Shit," Moss whispered.

I shouldered my pack and rose to my feet slowly, keeping an oven between me and the door. I peeked over and saw a large shape moving from the doorway slowly. It was large, maybe eight feet tall, and moved with a reptilian grace. It's head… it was a nightmare. It was dark, almost black in color. If you've seen the movie *Gremlins*, you'd likely recognize what I saw walking towards us, sniffing the air like a dog. It was an eight-foot tall *Gremlin*-looking creature with a long tail dragging behind it as it walked on two legs.

"We're so fucked," Moss whispered to me.

AWAKENED CONTROL

The creature's head snapped our direction, and we both held silent. After a moment it raised its snout again and made a coughing sound as it opened its mouth. That half a moment with my adjusted vision was enough to see rows of sharp pointed teeth, and eight-inch talons on what went for hands. Three fingers, one thumb. Four of the deadly looking claws to rip and render flesh on each arm. My joke with Moss about the T-Rex a couple days ago felt stupid now. Here was the real predator, the real monster.

There was another coughing sound further back, and another one strode in the door that was swinging shut. The door banged against the wall again, the handle embedding into the sheetrock that still lined the interior. Two. Now there were two, and the first one was the baby judging by the size of the second. I started walking, using the long narrow machines as cover. I felt Moss tap me on the shoulder, and she pointed. There was a ladder set into the wall, and I followed that up. There was a small catwalk against one side of the building. Pipes ran across the ceiling, probably carrying electricals, natural gas and exhaust in and out of the building. A maintenance convenience. I followed the catwalk and saw that it led to the far side and towards the only exit I was for sure of, the one the Stalkers were covering.

"Let's go," I whispered loudly.

Smooth move, Alice chided. *That got their attention.*

"It was supposed to," I hissed, and started running.

I heard what sounded like a scream that shut off

quickly behind us, and Moss whimpered in fear. I shoved her in front of me and pushed her towards the ladder. I turned and saw the things of nightmares moving and moving fast. I gave half a glance as Moss's waist passed my head and then focused on the charging Stalker. Its scales were a mottled gray and black in a pattern that reminded me of a rattlesnake. Its mouth was open and its long arms and talons were in front of it. It was followed by the second and larger Stalker, but that one was twenty feet behind it. It almost reminded me of a dinosaur from Jurassic Park the way it was coming on, and I realized I didn't have time to follow Moss up.

I took aim with the LRG and put the dot between the charging creature's eyes and pulled the trigger. The weapon discharged, and I mentally thought "pew pew pew" and had to jump. The slug of metal hit the creature between the eyes, more towards the top of the head. The slug had ricocheted off, and the creature dropped. The problem was, its mass and momentum kept it coming. My jump was half-hearted and I tried to scramble up the ladder as the creature hit. It shook me, and I almost lost my grip but scrambled up the ladder like a monkey who'd had three triple espressos from Starbucks and was jonesing for some banana fritters.

What? That's a thing.

"Hurry," Moss called without looking back down.

I looked up and kept moving, despite admiring the view, and that was when the second creature hit the wall the ladder was bolted to. My feet came free, and I was suddenly hanging onto the ladder by one hand. It roared, and I saw it was three feet under my boots as I desperately grabbed for another rung, and pulled myself back onto the ladder. The fucker had jumped. I felt something grab onto my leg for a moment, near the knee.

I screamed in pain as it felt like my whole leg was on fire and I looked down in fear and shock expecting to see my leg torn off, but the Stalker had simply sunk its talons into my leg and ripped. The problem it had was its talons were too sharp, and it didn't pull me off. The problem I had, was the talons were too sharp, and had gone through my shield and almost cut my leg off. I tried to go as it bunched up for another leap. I felt a pulling motion but not from below, from above.

Moss had grabbed the drag handle on my vest and heaved. I never ever would have expected it, but she heaved me, plus my gear, bodily up just as the creature leaped. Its talons scored scratches in the bottom of my calf, and again I screamed in pain and then I was trying to help her, pulling myself up hand over hand until I was laying down across her on the catwalk, looking down through the mesh at the two creatures below.

The one I shot was stirring.

Healing damage. First, though, I'm blocking out the pain as best as I can.

"Thanks," I said aloud, tears streaking my face from the shock and pain.

"You would have done the same for me," Moss said and kissed me and pushed me off.

"How long until you can move?" she asked.

I looked down and rolled to my side. Somehow I had kept hold of the LRG, the strap of the sling around my right arm. I pulled it ready and made sure it didn't have damage to the end of the barrel before I answered her.

"I think I can now. It got me pretty bad, but I'll heal."

"Good."

Below, the standing creature was making a sound to the one I had shot. Was it communicating? I looked at it the same time it looked up at me. Pure evil and malice, mixed with a dash of hatred returned my look, and I shivered involuntarily as I pulled myself to my feet shakily.

"Those pants are shot," she quipped.

You are 90%, Alice told me, *Move your ass.*

I moved and made sure the timer was reset on the LRG and watched as my shield regenerated until it flashed it was back up and online. I shuddered to think what would have happened if I hadn't had even the minor protection it gave me against the four hundred pound sack of quivering alligator donkey dick.

"Yeah, let's see if we can keep them there. It looks like I knocked the one out, but the other…"

The shotgun boomed, and the larger stalker flinched and looked up, and its focus settled on Moss for the first time. She moved sideways while pumping it and fishing a shell out to reload.

"Save your ammo. I think it's going to stay with its mate."

"It's mate?" Moss said in horror.

"Move, we'll talk later," I told her.

AWAKENED CONTROL

The creature roared as we moved across the ceiling of the building via a catwalk. It was unnerving to be up here and seeing the floor below. Still, the Stalker stood by the downed one and kept nudging it with the back of its head, pushing and rolling it side to side. Its eyes only left us to do that and for the first time I wondered how intelligent they were. I had noticed a difference in sizes, and at first, I'd thought the first one was big… but I suspected that that was because, like a lot of animals in nature, it was bigger than its mate. That was my basis and how it seemed to be waiting for the other one to wake up as if it was a family member.

"Almost there," Moss whispered.

"Slide down the ladder and hit the door running," I told her. "If it comes for us, we'll have to find someplace to hide."

"Gotcha," Moss whispered back.

The second creature was getting to its feet shakily now, and I took aim. I feathered the trigger and sent another slug of metal across the factory floor now. I hit the Stalker in the back of the head, and it dropped again. Once again my slug had ricocheted off, but I'd had a different angle and not head on. It wouldn't have had as much force. Still, the creature was down, and I hoped I had bought us enough time to get out of here and not piss the big one off. Moss grabbed the sides of the ladder with her hands and feet and slid down. I did the same after slinging the LRG, and came down hard my knee buckling.

I got up and shook my leg as I scanned behind me. I couldn't see the creature anymore, but I heard

a scrabbling of claws and another of those shriek-
ing sounds. We didn't wait around to see what it was
and tore out of that factory like our asses were on fire
and our hair was catching. Gone was any pretense
of moving cautiously. Now we were running for our
lives. One block passed us in a blur, two blocks. We
were near where the bodies had been left. I wasn't
surprised to see that one of them had been dragged
away by something. More tracks in the cracked earth.
Four toes per giant foot. The drag marks moved off
in a different direction, and we paused at the back of
that building to catch our breath.

"You shot one... twice... in the head..."

"Didn't kill it," I told her, gasping but my breath
was coming back fast as Alice was working overtime.

"Never... that second one... bigger... my alpha
wasn't that big..." Moss said panting, her chest heaving.

We were trying to be quiet but an inhuman roaring cut the air, and it wasn't that far off. We looked at
each other with a DAFUQ look on our faces and then
we took off at a dead run. I knew where the buggy
was without having to think about it and I angled my
way towards it as we left the outskirts of town. The
pack and LRG were pounding my back and kidneys
mercilessly, but I kept going, urging Alice to keep me
fueled enough to make it. That was when I looked
back.

Moss stumbled. That was all it took. A stumble.
The Stalker that had been chasing us was a good forty
yards behind her, but when she went forward, probably tripping on a rock she hadn't seen, she tucked

into a roll and came down hard on her stomach from the speed of her run. I dropped the pack and shouldered the LRG. I could have maybe gotten away, but not before the creature killed her. I'd be leaving her behind to save myself. I wouldn't do that, couldn't. If I lost her, I'd go down fighting myself.

The red dot was hard to keep on target, and I only hesitated a full second before firing. Time seemed to slow, and it was almost as if I watched the slug go downrange in slow motion. It had a slight right-hand twist to it, and the rounded depleted uranium and tungsten slug of metal hit it in the throat in one of the upward bounds, just above where a human would have a collarbone. Bright red blood sprayed out, and the creature fell, rolling to its side before coming back up on its feet and moving again. I felt somebody tug at my arm and saw it was Moss. I didn't have time to run, neither did she.

"Run!" I screamed, trying to buy her time as the creature started off slow and started running towards me again. Three seconds on the LRG. Two large steps and it closed a good six feet of space with only twenty left to go. Two seconds and it had closed to within ten feet. Not enough time. I dropped the LRG and pulled the Beretta and started firing with my right hand as my left fumbled for a full magazine. I hadn't reloaded earlier, and my mistake might be what would kill me. The creature rose to full height, one clawed hand behind its back to strike when the shotgun roared, and the Stalker flopped on its back, a gurgling cry loud in my ears.

"In the throat," Moss said, racking the slide on the

shotgun. "You found its weak spot with the first shot."

"I was aiming for its eyes," I admitted.

"Well, your aim might suck, but now we know. Get your stuff, the other one might be coming."

I looked around nervously and let Alice slow my breathing some. I walked over and picked up my LRG, shaking the barrel, making sure nothing was in it, and topped off the mags of the Beretta before putting my backpack back on. I squatted down next to the dead Stalker and looked at it and pretended that I couldn't see how impatient Moss was getting.

"You know how to skin one of these things?" I asked her.

"You can't be serious," both Moss and Alice chimed at the same time.

I laughed, and neither of them could understand why. That joke, that one I'd keep to myself.

CHAPTER
15

We stopped at the spot Moss had shown me. I used what little water was left in storage here to wash the stalker blood off my skin. It tingled like it was acidic. Alice said it had a bit to it and it was draining my resources. Using sand to try to wash it off hadn't worked as well as I'd hoped and just made my skin raw, but I had the front and back side of one giant assed lizard that had tried to eat us. That, and the claws. They were so sharp, I figured they might have good trade value on the black market. There was something I wanted besides the servos, and that was every advantage I could get against Magnus. That meant upgraded weapons, shields, armor, more guns... better guns... maybe some mercenaries. All could be had as long as the credits were legit.

Mine were. So far. I just didn't have enough, though I thought I could trade the hide of the Stalker for at least a new shield generator and some of the crazier looking tech I saw there. Once I was done cleaning up, I stripped out of the torn white pants I'd taken from the Order of Purists and changed them out with an old set of brown robes and homespun pants made out of the same material. It was scratchy, but I was able to get the shield generator on the vest under the robes. A plan was coming together, a crazy one, but I thought I might have a way inside the ville, Moss too, if we played it right.

"So what are you thinking?" Moss asked.

"How much do you know about the changers?" I asked her.

"You tap the middle to activate it, tap it again to scroll through the options and if you go to the end it shuts it off like it is now."

"Good," I said and tapped the center twice.

The shield generator was invisible, but one of the mods was a changer, and it changed the appearance of my skin. Now I was a nut brown ale color, more tan and red than chocolate. I tapped it again, and my skin turned ebony. Too dark. I went back to the first option and wished I had a mirror.

"You know, with your hair growing out on top and kinda covering your scar, you don't quite look the same."

"You're going to tell me I'm hot, probably like an ex or something. Yeah?" I asked her, joking.

"No… you don't. Sorry."

Burned!!!!!!!!!!!!

AWAKENED CONTROL

"I hate you sometimes," I said mentally.

hahahahahahahahahahahah—

I ignored her and turned to Moss. "I can't fool Magnus, but what about the guards?"

She gave me the once over and shrugged.

"So that's a maybe?" I asked as she took one of the trail crackers and scooped a big dollop of Yana paste on it.

"It's a maybe," she answered, and devoured the whole glob in one bite.

"Now we have to figure out how to get you snuck in."

"If we're sneaking in, why don't we just take the secret passage?" she asked, around chewing her food.

I stopped what I was doing and stared at her. She swallowed and looked back up at me, with her head tilted.

"What?"

———

"This is insane," I told her for the third time.

"Trust me, I've done this before."

I trusted her, but I didn't trust myself. We'd stashed the buggy a ways back and were now approaching the bottom of the hydro dam near Lake Powell and the Colorado river.

"I feel naked without my guns," I told her.

"They stick out and mark you. You still have your hand shooter," she told me with a smirk and turned to go to the shoreline.

But... but... but...

Suck it up buttercup, Alice interjected. *She told you the plan, and you agreed.*

Grrrrr…

I followed Moss as close as I could. The sound of the water falling and hitting from where it came out was loud. It came down in a spray, a lot like a water-fall. The dam up close looked like it'd been patched and repaired dozens or hundreds of times since the big war and I could see that there were cracks in the concrete where water seeped through. This wouldn't last forever. Hell, I'd be surprised if this marvel would be here in another year. I walked on a concrete ledge no more than a foot wide now, at the base of the dam.

Moss turned to face the river with the dam at her back and inched her way to the left, towards the eastern side of the river. I followed suit the best I could. If I'd been wearing my pack instead of stashing it, I'd have never fit. As it was, my booted feet hung over the ledge a bit. As I passed the water coming out a foot from my face, Moss called out.

"Don't touch the water. Force of it will throw you off. There are rocks down there," she said without looking, and it was all I could do to not shuffle a little faster.

It took ten butt-clenching, gut-wrenching minutes to crab walk to the other side of the water and start walking the opposite shoreline. From the other side, the small shelf in the rock face wasn't visible, but what was right under it was. An outflow pipe almost eight foot in diameter.

"In there?" I asked her.

"Yep," she said grinning, and knelt down and held

onto the edge of the ledge till her feet dangled.

I watched as she dropped to the top of the outflow pipe and then she repeated the action. Before she dropped, she swung her body, and the inward swing took her out of my sight as she entered the pipe.

"Why did I think this was a good idea?" I asked myself.

Because you love spiders, rats, mice, oh, and you really love centipedes, Alice said hitting every creepy crawlie note that freaked me out.

"I really hate you sometimes," I said and mimicked Moss's motions until I was swinging into the outflow pipe.

Moss was in there about ten feet back where it started to get dark, and I saw her pull something out of a pocket and bend it till I heard a snapping noise and she shook it. Another chem light. She held the green stick up over her head in her left hand and pulled a knife in her right. I was thinking about my Beretta, but she'd told me no gunfire. The sound would echo all along the ville. Apparently, this was an emergency storm drain if the dam overflowed and was going to flood the town. It had happened from time to time but not in recent memory.

Still, it was dank, dark, smelled like a sewer and what the fuck just slithered by my foot? I jerked around, pulling the stiletto instead of the gun as something slithered out of sight and dropped into the water behind me.

"What the ever-loving—"

"Shhhhh, it was just a snake."

Add snakes to the creepy crawly list. I hurried up

and put my free hand on her shoulder and tilted my head up in the lead on gesture. I mean, she had the light. She could… go first. She had big stompy man boots. Did I mention I hate things that creep and crawl? I did? Good.

We walked slowly about twenty more feet and turned left at a fork. We walked there, and it wasn't long before I became hopelessly lost. Left fork, right fork… crawl up a short ladder to another set of pipes… Alice assured me she was taking note but I was starting to wonder if Moss was lost too.

"This is new," she said after a minute.

There were several crates stacked and what looked like a bedroll laid out on the top. A lumpy pillow was on top of that. The smell here was worse than the areas that had water. Somebody was living in this portion, and it smelled like they used it as a latrine, and nearby. I checked my boots just to be on the safe side. Alice motioned for me to follow. I stepped wide of the makeshift bed, and she led me to another intersection. It was a three-way intersection, and two of the tunnels rose up in slope. One ran down.

"The right one," she said and pointed, offering me the glow stick.

"Aren't you coming with me?" I asked her, confused.

"I'll meet up with you," she said. "This tunnel leads to a grate in Blakely's shop. You should be able to get in. Come on back down, and I'll meet you here in two hours."

"What are you going to do?" I asked her.

"Rogue healer. I have to get a new flesh cast. My wrist…"

Dammit, I should have guessed. It was my fault she was in it and now that I thought about it, her hand had been functional, but she'd been favoring her good one after the ladder escape.

"Yeah," I said and pulled her close. "Meet me here. Two hours."

"You know what to do if I'm not here?" she asked.

"Burn the town down, kill the outsiders, nuke the whole canyon."

She let out a laugh, and for the first time, I saw what she would have looked like as a little girl. I pulled her close and squeezed her tight. No day was ever guaranteed, but moments like this were now what were keeping me going. Oddly, Alice was silent with Moss around. The AI was probably perceptive enough to know when I needed her and when I needed a joke or a poke in the ribs. The tender moment was broke as Moss's knee came up and at the last second I brought my knee up and twisted so she caught me in the outside of the thigh.

"Son of a bitch," I cursed, and hopped around on one leg a couple of times, thoroughly Charlie horsed.

"You come back too, or I'm going to do much the same."

Freaking psycho hottie. That hurt. I wasn't going to say that out loud, but she was going for full contact with my balls. Not cool. We'd have to discuss safer methods of PDA. My balls in danger were no longer on the table. Errr… never mind. I took the tunnel and wondered if she'd had another glow stick or if she even needed it now. Moss was stuck in my thoughts. It was the first time since Alice that I could remember being stuck on a woman the way I was on her.

She was everything I'd never set out to find. Wild, crazy, literally crazy, passionate and off her rocker violent. She saw nothing wrong with taking a swing or kick at me in play, or a knife for that matter. Her moments of tenderness were disarming and more than once, when I thought I was falling head over heels for her, did the small quiet voice in my head… and not Alice's… wonder if I was being set up.

Dark thoughts swirled through my brain as I slowly traveled up. If the pipe had been smooth there would have been no way to climb, but it was ribbed like a culvert pipe but larger. The pipe reduced and then reduced in size again and stopped at a large floor and wall grate. The grate was literally a 90-degree affair, round like a manhole cover that had been bent. I pushed and was surprised when it slid away. It made a screeching noise and I hurried and got up to find Blakely looking over at me with HUGE eyes.

"It's you," he said as a statement.

"Yeah, I'm back."

"You find the servo motors?"

"I've got two of them. You wouldn't believe me if I told you how much trouble it took me to get them."

"Probably not. Let me guess, it was in the middle of a stalker nesting ground, right?"

I stopped and stared at him. He seemed to shrink back and could probably see that I was pissed.

"Yeah, how did you ever guess?" I asked, my voice low.

AWAKENED CONTROL

From my side, I pulled a rolled and tied shut package of black scales. Blakely flinched and watched my hands and the package as I untied it.

"I heard things, but I didn't know if it was the same place," he admitted. "We don't have maps to verify anything."

I sighed. That was believable. I put the gory bundle on the table and unrolled it, showing the two motors that had been wrapped in the shredded white cloth from my pants.

"Oh hey, these might work just by plugging them up," he said and took them.

I followed him over to a bench where he sat both of them down. He used a wire stripper to expose the copper wires of the motors and used the same alligator clips to attach to the motor. The first one whirred to life. The second one when tested resisted at first and then it started whirring. I smiled grimly.

"So I can grease this one up, but you don't need me to do anything else really. Twenty credits?" He asked.

I made it 20k and bumped bands with him. His face lit up when he saw that and then looked at the stalker hide for the first time.

"You took out an alpha?" He asked, his voice filled with awe.

"Took teamwork, but yeah. He got so close, I could smell the last victims BO on its breath," I admitted.

"That's so gnarly," he told me, and I had to bite my cheek.

"I'm headed upstairs to sell it and buy some stuff.

Can you have that second motor ready to go in an hour or less?"

"Oh yeah," he said smiling. "This is no problem, and for good measure, I'll do the same with the other one. You can never be too careful."

That's for damned sure.

Two is one and one is none, Alice said from the peanut gallery.

"Thanks, Blakely. I'll be right back," I told him rolling and tying the hide again.

He got to work, and I left, the same way I'd come in before. I went up one level, and when Jonald saw me walking, his eyes got huge. He must have recognized me and that was when I remembered he'd seen me and Moss up close and personal, rolling around. No fooling this guy. Still, I slowed to a stop by his table.

"Anything good, Jonald?" I asked.

"You are crazy for coming here. Boris is down here somewhere."

"Who're the most honest dealers down here? I'll give you 10k for the information, and I'll leave you alone."

He hesitated and then nodded. I worked for the band and then bumped it to his. He double checked the deposit and then told me. He pointed out three dealers after I told him some of what I was looking for. I thanked him and left quickly as promised. As I did, I saw him wipe sweat from his brow. I made the poor dude nervous.

The first table was the one I had passed days ago. It had shield generators and bits of reactive armor. It was run by a younger woman with what could have been her mom standing behind her.

"Hi," I said softly, taking the hide out and undoing the ropes.

"Hi, what do you have… Oh, my," the mother said.

"Is that what I think it is?" The younger woman asked.

"Adult Alpha Stalker hide, fresh."

"We can't afford that," the mother told me.

"What if I wasn't looking for just cash?" I asked her.

They both leaned forward.

———

"They both check out fine, and the modifications to your changer are working. Shield is now three times as strong as the first one. You still need to avoid blunt force trauma, but it's a vast improvement. Also, the augmented healing envelope will work well with your nanites. It'll also slow down how many calories you need to consume to keep me functioning, as it'll take some of the load off."

"Too bad they didn't have another set," I grumbled.

I'd traded one-half of the hide, the front, for an upgraded shield generator, modifications to my changer and an IOU from them for a good forty thousand credits worth of materials. I hated to leave it like that, but to buy what I wanted straight out would have wiped out my credits entirely, and it was the next vendor that I needed them for.

He was across kitty-corner from where I'd bought the shield, and most of his merchandise was covered by a black tarp making lumpy shapes on the table.

"Looking to deal a little death? Banish some badasses?" he asked.

"I need something that'll disable Exosuits," I told him quietly.

Since the Outsiders were the only group that had Exosuits, it was obvious to him I was prepping for something nefarious. I was hoping he would approve. He looked left and right nervously, and made a subtle gesture with his finger, urging me closer.

"Fifty thousand each," he whispered, "and I've got two."

I played with my band and bumped it to his.

"Well, where you gonna put them?" he asked, handing me two round globes.

"I dunno, hadn't…"

"Amateurs," he muttered and turned. When he turned back to me, he was holding out a utility belt.

If Batman could have a badass belt with pockets for everything, so could I. I put it on above my other belt, the pouches hanging down at arm's length. I liked it. My vest under the robe could hold the grenades, but it would be bulky in the wrong places… plus I liked looking like a superhero.

You know you're lame right? Like the lamest of the lame? There are losers out there who don't even know who Batman is and you're fangirling all over an exaggerated fanny pack?

"Shut up," I told her aloud, by accident.

AWAKENED CONTROL

The man looked at me curiously and then shrugged.

"Sorry, the voices," I said and grinned.

The man paled, and I grinned and walked on, in my fancy new superhero belt, the grenades a comforting weight. They were EMP grenades, something Moss had told me about. You twisted them from the middle and threw them. They sent out a pulse of EMP energy contained within a fifty-foot circle. Alice told me she'd be shielded by it, but things like power armor and non-military electronics would be knocked offline or stunned. They weren't powerful and had been designed to disrupt and not destroy. I hoped.

I turned and went two more stalls down to where a man was wearing a bandolier of thirty caliber shells crossed over his chest. He once probably had blonde hair, but it was turning gray as evidenced by the chest hair that seemed to be trying to overgrow the shells.

"Can I get ya?" the man asked.

"Nuke cores," I whispered to him.

He didn't look surprised but just nodded and the pointed to the hide.

"What you got there?"

"Adult alpha male stalker hide. This is the backside as you'll see from the ridges, the thickest and strongest part of their carcass."

The man was nodding as I unrolled it. I held it up as high as I could, skin side to me so he could get a look. I wasn't tall enough to spread it all out, but I thanked the stars that my dad had been a hunter and taught me how to skin out beasts... well, not this kind of beast but you know what I mean.

"That's the best one I've seen yet," he told me, "Good coloring, tiger striped with a diamond pattern. Natural camouflage."

"How many?" I asked him.

"Two," he said without looking me in the eyes, and reached out to caress the scales.

"Four, and an undamaged data core."

The man jerked as if I'd yanked on something delicate.

"No," he said. "I don't know what you're into, but nobody sane around here would stock that. Two fusion cores and that's it."

"Three cores and one data core."

"What are you going to put on the core?" The man asked me slowly, his gaze finally meeting mine as he pushed the hide down and onto the table.

"What if I told you that I am going to try to put an end to the information repression that the Outsiders have been doing forever?" I said.

"Well, I don't know about that. Too much gets out, it'll put guys like me out of business," he said.

I hadn't thought of that, but Alice whispered something and I agreed.

"Not everyone is going to know how to read or interpret the information. They are going to need men like you and Blakely. Tinkerers and deep thinkers. I need the data core to transfer information."

"Then what are you going to do with it?" he asked, his voice rough.

"I'm going to give it away, broadcast it across the network to anybody who wants it."

"Magnus will kill you first."

"He's tried twice, once in the arena and once when I broke out of here."

"Aye, I thought it was you," he whispered. "If I didn't know you by your past deeds, I'd be turning you in myself, Augment. As it is—"

"As it is, people will suffer and die. Women and girls are abused at the whim of the Outsiders' desires… the Order of Purists is a little better, but they are so stuck in their religion they are almost as oppressive…"

A smile broke out on the man's face, and he held up a finger. He turned and fiddled on his shelf, and a section of the back wall slid back. He reached in, pulling stuff out.

"Here's three, with one data core. If you are who I think you are, Moss will tell you how to use this stuff. I'd get you a damn Exosuit if I could."

I handed him the hide, and he rolled it up quickly and placed it behind the table somewhere in the shadows. How had he known about Moss and I? Was there an underground resistance I needed to tap into? My thoughts swirled.

"Do me one favor, though," the man said leaning forward to whisper and held out his hand. I held mine out, and four cardboard boxes the size of old school fuses were dumped in my hand, "make sure you kill him hard. Magnus, I mean."

"That's the only way I kill," I told him. "Dumped a damn container on that cyborg's head last time they tried me. Magnus? I'll have to be creative."

"Saw it, now scat. Boris's coming."

I shot a glance over my shoulder and saw the big

man pushing his way through the crowd. He was looking around wildly, but his eyes passed over me twice.

"Thanks. I'll see you," I said and started making my way back to where I had been.

I tried to walk casual, but it was difficult. How much would he remember me? It sounded like he'd been alerted by somebody, but I had no idea who. Also, he'd not seen this face, I hadn't had the changer when I'd put his boy down hard in the arena. He was looking for a very light skinned man, and I looked at least as dark as the people of Lakeville. Still, I was an unfamiliar face, and it might be enough to trigger him to look closer at me.

I timed my passing to bend and look at shield generators as he walked by. The mother and daughter dropped me a wink and then motioned with their heads as he walked past. I hurried back to the back staircase and within moments I was back on the lower level with Blakely.

"Boris was down here a little bit ago," he said in a dull voice. "I think he might have been looking for you."

Something about his voice was familiar, and had been for a while, but all of a sudden, it clicked. He sounded like the dude who played Napoleon Dynamite. I almost cracked a vote Pedro joke but held back.

"Well, I'll be out of here if you're done."

"Oh yeah, here ya go, watch," he said, and clipped the power leads to the motor.

It started up and started humming smoothly.

AWAKENED CONTROL

He unplugged it and handed me both servo motors. I thought about it for a sec and picked a different pouch for each, balancing the weight on my new Spiderman belt.

You said Batman last time, Alice chirped.

"Shut up," I said mentally, and I got a feminine chuckle in reply.

"So, uh, he's headed back this way. See?"

I'd missed the small screen of a CCTV monitor, and saw that he was about ten seconds away from the door. I took off in a dead run for the corner and slid the grate out of the way. I dropped down into the hole and heard the door open as I was pulling it closed. Instead of dragging it, I picked it up, straining my arms, trying not to drag it and make a sound. I got it lined up and lowered it slowly as I heard the voices above.

"Detectors show that the CEPM who killed a member of my family is somewhere down here. You have telemetry readings so we can zero in?"

"I'm shutting down for thirty seconds," Alice said in warning, and I was alone in my head once again.

"Uh… for sure. Here," Blakely said, and I heard shoes scrape.

"Hm… It shows it was near the front door the last ping. No trace now?"

"No man, I don't see it on the screens. Do you?"

"You're the tech guy, mister fix it… Did he buy anything from people?"

"I don't know," Blakely lied, "But I'll send you a ping as soon as he comes back on telemetry."

"That's good, thank you," Boris said.

I heard a door open and close and started down

the tunnel to the meeting space. He'd lied for me. Maybe there was something going on. I needed to talk to Moss.

———

Somebody was going to die. That's all there was to it. I'd waited two hours and was now making my way topside. As soon as Alice had come back online, she'd started checking the networks for who had been tracking us and how. She theorized that there had to be a new kind of technology that gave a rough idea when a CEPM was in the area and active. It was how they had been alerted when I'd first made my way out of the Data Arc. Regardless, Moss wasn't back, and I was heading topside to make my promise to her good.

I followed the upward slope and came to a T junction. For a moment, I couldn't tell which way she'd gone, but then I noticed about four feet down the right intersection that a spot on the wall had been brushed smooth as if somebody had bumped it and wiped the grime clear of the side. I headed that direction, Alice assuring me she was keeping track of the directions I was taking so I could come back in a hurry if I needed to. That pipe seemed to run on for what felt like hours until it abruptly ended. A small ladder had been propped against the wall, and there was a grate above, set into an old crumbling concrete sill.

I pushed the grate up when I got to the first couple of steps and pulled myself up slowly. I was behind a ramshackle building the size of a shed. Corrugated sheet metal, black tar paper, and plywood seemed to be held together with bubblegum and baling wire into some sort of three-sided structure with a roof. Still, it gave me cover, and I got to my feet, my hand itching for my gun. I left it under the robes and considered closing the grate. I knew I might have to come through here in a hurry, so I left it open despite the chance somebody could find it and figure out how I got in.

I walked around the side of the structure and saw I was back on the market. I pulled my hood up over my head to keep the sun off me, and to give me more cover and started walking. Somebody bumped into me. A boy maybe… and then when he turned to apologize I saw it wasn't a boy after all, but it was the girl… the one who'd thought my pale skin was unusual and amazing a couple days ago. One problem, though, was that now I didn't have the same skin tone.

"Sorry mister—"

"Oh hey," I said, "no worries."

Something in my voice made her give me a second look, and her eyes shot wide. I figured she was going to bolt or scream and I didn't want to have to conk her out or chase her and make a big scene. Instead, she stepped forward.

"You're the guy who beat Boris's men in the arena? The one who usually is pale?"

"Yes," I whispered to her, mindful that there were people walking all around us.

"You look so different. Not bad, just… This is not a good color for you."

Despite the nerves and fear, that caught my funny

bone, and I gave her a grin.

"Hey, can you tell me where the rogue healers operate?" I asked her.

She looked at me nervously and then over my shoulder.

"On top of the dam, on the walkway heading towards the water and Mesa," she said, and then ducked under my arm and was lost in the crowd.

I spared a look behind me and saw Boris walking through the market, pushing people out of the way, looking for something. Someone. He hadn't seen me, but once again his eyes roamed over the area I was at. Time to move.

I started walking. With Lakeville built on the west side of the Dam and partially over the water, it was easy to find the walkway that crossed the dam. Fishermen threw their lines on the lakeside and dotted every spare inch of wall space. Most had nothing behind them, but a couple had pulled up what looked like a mutated walleye, their eyes huge and glassy, spaced on their heads like flounder. I tried not to look too closely but put distance between myself and Boris. If he was here, Magnus was probably rounding up troops to capture or kill me.

Note to self, watch out for power armor. Not a good way to get killed.

Soon, I saw at the end of the walkway that headed north, behind several sets of tents. Most were old canvas, the wind and elements having almost shredded them to bits. I looked behind me and didn't see anybody obviously following, and ducked into a green one. With the shredded canvas, it was bright inside as the light came through cracks and tears in a hundred places. A pair of stools were on one side, and somebody was sitting with their back to me on a rolling stool of their own.

They spun around when they heard me, and I saw it was a young woman, dark skinned and dark haired.

"Good 'un eh? What ails ya?" Her voice had an accent to it that sounded a cross between Appalachian homeboy and something exotic…

"Your ancestors were Australian?" I asked her.

"Isn't polite to talk about me parents as such. Daddy came from Scottish stock and my momma was a mutt, probably a barrel woman for the Aussies, yeah."

Uhhhhhh… what?

"So what can I fix on ya, or are you having a problem with your wee baron?" She asked, pointing down at my crotch.

I cupped it instinctively and backed up.

"No, I'm looking for somebody," I told her, "Moss. Have you seen her?"

"Aye, she's two tents over. Come with me, I have to check on a patient and then I'll wake her up for ya."

She stood, and I followed her. There were four tents in a line, but despite knowing where Moss was, I followed. Part of me felt relieved, but I did wonder why she was asleep. Did she not believe me when I said I'd nuke the canyon? I followed the doc into the second tent. I tried not to stare, but there was a man and a woman who looked close enough to be twins in their features. Both were stripped to their waists and IV lines were running from one to the other. Blood transfusion? Why were they…

"His sister has a clotting issue he doesn't have. I strip them to watch for a reaction. These two are twins and grew up in the same house. Nothing they haven't seen before," the doc said, and proceeded to check on them both.

She pressed two fingers to their throats checking their pulse and then looked at their backs. I stood there and waited. I guessed bedside manner was different in the future. As the doc turned to leave I went to follow were both brother and sister raised their right hands and waved in the exact same manner and speed. I tried not to get creeped out. Failed that.

And now we were walking into the third tent where Moss… wasn't.

There were a cot and a rolling stool in this one. A metal cabinet on the side held old medical supplies, probably needles and cloth bandages preserved in plastic. Still, no Moss...

"She must have left?" the doc said. "She paid me for a new cast, one that'll last to the end of the healing and then…"

I tore out of there and into the last tent. The smell of chems and something sickly sweet hit my nostrils. There was what looked like two cauldrons set onto the concrete. One had a milky white liquid in it, and the other was clear with what looked like long strips of white cloth in it. An IBC tank filled with something was also set off to the side with a black box and a set of wires and a tub running into it. Tech. No wonder the doc was called a rogue… Still, as long as she was patching people up, Magnus might have looked the other way...

"Where is she?" I asked the Doc who rushed after me and tried to pull me out of there.

"You can't be in here," the doc said.

"Where is Moss?" I asked her, shaking her hand off my arm angrily.

"She must have left."

"Why was she asleep?" I asked.

"She…" she looked around, and her eyes settled on the tote, "She asked for a new flesh cast and a hot shot."

Drugs?

I don't know what she means, Alice told me mentally.

"What do you mean a hot shot?" I asked her, my voice suddenly very calm and very quiet.

The doc noticed the change and took a step back.

"You're with the Order?" she asked me, real fear popping out in her voice.

"No, and before you ask, I'm not with the Outsiders either," I said in a low growl.

"It's just that Brother Gregory was here earlier asking about her, he knew she'd been around here. Doctor-patient confidentiality and all, so I didn't…"

I tore out of there, knowing a load of bull when I heard it. There was no doctor-patient confidentiality, not that she'd shown me so far, but she'd been afraid and slipped. She may not know what had happened to Moss or when, but she'd put the pieces together. The same damned way I was doing. I remembered how the second in command of the Order of Purists was. He hated Moss with something so pure it was plain for all to see. I know that Doctor Nicholas Sparkman, aka. Brother Tims was in charge, but he was old and almost completely blind. The scientist may not even have known what was going on. If that was in fact what was going on.

I broke out into a dead run, all pretense of stealth was gone. I clipped people as I ran past, sometimes bowling others over. I knew where I had to go and it wasn't going to end well. The brothel took me ten minutes of sprinting to reach, and I was debating what Gregory might have done. He'd been more enraged when he heard I'd planned on freeing her, but I wouldn't put it past him to have one of his acolytes hold her and possibly kill her. Order or brothel? Indecision was killing me, and finally, I made my mind up and went running to the Order of the Purists.

I didn't slow down when I got close to the door. Instead, I lowered a shoulder and counted on Alice healing me, and hit it with all of my two hundred and fifteen pounds at a dead run. The jam shattered and the door went flying backward. I blocked out the pain before even Alice could.

"Gregory!" I bellowed.

There were startled men from the order in what looked like the front of the old church, but they scattered with my shout. I strode forward, wishing the grenades in my pouch were conventional. Killing somebody for eating the wrong fish? These backwoods shitheads were just as bad as the outsiders in their own special snowflake kind of safe spaces way.

"Gregory!" I shouted again.

Several younger men came running out towards

me from what had to be the main church with wooden clubs in their hands. Their idea of guards. The clubs seemed to be wrapped with what looked like barbed wire. They must have seen old reruns of The Walking Dead … The first one swung as I stepped in and dodged under the blow. The second man was winding up, and I hit him as I was coming back up to my full height. I didn't hold back and was surprised that he flew backward, his head hitting the old wood door that led to the church.

I side kicked the man who'd missed me first, my boot connecting with the side of his knee and it made a sickening crunching sound, and his leg went the wrong way. He screamed and dropped the bat. He was on one knee and had both hands on the ground when I punched him in the back of the head. The screams stopped. I flexed my hand, making sure it wasn't broken, and then pushed the double doors open and shouted again.

"Gregory? Where is Moss?"

I saw red and the men and women of the church scattered. I saw two hunched figures talking to each other near the altar. I made a beeline for them. A couple of men came towards me, their hands up as if to ask me to stop. The robe I was wearing was loose enough, and while I'd been striding forward, I'd reached into the fold and gotten the Beretta loose.

"Move out of my way," I said, not breaking stride.

They babbled, and I realized they were speaking in Navajo.

"Move out of my way, only warning," I said in their language.

BOYD CRAVEN

The man gulped, "You must not do this, it is a house of worship—"

While he was looking at the pistol, I sucker punched him with my left hand in the throat. Not hard enough to crush his windpipe, but enough to drop him and make him gulp. The other two men beside him lifted their hands up high, now in the universal gesture of don't shoot. I stepped over the fallen man and kept an eye on the other two until I had to turn to see where the old priests were. They were still talking, but the younger one was pointing at me and shouting something.

A mixed group of young adults swarmed me, and I did the best I could to push them back, but when that didn't work, I fired a shot off over their heads with my right hand. A young man who was probably no older than 18 was in the middle of throwing a punch my way when I shot him. Bits of the finger and his fist splattered and the bullet embedded itself in the wall behind him. The screams and shouts were loud and overwhelming. I pushed and kicked people out of the way. Apparently mass had been in session when I made my entrance.

"Gregory," I repeated but didn't have to yell it this time.

I had made it to the front of the church, and most of it had cleared out. Friends of those I'd hurt and maimed were trying to get their people out of my range. The smell of burnt powder seemed to have followed me, and I could see Nicholas using the Altar to hold himself up, hyperventilating. Gregory, on the other hand, his chest was heaving, but his face was bright red with rage.

"You dare?" he fumed, spittle flying out of his mouth.

"Where is Moss?" I demanded, raising the Beretta.

"You mean the whore of Babylon? The lying, cheating, murderous, psychotic, torturer?"

I fired once. The round hit between his feet and he jumped back a step and lost his balance.

"You call her a whore again, and I'll shoot your balls off," I told him as I strode closer.

"Listen to me Tony," Nicholas said, "This is doing more harm than good."

I turned the Beretta on him and made sure it was close enough that he had 9mm to look down and see his own death.

"Where is Moss?" It was a question that had an unsaid promise behind it; tell me, or it's over.

Right here, right now.

"I didn't take her, Gregory was just telling me that she was seen in town and he had some of the—"

"Where is she?" I asked Gregory, turning the pistol on him.

He started laughing and shaking his head no. That was when I burned through a whole clip. I didn't delight in torture, but sometimes you need to prove to the other person that there are worse things than death. There is wrath, and today I took up that mantle. I shot off parts that he would need, I shot off digits and crippled joints. He quit laughing after the first shot, but I had a point to make. He would die of these wounds, I had no doubt, but I didn't hit anything vital. Yet.

He screamed incoherently in pain, trying to pull himself into a fetal position, but it hurt too badly.

"Last chance," I said, changing mags. "Where did you have her taken?"

"Brothel," he gasped.

I fired once more and walked away. I turned once to look at my handiwork and saw the blood splattered face of my surgeon Nicholas looking in my direction.

"It didn't have to be this way," he whispered.

"Sometimes, it does," I said and spat.

I'd like to say I remembered my walk to the brothel but that would have been a lie. Somewhere between the central part of the church and the front door I was intercepted by a mix of ville guards and toughs from the church. The fight was bloody and fast. I wasn't going to waste time. No one was armed with more than an electrified trident and nobody was wearing body armor. When I started walking bullets into bodies at close range, they fought on for another half a second before they turned and ran. I didn't stop to see how many I had downed, but I did a mag change and pulled a handful of shells out of the box in my mostly flattened dump pouch and started reloading the mags with the Beretta held in my left armpit, ready for easy, quick use.

There were screams as I stood there and when I was done reloading and, watching everyone scatter from the front doors of the brothel, I picked up a trident and walked in. Actually, more like I kicked the door in.

Tony, you are in a rage. Stop, Alice tried to plead.

"This is the one place, the one fucking place she

was terrified of!" I screamed aloud.

I saw movement and turned, firing. My shot missed, but the big woman who was mostly torso flipped over backward trying to dodge. The cart she was on rocked, and I ignored her. The dance floor was mostly empty with bodies fleeing out of any door possible. I caught sight of a big form across the room and tucked the Beretta in my holster. I hefted the trident and triggered the button to turn on the sparks and threw it like a spear.

Boris roared like a bear as the three tipped spear hit him in the shoulder. He ripped it out, spraying the already red lit room with his own crimson blood and spun, his hand coming up with what had to be an old Smith and Wesson .500. I'd pulled the Beretta immediately after my throw and faced him.

"Where's Moss?" I asked him.

"She's upstairs," he said, closing the distance between us.

"There is no upstairs," I replied, taking aim.

He shrugged, but there was no humor or amusement in his face or eyes. The trident had to have hurt, and he was bleeding freely, but I could see it wasn't a critical wound.

"Some jerks believe me and spend hours looking. She's in my quarters. I was on my way to break her in."

"She's not your property," I told him.

"She's not yours either," Boris said, cocking the big gun. "What was it you told us here? How you adopted the motto of Lakeville. what was it again? Keep what you can? The bitch is mine."

He fired the same time I did. It felt like I was hit

by a locomotive.

Shield's down to 24%, you cannot take another hit like that, or it might kill you.

"I'm working on getting my heart to beat and starting to breathe again," I told her mentally.

This conversation took a millisecond, but as I hit the ground, I saw my bullet had grazed the cheek of the big man, his heavy slug throwing my aim off as he hit me first. He wiped at the blood with one hand and thumbed back the hammer of the massive revolver. I rolled to the right, trying to stay out of Boris's sight picture while the shield recharged.

"I see you've gotten a tan," the big man bellowed. "It's too bad you won't be around to enjoy it."

He fired, and chunks of concrete flew up. They did almost as much damage as the bullet would have and it discharged the shield in a bright flash and several sharp slivers cut my face and arms. I cursed and rolled one more time, firing off the Beretta.

I emptied the mag point blank into him when he shot me. The bullet hit me in the left of my chest, and I felt the shock of the 300-grain bullet blow all the way through my body. The vest couldn't stop the big bore hand cannon from point blank range.

Tony, you can't... I'm not sure...

Alice's voice faded as I saw that I'd hit Boris from waist to his throat in a diagonal stitch, emptying the magazine. He looked at me, with a wisp of smoke coming out of the monster revolver and then fell face forward, landing next to me and making the ground vibrate.

"Not yet," I told Alice and rolled to my side and

vomited.

The shock was doing horrors on my body, but the trauma was already being repaired. I took deep breaths and blocked out the pain. Alice could do this, I know she was probably just too busy working to talk to me.

Shield recharged, healing assist is working as asked. You should be back up to full strength in ten minutes.

"Why so long?" I asked her, glad to hear her voice again.

That one nearly clipped your heart, and you lost a lot of blood. I know you're in a firefight, but you need food and something to drink soon so I can have your body—

"Yeah, yeah," I said and got to my feet. I wobbled over to the big man and pulled the S&W out of his cold dead fingers and patted down his pockets. I found two speed loaders. So that meant I had one or two more rounds in here... I reloaded the gun, putting the spare speed loader and the two loose rounds in the superhero belt, and ignored Alice as she tried to make light of my apparel choices.

Something came through the front door. Actually, it was a little too big to come in through the front door, and part of the wall disintegrated as a suit of power armor made a hole big enough for it to come in. Now, I'd seen Moss's set of armor and then again the set she'd stolen. They had been lithe things, minimalist but still big. This thing was huge. Like it was built for a giant. It roared at me and started stomp smashing its way in my direction, the helmet dragging on the ceiling and knocking down sheetrock

BOYD CRAVEN

and drop ceiling tiles. Sparks flew as lights shattered in the giant's onslaught.

Um, run, Alice advised me.

I was about to when I saw dozens of the Outsiders guards and officers pour in, with two more suits joining the party. That's when I ran. And screamed and…

"I'm in their network. Boris's apartment is off to the left and through those doors down a hallway and…"

I didn't hesitate, and the walls and floor erupted as the men with guns opened fire. I took two shots to the back that made me stumble as I got to the door, but they weren't enough to discharge my shield the way the big revolver did at point blank range. I got through the door and saw a crash bar on the other side, almost like the eye beam in Moss's hideaway. I put that in place just as the men hit it and started trying to open it. The giant in the suit or the other smaller Exosuits could smash their way through, so I ran.

"Give me an overlay," I told Alice, wanting to not have to think about directions, just see it. She showed me, and I ran.

Men ran out of doorways where they'd been hiding when they'd been caught with their pants down, literally. If they weren't armed, I let them pass. If they were, well, I had a pistol in each hand now, but I was saving the big bore revolver, just in case. I heard splintering behind me as I reached the door where Boris's apartments were and knew they had crashed through. I shot the lock and kicked the door, making my own noise. I ran into a lavishly decorated one bedroom apartment. Hogtied, but intact, was a struggling Moss, tears streaking her face and dry heaving from the gag in her mouth.

I pulled the black stiletto I'd taken from her after our first date, and roughly cut the ropes on her hands. She immediately went for the gag, and I cut the ropes holding her feet. She was still clothed, but she had dried blood across half her face where she'd had her nose broken. Probably she'd been beat on, but she was alive. A new cast covered her broken wrist, and I could see she'd been using the rough side of it to try to saw through the rope, as evidenced by the fibers stuck to it.

"Tony, you shouldn't have come," she said, throwing her arms around me in a crushing embrace.

"I told you, kill everyone, nuke the canyon. Come on."

I could hear the giant advancing. Part of me wondered if we were about to be overwhelmed with men, but it hadn't happened yet. I pulled her, and we fled out the door. I heard what sounded like a high RPM whine start up and pushed Moss down and fell on top of her. An electronic Gatlin gun, the big brother to the chain gun Moss had used, opened up. It shredded everything from knee height and up as the giant sprayed everything in front of it. The depleted uranium rounds blew through walls, and there were screams from outside the brothel and within as people were hit by friendly fire. I heard the big gun spin down, just out of sight. I got up and pulled Moss up by her cast. I was running out of hallway as we twisted and turned and I saw an emergency exit. It was chained shut. We ran to it, and I pulled the S&W out and aimed at the lock.

The hand cannon almost jerked itself out of my grip from the recoil, but the bullet snapped the lock, and I was unwrapping the chain when something heavy crashed into the wall next to me. I fell from the shock and rolled to see the giant suit of power armor was right behind me. Its punch had missed me, but it had left a hole the size of a bowling ball in the wall. Moss finished unwrapping the handle as I scrambled to my feet and tried to get out of its range. I saw it try to bring its Gatlin to bear on me just as Moss pulled me by the hood, out of the door. The giant couldn't get the gun up, the wall was in the way in the tight quarters, and we fled.

"Where's the closest exit?" I screamed at her.

"We have to go closer to the market—" Moss screamed and then I heard the report of the gunshot, then she slumped to the ground.

I turned to see Luca, with an old pistol in his hands and murder in his eyes. "You were my friend, and you killed the—"

I started firing the hand cannon. My first shot hit him in the chest, the second hit him in the shoulder as he spun and he hit the ground. Then I put one in his head from ten feet away. Parts of hair and his skull sprayed out the back. I dropped the hand cannon and turned to Moss. Her vest hadn't been done up in the front, and she had a dark stain low in her stomach, just above the leather pants that would have protected her.

I heard a metal roaring behind me and saw part of the brothel's ceiling collapse. Brick and wood came down in a crash, and I had to hope the Exosuit was under that mess. If not dead, slowed. I turned back towards the church where the Order had been. Nicholas Sparkman was walking towards me, having already passed the corpse of Luca. There were tears in his eyes. I didn't have time for that.

"How bad?" I asked her, ripping the sleeve of my robe and then cutting it with the stiletto and using it to put pressure on the wound.

She screamed at the pressure and then looked up at me. "It's bad, you should go." She coughed.

I could smell what the bullet had done. She was gut shot, and it might take a day, it might take a week, but without help and surgery, she was as good as dead. I was not going to accept that. No way in hell.

"Hold this here," I said and advanced towards Nicholas.

Guards came rushing around from the front of the brothel, and I emptied the magnum and fired the Beretta into the crowd of them. Some fell, some were slightly wounded, but they all took cover.

"Nicholas my man. How's the sight? You ready for some surgery?"

"You shouldn't have done this," He said, horror-stricken.

"I need a way out of here, and you are coming with me," I told him. "I need to get to the bottom of the dam, and it needs to be now."

"I cannot leave my flock, the people here need me…" he said, sounding feeble.

"You believe the twisted religion that's sprung up here? Because of your people, Moss is dying."

"What's one life, that of a murderer, versus what you've done here?"

"I'd kill everyone in your precious church to save her," I said, putting the hot barrel of the Beretta against his forehead.

He closed his eyes and said nothing for a full three second count. I could hear Moss moaning, and a scraping, and then she was beside me, hunched over.

"Don't kill him, this was Greg…" she coughed, "Gregory's fault," she said, leaning against me, her head on my arm.

"I can get you out of here. I can probably even manage the surgery, but I can't do it here."

"I have what I need to fix the ARC," I told him simply.

He nodded, and I pulled the barrel back and holstered the gun.

"Follow me," he said.

CHAPTER
16

The entrance to the storm drains was in a place that Moss and I hadn't seen before. The wily old man wasn't as crippled as he'd been acting and was actually pretty spry. It made me wonder how much of his appearance and blindness was an act too. He nearly outpaced me when I had to start carrying Moss to prevent any more injuries. Instead of coming out at the same location and having to shimmy across the causeway with the waterfall, we came out on the other end, once he had me roll a stone back. Both Moss and I had walked past this spot, and neither of us had detected it on our way in… and she'd grown up knowing these tunnels and passageways.

The entire city was up in arms now, shouts, screams, horns. I heard drums fire up in the distance and I threw Moss over my shoulder and ran. If I didn't have Alice tweaking my adrenaline and blocking out the pain, I never would have made it. She's not a big girl, but I was running full out for half a mile to the buggy. Despite being more nimble than he looked, I had told Nicholas to keep going, but I would meet up with him with the buggy.

I put Moss into the driver's seat and pushed her over to squish her in so I could keep her from falling out. She was in and out of consciousness, whether from the pain or from the blood loss and sepsis, I didn't know. I fired up the motor and took off. I found Nicholas a moment later, and he held onto the side as we roared out of the area.

Since we hadn't gone out of the gate, I was hopeful that nobody was watching the distance where we snuck out, nor saw the dust cloud rise from me holding the pedal down. What had taken me many days of travel was now less than an hour away with the tricked-out dune buggy. Moss moaned at every bump, but at this point, I was more worried about getting her to the ARC so hopefully Doctor Sparkman could do something with her stomach wound.

I was waiting for Murphy to show up. Murphy of Murphy's Law... Spiders, Vorryn, those weird purple scorpions I didn't know the name of... None of that happened. Despite the wild escape, we were able to drive up to the rock cave that hid the door to the redoubt and Data ARC. The stone would shield the buggy from casual view, but it was deafening to be in there with the motor running. I cut the motor and ran for the doorway. I chanced a look behind me and saw the old man getting Moss out. I found the hidden door entry keypad that Alice had told me about and punched in my code. The door rumbled open slowly.

"I got her," I said, taking her weight and moving in.

"Get your bag, doesn't it have the last servo?" Moss asked.

Yes, yes it did. I let Sparkman hold her up and grabbed my gear. I dumped my weapons inside the door but took the backpack and hit the close button. It was about to get pitch black, as all emergency lighting had been shut off. I heard a snapping sound and heard it repeated and then a green glow as Moss handed me a glow stick from her never ending supply. She held its twin up, her face covered in sweat.

"Got two more," she said quietly, coughing.

"Doc, I'm going to get the reactor online. You two start down and if I get the power back up, take the elevators. Where you going to be?" I asked him.

"Between levels 25 and 29, depending on what tools and supplies I can find," he said. "I'll get on an elevator as soon as the power comes online, I don't want to risk making things worse with the stairs."

"Moss, I like you," I told her, and kissed her hard.

"Like you too, you crazy bastard," she said breathlessly.

I ran. Three servos, three repairs. Alice told me as I started down the cement stairwells where and how to do the repairs. She promised me she would guide me as fast as possible. I believed her. Part of me wanted to just slide down a cable or the ladder in the elevator shaft, but in the dark, it would be hard to see,

BOYD CRAVEN

and I was going down and not up. I wasn't convinced that I could stop my descent if I got going too fast.

You're overthinking this, Tony.

"She's lost a lot of blood," I said, "and I'm worried about…"

Killing his second in command, putting a gun to his head, demanding help and then having to leave Moss with him as you make a mad escape down the darkened corridors of…

She droned on and on mentally, and I was surprised at how long it was taking to get to the message. Most thoughts just happened. Message sent, message received. Then it hit me, she was trying to keep my mind occupied. I let her droning go on.

"What are her chances?" I asked Alice after she finally went silent three floors later.

She lost a lot of blood, I think her intestines were ruptured, seems to be suffering shock and sepsis. She would have been critical an hour ago, but now it's… She's tough, Tony.

I ran harder, leaping down the stairwell. Two steps at a time. Three. Four. There was little to no hope saving her without getting the power on, so I tempered my need to get there with the fact I had to be in one piece to make repairs. It was balancing on the razor's edge now. One more floor. Never before had forty or so steps seemed to take so long. 25. 22. 19. 15. 11. 9. 5. 2.

I pulled the door almost off its hinges and ran for the control room. I almost missed Alice's directions and nearly went to the one after where the repairs were needed. The room was a mass of conduit, exhaust pipes, water lines and wires. Everything was labeled in clear and understandable gibberish. Which, to me meant Jack and Shit, and Jack left town… If Alice hadn't highlighted the part in my vision, I would have missed it. A water regulator. It had a computer controlled servo to control water flow. Frantically I started looking for something to unbolt it with when I remembered the pliers Moss had lent me. I didn't remember what had happened with them when the stalkers had attacked…

I started smacking at my vest, feeling the magazines, the stiletto and then a lump in a pocket near the dump pouch. I pulled out the pliers and started to work. Unbolting the first one wasn't difficult, and I could see right away the motor had burned out. Instead of the pin holding the shaft in place, it had a keyway cut into the metal that matched the indentation in the shaft. The new one slid right in.

"How did you know these would fit?" I asked Alice as I worked frantically.

It's the government. They use easy to find and replace parts in their critical infrastructure. This just happened to be the right servo. Now strip those wires and connect them. There's no current in them, and we can come back and wire nut them later, just don't let them short out on each other—

"Got it," I told her, and moved to do the second.

It happened so quickly that when I was done, I sat back in awe.

You have to restart the reactor dumbass.

I took off for the control room, which was close by. For whatever reason, I'd spent this entire week looking for those three little electric motors and now that I had them in, part of me was expecting the power to light up, for Moss to come out of surgery ok… boy saves the girl, and the world is saved. Nope. I had to start the reactor. I remembered part of the sequence of levers and buttons, and I worked at them frantically while Alice pointed them out as a green highlight in my HUD overlay. I hit the final button and ran to the terminal. Power flickered on.

"Type this," Alice said, and I pulled a chair out and flopped down to type.

The cushion had dry rotted, and I almost tipped out, but I managed to stay in there and started typing as fast as I could. The commands were in Urdu for all I knew, but Alice was fluent in whatever hack slash pound sign dash and gibberish she was doing. When she had me hit enter, I stood up and looked at the board. Green lights started showing where they had all been dark before.

"Did we do it?" I asked Alice.

"Mostly, we may have to monitor things while the new servos come online. I don't know how much Mr. Jones had to adjust the programming for the failing equipment before he died."

"Can't you just set it to factory default and let it fly?" I asked her, moving towards an old rusty toolbox.

I opened the lid and found it had electrical and plumbing supplies… I threw things over my shoulder until I found what I wanted. A roll of electrical tape and some wire nuts. It was pretty weird that it took three servo motors and some wire nuts to fix things when the world went to shit. I mean, the entire weight of human civilization might now rest on the fact I did or did not have access to wire nuts because the servo wires might short out and cause another catastrophic failure that—

Tony, calm down. You have six to do. Then go find Moss. You're driving yourself crazy, and I am having a hard time keeping your blood pressure down. You also need to drink, you lost a lot of blood yourself.

"I'll do that later," I told her, ignoring the dried gore on the front of my vest.

I covered the splices I made, wing nutted them together and wrapped the wires and nuts in electrical tape. It wouldn't last a thousand years, but hopefully, I wouldn't need this place this long. God, I hoped not.

"Status on Moss?" I asked her.

One floor up, one room over from yours. It's an auxiliary to the room you woke up in.

"Why is she there?" I asked in a panic.

"I can only monitor the systems. She's not hooked up to anything I can monitor yet, I'm working on… Oh…"

I ran again. Despite having an AI and advanced nanotechnology running through my system, I was weary, bone weary. The adrenaline started wearing off and my boundless energy left me in a rush. I almost collapsed with the come down from it. I grabbed the railing and climbed, no longer able to take two or three steps at a time. The elevator would have been nice, but I wasn't about to wait.

You're dehydrated, you're still weak from almost dying. You'll be there in thirty seconds or less, Alice assured me.

I hoped so. I made it to the top of the landing and started running towards the door she indicated. She cautioned me about going straight in and interrupting surgery, so I went into the viewing room. It was the one behind the one-way mirror. I went in there and saw Moss laid out on a table, machinery whirring all around her. Robotic arms with scalpels, sutures, suction and a light worked at the spoken direction of Dr. Nicholas Sparkman. It almost looked like a robotic octopus and it was the scariest thing I'd ever seen in my life. Belatedly, I realized I could hear him, and there was a speaker inside the room here relaying everything. I didn't know the medical terms and declined Alice's offer to translate it.

Then I heard the monitoring equipment to her heart rate stop making beeps and made one solid tone. I collapsed in the chair as I realized that her heart had stopped. Another surgical arm came down with what looked like a six-inch needle, and it pierced her bare chest over her heart and then Dr. Sparkman was using paddles. One shock, two. Moss trembled, started breathing again.

"Can you hear me? I see the light on in the viewing room." Sparkman asked.

"Yes," I told him.

"I can help her, but I have to… Only the nanites can save her now."

"I'd burn the world down for her," I told him. "Do it."

"You don't want to watch this part. I'll come find you when it's done."

I left the monitoring room. I didn't want to see

any more. I had to pray that the technology that saved me could save her. Seeing her filleted open like that killed something inside of me. For the first time that I could ever remember, I prayed.

Tony, you're dangerously dehydrated, Alice told me as I put my back to the door of the monitoring room and slid down.

I pulled my canteen from my pack and started drinking it. A quart of water down. Still, the sobs were without tears. The tears wouldn't come. I was so scared. Moss. Moss.

CHAPTER 17

I woke up when I felt somebody shaking me. Was it all a dream? I opened my eyes slowly. They seemed to be pasted shut, and I wiped at them with the back of my hand and looked up. Dr. Sparkman. Nope, not a dream.

"How is she?" I asked, my voice hoarse.

"She survived the surgery. She's been sleeping now. I wanted to speak with you. We can go in the viewing room now, I have things cleaned up."

I got up slowly, and my legs wobbled. The old man grabbed me in a firm grip and helped me up. We entered the door I had fallen asleep against. The first thing I noticed was Moss on the table still, the sides now up to prevent her from rolling off. She'd been covered with a white sheet, and I could see the steady rise and fall of her chest. A mass of wires was hooked up to machines all around her, but I couldn't see where they went.

"How is she?" I asked, leaning against the glass.

"She's stable. I had to implant an AI to make the nanites work. It was the only way to save her that was available to me."

"You had to cut into her brain?" I asked him.

"No," he said, "but I did have her opened up, so I tapped into her central nervous system through her spinal column. It's not a perfect system, but it works. As soon as we injected her with nanites, her AI started the internal work of repairing things."

"There's a but coming," I said.

"Yeah, there is. While she's healing, I had to use an advanced AI, like yours. Like the kind I couldn't steal back when I was running this program. It was in testing when I went into stasis."

"Ok, so she's got a quantum computer inside of her. What's the deal?" I asked him.

"The AI was not always… sane. It harbored psychotic tendencies and started developing a personality."

"A personality? That's not common?" I asked him.

"No, not at all."

I was silent, thinking of how cold and informal Alice used to be and how she was now using humor and—Wait, she now understood emotions too. She had kept me distracted while I was in my mad dash. She hadn't done anything to hurt me…

No, and I wouldn't. Humans are afraid of what they can't understand, Tony, Alice told me mentally.

"What about her AI made you think it was psychotic?" I asked him.

"In testing, it decided that humanity was best managed by enslaving them. It suggested that if implanted into a host it would start working towards that plan."

"But the AIs don't have access to our motor functions. They just run the nanite suites," I told him.

"Who told you that?" he asked curiously.

A dawning horror started to fill me with dread. Doctor Sparkman must have caught something in my expression because he backed up half a step.

Tony, I can't do it because I won't allow myself to, the voice said out loud, *the voice that came out of the speakers,* the voice that sounded exactly like Alice.

At the table, Moss stirred and murmured my name.

I left Doctor Nicholas Sparkman in the viewing room and headed into the surgical theater. Moss was starting to sit up on her own. As the sheet fell back, I saw the doc had put a gown on her front, but the wires were routed in from the waist. She rubbed her stomach in wonder for a moment, and then pulled the gown aside and looked at her unblemished belly. Then she looked up at me and our eyes met. She smiled.

"Tony," she said, and her eyes flashed blue.

AWAKENED CONTROL

LATER IN LAKEVILLE

"How is it he's still alive?" Magnus asked the rogue healer.

"The brain is a mysterious organ. I don't know. I was able to stop the bleeding, but I need to know what you want me to do here?"

The healer was terrified; her operation had not only been found out, but it had been moved into the Outsider's headquarters where Magnus lived, in the old circular shaped welcome center. Her vat of nanites and solution in the tote had been discovered, and she'd been co-opted. She wasn't even sure if her cooperation would ensure she wouldn't be put to death at a later date.

"I want you to work with my Technomages," Magnus said, pointing to a man in a white lab coat who was wearing what looked like latex gloves.

"Ok, what are we going to be doing exactly? It's not like I can grow back his brain?"

"Oh no, no need to grow one back. We're going to implant one," Magnus said with a wicked grin. "Mage Caldor, do you have the AI and the Augment nanites ready?"

"I do, Lord Magnus."

"Good, make sure Luca receives the best of the best."

"On it, Lord Magnus."

—THE END—

ABOUT THE AUTHOR

Boyd Craven III has penned over 20 books over the last two years, only recently deciding to take the plunge into publishing. His "The World Burns" Series has hit the top 10 in the Dystopian Genre in the USA, the UK, Canada and Australia. Boyd has made his home in Michigan with his wonderful wife and about a million kids, but travels to Texas to visit family as frequently as possible.

He hunts and goes fishing when he's not dreaming up post-apocalyptic nightmares to put his characters through. Fear not though, Boyd is a huge believer that in the darkest hour, there is always a glimmer of hope to hold onto.

In addition to being a modern day urban farmer, Boyd belongs to a co-op selling at the local farmers market, and lately has been experimenting with living off the grid - an excellent way to research for his series, as well as torture his teenage sons.

Prepare yourself by reading his books - they're a thrill ride, on or off the grid.

http://www.amazon.com/Boyd-Craven-III/e/B00BANIQLG/

38773726R00222

Made in the USA
Middletown, DE
11 March 2019